11/2

To

Enjoy the novel.

THE
PEACEKEEPER

Best wishes

JESS STEVEN HUGHES

Jess Steven Hughes

A HISTORICAL NOVEL

MILFORD
HOUSE

an imprint of Sunbury Press, Inc.
Mechanicsburg, PA USA

MILFORD HOUSE

an imprint of Sunbury Press, Inc.
Mechanicsburg, PA USA

NOTE: This is a work of fiction. Names, characters, places and incidents are the product of the author's imagination or are used fictitiously, and any resemblance to actual persons, living or dead, business establishments, events or locales is entirely coincidental.

For information about special discounts for bulk purchases, please contact Sunbury Press Orders Dept. at (855) 338-8359 or orders@sunburypress.com.

To request one of our authors for speaking engagements or book signings, please contact Sunbury Press Publicity Dept. at publicity@sunburypress.com.

ISBN: 978-1-62006-760-4 (Trade paperback)

Library of Congress Control Number: 2018943243

FIRST MILFRED HOUSE PRESS EDITION: June 2018

Product of the United States of America
0 1 1 2 3 5 8 13 21 34 55

Set in Bookman Old Style
Designed by Crystal Devine
Cover by Lawrence Knorr
Cover art by Tal Dibner (www.dibnergallery.com)
Edited by Janice Rhayem

Continue the Enlightenment!

Also From
JESS STEVEN HUGHES

———

THE SIGN OF THE EAGLE

THE WOLF OF BRITANNIA, PART I

THE WOLF OF BRITANNIA, PART II

THE BROKEN LANCE

DRAMATIS PERSONAE
(IN ORDER OF APPEARANCE)

IN ROME

Marcellus Tiberius Reburrus – Centurion
Crispus – Junior Cavalry Officer
Anicius Pedius Gallus the Younger – Roman Tribune
* Titus Flavius Sabinus – General/Senator
Priscilla – Jewish Woman
Aquila – Priscilla's Husband
Eleyne – British Princess
Candra – Indian Slave
Aurelia Severa – Wife of Sabinus
* Lucius Vitellius – Senator
* Tiberius Claudius Nero Germanicus (Claudius) – Emperor
* Messalina – Claudius's wife
* Titus Flavius Vespasianus (Vespasian) – General –
    Sabinus's Younger Brother
Camillus – Senator
Alexias – Greek Slave/Steward
Chulainn – British Slave
Budar – Marcellus's Uncle
Caecilia Juanaria – Marcellus's Mother
Porus – Greek Slave/Steward
Casperius Niger – Centurion
John-Mark – Christian Leader
Imogen – British Slave Woman
Young Marcellus – Marcellus's Older Son
Young Sabinus – Marcellus's Younger Son
* Sofonius Tigellinus – Praetorian Prefect
* Lucius Domitius Ahenobarbus (Nero) – Emperor
* Poppea – Nero's Wife
Soranus – Greek Physician
* Cornelius Martialis – Tribune
* Claudius Apollinaris – Roman Navy Admiral

* Historical Character

ROMAN EMPERORS – DATE OF REIGN

Tiberius Claudius Nero Germanicus – 41-54 AD
(Claudius)
Lucius Domitius Ahenobarbus (Nero) – 54-68 AD
Servius Sulpicius Galba (Galba) – 68-69 AD
Marcus Salvius Otho (Otho) – 69 AD
Aulus Vitellius – 69 AD
Titus Flavius Vespasianus (Vespasian) – 69-79 AD
Titus Flavius Vespasianus (Titus) – 79-81 AD
Titus Flavius Domitianus (Domitian) – 81-96 AD

GEOGRAPHICAL LOCATIONS

ANCIENT NAME	MODERN NAME
Britannia	Britannia
Hispania	Spain
Gaul	France
British Ocean	English Channel
Germania	Germany
Alexandria	Alexandria, Egypt
Ostia	Rome's Seaport
River Rhenus	Rhine River
Moguntiacum	Mainz, Germany
Baetica Province	Southern Coast of Spain

PART I

ROME
45 AD

Dressed in plain tunics, barely hiding our swords, we hiked along Tuscan Street, on a humid afternoon, between the Temple of Castor and the Basilica of Julius Caesar toward the Forum. A noisy stream of people jostled their way up and down its marble steps, in and out of the cavernous building's many entryways.

Crispus glanced in the direction of the usual idlers lounging about the vast double porticoes. He spat. "Can't believe some of those useless turds will soon be officers in the army."

For the space of a half-dozen heartbeats, I studied the young men in fashionable togas or tunics, now sweat-stained under armpits and down backs, looking for ladies of easy virtue. The daughters of Venus, licensed prostitutes who freely roamed the area, were easily spotted wearing blond wigs and saffron gowns.

"We've had this conversation before," I said. "When you're the son of a rich senator, you can get anything you want."

Even as we continued to walk, Crispus turned his head towards me. "What they want and what they should get is good thrashing by a centurion's vine cane on their backs and arses."

My hand reached for my waistband before I remembered I wasn't carrying a vine cane. I only wore it when in full uniform. "I'd be glad to oblige you if we were back in Britannia."

Crispus grunted. "Well, we ain't."

"That's right, let it go. Most of them won't join the army anyway.

"Thank the gods."

We continued to move through the sea of people. The pavement about the foot of the court was marked up in charcoal for gaming boards, busily played by people from all classes. Sounds of clattering dice filled the air, followed by exclamations of delight by the winners or groans and profanity by the losers. A pinch-faced member of the Equestrian Order shook his fist at the youthful winner in a ragged tunic as we passed. "You stole the last of my money, you cheat!" he yelled. "Your dice are loaded!" Onlookers either jeered or laughed.

Crispus and I grinned and kept moving.

Portable goatskin stalls lined the crowded lane. Shopkeepers hawked their wares to passersby. The smells of cooked sausages, meat turnovers, and honeyed cakes wafted on the light breeze. My stomach growled. After investigating a report on valuable stolen statues being auctioned at the Porticus of Pompey, we were heading to the home of Senator Titus Flavius Sabinus to report our findings. We came up empty-handed.

We had nearly cleared the huge, three-hundred-foot-long basilica, Rome's major law court, when I spotted Gallus coming down the marble steps. Dressed in a white toga trimmed in gold, he was escorted by an entourage of clients. Six bodyguards surrounded him—muscular, scarred-face, broken-nosed thugs—probably ex-gladiators. They wore white, linen tunics and embroidered on the right shoulder of each was the family symbols of Gallus, a golden rooster below the letter *G.* Beneath their tunics, obviously meant to be seen, were outlines of long daggers.

We stopped.

Crispus motioned his head in Gallus's direction. "Do you see what I see?"

"Aye, how could I miss him?"

A shudder raced through my body. *What did I have to fear from him?* Everything and perhaps nothing.

The conspiracy against the life of Emperor Claudius that Crispus and I had discovered had been instigated by Senator Gallus, the Elder. His son, the younger Gallus, had recently returned to Rome from the army's campaign in Britannia to pick up the political pieces left by his dead father. Since old Gallus had been pardoned, all the family estates were left intact. Would his father's old cronies rally around the son or shun him like a pestilence? I expected my former cavalry cohort commander, from our days of campaigning in Britannia, to seek me out. He did, sooner than expected. The hatred young Gallus and his father had for my family went back to when we were boys. Although the same age, he was Roman and I, a Spaniard.

Gallus stopped at the foot of the steps. He held up a hand, signaling his retinue to do the same. Spotting me, he glared then slowly wiggled a forefinger motioning me forward.

The fine hair raised on my arms and shoulders, sweat ran down my back. I stared back but refused to move.

Crispus was a half foot shorter than I. His copper face looked up to mine as he whispered, "Marcellus, it wouldn't be smart of you to refuse him. He's our former commander and a patrician and could cause you a lot of trouble. Senator Sabinus would have a hard time excusing your action."

I growled under my breath. "I better see what he wants." Being six years older and wiser than I, Crispus was right. Any sign of disrespect to Gallus would be excuse enough to break me as a centurion. I would never be admitted to the Equestrian Order. "Walk behind me and watch my back. His gorillas," I motioned with my head toward Gallus's bodyguards, "are looking for trouble."

Gallus waved his men to step a few paces away from him.

I turned toward Crispus. "At least he doesn't intend to harm me in public. He's smarter than I thought."

Reluctantly, I stepped forward, halted before my old cohort leader, and looked down upon him. Like me, he was twenty-five, but at six feet, I stood five finger widths taller than he. No longer pale, his slender face was sunburned and hardened by battle. Thin lines creased his forehead. A narrow scar sliced across the side of his jaw, and a tiny section at the bottom of his earlobe was missing. His pale-blue eyes still burned with hatred—no doubt for me.

"Now that I have returned to Rome, Centurion Marcellus Tiberius Reburrus, . . ." Gallus's voice was full of bile, "did you think to escape my attention so easily?"

"I don't know what you are talking about, sir." I stepped away, spat, and faced him again.

His face darkened. He raised his voice. "Did you think it would remain a secret?" He turned to his retinue and to passersby coming down the court steps. "Yes, here stands a lowly Spanish tomb robber! He and his friend, another Spaniard." He gestured toward Crispus who showed no emotion. "Broke into my family's mausoleum like common grave robbers!"

A gasp erupted from his people and others nearby who had stopped to listen. They were a cross-section of men and women, draped in a variety of clothing ranging from dirty tunics to immaculate stolas.

Gallus's face turned crimson. "Did you think to ingratiate yourself with the emperor?"

I returned his glare, seeing through him as if he weren't there—the murderer of Kyar, the woman whom I had loved in Britannia. I could play the same game. "The fruits of my search speaks for itself," I answered in a loud voice for all to hear. "Your father conspired to murder the emperor! His assassins nearly murdered Lord Sabinus and killed many in his household."

A louder gasp burst from the crowd of onlookers who inched closer, some so near I smelled garlic on their breath. Others reeked of strong perfume or the sour smells of dead cattle killed in the slaughterhouse south of the Forum.

Gallus looked about and motioned to his bodyguards who snarled like animals and violently shoved the people back.

I was grateful. Roman mobs had a reputation for getting rowdy, ugly, easily incited to riot.

A grim-faced Crispus turned from side to side, hand on the hilt of his concealed sword, as he surveyed the hostile gathering.

"If so, why did he pardon my father?" Gallus finally asked. He glanced to his entourage and to the rabble as if to elicit their sympathy. "He cleared my father because the evidence was planted by his enemies—those documents were forged! He had nothing to do with assassins!" Gallus gestured to the crowd as if it were obvious.

"You're grasping for air, sir," I said. "Where is your proof?"

"I have it, and you are implicated."

Despite being pushed back, cautiously, people stepped forward again seemingly hanging on to our every word.

"You mean you manufactured it." I laughed in a sardonic voice. "Don't you know?" I paused to scan the people making certain I had their attention. "Your father offered me a position on his staff?"

There was a stirring of voices in the crowd who seemed intrigued by this bit of news. They pressed closer, and I heard one man ask, "Is it true?" The bodyguards shoved them back again brutally, using their muscular bodies like battering rams.

I looked around for an escape route. Afraid the mob would turn violent, I kept a tight rein on my nerves.

Crispus gave me a nod as if to say he understood.

Gallus pinched his pale eyebrows together and glowered. "You? I don't believe it!"

I shrugged. "He offered me a position and promised me entry to the Equestrian Order providing I would be his little boot licker, which I refused. Now, even though the emperor pardoned your father . . . ," I paused for effect and raised my voice, "all Rome knows he plotted against him."

Jeers in the affirmative streamed from the mob.

"You may be his only son," I added, fixing my eyes on the crowd, "and had no part in his scheme, but still by custom *you* bear his disgrace."

Several in the mob shouted, "A disgrace! He's a disgrace!"

Gallus's features tightened. His gaze darted about the huge gathering. His bodyguards pulled back and surrounded his side and back, leaving his front open to

7

me. I was in striking range of him with my sword, but both of us knew I would not be so foolish as to strike him down in public. The thought was tempting, but I was no fool.

"You no longer have credibility, sir," I said. "Who would listen to you?"

"Many have listened," Gallus answered in a quivering voice, as if trying to convince the crowd. "And so will the emperor. I'm not sitting idly by allowing my family to be disgraced."

"It already is. Do you plan to purchase the Senate and Narcissus, the emperor's secretary, in order to change their minds?"

More jeers from the surrounding group.

A sinister smile crossed Gallus's lips. "Don't mock me, Centurion. When the time is right, I shall reveal my evidence." His grin reminded me of a wolf ready to pounce upon its prey.

Why was he telling me his plans, especially in public? Couldn't he keep his anger under control? What was the purpose? Surely, he knew he placed me on alert and I would inform Sabinus.

"You realize Senator Sabinus will do everything in his power to stop you?" I said.

Again, a cruel grin formed on his narrow lips. "Only this time he will fail. Be forewarned, my father's death will be avenged."

What else did he have in mind?

He turned, signaled to his entourage. His bodyguards shoved a wide space through the crowd for Gallus to pass, leaving an opening like the wake of a ship.

He walked a few steps but stopped and faced me. "I will do everything I can to see you never get another chance to enter the Equestrian ranks!"

* * *

We hiked out of the Forum and up Quirinal Hill to Sabinus's plush mansion where I also lived. The senator was also a general in the Roman Army. He had promoted me to the rank of centurion from cavalry sergeant after I had saved the life of my troop commander, Sextus Rufius, in battle. Since that time, Senator Sabinus used Crispus, now a sergeant, and me as his bodyguards and for special investigations working with Rome's police and fire fighters, the Watch. We also developed a unique relationship with the beggar king, Scrofa, who passed along information regarding the city's criminal elements. It had been on a raid to a hive of thieves living beneath the city that we discovered evidence leading to the possible overthrow of Emperor Claudius.

Meeting with him in the atrium, we reported the confrontation with Gallus.

"We knew this was inevitable," the balding, forty-one-year-old senator said. Nearly as tall as me, Sabinus wore a snow-white toga, with a broad, purple stripe down the center denoting his senatorial rank. He arrived a few minutes ahead of us from a meeting in the Senate. Walking next to him, Crispus and I strolled by the small, gurgling fountain at one end of the reception area near the entrance to the garden. Our footfalls echoed off the mosaic-tiled floor.

"Why did he wait six weeks to confront me?" I asked.

Sabinus turned to me, his mahogany eyes peering into mine. "He probably needed time after returning from Britannia to ingratiate himself with his father's old cronies. No doubt he pointed to his own *heroism* in battle when he and your old unit fought against the British rebels."

A revolt in western Britannia, led by the British king, Caratacus, had erupted the previous spring. Retaliation had been swift; the back of the rebellion was broken in two weeks.

"The credit should go to your brother, General Vespasian, who led the Second Legion in crushing the revolt," I said. "My old cavalry unit, First Hispanorum Vettonum, was only a part of the counter-offensive."

"True, but your old unit fought heroically," Sabinus answered. "Gallus cannot be faulted for his bravery. He has the scar on his face to prove it."

I snorted. "So I noticed he was trying to atone for his father's betrayal."

"But my sources tell me, old Gallus's friends have kept their distance—at least for now."

"They want to keep their own political hides out of jeopardy," Crispus said.

"No doubt, Sergeant," Sabinus said. "But since he has threatened Centurion Reburrus, I will send out spies to keep a close watch on him."

"And if he tries anything like his father did against you?" I asked.

Sabinus halted, as did Crispus and I.

A thin smile creased his smooth face. He eyed the two of us. "We shall be ready."

CHAPTER 2

OCTOBER 45 AD

More than a year had passed since the death of Gallus the Elder. Despite the confrontation with his son, two months ago, I had neither seen nor heard anything further about him. During that period, Emperor Claudius grew more distant and absentminded by the day. He spent greater time and money on gladiatorial games. However, Pallas and Narcissus, his Greek freedmen and secretaries, kept his peculiarities in check.

Information supplied by Scrofa and his beggars proved steady and usually reliable. As a result, the Watch seldom bothered the beggars and apprehended several notorious felons. Scrofa's money pouch swelled, but he stayed with the beggars—they were his people.

On a rainy October afternoon, after meeting with Scrofa to plan another raid on Rome's criminal element, Crispus and I took lunch at one of Rome's cleaner cook shops. The place stood in the Trans-Tiber area along the Portensis Way, on the west bank, near the Great Naval Arena, the Augustan Naumachia. Despite the rainy weather, the street teemed with people. On days like this, we wore our cloaks, and beneath our tunics, knee-length cavalry breeches, boots, and heavy woolen socks. Hot sausages, vegetables, and spicy Calda warmed us. The coals from two braziers glowed a sunset red, and its heat was a blessing. We sat at a table on the edge of the crowded sidewalk, protected from the elements by an overhanging canopy. As we intermittently chatted with the baldheaded proprietor, the rain receded to an annoying, chilled mist.

We discussed the validity of Scrofa's information while lingering over cups of mulled wine.

Someone screamed.

Startled, I turned and saw a tall, red-headed Gaul snatch a covered basket from a young woman wearing a long tunic. She held on, refusing to let go. He wrenched the basket away, slammed her against a shop wall next to the adjacent sidewalk. Her head struck with a loud crack. She slumped to the sidewalk. Dead.

Crispus and I were on our feet instantly. The thug dropped the basket and fled. We chased him as he dodged and shoved several cursing people out his way down the congested lane. A couple of times he stumbled on the wet, cobblestone street. We struggled to maintain our own balance as we splashed through ankle-deep puddles, seeping through our boots and socks. My sword, hidden beneath my tunic, scraped against my thigh with every step I took along the trash-strewn way.

The bandit ducked into an alley to the right, one that I knew to be a dead end. I motioned to Crispus to slow down. He nodded. Cautiously, we entered the alley enshrouded in shades of gray from the high tenement walls on both sides. The place reeked of decayed food, rotten fish and vegetables, feces, and urine. A filthy, narrow stream ran down the center, rain runoff from the apartment roofs.

In the gloom I saw the thief at the end of the passageway, his back towards us, his head looking up the side of the wall as if searching for a way out. Silently, Crispus and I moved towards him. He turned and faced us, pulled a hidden dagger from his waistband, and brandished it.

Big mistake.

My partner and I drew our swords, and before he could move, we were on him. Both of us ran him through the ribs. My weapon pushed against his spine and twisted until I heard a snap.

Blood spurted from his mouth. He dropped his weapon. We pulled our swords from his torso. A loud sucking sound escaped from his lifeless body as it slumped face-first into the muddy stream. We wiped the blood from our weapons on his dirty tunic.

"Leave him," I said. "Let's go back to the dead girl. Maybe we'll find somebody who recognizes her."

We returned and shoved our way through the crowd that had gathered around a weeping middle-aged woman. Shrouded in dark clothing, she cradled the victim in her arms. At once I recognized her as Priscilla, the one we had rescued from a robbery the day we'd arrived in Rome. For the space of a half-dozen heartbeats, I stared at the dead girl. Goose bumps crawled down my arms and back. This was a younger image of the distraught woman.

Priscilla looked up for a moment and recognized me. "It's you." She turned her head in the direction in which we had chased the bandit. "That robber killed her! He murdered my daughter!"

I kneeled on one leg. "He's dead, madam," I said quietly. "He'll kill no one else. I'm very sorry about your daughter, truly I am." I wanted to say more, but this was neither the place nor time.

Crispus nodded.

I scooped up the young woman into my arms and, along with Crispus, followed Priscilla to a nearby apartment. They lived on the second story above their tent shop. I laid the girl on a mat in a tiny bedroom. A small group of sympathizers, who had followed us, gathered as I left her side. Several women came to Priscilla and offered sympathy and began preparing the body for burial as Crispus and I departed.

Returning to Sabinus's home, we reported the incident to him. He shook his head saying, "What a tragedy that an innocent girl has lost her life," and complimented us on catching and killing the murderer.

* * *

That evening Crispus and I paid a visit to the home of Aquila and Priscilla to offer our condolences. Although we were under no obligation to attend, something within urged me to go. Out of curiosity, Crispus decided to join me. It was the Jewish custom to bury the dead within twenty-four hours. Cautiously, we trudged up the poorly lighted, rickety stairway that led to their flat. I knocked, and the door slowly opened, like a yawning lion. A dim light came from within. I saw in the poor illumination a sallow-faced, middle-aged man peering at us suspiciously through glaring eyes.

"You. Are you the ones who killed my daughter's murderer?"

We nodded.

He emitted an audible sigh and mumbled something about "an eye for an eye." I noticed his balding head as he peered back into the front room. "Please enter, gentlemen," he said. "You must forgive a father who grieves the loss of his daughter."

"Words are always so useless at times like these," I said. "We're . . . if there is anything we can do to convince you that we share your sorrow."

"Your coming has proven that."

Aquila led us through a small but immaculate atrium to the bedroom. Lying in peaceful repose cloaked in a white, woolen robe was the body of their daughter. A candle flickered at each corner of the bed, giving her face a ghostly effect. A stalk of incense smoked its thin, gray-white plume, pooling like fog along the ceiling. The wisp of smoke swirled only when someone entered or left the room. Priscilla, dressed in black garments, sat at the bedside motionless, her eyes fixed in a hypnotic gaze on the young woman. Unlike the incense smoke, she never wavered. We left her to her thoughts.

"We didn't know your daughter," I said to Aquila when we returned to the atrium. "We came out of respect for Priscilla. We regret that we could not have saved her—we were so close." We explained how we found the girl.

"My brother," Aquila said, "I would not worry, for she has found peace in a better place."

Crispus glanced about and up towards the darkened ceiling. "Beyond the stars?"

"A place far better. She is with our Lord in heaven, a place not of this Earth."

14

I balled my hand into a fist along the side of my thigh and opened it again. "Rubbish. Even the Elysian Fields are beneath Earth."

"Do you really believe it exists?" Aquila quietly asked.

For the space of a couple of heartbeats, I studied the elderly man's horse face and alert, dark eyes. Even in his time of grief, he appeared almost serene, as if accepting his poor daughter's fate. "No. Then again, I doubt the existence of Melkart, my people's god."

"Most Romans and Greeks that I have known long ago lost faith in their gods," Aquila said. "Our Lord Jesus, the Son of God, has told us that He lives."

"There are many among our religions who claim they are sons of gods," Crispus quipped.

Aquila pursed his lips and looked into my eyes as if peering into the depths of my soul. I shuddered. "There is only one real God and one true Son. He is the Son of God and Man. Yet He is rejected by his own people, the Jews. Even his disciples did not understand what he was trying to teach."

"Perhaps the Jews saw him for what he really was, a fraud," I said.

"On the contrary, it was the Gentiles, especially the Greeks, who seemed to understand what he was teaching, though few accepted him at first," Aquila said.

I was about to reply when Aquila waived his hand about the small room crowded with about thirty men and women dressed in shabby but clean clothing. They ranged from mid-twenties to early fifties. All the men wore beards, the women's heads covered with shawls. Many of them stared at us, scowling, because we were outsiders who didn't belong here.

"These men came to pay their respects," Aquila said. "It was they who tried to save our daughter's life. They killed her murderer."

Members of the gathering murmured among themselves and nodded in approval.

"But enough for now," Aquila said. "It is time, everyone is here."

15

He stood before the gathering of mourners and bowed his head. The others followed in unison. "Let us pray." Aquila proceeded to eulogize the dead girl describing her love for family and friends and her compassion in helping those in great need. He told about how she accepted the Jew, Christus, as her savior, the Son of a loving God. The last bit startled me. How can any living mortal be a son of a god? Did any god truly love the people? Not the ones I knew. I was skeptical of the existence of any god. I wondered if this was the one the Druid priestess warned me about. I shuddered. Was she warning me of some unseen evil, or something else? Was this the reason that drew me to this home tonight? Perhaps I was imagining too much. My old commander, Sextus Rufius, more than once said I did too much thinking. Maybe he was right.

I can neither remember all the events of his long tale about a Messiah who was the Son of God, nor will I try, only the gist of it clings to my memory. Even to this day, I doubt much of what he said. Aquila said this Christus had been accused of blasphemy by the Jews, sent to the procurator, Pontius Pilatus, to be tried and condemned to death. Even though Pilatus knew Christus to be innocent, he still sentenced him to be crucified, a Roman death, at the instigation of the mob. It puzzled me why he was tried by Romans when this was obviously a violation of Jewish law.

After a few more words, Aquila concluded his eulogy with a prayer. Many gathered around him and asked his blessing, which he gave.

Crispus shook his head and whispered, "This Aquila may believe what he says, but to me it sounds like another charlatan god from the East. I'll stick to Melkart."

I wasn't so sure.

We were about to depart when Aquila motioned us to wait. After the rest of the mourners were gone, he approached us.

"I'm sorry, Aquila," I said politely, "but it will take a lot more than what you said tonight to convince me that your god is different from the rest."

He nodded. "I regret I have failed to show you the way. I sense that you want to believe but you refuse to accept it. Perhaps, one day you will believe He is the true God."

"When do you bury your daughter?" I blurted, convinced he would not convert me.

"Tomorrow morning, we will take her body to the necropolis along the Via Triumphalis north of the city walls."

"Aye, I've heard of the place." I knew it to be a large burial ground with a mixed clientele ranging from slaves to middle class and foreigners.

"We cannot afford an expensive tomb out on the Appian Way," Aquila said, "but this cemetery is within our means and allows us to bury Rachel with dignity."

In other words, she wouldn't be thrown into a garbage pit with those too poor to afford a decent funeral.

"You have an enormous task ahead if you believe you can convert the people of Rome to your faith," I said.

"We know, but our daughter's death will give us new strength to carry on."

"Will it?" I asked skeptically.

"Yes, our faith is very strong."

"If it helps you overcome your grief, then your god is far better than many of the other gods," I said.

"Someday." He paused for effect. "It may be the only faith in Rome."

CHAPTER 3

LATE OCTOBER, 45 AD

My grief in losing Kyar had gradually faded to a sweet memory over the months since I arrived in Rome. She was a beautiful German princess, who was sold into slavery and prostitution by her father, the King of the Chatti tribe. I had purchased her while I was with the army in Britannia. But Rix, the treacherous Gallic pimp from whom I bought Kyar, murdered her while I was away on campaign. Before I could take revenge, my Uncle Budar, Crispus, and other members of my cavalry squadron, killed him. Later, I learned Gallus instigated the killing of Kyar. Foolishly, I had borrowed the money from him to purchase her. Even though she was dead, I repaid the loan at the exorbitant one hundred percent interest rate, which he demanded, much to his chagrin. I am from a wealthy family that owns a large *latifundia,* cattle and horse ranch, in Baetica, Southwestern Hispania. I could never prove Gallus was behind the murder, but someday I planned to take my revenge.

The duties required in being Sabinus's retainer kept me busy, and I had little time to dwell upon my loss. My relationships with women since arriving in Rome had been limited to an occasional slave girl who slipped into my cubicle after the household went to bed. Although satisfied sexually, an empty longing lingered in my soul. I became restless. Lonely.

As time went on, my feelings for Eleyne grew. Daughter of Verica, king of the British tribe, the Regni, she had been taken as a royal hostage to insure her father's loyalty to Rome. She was placed in the custody of Sabinus and his wife, Aurelia Severa, who treated her like a daughter.

During the journey from Britannia to Rome, we had developed a friendship. However, I followed Sabinus's advice and kept my distance. Yet, it had grown stronger after the death of her servant woman and friend, Karmune, who was murdered on the first night after we had arrived in Rome. Often, Eleyne and I passed one another in the hallways and stopped to converse in the presence of her ominous Indian bodyguard, Candra. He had been assigned to protect her after Karmune's death.

Being on call twenty-four hours a day as Sabinus's retainer, I lived at his home and dined with him and his family, which included Eleyne. But after the night the assassins attacked Sabinus's home, the previous November, I knew what I felt for her was real, she all but expressed the same for me. Had not Sabinus entered her room when he did, I would have told her of what, dare I say it, love.

Trained by Aurelia Severa, Eleyne had learned to sing and play the lyre. To the delight of the family, she caught on quickly and had a sweet, lyrical voice. Eleyne had many opportunities to display her new talents for the family when they celebrated Rome's numerous holidays. Her soprano voice stirred my soul as she sang in melodious tones of loves lost and found, and of heroic deeds by Rome's mythical characters, and those of her people's warriors. Her songs reflected simple stories and feelings— the way she liked it, and that's what attracted me. Honest and straightforward, just like her people.

The color of Eleyne's pretty, angular face reminded me of white marble, a contrast to her jet hair. But she grew more attractive as Aurelia Severa's training in Roman dress and mannerisms became more apparent. Sabinus's wife introduced Eleyne to the shops of the wealthy along the Sacred Way and bought her a number of elegant gowns and intricately woven tunics becoming her shapely figure. Still, Eleyne preferred making her own clothing and occasionally wore tartan tunics from Britannia.

The Indian bodyguard escorted the women wherever they traveled. Although Aurelia enjoyed the outings, Eleyne appeared oblivious to it all. She admitted later to being lost in thoughts about Karmune's death and yearned to return to her homeland.

* * *

I found Eleyne one day in the atrium as she played her lyre, the melodic sounds echoing through the corridor. I complimented her on her skill, and she thanked me. Turning, Eleyne motioned to Candra, who stood behind and a few steps to the left of her chair, to move out of hearing distance while we conversed. From his scowling face, it was obvious he was not happy about the situation. She gestured me to a wicker chair next to her. The essence of lavender radiated from her being. I glanced to Candra and back to Eleyne and commented on how protective he was of her.

Eleyne related the story about her slave guard. Though mute, by sign language and crude Latin writing, which Eleyne had taught him, she learned about his fascinating past.

"He's from a warrior caste in India called the *Rajput*," she said. "They're the house troops of the Indian kings. The red mark he wears on his forehead is a religious sign meaning life."

She further related how Candra, short for Candragupta, had been the personal guard to a warlord ruling the Land of Sind, along the eastern bank of the Indus River. After watching him kill the assassins with only his bare hands, during the November attack on Sabinus's home, I understood why he had been chosen to protect Eleyne.

"When the king's army was defeated by the Parthians," Eleyne continued, "Candra was captured and sold to a slave caravan traveling to Antioch. He attempted to escape but was caught, and the slave dealer cut out his tongue as punishment! Isn't that barbaric?"

"It's terrible. No one deserves to suffer that fate."

"I'm puzzled why he wasn't sold to a school for gladiators. He doesn't need to speak to fight."

"I don't know the answer, but I pray that he never will. He would surely die."

* * *

Candra was very protective of Eleyne when anyone, especially men, were present. Although the Indian viewed me like the others with suspicion, I gained his respect after the raid on Sabinus's home. At times, I wanted to grab Eleyne by her graceful shoulders, take her into my arms, and make love to her. I restrained myself as long as the dark Indian giant was present.

Nevertheless, I grew more drawn to her, and my thoughts and desire became stronger with each passing day. I needed to confide in someone about the fire raging in me before I did something stupid. Then Aurelia Severa came to mind. Each time I was in her presence, this wise, sympathetic woman placed me at ease. If anyone could give me advice, it was she.

* * *

I sent a slave with a sealed note to Aurelia one morning, asking to see her about a personal matter.

That evening, after Sabinus had gone for his bath, Alexias came to my room. "The mistress wants to see you at once. She waits in the tablinum."

I proceeded to Sabinus's office, located at the rear of the atrium. Nine or ten sputtering candles lit the brightly painted alcove where the senator greeted his guests and Aurelia kept his finances in order. She spent much of her day in the room. Two walls, covered from floor to ceiling with cupboard shelves and stacked with brass, circular book containers, held Sabinus's voluminous scrolls. Sitting on a pedestal in one corner was a small bust of Virgil. His works, especially the *Ecologues*, were the senator's favorite. Two chairs and a plain but highly polished hardwood table filled the rest of the room. Reed pens, papyrus scrolls, and two finely wrought inkwells made with bronze and gold

21

casings were neatly arranged along one edge. A smoky brazier rested on a small tripod in another corner, failing to generate enough heat to ward off the spring evening chill.

Dressed in a warm, white stola covering her matronly body, Aurelia sat behind the table. A red- and blue-trimmed *palla* draped her shoulders. She wore her hair curled into several neat, half-circular rows from the front to the back of her head and tied into a number of curving braids and a bun. Large, gold dolphin earrings dangled from her ears.

She greeted me with a friendly smile, revealing a slightly double chin in her plump but attractive face. "Come in, Marcellus. I have been expecting you. Please have a seat," she offered with an open palm.

"Thank you, Lady," I said, bowing slightly.

I drew up the other chair facing her across the table. A few minutes of small talk set me completely at ease. Those perceptive, wide, brown eyes searched mine as if she knew what I wanted to say.

"I'm flattered you sought my counsel instead of my husband's," she said. "How can I help?"

"I came to you, Lady, because it's a rather delicate matter."

A devilish smirk crossed Aurelia's mouth. "Oh? Then it must involve a woman."

"Yes, someone we both know."

Aurelia Severa leaned forward, placing a fleshy hand on her chin. "Who?"

"Well . . ." I hesitated, thinking perhaps I shouldn't say who it was, wasting my time and hers.

"Come now, Marcellus. If you want my advice I must know her name. Are you having an affair with her?"

My hands grew clammy, and my mouth became parched. "No, Lady, that wouldn't be proper. It's Eleyne."

She nodded slowly. "So I was right."

For a second, I stiffened, my eyes grew wide. "How did you guess?"

She chuckled. "My dear young man, I've seen the way you have watched her at dinner, and in the atrium when speaking to her." She paused. "After the night you saved her life, it became all too obvious, don't you think?" She pulled her hand from her chin.

"I didn't realize it was so evident. I didn't think I felt so strongly about her until that night." Her comments had jolted me. Was I making such a fool of myself?

"It's difficult to hide one's thoughts when you are in love."

I stiffened, my heart stuck in my throat. "But, Lady, I'm not in love."

She shook her head as if scolding me. "Nonsense, Marcellus. I'm old enough to be your mother, and I have raised two sons of my own. I know the looks, the yearnings."

"But I swear!" Heat rushed to my face like boiling sunlight.

"Don't bother with denials," she said. "You are only deceiving yourself. I saw the same mooning eyes in my son, Sabinus the Younger, when he was in love with a slave girl. The foolish boy wanted to marry her. Besides being impossible and against the law, the family would have been ruined. I broke up the affair by selling her." She sighed. "More the pity, because she was an obedient girl and a good worker."

"Naturally, you did the right thing," I sputtered, not caring at the moment for the problems of others.

Aurelia nodded. "Lord Sabinus said he felt the same about me, even though our marriage was arranged. Fortunately, the moment I set eyes upon him, I knew he was the only man I would ever want."

She smiled again. "Of course, you are in love. Now, tell me—from the beginning."

I took a deep breath, and everything poured from me. "Eleyne. I can't stop thinking of her . . . those times I'm in her presence at dinner and our eyes touched . . . I can't stand to be near her . . . and I want to kill that eunuch guard . . . and take her away . . . and it's all impossible. It has grown worse since the raid on your home. After I rescued her, I almost told her how I felt about her, but

Lord Sabinus entered the room. I said nothing. What am I going to do?"

I confessed to an accidental meeting late one night on the balcony above the moonlit garden when we were alone. It happened about one week before the assassins raided Sabinus's home.

"I should have left," I said, "but I was captured by her warmth and of sharing the starlit beauty of the garden with her."

My thoughts and words must have seemed totally unrelated to Aurelia, but I sensed a concern and understanding from her. I continued, confessing more than I meant to, adding that our passions nearly overwhelmed us when Eleyne turned to leave and her arm brushed mine.

"We seemed to inhale the night," I added, "and when our eyes embraced I knew that other women might momentarily possess me, but none could ever own the part of my soul that she had claimed with her gaze."

As soon as I spoke those words, I felt that I betrayed the memory of Kyar. But she was gone. I prayed she would want me to go on with my life.

I looked at Aurelia, who nodded for me to continue.

"Just for a few seconds," I said, "yet in those seconds . . ." I glanced at Aurelia to see if the ramblings had made any sense. Her eyes were locked on my sweaty, fidgeting hands, which I forced into a false state of calmness. Then I recognized I was putting into words feelings I had only thought before. Aurelia was right, but I refused to admit it to myself.

"What should I do? I realize because of Eleyne's position as a hostage, the political ramifications make our situation impossible."

"At least you have the sense to recognize her delicate position."

I nodded.

"I have been married to Lord Sabinus," she explained, "for over twenty years, and privy to many of Rome's intrigues. I have seen men far greater than you lose their lives for much less. You are wise to restrain yourself, but don't despair," she added in a more comforting voice, "things could change."

"I don't see how."

"Anything can happen in Rome and does," she said, lowering her voice. "Intrigues take many strange paths. It has happened before and will again, especially with an emperor . . ." She looked to the curtain-covered door and leaned over the table and whispered, ". . . as mad as Claudius. In the meantime," she said, sitting back and speaking once again in her beautiful low voice, "you will have to wait."

I took another breath. "If I must, but then again, she may not think the same of me."

"Don't worry. She has . . ." Aurelia broke off the conversation and eyed the doorway's flimsy curtains fluttering faintly in the still room. Outside came the sound of light footfalls scurrying away.

"Be a darling," Aurelia asked, "and see who was spying on us."

I raced into the hallway and saw Eleyne scampering down the corridor, but without her Indian guard. I called to her and quickly caught up. I grasped her elbow as she stopped and whirled around, trembling.

"Is Aurelia right?" she demanded. "Do you really care for me?"

I looked into her eyes and answered slowly, "Yes, I do."

"Didn't you guess I felt the same about you, especially the night you rescued me?"

"I guessed it, but wasn't sure. You said you wouldn't know what to do if anything happened to me. But I believed it was said in the heat of the moment. I had no idea."

She flinched. "You've saved my life three times, what did you think?"

"Is that the only reason?"

"No, but it won't work," she said in voice full of resignation, "not now. Not as long as I'm a hostage. Besides . . ." She turned away, tears filling her eyes.

"What else?"

"You know I'm betrothed."

"You're what!" My shoulders tightened, and I swallowed bile.

"Don't you remember? I was betrothed to Bodvak."

I swore softly. "That no longer binds you. He's a rebel, and Rome won't let him live."

"I know, but until I hear otherwise, I must honor my father's wishes. I can't do anything else. I can't." She grimaced, her alabaster face growing pinker with every tear flowing down her cheeks. Covering her eyes with her palms, she turned away.

"Oh, Marcellus, what are we going to do?" She wept softly.

I took her in my arms, a move she didn't resist, and said in a soothing voice, "It'll work out, you'll see. Alliances are broken every day, and in Rome, anything is possible."

She uncovered her tear-stained eyes and searched mine; for what, I couldn't say. "No, it's impossible. If ever I'm released as a hostage, I'll be sent back to my people."

As she nestled in my arms, I looked about searching for her guard, Candra. There was no sign of him. I said gently, "Be patient. My heart tells me things will change for the better," although not really convinced myself.

Eleyne wept a little longer and stopped. She pulled a lilac-scented handkerchief from within her waistband and wiped away the tears staining her cheeks. "Gods, my face must be a fright."

"No, it isn't." I smiled. "It's beautiful."

Eleyne blushed and turned away. She twisted around, and our eyes met. Holding her tightly, I pressed my lips to hers. A gentle first kiss, and then from within a stirring deeper than my passion erupted. A feeling that my soul had touched hers somehow, a warmth I had never known before. Nothing mattered but our moment together. She sighed and yielded momentarily. I realized I was taking advantage of her confused state, and reluctantly, with great control, forced myself to turn my lips from hers. In spirit, nothing could keep us from one another. Not Verica, her father. Not Rome. No living thing. Not even Kyar.

She placed the side of her delicate face against my chest. "What now, Marcellus?" she whispered.

I was at a loss for words but had to say something reassuring. "Nothing can change my feelings for you."

"I know, I pray to the gods for help."

"As do I."

Then she tightened. "Someone might see, what if Sabinus . . .?"

"He'd break me, and I'd be transferred back to Britannia." What irony. To return to the land of her people, and despite her earlier protestations, she could never go.

"Oh no. I would never see you again," Eleyne cried. She pulled away and asked softly as to herself, "What's the use? It won't work, Marcellus. Why did I have to fall in love with you?"

I felt hope in her words. "Then we will find a way."

"No! We can't! It's impossible. I'll always love you, but . . ."

"What?"

"I never want to see you again." She turned away from me.

I grabbed her by the shoulders and turned her towards me. "Impossible! We live under the same roof."

"Then you'll have to stay away from me. I won't speak to you again—ever."

"After what we've confessed to each other? Aurelia knows my thoughts. Gods know how many others must suspect," I answered calmly trying to control my emotions. I was angry and hurt at the same time.

She wiped the tears again with her cloth and placed it back in her waistband. "I don't care—it doesn't matter." She gave me a knowing look. "Go back to your slave girls. They'll take care of you. You don't need me."

For the length of a heartbeat my shoulders tightened. *No slave could ever take Eleyne's place.*

Before I could respond, Eleyne broke away from me, whirled, and fled down the hallway. It was all I could do to keep from swearing. When I glanced about, I saw Aurelia standing at the door, her eyes filled with concern. Only then did I realize she had heard everything.

"Both of you are fools," she called softly. "But so am I, and I will do what I can to help."

* * *

JUNE. 46 AD

One humid morning, Crispus and I joined Sabinus prior to meeting with his clients in the atrium of his home. Sabinus nodded to the scroll he held in one hand at the side of his thigh. Then his gaze brushed mine for a moment. "Eleyne's father, King Verica, is dead."

Crispus and I glanced at each other. My friend knew how I felt about Eleyne, and my first thought was for her. Now, she had lost her value as a hostage to Rome. What would be her fate? "How did he die?" I asked.

"Assassinated by his bodyguards while on a hunt."

"Who put them up to it, sir?" Crispus asked.

The senator shook his head. "We shall never know. Followers, loyal to Verica, fell upon the assailants and instantly killed them all."

I snorted. "Conveniently silencing the lot. Who is replacing him as king?" I knew the answer.

"Togidubnus, Verica's advisor, was appointed by the emperor," Sabinus said.

"I can guess who was behind Verica's assassination." I rubbed the itching scar on my face.

"Undoubtedly, you're right, Marcellus, but all further inquiries have been squashed like poisonous insects," Sabinus said.

I cleared my throat and swallowed. My mouth went dry. I couldn't understand why I found it so difficult to ask the question. I said in a rasping voice, "What about Eleyne? Her father's death will come as a terrible shock to her."

Sabinus's dark eyes pierced mine as if looking into the heart of my soul. *Does he know about my love for Eleyne?*

"Since she is my responsibility," Sabinus answered, "it's my duty to tell her with my wife beside me. The two have become very close, you know. Aurelia considers her to be

28

the daughter she never had." He paused and nodded. "I feel much the same way."

"Sir, may I be allowed to be present when you break the news? Eleyne and I are friends, and I would like to offer my condolences."

"Of course, Marcellus. With both of you under my roof, you're almost family."

I pondered Eleyne's future, our future. "What's to become of her now that Verica is dead?"

Crispus winced. No doubt he thought I was going to get myself in woman trouble—again.

"It's too soon to think about the matter," Sabinus replied thoughtfully. "Although it's the emperor's decision, he'll entrust the matter to me because Eleyne is my ward."

* * *

Since the day we first expressed our mutual love, Eleyne never passed me in the halls without a look of yearning. Then one afternoon back in April, I saw her strolling through the garden, with her ever-present and powerful Indian bodyguard, Candra, following at a discreet distance. Slowly, I approached her, not knowing if he would block my way. He glared and started moving in my direction. Eleyne spotted me and then turned to Candra. She motioned with her head for him to back away. He frowned but stepped back. A smile graced her delicate face when I halted before her. The smell of roses and lavender drifted on a light wind, and birds chirped in the nearby bushes and trees. Eleyne and I exchanged a few pleasantries before she quietly remarked, "I know I said I never wanted to see you again," she sighed, "but I know that's not practical, we live under the same roof. Can we . . . you and I still remain friends?"

I smiled. "Of course we can." Inwardly, I knew and she must have known it was a lie. Her eyes said she still loved me as I did her. I would be content with being a *friend*, but I didn't know how long that would last. Fortunately, Candra's presence made it easier for both of us to control our longing.

Eleyne exhaled, as if relieved. "Thank you, I'm so glad we still have that." Eleyne glanced about checking the garden, seeing if anyone but Candra was near. She trusted him.

"You know, Marcellus, there is something I have been meaning to ask you."

"Tell me." My forehead creased, curious about what was on her mind.

"I've told you before how much I miss my father."

"I know the feeling." My own father was dead, but I still remembered him fondly.

"I have only received official reports that he was alive and well, but never any personal messages. Are they true? I don't know what to believe."

"If there was anything amiss with your father, Lord Sabinus would be the first to tell you. He is an honorable man. He has told me he has great respect for Verica."

"I hope you are right. In the meantime, all I can do is pray to the gods, especially Mother Goddess, to watch over him."

* * *

That evening, Sabinus consulted Aurelia, who sent a slave to fetch Eleyne.

Dressed in a scarlet-trimmed, gold chiton, Eleyne came to the triclinium. Her jet-black hair was braided and curled on the top of her head in the latest Roman fashion. She seemed puzzled by the little gathering in the study of Sabinus, Aurelia, and me. "You wanted to see me, Lord Sabinus?"

"Have a seat, my dear," Aurelia pointed to a cushioned, three-legged stool beside her. I stood to one side of Eleyne. My hand trembled as I restrained myself from touching her.

Sabinus, his face stony, sat behind the office table and peered into her eyes. "Eleyne, I have bad news."

"About my father?"

He nodded. "I'm afraid so. He's with the gods."

Eleyne's hand pressed a hand against her heart. "I knew it." She bit her lower lip, glanced at Aurelia and, for a split second, back to me. "When did this happen, how?"

Sabinus told her briefly of the assassination.

Tears swelled in Eleyne's eyes, and her face flushed. She cupped it with pale, long fingers and began to shake. Lowering her head, she softly wept.

Aurelia reached over and placed an arm around her distraught friend. She pulled Eleyne to her. "We understand, Eleyne," Aurelia said quietly. "I know this is terrible to hear, and we are truly sorry."

I wanted to reach over and touch Eleyne, but thought it better to wait until Aurelia had calmed her feelings and grief as only a woman knew how. And I didn't want to seem too familiar in front of Sabinus.

"My dear," he said to Eleyne, "you are among friends, we grieve with you. Your loss is ours."

"What difference does it make?" she answered through tears. "My mother died of a chill in her lungs when I was five. Now, Father is dead. He was getting old, but I wanted to see him before he died."

"Your father," Sabinus interjected, "was a great warrior. I assure you, dear lady, that I mourn his passing. I preferred to have him as my friend and ally than my enemy. That is why we made you a part of our family. We mourn him because your presence has touched all of us."

"Then why am I a hostage?" She pulled herself from Aurelia's arm and glared at Sabinus.

"The emperor considers you a hostage, we don't. I took custody of you, so you wouldn't fall into the hands of Governor-General Aulus Plautius." Sabinus paused, taking a deep breath. "He has no love for the Britons, even one as innocent and beautiful as you, especially when Bodvac fled to Caratacus. I regret I wasn't at liberty to tell your father why I took you hostage."

Sabinus had no choice. Verica was suspected of conspiring with Caratacus. Eleyne could never return to Britannia with Togidubnus ruling in place of her father, he would kill her. As a foreign princess, and daughter of a loyal ally, Eleyne could be married to anyone the emperor chose. A number of senators visited Sabinus's home, and I had watched them as they cast their lecherous eyes upon her. News of her father's death would encourage them to ask for her hand in marriage. Although she had no wealth or power, marrying the daughter of a barbarian king was still considered politically prestigious.

Eleyne shook her head. Stray strands of her hair fell around her kohl-stained eyes. "I've brought you only grief and horror."

"Nonsense," Aurelia said.

"It's true," she insisted, "Karmune's dead, and I have been nothing but trouble."

"That is simply not so," Aurelia countered. "What happened was not your fault. We grieved for Karmune, but she saved your life. In her death, she saved the lives of many others, including my husband and the emperor. The gods work in strange ways, have you forgotten?"

"No, of course not, it's . . ." She sniffled and wiped tears from her eyes and then blew her nose in a cloth napkin Aurelia handed to her. "I miss my father. I want to go home!" She leaned over and buried her face onto her mistress's chest.

Eleyne raised her head for a second, and as our eyes met, I touched her arm with my fingertips, not of passion, but of support.

"Eleyne," I whispered, a plea from my soul to her heartache, and her name upon my lips spoke volumes of my true feelings for her.

Eleyne's grief overwhelmed her, but she did not respond. Yet I hoped that something deep within might remember my touch and know I loved her.

Sabinus motioned to the door, and we departed, leaving his wife and Eleyne alone.

CHAPTER 4

After Eleyne had been told about the death of her father, King Verica, I didn't see her for nearly a week. From then on, she hid her grief like a true princess. But she told me she no longer found any solace in praying to the old gods. I told her about Priscilla, and the loss of her daughter, and how she found comfort in the Jewish God and teachings of one Christus. A week later I took her to the home of Priscilla, who seemed to take to Eleyne as if she had been her lost daughter. Eleyne was near Rachel's age of seventeen. Since that first visit with Pricilla, Eleyne appeared to be more at peace with herself.

After dinner, one hot September evening, Eleyne and I sat beside the cool gushing fountain in the *peristylium*. The hissing fountain spray reflected the sparkling yellow-gold light of the torches surrounding the garden, giving Eleyne's pale face a radiant glow. I was almost too entranced by her to feel the misting air. At a discreet distance stood the ever-present giant, Candra, keeping a watchful eye on his charge. She took up her lyre and played a haunting melody, its tune mixing pleasantly with the scent of roses and other flowers planted in the garden.

When she finished, she laid her instrument on the bench beside her. She sighed and focused her dark-blue eyes on mine. "Now that father is gone, what's to become of me? It's been nearly two months, and I haven't heard a word. I'm no longer useful to Rome."

"The emperor is leaving the details to Sabinus."

"Don't I have a say?" Eleyne swung her head toward the fountain and stared at the eels swimming lazily among the lily pads.

"It's not so simple," I replied calmly. "Deals must be struck and favors exchanged."

Frowning, she turned and glared. "With my life?"

"Exactly, but you'll come to no harm. Sabinus and I will protect you." For the length of a few heartbeats, I paused, unsure how she would accept my next words. "However, the emperor has forbidden your return to Britannia."

Eleyne nodded, as if she had expected the inevitable. "There's nothing left for me in Britannia now. If I returned, Togidubnus would kill me because I'm a threat to his rule. The tribal council would rebel and elect me queen."

I didn't believe Rome would allow that to happen, but no doubt she would be murdered.

A few moments of silence elapsed. She sat quietly, hands folded in her lap. "What does Lord Sabinus plan to do with me?"

"More than likely Sabinus will arrange for your marriage to a rich nobleman." The thought sickened me, and I was determined to prevent such a disaster. My family was wealthy, if only I could find a way to enter the Equestrian Order, my chances of marrying her would increase ten-fold.

Eleyne bolted upright. "Married? I don't want to be married to some fat Roman. Why can't they leave me alone?" She looked into my eyes, pleading, and her soft hand touched my forearm. "You won't let that happen, will you?"

I knew what she wanted. Our feelings for one another had not diminished over these last several months, although we had learned to suppress them. No more. Determined not to lose her, I had to risk the consequences.

Taking her smooth hands in mine, I raised them to my lips, and lightly kissed them.

"We don't need to hide from one another any longer, Eleyne. Do you still love me?"

"You know I do." She moved softly into my arms. Her hair, lightly scented with lavender, brushed against my face.

"Become my wife, Eleyne. I'll do anything for you and protect you always. We don't dare to wait any longer. I don't want Sabinus marrying you to anyone but me."

It came in a flash. I needed his aid in being admitted to the knighthood. Would he help me? Did he honestly want Eleyne married to some political hack?

Her grasp tightened on my arm, as if at once elated and alarmed by my proposal. "Is it possible, darling? Will they let us marry? I'm afraid you'll get into trouble for asking."

"Let them stop us!" I boasted, more confident than I felt. "If Sabinus has the power to make the choice, he should think enough of you and me to grant our request. You are the only woman I want." Now I silently prayed to the gods the senator would aid us.

"I'm so happy, Marcellus. I've loved you for so long. Had you found another woman, I would have died. Lord Sabinus thinks highly of you—Aurelia told me."

She stepped forward and threw her arms tightly around me, her lips pressing mine.

Candra winced.

I motioned toward the stairs near the entrance to the garden, leading to my room. Without a word she followed me up the steps. At the door to my cubicle she turned to Candra who had dutifully followed. "You can go, Candra," she commanded. "Come back for me at dawn."

He did not budge. His eyes flicked from hers to mine, threatening me with all warnings his lips could not utter, and for a fleeting moment my hand slipped to the hilt of my dagger.

"Candra," she ordered, "I said *you can go!*"

He frowned, glaring at me with large, black eyes. In that moment I wondered if he, too, loved her. Perhaps he did. Finally, he trudged away. He kept peering back over his shoulder as he descended the stairs, eyes mixed with hate, loyalty, and uncertainty. I knew then he did love her, but she was mine alone.

* * *

The next morning, after breakfast, I encountered a grave Sabinus in the atrium. His mood put a damper on my high spirits, but no matter what his decision, I was determined to have Eleyne as my wife, claiming her by force if necessary.

"You look as if you've seen old Charon the boatman, sir," I said. "Is there something wrong?"

"Unfortunately, yes." His hands gripped my shoulder. "Marcellus, Senator Vitellius received permission from the emperor to marry Eleyne."

I froze in my boots. I remembered the first day in Rome when that fat, pompous excuse for a senator welcomed Sabinus at the docks. Vitellius expressed interest in Eleyne, but I thought it was windblown rhetoric.

"But, why?" I stammered, twisting from his grip.

"Why not? She's beautiful and no longer valuable as a hostage."

"Can't you stop it?"

Squinting his forehead, he eyed me quizzically. "Why should I? After all, she's Rome's hostage. Although I admit being fond of her, my responsibility was to keep her out of mischief."

"If she's no longer a hostage, isn't she free to do as she pleases?"

"What are you trying to say?"

I hesitated. My heart pounded, and a feeling of desperation swept over me. My mind raced. I considered taking her away this very moment, even if I had to slay Sabinus.

"I realize I'm being presumptuous, sir, and were it not for Senator Vitellius, I wouldn't ask so soon. The hourglass is running out. I'm asking permission to marry Eleyne."

For a fleeting few seconds, Sabinus's face darkened.

"You are bold, aren't you? The emperor can marry her to anyone he wishes."

"Yes, sir, but if he doesn't make the right choice, she'll be miserable."

He waved the remark away. "Emotions have no place in marriage arrangements. What makes you think she wants you for a husband?"

"I asked her, and she accepted."

"You took it upon yourself, did you?" he said sternly. "That reminds me of when you disobeyed orders in Britannia and attacked the Druid temple. You always were impulsive."

"No one said I couldn't ask her, so I did."

36

A grin crossed Sabinus's face. "You know, Marcellus, Aurelia told me months ago about you and Eleyne. Neither one of you have hidden your fondness for one another. I'm not blind to the looks you two have exchanged."

"Lady Aurelia said the same thing."

He nodded. "So she told me. To be honest, Eleyne will be a fine wife. It's time you settled down."

Instantly, I was ashamed of my thoughts of violence towards him, and relief brought me near tears. "Then you approve?"

"I do, but it will take some effort to change the emperor's mind. I may have to reward Claudius's secretary, Narcissus, to help me in the process." He spat.

"Can it be done?"

He explained his plan.

Later, I broke the news to Eleyne about Vitellius's intentions.

"I would rather be eaten by a lion in the arena than marry that bloated ox!"

I took her hand, lightly stroked her face, and managed to calm her down while I explained Sabinus's plan.

"It had better work," she answered. "Oh, Marcellus, I'll die if I can't marry you."

CHAPTER 5

The plan, involving Vitellius's dull-minded, soon-to-be-divorced wife, Lollia Appolonia, nearly failed.

A week later, I was summoned by Lady Aurelia Severa to meet her in the library. She directed me to a chair across the desk from her. Nearing forty, light wrinkles circled intelligent eyes in her plump but still attractive face. Specks of gray mixed with her jet hair, which was wrapped in circular tresses on top of her head. "My husband will fill you in on the details later, but I have news directly affecting Eleyne's fate."

My body tightened at the thought of losing her. "What's wrong?"

"Nothing so far," Aurelia answered calmly. She tugged at the sleeve of her white stola girded beneath her bosom. "But I finished speaking to Lollia Appolonia less than an hour ago, and we have a problem."

I pitied Vitellius's frumpy wife. Aurelia said the woman had been treated shabbily by her husband for many years.

"The day after my husband revealed his plan," Aurelia continued, "I approached the senator's wife. Poor dear, she was beside herself, can you blame her?" She stared through me with her wide, walnut eyes as if I weren't there.

I started sweating, my shoulders tensed. Her piercing look unnerved me. "She must be at a loss to prevent the divorce," I said.

"Yes," Aurelia said, "that is why I suggested she demand the return of her dowry and all interest accumulated in the savings banks." Aurelia lowered her head and pulled a metal stylus from an open compartment, part of the wax tablet on the desk, and examined it. Then she returned it to the same place. She studied me again with the same intensity. "As you can imagine, Senator Vitellius's wife agreed instantly."

"That's encouraging," I said in a guarded voice, suspecting she wasn't finished.

Aurelia sighed and silently slid two gold bracelets on her left arm up and down between the wrist and elbow a couple of times before she stopped and dropped her hands upon the desk. "When I saw her the following afternoon, she said Vitellius had remained adamant about the divorce. Earlier, Lollia thought she had won."

My chest tightened. "What changed Vitellius's mind?"

"That evening at dinner, after our first conversation, Lollia confronted her husband." Aurelia licked her full lips. "She demanded the return of her dowry if he insisted on a divorce."

Aurelia continued to tell me that Vitellius was initially shocked and dismayed, obviously never thinking his wife would make any demands. He vacillated at the last moment. Deciding to think the matter over, Vitellius left Lollia reclining on the dining couch, her fat bulk in tears.

"In other words, the situation got worse," I said and clenched a hand into a fist, wishing I could have smashed it into Vitellius's bloated face.

"It did," Aurelia said. "The next morning, Vitellius informed Lollia that after the bankers drew up all the necessary papers for transfer, he would return the dowry."

"You mean, despite his greed, he'd still give up a fortune to marry Eleyne?" I asked. My throat muscles tightened, the vocal cords seemed to scratch as the words poured out.

Aurelia raised her hand. "Calm yourself, Marcellus, I'm not finished. To say the least, Lollia was stunned. Her husband had capitulated too easily, and she suspected he was receiving financial support from someone else. He had to, else he would be penniless."

Aurelia explained that Lollia Appolonia had discussed the situation with her loyal house steward, a Persian freedman. I had heard he was devious by nature and had ways of getting to the bottom of the matter. The steward, who Aurelia believed was Lollia's lover, had contacts with slaves in many of Rome's wealthiest households, including that of Gallus. Not surprisingly, he learned Vitellius had made several late-night visits to the Gallus home. By means of bribery, the steward ascertained from slaves within Gallus's house that he was financing Vitellius. Aurelia finished by saying, "Lollia couldn't understand why."

I knew the answer. I realized I gripped the handle of the dagger, hanging from my belt so tightly my fingers grew sore.

"But I correctly guessed the reason," Aurelia continued. "Gallus knew that upon the death of his father, Vitellius became one of the most influential members in the Senate and considered a *Friend of Caesar.* Using his power, he could subtly enhance and advance the restoration of Gallus's family name to good standing, which he did. Why do you think he inherited his late father's seat in the Senate so quickly? It matters not that he has to wait until he is thirty years old before he can participate in their proceedings," Aurelia added in a disgusted voice.

"What else, Lady?" I asked, puzzled by her abrupt stop.

"Gallus learned of your intentions to marry Eleyne. Out of spite, he is helping Vitellius to take her from you."

"What can we do to stop him?" It was all I could do to control my anger and fear. This monster, who had been hand-in-glove in the murder of Kyar, now attempted to destroy my marriage with the only other love of my life, Eleyne.

"Tomorrow, my husband meets with Gallus. Sabinus summoned that insufferable young man after I informed him of Vitellius's betrayal."

"What's to stop him from ignoring Lord Sabinus's request?"

Aurelia smiled. "My dear Marcellus, it isn't wise to refuse an invitation from a senator."

* * *

The following morning Gallus arrived at Sabinus's home, followed by a retinue of freedman, slaves, bodyguards, and other hangers-on. To Gallus's consternation, only he was admitted to Sabinus's home. The rest were summarily commanded to wait outside the front gate.

As I listened through the parchment-thin walls of an adjoining room, Sabinus confronted Gallus. Gripping the handle of my dagger, I waited eagerly for the senator to put Gallus into his place.

"Remain standing, young Anicius Pedius Gallus," Sabinus said in a firm voice. "This won't take long."

I heard the shuffling of sandals on the mosaic floor. "As you wish, sir. Why did you send for me?"

A hand or fist slammed down upon the desk, echoing through the house. "I will ask the questions," Sabinus said. His cushion squeaked as he readjusted himself in his chair. "I hear you're making Senator Vitellius a substantial loan."

"With all due respect, Senator Titus Flavius Sabinus, I consider financial affairs a private matter." Gallus scraped his shoes on the floor.

"So do I, when a loan is involved. However, I consider replacing the dowry of Vitellius's wife an outrageous bribe."

A gasp escaped Gallus's mouth. "What in Mars are you talking about?"

"You know exactly what I'm talking about—influence-peddling, anything else you want to call buying favors," Sabinus answered coolly.

A pause. I wondered why neither spoke. Finally, Gallus said, "Senator Sabinus, your accusations are very serious. Do you have proof?"

Sabinus pounded the desk again. "Enough to see that you are never readmitted to the Senate, and your family name struck from the Senate list forever."

I nodded as if in their presence. *Good.*

"I have committed no crime," Gallus answered in a surly tone. "I am helping a man made a pauper by his scorned wife. After all, he isn't the first distinguished senator left without means in Rome."

I wanted to laugh. Gallus didn't have a charitable bone in his body.

"And he won't be the last," Sabinus said. "However, you can explain your reasoning before the Senate, where I plan to bring you and Senator Vitellius to trial."

My breath caught in my throat. This last remark took me by surprise. Would Sabinus follow through with his threat?

Gallus scraped his feet again and cleared his throat. "That isn't necessary, Senator Sabinus. I shall inform Senator Vitellius I have reconsidered the matter and must deny his request for a loan."

"A wise decision."

"Then you will drop the charges?"

"If you follow through on your promise," Sabinus growled.

"I will, but what about Senator Vitellius? He can ask others for a loan."

"I shall deal with him. He'll see the virtue in staying with his wife. He couldn't afford the outrageous interest rates charged by the money lenders, in any case."

"What is to become of the barbarian princess?"

"Does it matter?"

A pause. "No."

"Since her well-being is my concern, I'll see she marries the proper person. Unlike you, it will be someone who considers her the civilized woman she is. Now leave me."

I heard the squeaking of shoe leather, and then shoes stomping as Gallus left the library and stormed out of the house.

* * *

Later, Sabinus told me of his confrontation with Vitellius. The bejowled senator understood the implications of his association with Gallus and backed away. He told Sabinus he couldn't afford to lose his status as Caesar's friend because of his involvement with the son of a senator who had conspired to kill the emperor.

Sabinus had bluffed Gallus and Vitellius. "Had I brought charges against the two in the Senate," he explained, "more than likely, I would have lost the case because of Vitellius's influence. I depended on his dislike of public scandal to force him to capitulate.

"The so-called proof of Gallus's bribing Vitellius," he added, "turned out to be no more than rumors. However, I was certain they were true, and willing to stake my reputation and gamble with a bluff. Thank the lucky twins, Castor and Pollux, it worked."

Within days, I received word Gallus seethed upon discovering he had been tricked. I knew he would quietly mark his time until another opportunity arose to regain his influence.

* * *

Early Monday morning, a couple of days later, Sabinus's entourage of freedmen, slaves, as well as Crispus and myself, milled about the Imperial palace's cavernous audience room. Other groups of noblemen and their retinues were also present. A cool breeze swirled in through the open windows high in the walls, mixing with the murmur of voices in low conversations. I shuddered as a chill ran through my body and wrapped my cloak about the shoulders. As we waited for the emperor to appear, balding, triple-chin Vitellius, wearing a white toga trimmed with a broad, purple edge, approached our little group.

"Watch this," Sabinus whispered to me.

"I have the most terrible news, my dear Sabinus," Vitellius said in a distressed voice that echoed through the yawning chamber. The little clusters of noblemen and lesser people, scattered about the great room, halted their conversations, their ears in our direction.

"What's the trouble, my friend? You look as if you've seen the face of Medusa," Sabinus said.

Vitellius's jowls shook like gelatinous grease as he flung his hands up in disgust. "You must be talking about my wife, the miserable cow. No, unfortunately, I can't marry your lovely barbarian."

"Why, you must be devastated," Sabinus said in feigned sympathy. "What happened to your plans?"

Vitellius wiped his sweaty forehead with a silk cloth that had been handed to him by one of his nearby slaves.

43

He tossed it back to the servant. "My wife refuses to give me a divorce."

"A mere inconvenience," Sabinus answered with a flick of the hand. "You don't need her permission."

"That's not the reason," he replied, placing his plump fingers on Sabinus's forearm. "It's a matter of finances."

"You're a wealthy man."

Vitellius cast his eyes on the polished floor and sighed. "The fortune, all that wonderful gold and those precious gems, belongs to my wife. It was her dowry. If I divorce her, I must return every last quadran. I'll be ruined."

"What a shame. You're a good man, Lucius Vitellius. I can't wish ruin on one of my best friends."

"You're most kind, Flavius Sabinus." The fat senator shrugged. "Oh well, perhaps it's for the best. After all, she is a foreigner," he added with a sneer as he glanced in my direction, "and belongs with aliens."

* * *

Upon leaving the palace, Sabinus's entourage strolled through the crowds in the noisy Forum. Jostling our way past the trading booths bordering the Portico of Gaius and Lucius, Sabinus acknowledged Vitellius had to publicly place the blame on his wife for refusing the divorce. He had to distance himself from any admission to debts and to Gallus. However, as a concession for refusing the divorce, Lollia Appolonia agreed he could buy the most beautiful slave woman in Rome to become his mistress.

"Your proposal to Eleyne was very timely," Sabinus said to me as I strolled beside him. Crispus followed behind us. "Because of her father's death, I didn't expect you to ask for my permission so soon."

"I thank the twins I didn't wait," I said, thinking of her with Vitellius. I nearly choked.

"You had the vision of a Chaldean astrologer."

"Won't there be talk among the nobility of her marrying a centurion?"

"Of course. But they'll keep their traps shut if you're a knight."

The impact of a missile from a ballista could not have been greater than Sabinus's announcement. I stopped in my tracks and stared at Sabinus. Crispus pushed into my back, and I momentarily staggered before regaining my balance. I looked about as the crowd moved around us. Despite the shouts of a hawking bronze-wear dealer in my ears, no one paid us any attention. What I coveted for so long would become a reality and a fulfillment of my parents' dreams. A knighthood meant promotion to the higher ranks within the army, and even the rank of legion commander would no longer be out of the question. Gallus's position was too weak to interfere with my elevation to this illustrious order. To his consternation and by the time he gained power, my position as knight would be secured.

"I'm deeply honored," I finally stammered, "I had no idea—"

"You deserve it, Marcellus," Sabinus said, as we moved away from the boisterous trader.

Crispus, who came around to my side, nodded. "The senator is right, good friend."

"You've proven your value," Sabinus continued, "and your family has the qualifying income. A knight marrying a princess, barbarian or otherwise, is an honorable union, and received with great favor in Rome."

"But how will you achieve this?" I asked. "After Gallus's threats, I didn't believe it was possible."

"Gallus has influential friends but no real power, not yet," Sabinus answered. "I, too, have influence. Much as I despise him, I have been cultivating a friendship with the emperor's secretary, Narcissus. He is willing to assist us because he hated the Elder Gallus and has no love for his son."

"No doubt a few pieces of gold wouldn't hurt either," I said.

Sabinus shrugged. "Unfortunately, with Narcissus, *friendship* carries a price. No matter, it shall be done." For a second, his hand touched my shoulder. "As a loyal soldier and citizen of Rome, you deserve no less."

I remained speechless, humbled by his compliment. Finally, I mumbled, "Thank you."

"I agree with his lordship," Crispus said.

I stared at Crispus and grinned. Turning about, I heard people shouting at us to move out of the way. Then Sabinus said, "Come on, let's go to my home."

Although I knew Sabinus's compliment to be sincere, most Romans still considered Spaniards little more than barbarians. Even though we had been part of the empire for nearly two hundred years and most were Roman citizens, I doubted if the aristocracy cared one quadran if I married a British woman. At least, no good Roman blood would be diluted.

Returning home, Crispus and I followed Sabinus through the atrium to the library where we found Aurelia sitting behind the desk studying a wax tablet. She looked up into Sabinus's eyes and smiled.

After the usual greetings, Sabinus asked his wife, "Where is Eleyne?"

"She's in the garden playing her lyre, I suppose. Why do you ask?"

Sabinus grinned. "Perfect." He held out his hand to Aurelia. "Please join us, my dear. Marcellus has something important to say to our young ward."

"Does he now?" Aurelia gave me a knowing smile as she came around from behind the desk and took her husband's hand in hers.

Sabinus motioned to Crispus and me to follow.

Sitting on a cushioned, marble bench, at the end of the short, graveled path, Eleyne, dressed in a long, pale tunic trimmed in gold, strummed her lyre and hummed a quiet tune. Nearby, an artificial brooklet, surrounded by a miniature forest of small pines and bushes, gurgled its way into a little pool containing tamed eels. A light breeze rustled through the foliage and caressed our faces. The peaceful setting nearly made one forget the noise of the city street just over the high wall from us.

As we approached, she peered in our direction, stopped her playing, and carefully placed the instrument on the bench beside her. She stood and studied us as if unsure why the four of us were there. For the space of a heartbeat, she turned to Candra, who leaned against the garden wall next to an old boxed tree.

Turning about, she bowed slightly to Sabinus and Aurelia. "Lord Sabinus and Lady Aurelia, good afternoon." As an apparent afterthought she added quietly, "Marcellus." She nodded to Crispus. "Begging your pardon, Lord, why are you all here? The last time you gathered like this, you brought me news of my father's death. Do you bring more bad news?"

"On the contrary, my dear," Aurelia answered. She nodded to me. "Marcellus?"

I stepped forward and admit I was a little nervous, my throat suddenly dry, tiny bumps raised on my arms and back. I licked my lips. After all this time, I didn't think it would be so hard to say. "Eleyne . . . ," I stammered, "Eleyne, Lord Sabinus has given us permission to marry."

"He has?" she said with a squeal of delight. "You mean I don't have to marry Senator Vitellius? Marcellus!" She flung her arms around my neck and hugged me.

Remembering our company, she released her hold and turned to Sabinus. "Thank you, Lord. I'm so grateful." Words seemed to fail her as she quickly hugged Sabinus. He flushed red and laughed heartily. She fluttered to Aurelia, bouncing like the young girl she was. I was overjoyed with her happiness.

"Eleyne," Aurelia said, "we are so pleased for you and Marcellus. At last you have found the joy you deserve." She kissed Eleyne on the cheek.

Crispus came forward, gave me a big, toothy smile, and shook my hand. "Congratulations, old friend, you deserve the best." Then he stood back.

"When do you wish to be married?" Sabinus asked.

"With your permission, sir, as soon as General Vespasian returns from Britannia," I answered. "If I'm not being too presumptuous, I would be honored if he would attend the ceremony." Sabinus had received reports that his younger brother, commander of the Second Augustan

Legion had waged a successful campaign in southwest Britannia. He was being recalled by Emperor Claudius and would receive a ceremonial ovation upon his arrival in Rome.

"I'm sure arrangements can be made," Sabinus said. "My brother is very political, but now that Eleyne no longer has value as a Roman hostage, he will want what is best for her."

Eleyne's body tightened, and she clung to me and placed her head against my chest.

I prayed that Gallus would do nothing to jeopardize our happiness.

CHAPTER 6

After a successful campaign in Britannia, Sabinus's younger brother, General Vespasian, returned to Rome. The Emperor Claudius publicly thanked him in a ceremony on the steps of the Temple of Apollo. Then Claudius and Vespasian sacrificed fifty oxen at the altar of the brass god of healing and prophecy.

That evening, as guests of Sabinus and Aurelia, Eleyne and I attended a palace banquet given by Caesar in Vespasian's honor. Basking in the smoky light of a thousand olive oil lamps and candles, the halls and great dining room overflowed with senators, knights, and wealthy citizens, as well as aliens and their guests chattering in a dozen languages. Tastefully arranged in multicolored displays, a legion of flowers and their perfumed scents gave the monumental room an aromatic garden atmosphere.

At their beck and call, Imperial slaves and personal attendants waited on guests, serving wine, sweetmeats, honey cakes, and other delicacies. Before reclining on thickly cushioned couches forming a three-sided square, servants removed our sandals and washed our feet.

Upon the raised dais, the Emperor Claudius and his cat-eye empress, Messalina, nearly thirty years his junior, feasted with their honored guests, General Vespasian, his wife, and intimate guests. Eleyne and I dined with Sabinus and Aurelia on the main floor across from the emperor, with Vitellius and his equally obese wife, Lollia Appolonia. Together, they severely punished a couch, adequate for three people. It visibly sagged. Vitellius's new mistress, a tall, stately German girl from the Marcommani Tribe, eagerly awaited to serve her master. The yellow-haired beauty stood behind his couch while many of the male guests shamelessly leered at her.

Close by, Candra, his arms folded across his tunic, kept watch over Eleyne.

Gallus, wearing a brocaded silk, white toga, had been invited to the feast by one of his father's old senator friends, Lucius Camillus.

I motioned to Sabinus, as Gallus and the senator engaged in a conversation. "Why did Senator Camillus bring Gallus to the feast, sir? He's asking for political disaster."

"Camillus slipped Narcissus a substantial sum of gold to place a favorable word on Gallus's behalf with the emperor."

"Obviously it worked," I whispered. "But I thought he loathed Gallus as much as his father?"

"Unfortunately, Narcissus's greed is insatiable. Money always speaks first," Sabinus said in a grave voice.

Two attractive young ladies known for their amorous adventures reclined with their elderly senator husbands on a nearby couch. They gave Gallus inviting glances, but he paid no attention. Leaning against a pink striated pillar, one of Gallus's young, pretty male attendants eyed the women jealously.

Gallus caught sight of Eleyne and stared at her for a few seconds. Acting as if I didn't exist, he smiled and nodded before turning to Senator Camillus. His eyes kept returning to her.

"Marcellus, why does Gallus keep staring at me like that?" Eleyne asked.

"I would like to think it's because he has good taste," I answered. Girdled around the waist with a yellow palla, Eleyne's long, sleeveless, green tunic contrasted with the pale, red ocher lightly daubed on her white cheeks and lips. Little, golden duck earrings dangled from her small lobes, and a gilded necklace of deep-red garnets encircled her neck. Combed into a Celtic-style single braid, her jet-black hair dropped to the middle of her back. A small, jewel-encrusted, silver tiara crowned her lovely head.

I wore a new linen toga with a narrow, purple stripe running down the middle, denoting the rank of knight. Two weeks before, I had been elevated to the Equestrian Order by the emperor. Adorning my right hand was the coveted golden ring marking my new status. Although proud, I made it a point to show humility, avoiding the role of a boorish snob. But from the moment Sabinus announced my promotion to his friends and clients, people seemed to treat me with greater respect. Thank the gods Crispus regarded me no differently—I valued his friendship too much for anything to change between us.

I had written my mother and informed her of the promotion, but several weeks would pass before I received a reply. She would be pleased and proud, because I was the first in our family to achieve this high honor.

"What else were you going to say about Gallus?" Eleyne asked, pulling me out of my thoughts.

"Gallus's preference is for young males," I told her. "That's well known. He's up to something."

"Nothing good, I'm sure," she said.

We struggled through the fifty-seven-course dinner, the *fercula,* each course more extravagant than the last. One choice featured a lion made of Corinthian bronze, standing on a sideboard with large baskets propped on both sides of its back. One side held expensive oranges from Joppa, and the other red, polished apples from the Isle of Chios. Two silver dishes containing little dormice rolled in honey and poppy seeds were supported on miniature bridges crossing between the baskets. Then came a large pig stuffed with steaming sausages and blood pudding on a bronze grill, followed by a silver tray filled with dark-blue plums from Syria and seed of red pomegranates from Egypt. A fat chicken and goose eggs were served to each guest. On it went. Awed and revolted by the cuisine, Eleyne took only small nibbles from each course. I ate with gusto.

Vintage wine such as good massic and expensive Falernian—the nectar of gods—chilled in mountain snow, topped each course. I enjoyed them too much.

No sooner had the meal ended when scantily attired Spanish dancers appeared. The gaze of every man in the room, including mine, locked on to the lascivious maidens from Gades. Wantonly, they enticed every man with cat-like eyes, as their young, lithe bodies floated from couch to couch. Gliding around the marble floor, their nimble fingers clicked wooden castanets, in a frantic, rolling beat. The sound echoed throughout the palace. Exciting the crowd, these lusty nymphs of Venus gyrated their well-proportioned bottoms, just out of reach. Loud moans and sighs came from the lecherous besotted guests. When the performers leaned back and seductively stroked their exposed, ample breasts, a riot nearly erupted. Several noblemen had to be restrained by their wives.

Only when the emperor ordered these female devils out of the dining area did things settle down.

Afterward, the party wasn't the same. Jugglers from Ethiopia, a poor substitute, were jeered away, as was a hack poet who read a tome praising Vespasian's campaign in Britannia.

Eleyne saw my disappointment and nudged me in the side. "Don't worry, before the night's over you'll forget those sluts, I promise."

I turned to her. "There is no way they could ever replace you, darling. Never!" I meant every word.

She smiled and kissed me.

Claudius retired after falling asleep three times during the festivities. Before leaving, he begged the celebrants to stay and enjoy themselves. However, upon his departure, guests began to leave. One of Vespasian's retainers cornered me regarding a security matter, and I had to excuse myself from Eleyne.

"Steady yourself, you had too much to drink," she said.

Eleyne was right. Lightheaded, I had difficulty maintaining my gait. The horse-faced centurion's security matter was little more than an officer making a fool of himself.

As he droned onward, my soggy brain heard Eleyne's cry. "No, Candra! Don't!"

A shuffle and noise came from the direction of our couch. "How dare you touch me, filthy scum!" The voice of Gallus.

My bleary eyes saw Candra standing between Eleyne and Gallus. Dropping his massive hands to his side, he looked menacingly down upon a disheveled Gallus and a few of his indignant friends. However, none made a move to touch the giant.

"Who is your master?" Gallus demanded. "I'll have you crucified!"

A crowd, including Sabinus and Vespasian, gathered around the three.

I staggered to Eleyne's side. "He pushed Gallus," she whispered.

A fatal mistake.

Sabinus ordered Candra to step aside, but he hesitated, and Sabinus ordered him again.

"Please, Candra," Eleyne pleaded, "do it for me."

He did.

Gallus turned to Sabinus. "Lord Sabinus, this is an outrage!" he exclaimed in a drunken slur. The bloodshot eyes glowered with hate. "How dare he, a slave, touch me?"

"Is this true?" Sabinus asked Eleyne.

"Please Lord, he was protecting me. He didn't like Tribune Gallus's remarks to me."

"I assure you I said nothing insulting," Gallus arrogantly replied. Reeling, he was steadied by a friend.

"What did he say, Eleyne?" Sabinus questioned.

"He said I was a barbarian who had wormed Roman citizenship out of your lordship and the emperor. He put his hand on my shoulder and said, 'I can see why.' I told him to keep his hands to himself, but he only laughed. That's when Candra shoved him back."

"That's a lie!" Gallus yelled. "I didn't touch her. I said nothing! She lies like all Britons. He must die!"

Calling Eleyne a liar was more than I could stand. My hand reached in reflex for a sword that wasn't there. Why did he want to upset her, knowing Candra was nearby? Because of our betrothal, was he attempting to provoke an incident with me? Was he too drunk to realize I had left her side only for a moment? Did he believe I would attack him if he bothered her, and in so doing discredit myself with the Equestrian Order? The idea of using the woman I loved to humiliate me was a cowardly move, and it fired my anger all the more.

"That is for me to decide, Anicius Gallus," Senator Sabinus replied sternly. His hand raised to stop my forward movement. "He is my property, and in your drunken state you had no right to insult or lay a hand on my ward."

"I'm not drunk," Gallus slurred.

"Don't argue with me, man, or I'll do nothing," Sabinus answered, glaring menacingly into the younger man's eyes.

"You heard Senator Sabinus," Camillus said. "Do as he says, Young Gallus."

Gallus's mentor, Senator Camillus, shook his head. "Flavius Sabinus, it's true he touched the lady, but the slave."

"Yes, I knew she didn't lie, but you're right." Sabinus hesitated, drew a breath, and turned to a pleading Eleyne. "I'm sorry, but it won't make any difference, my dear. Candra touched him, and that's enough to put him to death."

"Oh no, Lord! No!" she cried.

"However," Sabinus turned and pierced the watery eyes of Gallus. "Since I'm his master, it'll be done my way. Candra did his duty in protecting his mistress from the likes of you. You are fortunate to be a Roman patrician. Were you not, Roman citizen or otherwise, I would have allowed him to kill you!"

A torrent of gasps escaped from the group and protestations from Gallus's friends, but Sabinus ignored them.

"You'll have your satisfaction but not by crucifixion. He goes to the arena as a gladiator."

I disagreed with Sabinus, but kept my thoughts to myself. Candra didn't deserve punishment for protecting Eleyne, but I was relieved that he would not be summarily executed. Although remote, by fighting in the arena, he stood a chance of survival and obtaining his freedom.

"That's outrageous," Gallus protested. "He touched me—shoved me. I demand his death, now!" His friends echoed his sentiments.

Sabinus turned to the group. "Roman law leaves it up to the master the manner of death a slave suffers. He properly performed his duty. You know I speak the truth." Sabinus's friends voiced their support, including Vitellius.

Gallus fumed. "How can you side with a barbarian?"

"She's a princess, and betrothed to a Roman citizen, a knight. That gives her the same rights and privileges you infringed upon. Be fortunate I'm punishing him at all."

He turned to Eleyne. "I'm sorry, my dear, but Candra must be taken away."

"Guards!" Sabinus motioned to the Praetorians who came forward. Candra's silent eyes pleaded with Eleyne.

"Candra, you'll have to go with them," Eleyne said in a shaking voice. "For my sake, don't resist. Please. I'll come and visit you, I promise."

The dark giant appeared reluctant, glaring at Gallus. His scowling face and angry, black eyes said what his mute lips could not.

"Take him away," Sabinus ordered when the guards approached. "Use no brutality, and he'll go peacefully." They saluted, and six burly guardsmen took the big Indian in tow.

"Come near Eleyne again, and I'll finish what her bodyguard started," I said to Gallus as he was about to leave. Angered by the whole affair, and my tongue loosened by the grape, I wanted to smash him to a pulp. But I wasn't too drunk to realize the consequences of such an act.

"Insolent as ever, I see, Marcellus Reburrus," Gallus said in contempt. "No matter, you're no better than she, a foreigner. Don't meddle in my affairs!"

I placed my hand beneath my toga on the hilt of a concealed dagger. I started towards Gallus, but Vespasian's firm grip on my shoulder stopped me. "Don't act stupidly—you'll regret it."

I backed away. "When it concerns Eleyne," I said, glaring at Gallus, "it's my affair, she's my future wife!"

"A perfect match," Gallus sneered. "Barbarian for a barbarian, and a grave robber besides."

I lunged at Gallus, but was caught by Vespasian as Eleyne cried out, "No!"

Gallus grinned. I realized I had played into his hands. "Your temper hasn't changed a bit. A man who won't honor his word can't control his temper. A man without honor, you jump from the skirts of a whore to those of a foreigner."

We lunged towards one another but were restrained forcefully by our friends.

"I suggest you learn control," Gallus said, "because I've not forgotten what you did to my father."

"Just stay away from Eleyne!" Although I could have broken Vespasian's powerful grip, something inside said the time was not right.

"Oh, I will," Gallus responded with a sinister grin, "but you haven't seen the last of me."

Senator Camillus and his companions urged him to leave, and he staggered, with their help, between the groups of onlookers.

People drifted away, as Sabinus and Vespasian stood admonishing me. I apologized for my conduct, and they seemed to understand. I couldn't remember when anyone had enraged me as much as Gallus. The animosities of our fathers had carried over to a new generation, and now we were enemies for life.

"It's all my fault," a tearful Eleyne cried. "Trouble follows me wherever I go. Now I've lost Candra. Oh, Lord Sabinus, I've been nothing but grief to you." Tears slowly rolled down her cheeks as she caught my eyes. "Darling, how can you marry me?"

"Eleyne, it wasn't your fault," Sabinus said. "Candra was a loyal slave, and I'm sorry to imprison him."

"Yes, I know. Why did Gallus act so horribly with me? I don't understand."

"I think I know why," I said. I told Eleyne and Sabinus the conclusion I'd drawn.

Sabinus stared into the direction in which Gallus had departed before turning back to me. His mouth tightened into a thin line, and he shook his head. "If that's true, Marcellus, then Gallus is a miserable coward for using Eleyne to discredit you."

I gestured with on open palm. "It's the only logical reason that comes to mind. However, he didn't count on Candra interfering."

"And Candra is to suffer for it," Eleyne added bitterly.

The big Indian should have killed Gallus, but I said nothing.

Eleyne stepped closer and placed her soft hand in mine before she asked, "Doesn't Gallus bring disgrace upon himself by his own conduct? He made a fool of himself."

"He doesn't care," Sabinus said. He looked about, but no one outside of our group was close by. "So long as Pallas and Narcissus are the emperor's advisors, he can buy respectability whenever it suits his needs."

Aurelia, who stood nearby, quietly nodded in agreement with her husband.

"Then one day he'll buy his father's seat in the Senate?" I asked.

"Since his father was pardoned, he doesn't have to, it's hereditary," Sabinus said. "However, he can't take possession until he reaches thirty."

"Then things will get better, at least for a while." But I didn't believe my words—a lot could happen between now and then. The whole affair had sobered me.

* * *

That night as we lay together, a habit we pursued with discreet caution, I held Eleyne gently in my arms. As wagons clattered past in the dark street below, both of us were lost in thought. After making love, she rested her head on my shoulder and stroked my chest with her hand.

"Candra, a gladiator," she said. I listened silently, knowing she thought of little else. "I hate the games. How can Romans pit one human against another for sport, like animals? I don't know which is worse—suffering a painful death on the cross or fighting until you're killed in the circus. Why didn't they execute him and be done with it?"

"I believe Sabinus thinks Candra can win his freedom."

"Is that possible?"

"I don't know, but as long as he remains alive, there's hope. I've no stomach for the games, either. War is one matter, but killing people for the bloodthirsty mob is a terrible waste."

"It's horrible. My people never engaged in such barbaric practices. A man died on the battlefield, honorable, not as a blood sport. Yet they call my people barbarians!"

"Candra's a warrior. He won't die easily. He's too skilled and powerful. Many will fall before he does. If the gods are real, maybe he will survive."

"What an awful way to go. Killing to live isn't right."

"He's a slave, nothing to the Romans. Slaves don't have rights, they're cattle."

Eleyne rolled onto her side, and slowly I massaged her back. "First, it was Karmune," she said with a bitterness in her voice, "then my father, and now Candra. Marcellus, I don't want anything happening to you! I couldn't bear it."

A quiet moment passed until she turned back and moved closer to me. She snuggled, and I responded anew to her. No man deserved such happiness. We fell into each other's embrace, soaring to the peak of oblivion. I could never be without her. In my soul, we were man and wife. Nothing could ever change that.

Awakening late in the night, I went quietly to the balcony overlooking the city. Even asleep, Rome was awesome. Cleaner and softer, draped in her cloak of darkness, firelights sparkled like stars. Deep in my thoughts of Roman beauty, wars, and life, I felt Eleyne's arms glide about my waist and her head rest against my back. She seemed to sense when I needed her. Saying nothing at all, that quiet shared moment alone is one of my most treasured memories. The taste of salt still upon my lips renewed memories of our lovemaking and gave rise to a sudden fear that should we ever part, I would lose this woman who owned my love so completely.

For several minutes we stood quietly. "Marcellus, you know I have never known another man except you," Eleyne said softly. She paused, as if searching for the right words.

"What I mean, was there another woman before me? One you cared for?"

I sighed heavily, not knowing how to begin. I had loved before, deeply. In spite of all that had happened since, I loved Eleyne with all my being, at the very time I had given up hope of ever loving again.

"Yes, there was another, a lifetime ago," I began, and told her about Kyar.

Afterward, we escaped from our problems, returned to our lovemaking and passion, and drifted peacefully asleep.

CHAPTER 7

JULY, 47 AD

As the wedding drew closer, I rented a flat for the two of us in one of Rome's better apartment buildings. Most of the city's population lived in decrepit, wooden tenements six or seven stories high. Situated on the first floor, the dwelling was the most desirable and expensive in the building, with ample living space, running water, and quarters for ten slaves—amenities lacked by the tenants in the upper floors. Located on Minerva Street, close to the Quirinal where Sabinus lived, I had only a short walk to his mansion.

In March, five months after the banquet, I moved into the new home. Although we were lovers, Roman custom and etiquette prohibited Eleyne from moving in with me until we were married. Although technically no longer a ward of Sabinus and Aurelia, she still did not want to cause them embarrassment or scandal.

I wrote my mother of the forthcoming wedding. We corresponded regularly but had not seen one another in years. Duties with Sabinus kept me from returning home to Abdera, in southern Hispania. Mother's dislike for cities, plus overseeing the latifundia, prevented her from traveling to Rome. However, she promised to come for the wedding, escorted by Uncle Budar. I looked forward to the gathering of my closest friends and relatives.

* * *

After moving into the apartment, Sabinus's steward, Alexias, and I went to the great slave market of the Fora. The place rambled amid the porticoes of the *Septa Julia* on the *Via Lata*. Organized like a cattle market, numerous pens and stalls stood beneath the dusty, vermin-infested arcades. Noisy crowds of buyers and spectators elbowed in and out of corrals that reeked of urine. A stale, fleshy odor, as from confined animals, drifted from many of the stalls. At the entrance of each pen, notices written on white boards with red chalk recited the nature of the slaves inside and their hour for sale at auction.

Races of all ages and both sexes from every part of the empire and from the rest of the world were represented. Besides captives of war, they included victims hunted down by slavers. The greatest tragedy were the children, sold by greedy or destitute parents. Laws that prohibited child molesting didn't include slaves, and rich perverts paid a premium for these little urchins.

Alexias and I entered one of the fetid, wooden pens to examine the chattel. I considered the Greek an excellent judge of human flesh and relied on his advice for such matters. Fettered in chains, the men were stripped except for a loincloth. Men and women were examined like horses. Brothel owners closely scrutinized particularly attractive females, forcing them to disrobe for more humiliating examination prior to purchase. The more fortunate ones, such as Vitellius's young German mistress, were sold as concubines to members of the nobility.

We approached a group of young, muscular British captives, dirty and smelly, standing in line on a raised brownstone platform. Chalk covered their feet, meaning they were available for immediate sale. Among them I spotted a youth of about fifteen. Tall and wiry, his sunburned face covered with light-red down, the beginning of a beard. Long, shaggy auburn hair touched his shoulders.

"Take a look at that one," I said to Alexias.

"Why him?" he asked. "The rest are older and stronger."

I furrowed my eyes and nodded. "There's something familiar about him, but I'm not sure what."

"His eyes are filled with hate," Alexias observed.

"Can you blame him? He's like a trapped wolf who's lost his freedom." Yet I sensed his bewilderment. Lost and out of his world, he continued twisting his head from side to side, as if searching for a place to run.

Alexias examined and questioned the boy in the lilting dialect of the Celts. The youth pulled away from his touch. Alexias growled a warning and slapped him. The boy yelped and went into a crouch. He balled his shackled hands into fists and shook them in challenge. A guard struck the youth with a leather prod. He doubled over, falling to his knees. The guard cursed the boy's defiance, but the youth had enough sense to unclench his fists and prostrate himself upon the floor. A few minutes passed before he stood and mumbled something to Alexias.

The steward turned to me. "He has a fire for living, unlike most sold on the block. Despite his defiance, I think he's trainable."

"What did you say to him?"

"I asked his name, and he replied, *Wolf Runner*."

I pursed my mouth. "A warrior's name."

"That's why I slapped him. At first he refused to tell me his real name."

"What is it?"

"Chulainn." For a few heartbeats, Alexias viewed me quizzically. "Do you know him?"

Was this the same boy whom Obulco found hiding in an oven after his relatives were slaughtered by the Durotrigian raiders? "I once knew a Chulainn," I answered thoughtfully. "He'd be about his age, but he lives with a free farmer."

"I'm told the name is very common, sir."

"It is." That didn't quash my curiosity. From the sign posted above their pen, they had been captured by Vespasian's troops in a skirmish against Caratacus. Why had this boy joined the enemy when he lived with free people? I would question the new slave further after Alexias had trained him to be a good household slave.

Alexias continued examining the youth. "Wiry as he is, he's strong as a bull, and free of disease. Feel his muscles—they're like iron."

I grasped the youth's biceps, and after a moment nodded. The boy seemed to eye me with a mixture of suspicion and puzzlement.

"He'll be a good one for you and the new mistress—if he doesn't run," Alexias added.

"We'll know soon enough."

Alexias checked his teeth and nodded in satisfaction. "They're good, too, which reminds me, he'll need to learn Latin."

"Eleyne can teach him."

I purchased Chulainn, and against the advice of Alexias, other Briton slaves for the household. Although they might be a danger if left in the household, I knew Eleyne would be happier with her countrymen, and more able to control them.

"But, sir," Alexias insisted, "not only are most Britons chronic liars, they are unreliable and un-trainable."

"You forget that Eleyne easily learned to read and write Latin and Greek while she still lived in Britannia," I reminded Alexias, "and the Britons have become excellent auxiliary troops since their posting to the Danubus frontier."

Alexias mumbled an apology. "Still, you should have bought Syrian slaves. They're intelligent and learn quickly and, above all, they are docile."

"Eleyne insists on Briton slaves," I countered. Her tribe, the Regni, along with other Briton tribes had enslaved each other's peoples through countless wars. Most of those captured by Vespasian were tribal enemies of her people. Nevertheless, I knew she felt at ease with slaves from Britannia, especially since she understood most of the southern tribal dialects.

* * *

Along with hired guards, I accompanied Alexias and the slaves to Sabinus's home where they would be housed until Eleyne and I were married. At the slave quarters,

Alexias and his effeminate assistant, Mironos, examined Chulainn and the rest closely for additional flaws.

Within the hour, as I conversed with Crispus in the atrium, Alexias returned and handed me a silver boar's head ring. "Not only is the boy disrespectful," he said in a voice of disgust, "but he steals. I strongly suggest, sir, you return the savage to the slave market and demand a refund. After all, he guaranteed the slave wasn't a thief, and by law, he has to refund your money if he made a fraudulent claim."

"Is this the one you told me about?" Crispus asked. He had returned from a meeting with Scrofa the beggar king.

"The same," I said.

I examined the ring and turned to the old man. "No, I won't—not yet. Where did you find this?"

"My young assistant, Mironos, checked Chulainn's body too enthusiastically for my taste."

He related how the youthful Greek pawed Chulainn's body, supposedly testing his muscle tone. The slave ordered Chulainn to remove his loincloth and groped his testicles and manhood. The servant grinned at Chulainn, who narrowed his eyes and curled his mouth into a hateful sneer. Alexias sensed Chulainn would attack any moment.

"Seeing Mironos's indiscretion," Alexias continued, "I immediately ordered him to stop. But as he removed his grasp, his fingers snagged a string beneath the slave's scrotum. He pulled the twine and out popped a ring from his buttocks. I demanded to know where he had stolen it." Chulainn claimed the ring belonged to the murderer of his uncle, but it had been given to him by a Roman soldier. He was afraid it would be confiscated.

"Naturally, I knew he was lying," Alexias said, "so I slapped him and grabbed the ring. He cursed me, and I slapped his face again. I threatened to kill him where he stood if he didn't behave. He had the sense to relent." Alexias looked at both of his hands. He crinkled his nose and grunted. "I still have to wash them."

"He stays, Alexias," I insisted, recalling the small boy and a similar ring from two years before. At the time, he said he was twelve. If this is the same one, then he lied. This youth had the build of a sixteen-year-old.

"Sir, you are making a grave mistake."

"I know what I'm doing."

When Alexias departed, Crispus slowly examined the ring. "I've seen this ring before—Britannia, right?"

I nodded to Crispus and placed the ring in my palm, admiring its fiery stone eyes. Was it a coincidence that our paths had crossed once again? "It is the same ring."

CHAPTER 8

Eleyne and I arrived at Uncle Budar's home on Vatican Hill mid-morning to see my mother, Ceacilia Juanaria. Sailing from Hispania, she had docked in Rome the evening before, but we hadn't received word from Budar until earlier this morning.

Although early September, Rome was still enshrouded in stifling summer heat. To save ourselves from getting sweaty and dirty as we crossed through the heart of the city and over the Tiber, we borrowed two of Sabinus's litters and had been carried to Budar's home.

An ankle-length tunic covered by a light-blue, woolen gown trimmed in silver covered Eleyne's willowy frame. Draped about her shoulders was a light-weight, yellow cloak. Small, gold, duck-shaped earrings hung from each lobe. A beaded necklace of long, narrow strips of umber and round, red garnets strung on a thin, gold band draped her alabaster neck.

I wore a simple knee-length, white tunic. A narrow, purple stripe ran down the right side indicating my status as a Roman knight. Hidden beneath my garb, a dagger clung to a waistband.

Budar's large villa stood across the Tiber, beyond the smoky haze that hung like an umbrella above the city, its back along the edge of a huge public park, the Garden of Caesar. A tall portico divided by the entrance ran in a half circle along the front. A graveled driveway bordered on both sides by poplars snaked its way up to the front of the mansion. As we went up the driveway, noisy, yellow-striped pipits flit from tree to tree. The chirruping sounds of skylarks added to the racket. A gray squirrel scampered across the path and disappeared into a box shrub along the side. A couple of slaves wearing wide-brim, straw hats and protective leather gloves carefully trimmed the thorny stems of late-season roses planted in a neat row beyond the trees. On a light breeze wafted the smell of resin from clusters of pine trees growing the park.

Originally, the house belonged to Budar's wife, Helvia, an older, rich widow he had married for money when he retired from the army. Yet he must have developed a genuine affection for her. When she passed away four months ago, he took her death hard. He wept, and for a month he sat around the house, listless, barely stirring from the premises to do anything. Then one day he snapped out of his doldrums and returned to being his loud, cantankerous self, the way I liked.

Because Helvia had no other living relatives except Budar, he inherited her fortune and properties. He told me that when it was his time to cross the River Styx, I would get everything. I said I was in no hurry. "Good," he growled, "I ain't in any hurry to leave." I chuckled.

Arriving at the front door, we stepped out of the litters. I dismissed the doorman as I knew the way to the atrium. After suffering in the stifling heat, the cool reception hall seemed like a present from the gods.

As we strolled down the hallway, Eleyne turned to me. "I hope your mother will approve of me, Marcellus."

I grinned. "I'm sure she will. I wrote her several letters describing how wonderful you are."

Eleyne blushed. "Oh, please, you didn't. You said she was very particular about young women."

"Mother can be. But if she believes what I wrote, she will like you."

Eleyne lightly jabbed my upper arm.

"Besides, by now," I continued, "Uncle Budar has probably described you as only he could to Mother."

"I hope that's good."

"After the way he took to you, I can almost guarantee it will be."

"Even though I'm from Britannia, a *barbarian*?"

I shook my head. "You are no barbarian. There are many Romans that still regard Spaniards as barbarians."

"Including that despicable Gallus, right?"

"Him above all else."

"Well, I'm not one and neither are my people."

I nodded. "We'll just have to wait and see what Mother says."

We entered the atrium and approached the impluvium. Bright sun pierced through the slanted roof opening over the shallow pool lighting up the reception area. Colored pieces of stone and glass making up the tiled mosaic floor sparkled like an array of pulsating stars. I spotted Mother and Uncle Budar sitting together on a cushioned bench, heads bowed in close conversation. At the sound of our footfalls, they turned our way. Uncle Budar stood and stepped towards us. Mother winced as she stiffly got to her feet.

As the old, bearded, crusty-face veteran stopped in front of us, his dark eyes narrowed. "It's about time you two got here," he growled. "Not right keeping your good mother waiting."

I stiffened. Eleyne and I looked at one another.

Budar broke into a loud horse laugh and hugged me in tight bear-grip. He released me and backed away. He turned to Eleyne and did the same. "It so good to see you again! Why haven't I been graced with your presence since the engagement? After all, you are my little princess."

Eleyne blushed again. "Uncle Budar, please."

"Well, you are, never forget that." He moved back.

In a softer voice, he said, "I'm glad you two are here, let's not keep your mother waiting." He turned, and we followed.

Mother wore a white, ankle-length, pleated skirt, the hem trimmed in embroidered gold and red. A scarlet mantle, covering her shoulders and draping her arms, reached down below her knees. A simple string of bright, silver pearls circled her neck. As usual, she wore her hair in a tympanum style, curved against the nape, gripping the neck as far as the lobe of her ears. Although invisible,

I knew a small rod on a pedestal held her folded hair in place. The whole of it was covered by a black veil. Long, gold, triple teardrop earrings dangled from each lobe.

Her face startled me. The years of overseeing the latifundia had drained Mother. Strands of aging, yellow-gray hair fell down her forehead. No longer was it the auburn hair of which she had been so proud. Barely forty-four, scores of wrinkles crawled like river tributaries across her sunburned olive face. The luster I knew as a youth had vanished from her large, umber eyes. The spring in her walk missing as she approached me. Mother hobbled to my side.

"Mother," I said.

Her smile revealed a mouthful of brownish teeth. "Marcellus, Son, it has been so long."

We hugged. Instead of feeling the solid body of a woman who worked alongside of her servants and slaves, I felt a frail, bony frame.

She touched the purple stripe on my tunic. "And now you are a knight. I am so proud of you."

I nodded. "It's what the family wanted."

"Yes, but you earned the right. It wasn't money alone. Budar told me about your bravery in battle."

I didn't want to think about those memories of bloodshed. "Yes, of course," I said.

I turned to Eleyne and back to Mother and smiled. "Mother, this is Eleyne."

Mother didn't say a word.

Eleyne raised her black eyebrows and glanced to me.

I shrugged.

Mother's face turned sober as she examined Eleyne almost as if she were a slave. She moved her head up and down, right and left. I was almost surprised she didn't check Eleyne's teeth.

"Turn around," Mother ordered Eleyne.

Eleyne glared at Mother and opened her mouth as if to say something, but closed it a heartbeat later. She turned a full circle.

Mother paused and looked Eleyne in the eye. "So, you are the young woman my son wants to marry."

For the length of a couple of heartbeats Eleyne stared at Mother before bowing her head slightly. "Yes, my lady."

Mother shook her head, and a smile crossed her full lips. "No, none of that. If you are marrying my son, you must call me Mother."

Eleyne and I looked at one another. She sighed in relief. So did I.

"I can tell that not only are you beautiful, but you are a bright young woman," Mother said.

Eleyne's bowed lips formed a smile. "That is kind of you . . . Mother?"

Mother opened her arms. "Come, give me a hug."

Eleyne turned her head toward me. I nodded. She stepped forward, and the two embraced one another. Both about the same height, five finger widths shorter than me.

The two released one another.

"You are not like those coarse, Celt-Iberian women who live in the center of Hispania," Mother said. "I had heard British women were similar, but you are different."

Eleyne stiffened. "I certainly think so."

"Is it true your father was a king?" Mother asked.

"Yes, he was, but he died several months ago."

Mother shook her head. "I am so sorry, but now you will be part of our family. We, too, are descendant from royalty."

"You are?" Eleyne looked at me and then mother.

"Mother, please," I said.

"Has not Marcellus told you?" Mother asked. She glanced in my direction and frowned.

Eleyne sniffed. "No, he hasn't."

"I can trace my family back to Hannibal," Mother said. "You have heard of him, have you not? He is the Carthaginian king who almost conquered Rome."

"So, I have learned from my tutor," Eleyne said.

"He was my uncle many times removed." Mother turned to me. "Yours, too, Marcellus."

"He and his people are long gone," I said. "Now, Rome rules the world."

Mother's nostrils flared. "Perhaps, but his memory lives on, and I am proud to be one of his descendants. So should you." She touched Eleyne on the forearm. "When the day comes that you have children, tell them royal blood runs in their veins from both sides of the family."

Eleyne nodded to both of us. "I will."

"Go ahead," I said, "but it will be my duty to see that they become officers in the army and serve Rome with honor."

Eleyne reached up and kissed me on the cheek before facing Mother. "If their father were someone other than Marcellus, I would have had my doubts. But I know they will take after my future husband."

CHAPTER 9

LATE SEPTEMBER, 47 AD

Because Roman law and custom prohibited weddings during certain weeks of the year, Eleyne and I were not married until the end of September, at Sabinus's home. Except for Mother, Uncle Budar, Crispus and his Numidian woman, Apulia, and General Vespasian and his wife, most guests attending were Sabinus's friends. Perfume from hundreds of bright bouquets, including roses from Campania, sprayed with sweet Arabian incense, scented the atrium. At the far end the ceremony was conducted in the alcove of the garlanded tablinum. Hundreds of people jostled one another for a better view in the crowded study room.

Crispus, dressed in his best white tunic, along with almond-complected Apulia, who wore a long emerald chiton girdled with a brass-colored belt, managed to push their way through the guests to the front. They stood beside a stuffy senator and his frumpy wife who didn't seem happy about having a couple of foreigners next to them. My friend winked, and I grinned.

Sabinus, representing Eleyne's family, waited with me at the simple, wooden altar framed by plain, little statues of Jupiter and Juno. Admittedly, I was a little nervous—the reality that Eleyne and I were finally getting married struck me. I prayed the ceremony would go as planned and the omens from the forthcoming sacrifice would be favorable for a long and prosperous marriage.

Next to us stood the long-robed and shrewd-eyed entrail reader, the *haruspice*. A few feet away, near the marbled impluvium, the household well, two acolytes held a white sacrificial sheep by a frayed, brown rope.

"*Salve!* Greetings!" erupted from the atrium. The group parted for Aurelia Severa.

She paraded like a matronly queen in her white and purple stola of finest linen. In her shadow trailed a nervous but smiling Eleyne, adorned in a finely woven, yellow gown held about the waist by a band of wool. Braided into six locks, her long, black hair was tied with blue ribbons and weighted down with shining pearls. Roman custom required her hair to be parted with a spear. Barely visible beneath the hem of the gown, I glimpsed white shoes of fine leather. A billowing, scarlet veil, one of Aurelia's treasured possessions and gift to Eleyne, covered her head. Held in place by a simple garland of blue and yellow flowers, the shroud fell gracefully down her back and sides. As tradition dictated, she had personally picked the blossoms for good luck.

I wore a plain, white toga, edged in thin, purple trim—symbol of the Equestrian Order. The day belonged to Eleyne.

As the women halted by the well, Eleyne took Aurelia's fleshy arm and slightly bowed her head. With help from his assistants, the entrail reader dramatically sacrificed the unsuspecting ewe. Although Eleyne had been accustomed to butchering animals in Britannia, she still paled at the slaughter and the sight of the quivering entrails as the blood dripped into the water. She tightened the grip on her mistress's arm but regained her composure.

The old priest examined the corpse as dark blood poured into the spraying fountain. No one seemed to notice, but for an instant, he blanched. He eyed Aurelia who gave him a sharp nod. He chanted something unintelligible passing for Etruscan, and solemnly proclaimed, "*Bene!* The omens are good for the marriage!" The old charlatan dared not claim otherwise, because if he did, the wedding could not proceed.

As the carcass was being removed, Aurelia led Eleyne to my side, and we joined hands. I cleared all thoughts of evil omens from my mind—no doubt the figment of a bridegroom's nervous imagination. Eleyne's hands felt cold and clammy in mine. Her sea-blue eyes shimmered through the flaming veil and looked deeply into mine. As she smiled, her small mouth slightly parted.

Sabinus, dressed in a flowing, white senatorial toga with its wide, purple stripe, lifted a tablet enclosing the marriage contract from the altar and faced us. With a somber expression, he glanced from Eleyne's face to mine. He opened the cedar-wood framed parchment and holding it in both hands read with all the gravity his voice could command. For a moment, I thought we were in a court of law. When he finished, Sabinus nodded to me—time for simple vows.

I paused, gazing into Eleyne's eyes, and thought of how much I loved her. "Will you be my *mater familias*?"

"Yes," she answered, squeezing my hands.

"And will you be my *pater familias*?" Eleyne invited with a slight quiver in her voice.

With my "Yes," we became husband and wife.

A boisterous round of applause and cheering by the guests swept the atrium. A weeping Aurelia hugged the bride, while Sabinus and I clasped the inside of one another's elbows in traditional Roman manner.

Seconds later, hand in hand, Eleyne and I glided to the altar where we placed a cake of coarse bread for Jupiter and Juno and offered brief prayers to bless our marriage and new home.

Followed by shouts of, "*Felicitas!*" and "Good Luck!" we were mobbed by the colorfully dressed crowd.

After being inundated with kisses and shaking hands, I found Eleyne. Gently taking her by the forearm, I turned to the group and raised my other hand. A hush fell over everyone in attendance. "Most noble and gracious guests," I said, "will you please do us the honor of joining my wife and me for the wedding feast!"

A hearty cheer echoed through the courtyard, and eagerly they followed us into the dining area.

The wedding feast lasted until late in the evening. Afterwards, a wedding party escorted Eleyne and me to our flat. A squadron of flute players and torch bearers led the way. Members of our group sang lewd and ribald songs, echoing through the streets. Our ten new slaves, including Porus, my new Greek steward, and Chulainn, mustered to greet me and their new *domina*, the mistress Eleyne. She stopped at the front door and wound the pillar facades with bits of wool, touching them with a daub of oil and fat, given her by Aurelia, to symbolize our future prosperity.

Then as the wedding party and the tenants of the apartment looked on, I lifted her into my arms and carried her across the threshold for good luck. It wasn't until much later that night the noisy escort, who had been shouting course jokes, singing, and dancing, left us in peace.

* * *

Late the next morning, Porus informed me two sweating acolytes who had attended the wedding were running circles around the apartment in stripped-down tunics. He inquired as to the reason and learned it was to ensure good luck in our marriage. They had been instructed to continue their marathon for twenty-four hours.

"That's not the true reason," I said to Porus. "The entrails reader saw something ominous in the sheep's liver."

My forty-one-year-old steward raised his black, droopy eyebrows, the sagging muscles of his blotchy face growing tense.

"If she asks, you are to say nothing about this to the mistress. Do you understand?"

I paid the acolytes to run somewhere else, lest Eleyne learn the true reason from the tenants in the rest of the apartment building.

* * *

Unwilling to alarm Eleyne, I waited a week before seeing Aurelia Severa, who had hired the priests.

"You are quite right, Marcellus," she said, as we sat in the library. For the space of a few heartbeats, the matronly wife of Sabinus studied me from behind her desk. "After the reading, the priest told me he had discovered flukes in the liver."

"That's a terrible omen."

She leaned a little closer across the desk. "By the household gods, *Lares* and *Panates*, indeed. However, since I paid him well, he followed through with the ceremony. Of course, he said he didn't like to lie!"

I nearly choked at her last words, knowing he was easily bought.

Aurelia motioned toward the door with her head. Guessing what she meant, I got up and stepped to the entrance and looked out toward the atrium. No one was about. I returned to my chair, sat, and shook my head.

"At first," she continued, "he was reluctant to tell me about his find, but I threatened to have him arrested for sorcery if he did not."

"What did he see?"

She pursed her fleshy lips. "He saw in the flukes . . . your death."

My chest tightened, and tiny bumps rippled along the length of my arms and up my back. I took a couple of breaths. "By what means?"

"A dagger in the hands of your enemies. And in his vision, he said he saw fire and effigies of great men tumbling and stars falling. His vision faltered from there."

"It's Gallus's curse from the grave," I said.

"Maybe, but I have never put much credence in curses." Aurelia picked up a rolled parchment on the desk and turned it about a couple times in her plump hands before laying it down. "At the same time, I could not risk angering the gods. Eleyne and you are too dear to me. So, I was determined to neutralize the omen with a special sacrifice. I paid the priest to run around the Temple of Jupiter Greatest and Best, and his acolytes to do the same around your home. I threatened to cut out his tongue if he told you or Eleyne the truth."

"I guessed the reason right away."

"I supposed you would, but I could not take the chance of anything happening to the couple I hold most dear to me after my husband and sons."

"And I'm grateful."

I don't know how much the priests or acolytes suffered in running, for none of them were in good physical shape, but I knew I would have to take whatever precautions necessary to ensure the prophecy did not come to pass.

CHAPTER 10

EARLY OCTOBER, 47 AD

The following two weeks, after speaking with Aurelia, I watched Rome's days become enshrouded in sweeping rains and chilly nights. Because of my growing concern for my mother's failing health, I slept poorly. Outside, the rainfall pummeled the apartment walls and dripped through the wooden screens overlooking the central well. Hanging from each of the six floors, the shrouds were a necessary measure to keep the more irresponsible tenants from dumping filth and trash into the courtyard adjacent to our flat.

It seemed as if I could hear every fat drop falling against the shutters attached to the high window framed just below the ceiling. A baby's cry echoed from one of the rooms above, and the curses of an arguing man and woman drifted from another flat. A couple of drunks on the third floor loudly sang a lewd song to the goddess, Diana. Wagons clattered down the street on their nightly trips to the markets and warehouses, delivering goods for tomorrow's shopping.

Tightly gripping the woolen blankets, I tossed and turned in vain as if they would help me fall asleep. Occasionally, I opened my eyes and saw the dim, shadowy light coming from the oil lamp clamped to the tall, bronze stand in the bedroom corner. Eleyne and I preferred a little light in an otherwise pitch-black room.

Mother's image kept appearing in my mind. Ever since that first meeting here in Rome when I introduced her to Eleyne, her failing health alarmed me. But she refused to admit to any problems. In Hispania, Mother confided only in Uncle Budar. Before the wedding, I had taken Budar aside. Since he was planning on returning home with her, I asked him to keep a close watch on Mother.

In spite of my restlessness, Eleyne slept peacefully curled by my side. Sprawled by my wife's feet purred Nefer, a tamed Egyptian wildcat. A wedding present from Aurelia to her, the brownish-yellow feline with dark, tabby markings took an immediate liking to Eleyne, tolerated me, and despised everyone else. If a hapless slave came too close to her, Nefer, who was little bigger than a domestic cat but stronger, growled almost like a dog, intimidating the slaves with ugly, yellow fangs.

At first, I loathed the animal. When I expressed my disgust to Eleyne, she made excuses for the cat's horrible disposition and the shredded drapes. The creature seemed to lift her spirits, which had drooped somewhat since the wedding. Adjusting to our marriage and living in the apartment, Eleyne missed Sabinus's home and Aurelia's company. She had visited Aurelia several times since the wedding.

Slink-eyed Nefer insisted in sleeping on the bed. Every night I kicked her off, but the persistent cat returned within a short time, placing the full weight of her body against my feet. Each time I swore I was going to get rid of Nefer, Eleyne came to the cat's rescue and scolded me in the process. This arrogant feline from the Lower Nile Delta would purr against her, as I sat scratched and welted. Nefer's smug expression seemed to reveal that she sensed I was not confident enough to know whether Eleyne would choose her or me. In disgust, I gave up. Ironically, thereafter, Nefer slept only on Eleyne's side.

Nefer rustled on the bed—something stirred her sleep. She sprang to her feet. The animal's long, amber and gray stripped tail slashed back and forth, her back fur standing on end. The cat emitted a ghoulish yowl, sailing through the apartment. She darted from the room.

Twisting, I saw the outline of two shadowed intruders framed in the lamp's dim light. Both rushed forward, daggers glinting in their hands. Suddenly, they split just before reaching the bed, one going around each side. I

yanked the blanket from Eleyne and myself and threw it
over the head of one intruder, momentarily blinding him.
I whirled to the right, barely evading the blow of the other,
and grabbed my dagger from the wooden stool beside the
bed. As I snatched it, he raised his weapon and lunged
toward me. I shoved my feet upward, kicking him in the
groin. He howled, dropped his blade, and doubled over
onto the cold, tiled floor.

Awakened, Eleyne screamed. The other assassin tore
the cover from his head and lunged straight for my face.
I jumped to my feet, whirling beneath his thrust, and
plunged my weapon deep into the middle of his rib cage.
A piercing wail shot through the house as warm blood
spurted from his side onto my chest. Tumbling over me, he
fell heavily to the floor with a thud—dead.

I leaped over his prostrate body and grabbed the throat
of the other intruder. Jerking him to his feet as he choked,
I slammed him against the mural wall. His knife clattered
to the tile. Raising my dagger, I was about to cut his throat
when I recognized the assassin. My slave, Chulainn. He
deserved to die. But before he did, I was determined to
learn who planned my murder.

At the same moment, bounding naked from the bed,
Eleyne also recognized the young slave and screamed
something in Celtic. At that moment he went limp, and
she yelled at me, "No, Marcellus, don't kill him!" Eleyne
pleaded. "It's all right, I told him who you are—about
Britannia! Don't kill him—please!" She picked up the
blanket and wrapped herself.

I forced Chulainn down, twisting his left arm in a
hammerlock, keeping my weapon to the side of his throat.
My chest heaved, and my heart pounded furiously.
Perspiration flowed down my face and along the tightened
muscles of my neck.

"Why shouldn't I finish off the sneaking bastard?" I
snarled. "Alexias warned me, and I was a fool not to listen."

Doubt and confusion rippled across Chulainn's face
as he wrinkled his light eyebrows and ruddy forehead. He
talked in a native, guttural tone.

Eleyne spoke to him and turned to me. "He doesn't believe you knew him in Britannia. I told him it's true, but he wants proof."

"I'll give him proof." I brought my blade up to his throat and tickled his skin as he held his breath.

"No, Marcellus! Please, for my sake."

I attempted to compose myself and collect my thoughts—this was no time to let my anger run wild. Then I remembered something no one in Rome but Crispus and I would know.

"Tell him," I said as my breathing steadied and muscles relaxed, "we should have left him cowering in the oven instead of saving his worthless body."

She did.

Chulainn shook his head as if he could not understand the implications of my remark. I shoved the boar's head ring on my hand in his face. "Remember this?" I asked.

He studied the ring for the length of a few heart beats and nodded, apparently guessing my question. He said something to Eleyne, and she translated that the ring belonged to his uncle.

"Who returned it to you?" Eleyne asked in Celtic.

"Soldier," he replied in shaky Latin, eyes clouding with moisture.

"Look at me," I pushed his head in my direction with the side of my dagger. "Look closely."

His terrified face studied mine, and seconds later tears filled his hazel eyes. He dropped his head as if in shame and sobbed.

"Darling," Eleyne said, "he's begging for your forgiveness. Now, he knows who you are—really."

Chulainn wept as he spoke to her. "This isn't his fault," she explained.

"He tried murdering me, and it's not his fault?" My rage again mounted. "Why are you making excuses for him?"

"You don't understand. He was put up to it. He and—"

"What's he saying?" I demanded.

"No! It can't be!" she exclaimed. Quickly, Eleyne lit the olive oil lamp on the nearby table and examined the scarred face of the dead assassin. "It's Bodvac," she gasped, "my former betrothed!" Momentarily, she turned her head. I thought she was going to weep, but she quickly recovered.

"All the more reason I should get rid of this one!" I spat.

"But this was Gallus's idea!" she asserted jumping to her feet.

My muscles tightened again at the mention of his name. I exhaled in disgust. "Will I never be rid of him?" I wanted to kill Gallus and be done with him once and for all. But that was foolishness. I would not lower myself to his level of depravity.

"Chulainn says he bribed them," Eleyne offered, "and when Bodvac heard I had married a Roman, he was determined to free me and kill you."

"But how? Chulainn hasn't left the house since we've married. It's common knowledge that Gallus and I are enemies."

"Remember the day you bought him?"

"Of course."

"One of Gallus's freedmen was in the market, too. He bought Bodvac from the same slave dealer."

"So?"

"Don't you see?" she gestured with a free hand, the other holding a blanket around her body. "Gallus learned Chulainn and Bodvac were friends. Through the freedman he made an agreement if he and Chulainn killed you, they would be released and return to Britannia."

"Knowing Gallus, he would have murdered them instead. What else?"

"He said if he had known it was you who had avenged his family, he would have refused to have any part of the plan. He wanted to return to Britannia. He's dying of homesickness—can you blame him? He won't try anything again, he promises."

"Rubbish!"

"It's the custom of our people," she said impatiently, "to remain loyal to those who have returned our honor and avenged the deaths of our loved ones. No, Marcellus, he is—was—one of my people. He recognizes me as the true queen and ruler of the Regni, not that it means anything now," she added in a bitter tone. "But I promise he will never attempt anything like this again."

I considered Eleyne's sentiments and mine. If I allowed Chulainn to live, what would stop him from making another attempt on our lives? Wouldn't he kill Eleyne? Didn't he consider her a traitor for marrying a Roman?

"This is against my better judgment," I answered after a moment, "because I don't tolerate assassins under my roof, but for your sake, I will spare him."

"Oh, Marcellus, thank you!"

"However," I emphasized gravely, "these are my terms. He must prove his loyalty, and I swear by the gods who followed my father to his grave, should he again prove disloyal, he shall die by my hands very S-L-O-W-L-Y."

Eleyne nodded. "Of course, dear, I understand."

"That is not all," I continued in a slow and deliberate manner. "For the time being, he will be shackled by the legs and chained in the cellar at night."

Eleyne's hand flew to her mouth. "Marcellus, please don't!"

"He's a slave! I won't risk our lives—he has to earn our trust. He's fortunate I don't whip him to death like a common criminal or crucify him." I didn't mention under Roman law I could extract a confession by torture, because he was a slave, and use the evidence to link the freedman to the assassination attempt. But it would be of little value, because I could not directly tie Gallus to the conspiracy on my life. Therefore, he could not be charged with a crime.

For a few minutes, I remained silent as I regained my composure. Nefer slinked back into the bed cubicle. She looked about sniffing the air. The cat glared at me, growled at Chulainn, and jumped onto the bed where she hunkered down and stared at both of us. Strangely enough, I felt calmed by her presence.

"You tell him, Eleyne," I continued in a steadier voice, "when he proves his trustworthiness, I'll remove the chains. Keeping him chained is degrading, but to keep the other slaves in line, he must be made an example."

"Don't be so cruel, Marcellus," Eleyne said in a voice full of sorrow.

"Would your sentiments have been the same had he succeeded in murdering me? Would you have cared if he had not been a Briton—a Regni?"

Silence.

I shouted for the steward, but the cook, gripping a long butcher knife, and the maid, Imogen, arrived first, apparently having heard Eleyne scream. They lit the other bedroom lamps. In the shadowy, smoky light, I saw the despondent face of my captive and the scowl of Eleyne's dark eyes glaring at me. I was confused as to why she would side with a slave against me.

"Porus, where are you?"

"Here, sir," called the short Greek. Gray and streaked hair proclaimed his age. Old for his forty-one years, he shuffled into the room. "Forgive me for taking so long, I came as fast as I could," he added in a soft voice, breathing heavily.

"Never mind," I said. "Help me take Chulainn to the cellar."

Roughly, we dragged him from the room, with Porus cuffing his ear every other pace and the cook following with his knife.

In the dark hours of the same morning, I ordered Bodvac's body taken to the cramped cellar cell and thrown in with Chulainn for about an hour. Before dawn, the corpse was secretly spirited away and dumped in front of the gate to Gallus's mansion.

Eleyne would not speak to me the next day. She was furious with Porus, who pleaded with me to execute Chulainn as a warning to the other household slaves. Old tribal loyalties still simmered beneath her pretty countenance, and an incident such as the assassination attempt was enough to bring the old ways to the surface. Chulainn represented a link to her past. Fortunately, her anger subsided and about a week later she admitted I was right in shackling Chulainn. However, I had the feeling she would never completely forgive me. Britons! Women! Exiled queens! Gods, I would never understand any of them, and my wife was all three!

In the excitement of the night, I had failed to learn from Chulainn how Bodvac approached him with the proposition. Eleyne learned the circumstances. Bodvac contacted him five days before, while she and I were shopping along the Sacred Way. He and Chulainn planned to flee to Britannia after killing me and giving Eleyne her freedom. Little did the fools realize Gallus would have silenced them.

Eleyne's former betrothed told the maid, who had answered the door, he wanted to see Chulainn. Against strict orders to allow no one in during our absence, the maid, who found him handsome and taken by his crude charm, let him enter. After he and Chulainn agreed on the plan, the maid was bribed not to disclose the visit. For her disobedience to my commands, I sold her to the wealthy owner of Rome's largest private bath. She would spend the rest of her life cleaning filth-laden latrines.

I summoned the rest of the household slaves together, who probably knew of Bodvac's presence, and warned them of the consequences of further betrayal of their mistress and me. They would suffer crucifixion.

The question remained, would Gallus use assassins again in an attempt to kill me?

CHAPTER II

MARCH, 52 AD

Sitting alone in my small office at Station One of the Watch, headquarters of the prefect, I studied security plans for the approaching Julian Festival. Minutes earlier, I had dismissed Chulainn after he delivered a message from Eleyne. Getting up from my hard-backed chair, I stretched my cramped legs and stepped to the office door. In the hazy morning sun of October, I watched as Chulainn disappeared in the distance through the *Porta Ratumena* gate off the *Via Lata*. Had it been nearly five years since we nearly killed one another?

As Eleyne promised, he had proven his loyalty. A few weeks after the assassination attempt, Eleyne persuaded me to remove his shackles so he could escort her to the Great Market near the Forum. The possibility of escape existed, but Chulainn's fear of the city and crowds minimized the likelihood.

On a cold November day, he and three other slaves had accompanied Eleyne to the street of the silversmiths, where she purchased an expensive candelabra. One of the escorting slaves carrying the item fell behind on the busy street. Two thieves emerged from the crowds, clubbed the little man, and sent him sprawling onto the trash-filled pavement. Sweeping up the prize, they fled as the bleeding slave futilely cried for help.

Disregarding the danger, Chulainn chased after the felons. The fugitives ran into a nearby neighborhood considered so dangerous even the Watch feared to enter without heavy reinforcements. Cornering them in a dingy alley, Chulainn proceeded to beat the thugs within an eyelash of their worthless lives. Suddenly, three or four young toughs attacked him with daggers. Seasoned in battle against the Roman army, he fought like a savage warrior. He slammed one bandit's head first against a brick wall, knocking him unconscious. Disarming two others, he used their weapons to inflict a score of wounds on the rest before they finally escaped. A bruised and bleeding Chulainn returned a dented but still shining candleholder to a delighted Eleyne. He never wore another chain.

I had heard a rumor that much to Gallus's consternation, even though Eleyne's former slave, Candra, had been condemned to the arena five years earlier, he had survived undefeated as a gladiator. Game after game he packed the wooden stadium of Statilius Taurus with fifty thousand spectators to watch him slay Rome's finest gladiators. Only fools wagered against him. Women came in droves to admire his immense physique, and he had the choice of wenches. Dressed in a loincloth, he fought with a long trident, a dagger, and a large fishing net—costume of the *Retiarii*. The mob worshipped him as a god.

Another conspiracy against Emperor Claudius's life had been uncovered. Plotted by his libertine wife, Messalina, and her lover, Consul Designate Gaius Silius, the attempted overthrow occurred in the full of autumn about two years after Eleyne and I were married. Stunned to learn his conniving wife planned to replace him as ruler with Gaius Silius, Claudius allowed his secretary, the clever Narcissus, to handle the crisis. Although illegal for a freedman, the emperor gave him permission to take command of the Praetorian Guard for one day.

At the sight of the mock wedding being performed between Messalina and her paramour, Gaius Silius was immediately executed. A bloodbath ensued. Four hundred people attending the ceremony were slaughtered on the spot as traitors. Escaping the carnage, Messalina fled to the home of her unsympathetic mother. Discovered by the Praetorians, an officer of the Guard gave her the option of committing suicide. When she refused, he did his duty by slicing off her lovely head.

That same evening, a dazed Claudius was known to have asked Narcissus, "Why is her ladyship not present for dinner?"

"You had her put to death, Caesar, don't you remember?"

"Oh, but of course—I had forgotten . . . gods, I had forgotten," he answered, his voice trailing away.

Most startling of all, especially to Sabinus, was the execution of his friend, Decrius Calpurnianus, the Watch prefect. Sabinus had been totally unaware of his complicity in the Messalina-Silius intrigue. Concerned that he might be wrongfully accused of treason, Sabinus hurried to the emperor's side and reassured him of his loyalty and disavowed any knowledge of the conspiracy. Fortunately, Vitellius, who had been attending the emperor through most of the ordeal, vouched for his long-time friend's integrity.

"Now, the score is even," Vitellius said to Sabinus later.

"In what manner of speaking?" a puzzled Sabinus asked.

"You saved my friendship with the emperor when I was willing to sign my political and financial life away to young Gallus. Remember how much I wanted to marry the barbarian woman, Eleyne?"

"Aye, and I would help you again."

"I believe you friend, and that's why I returned the favor. You and Decrius Calpurnianus were known to be friends. If I hadn't known you better, your association with him would have spelled disaster. I have, to put it coarsely, saved your hide."

Then rumor had it that Claudius swore he would never remarry, but within a year took his fourth wife, Agrippina, niece by another marriage. It was common knowledge that she was calculating and treacherous, far more dangerous than Messalina. She set her beautiful but wicked eyes on the throne for her young son, the headstrong Nero, instead of young Britannicus, Claudius's son and rightful successor. Agrippina seduced the old man into making

Nero, then twelve years old, heir to the throne. Many already feared Rome would rue the day.

Nearly two years later, reports came to Sabinus that Caratacus, who had eluded capture for many years, was betrayed. Leading an army drawn from the remnants of several British tribes, and a band of mercenaries recruited from the western part of the empire, he made his final stand against the Romans in Western Britannia. Badly defeated by the Imperial governor, General Ostorius Scapula, and Legion Fourteen Gemina, Caratacus escaped. His downfall came when granted asylum by Eleyne's distant cousin, Cartimandua, Queen of the Brigantes in Northern Britannia. Less than a week later, the flaxen-haired monarch was arrested and handed the renegade king over to the Roman Governor, who sent him to Rome in fetters.

Impressed by the British leader's defiant courage and impassioned speech before the emperor at the Praetorian Barracks, Claudius pardoned Caratacus and allowed him to live with honor in Rome. As Sabinus predicted, Caratacus fell into Rome's hands when least expected. What a strange tangle is the web of politics and war. Stranger still was when I saw Rome's one-time sworn enemy, hand in hand with his wife and little daughter, browsing the market place as a guest of Rome.

A short time later, based on lies that rumor said came from Claudius's friend, Herod Agrippa, King of Judea, the emperor expelled the Jews from Rome. He accused them of disturbing the peace of Rome at the instigation of the dead prophet, Christus, a god to whom Eleyne had grown attached.

The exile of those strange but good people, including Pricilla and Aquila, embittered Eleyne. As she became more involved with the Christians, as they called themselves, their influence on her swelled. So long as the sect's activities did not affect our family life, and its members obeyed the laws of the state, I didn't care which god Eleyne worshipped.

I jumped at the arrival of a messenger. Lord Sabinus requested my presence immediately. As reward for his loyalty during the conspiracy by Messalina, the emperor had appointed Sabinus acting Watch prefect, a position normally held by a member of the Equestrian Order. It was partial fulfillment of his original promise to make him city prefect six years before.

Arriving at Sabinus's office, I took the chair he indicated as he finished reading a report. Dropping the parchment to the table, he turned to me. "Drusus has been murdered," he said evenly.

"When did it happen?" Drusus had been tribune and commander of the Seventh Cohort. Tribune Faenus Rufus, who had since transferred to the Praetorian Guard, had warned me about Drusus's sympathies to the Gallus family when I had arrived in Rome.

"Not more than an hour ago."

"Any arrests made?"

Sabinus shook his head. "None. No witnesses—at least none who would come forward."

"Where was he killed?" I gestured toward the office door.

"The Trans-Tiberina District."

"What part?" Located on Tiber's right bank, the district was the poorest and most crime-ridden precinct in Rome. An area of mixed races with people from all over the empire—they had no love for the Watch.

"Happened on a lane ironically named Mercy Street," Sabinus answered.

I raised my eyebrows. "What were the circumstances?"

Sabinus explained that Drusus was riding his horse, escorted by a contingent of ten Watchmen, when a dagger, hurled anonymously from the jostling crowd struck him in the neck. He toppled to the trash-littered pavement, dead, and lay there as the panicked crowd scattered.

"Centurion Casperius Niger," Sabinus continued, "was part of the dead tribune's escort. He took charge of the investigation, ordered his troops to detain and question everyone in the area from which the knife was thrown."

"None too gently, I would guess." Casperius had been promoted from sergeant to centurion since the raid in the caves that had uncovered old Gallus's conspiracy against Claudius.

I smirked.

"No one admitted to seeing or knowing anything," Sabinus said. "I expected as much, even on a sunny day, with the street teeming with people."

"Why was he singled out?" I asked.

Sabinus snorted. He picked up the metal stylus laying by the wax tablet on his desk and fingered it before putting it down again. "As far as Centurion Niger can ascertain, Drusus was involved with a worthless slut—the kind who follow the troops."

"How does a street follower fit in?"

"Drusus killed her father after he returned home from the corner tavern and caught them in bed." Sabinus shrugged, and then a malicious smile crossed his lips. "He couldn't believe his daughter was that kind of girl. Seems like the drunken, old fool pulled a knife on him—a fatal mistake."

I shook my head.

"Calpurnianus should have gotten rid of Drusus years ago," Sabinus commented ruefully. "I couldn't because he was an Imperial appointee—the most inept and corrupt of my tribunes. The Seventh is the worst disciplined cohort in the Watch. However . . . " He paused as if for effect. "That's about to change."

"Sir?"

He leaned forward, his elbows touching the desktop, and clasped his hands together. He pursed his chapped lips as his hawk-brown eyes studied my face for the length of a few heart beats. "I'm appointing you the new commander of the Seventh Cohort."

A sickening feeling churned the pit of my stomach. Traditionally, an Italian-born tribune was promoted to the command. Somehow I had known, during the course of the conversation, he would pick me. As member of the

Equestrian Order and a tribune, I expected to receive a command, but not in the Watch.

I faced an enormous challenge in retraining the Seventh. For a moment I studied the black, marble bust of Cicero on the pedestal behind the prefect. Although a Republican, he was Sabinus's favorite statesman and politician. I speculated as to how he would have handled the situation—no doubt, roll up his proverbial sleeves and take immediate action. I was determined to do the same.

"You honor me, sir," I finally answered. "May I prove worthy of your trust."

"You will," Sabinus answered. "I don't expect miracles overnight." He shook his head. "They're a bad lot, but you're the right man for the job. Curse Drusus's soul—may he drown crossing the River Styx."

"I'll whip them into shape," I promised.

"Literally. From the information I've collected, Drusus's men haven't felt the sting of a vine rod across their backs in ages—surprise them."

* * *

Late afternoon, I arrived home with mixed feelings about the day's events and twists. Despite confidence in my abilities to command the Seventh, my gut feelings said Sabinus wasn't being realistic. I needed months, not weeks, to restore the cohort to the discipline and efficiency for which the Watch was famous.

Horse-faced Porus greeted me at the door. "Good afternoon, sir. I trust your day went well?"

I gave him my scarlet cloak and stepped into the small, lamp-lighted vestibule.

"It could have been better," I answered. I touched the smooth, bronze statue of *Lares*, the little house god, in the wall niche near the door for good luck. Eleyne no longer believed in the Briton gods, let alone Roman ones, but I refused her request to remove their images from the home. I found a strange comfort in their presence—perhaps as a reaction to Eleyne's invisible Christian God.

"I'm sorry, sir," Porus said in a sincere voice. His long face contorted as if in sympathy. "Is there anything I can do?" I could have complained of constipation and been met with the same reply. But his loyalty to our house was priceless.

"Bring me wine, Porus, and tell the mistress I'm home."

"Right away, sir."

"I'm here, darling," Eleyne called as I entered the flat's small atrium. "I'm almost finished with my sewing." She sat on a cushioned, high-backed chair. Nearby a brazier rested on an iron tripod, heating the otherwise chilly room. Black smoke formed thin strands curling their way up to the outside vent. Fading remnants of winter light filtered through the high, iron grill of the apartment wall. The small tapestry draped across her legs depicted a hunting scene of horsemen armed with spears and shields chasing a wild boar. Close on the beast's tail ran four hounds, followed by slaves carrying nets. Nearly as colorful was her green, tartan skirt and top, embroidered in gold trim, which she wore. Mother had sent a weaver to instruct Eleyne in the art, and her natural skill bore fruit with prized works illustrating life in Britannia.

Nefer sprawled next to Eleyne. She awarded me with an indifferent glance, twisted around and licked her paws. At least the cat no longer growled when I approached Eleyne. After warning me about the assassination attempt five years ago, I gladly tolerated the cat's sometimes obnoxious behavior.

Gazing at me, Eleyne smiled and set aside her needle and thread. As I bent down and kissed her lips, I noticed she wore the gold Celtic torc she'd brought with her from Britannia. It matched the armlets above the elbows, which encircled her pale neck. Now a citizen, and considered an honorable Roman matron, Eleyne's British ways still died slowly.

Since our marriage nearly five years before, Eleyne had given birth to our sons, Marcellus, now three, and Sabinus, two. The two boys were a contrast. Small and dark, young Marcellus would grow to be lean and wiry. A quiet child, he seemed to possess insight beyond his years. But young Sabinus was born big and noisy. He was happy and outgoing from the moment of birth. Fair like his mother, his long face and chin resembled his grandfather, Verica, Eleyne's father.

"I heard you talking to Porus," Eleyne said, bringing my mind back to the present. "Was your day so distressing?"

"Depends on how you view it," I answered glumly. "I should be thankful, but I'm not."

Her face tightened, and for a few seconds she remained silent as if pondering my situation. Despite birthing two children, she had gained little weight. Her delicate face contained few expressive lines at the corner of her mouth and eyes.

"Here, sit down," she suggested an instant later, "you look awful. Tell me what happened." Eleyne reached over and stroked my stubbled face with her soft hand.

I took the chair next to her and described the murder and my promotion.

"Drusus didn't deserve to die so horribly." She was more forgiving than I.

I nodded, not really meaning it.

"I'm happy you received the promotion," Eleyne said. "You've earned it." She planted a kiss on my cheek.

I smiled weakly. "Then pray to your God to give me strength. I'll need his and that of Achilles to restore discipline."

"Are they so wicked?"

"Aye, that's why he was popular with the Seventh." I exhaled. "They literally got away with murder."

"Is it any wonder they are hated by the people?" Eleyne said. "My Christian friends have been badly treated, too."

"They're treating everyone the same. Keeping the peace, calming disturbances, and fighting fires are their primary duties, but they've been derelict. They extorted the shopkeepers far more than other cohorts do. That ceases immediately."

We fell silent as Porus entered. He carried a bronze tray, containing two silver cups and a small, blue glass

94

amphora containing a dark Tuscan wine. An earthen jug of water to dilute the heavy drink accompanied it. Placing the server on the ornately carved oak table, he filtered out the resin with a strainer, filled the cups, and waited upon us.

Eleyne and I quietly sipped our wine.

"It isn't a problem that can be solved overnight," I continued, after Porus left the room. I held my cup with both hands. Then I realized I was holding it so tightly my fingers had turned numb. I loosened my grip. "The Julian Games start in six weeks, and there isn't any way they'll be ready to handle a major disorder."

"But there have been riots at other games and festivals. How did the Seventh manage then?"

"Drusus assigned the troops to patrolling the outskirts of the city during the festivals, through bribing tribunes from other cohorts to take their place."

"Didn't Sabinus know about it?" She took another sip.

"His spies only recently uncovered the truth. Sabinus was in the process of building a solid case against Drusus. The emperor would have had no choice but to dismiss him."

"Now, he's dead."

I lifted my goblet and took a long swallow, the slightly acidic wine warming my insides. "Aye, I'll have to gain the confidence of the Seventh, but at the same time be decisive and firm."

"I know you'll set a personal example as did my father. His warriors trusted and respected him," she said. Her mind seemed to wander back to perhaps happier times.

"He stood," she continued, "right in front when they went to battle. He didn't expect his men to do anything he wouldn't do himself."

"Your father was a noble man," I said, thinking of the assassination by his own bodyguards.

"By the way," Eleyne added, "Aurelia has invited me to the naval games."

I raised my eyebrows, and then studied her face. "Since when have you taken an interest in gladiator shows? Aren't they against the beliefs of your god?"

95

"They are, but Aurelia pleaded with me to go with her. It will be *the* event of the Julian Festival, so I said I would." She sighed and gestured with a hand. "Poor dear, she seemed so lonely and depressed—I don't know why."

"Doesn't she have lady friends among the senators' wives?"

"Yes, but she says they're boring, and she'd rather have my company."

"Very thoughtful of her. It's obvious she loves you like a daughter."

Eleyne blushed, and then smiled. "I know, and it's very flattering. She has been like a mother to me." Earlier, Eleyne had related how she lost her real mother when she was five years old. A chill had settled in her lungs, leading to her death.

"You know Candra will fight in the games?"

She lowered her head and stared at the shining, tiled floor. "I've seen the posters—they must be drawn on every wall in Rome. I've never wanted to see him fight, because I'm afraid he will be killed."

"What if it happens?"

"I don't know what I will do," she answered gloomily. "Of course, since Gallus is sponsoring the games, I'm sure he would celebrate his death."

Quietly, Gallus had regained the emperor's favor. Working his way through the junior offices, required for readmission to the Senate, he currently held the office of *Aedile* of the city water works. Appropriately enough, the finale of the Julian Festival was the naval games in which Candra was scheduled to fight. Next year, Gallus would take his dead father's seat in the Senate.

"I'll pray for Candra's survival," Eleyne continued, "even though the chances are great that he will die."

Sensing her uneasiness, I changed the subject. "Let's not talk further about Candra tonight." Somehow, I doubted the thought of his possible doom left her mind.

CHAPTER 12

My promotion to commander of the Seventh Cohort created bitterness among the troops. I ordered to muster the Seventh for roll call and inspection on the first morning of my command. Nearly one thousand men formed ranks on the small parade field by the cohort's barracks, in the Trans-Tiberina District near the *Via Aurelia*.

Ten centuries, each containing nearly one hundred Watchmen, lined up in the usual *contubernii* of ten men in ten columns. Unlike the undermanned army, the Watch was kept at full complement.

As I approached the formation, followed by a trail of centurions, another officer called the men to attention. The loud clattering of chainmail, stomping of hob-nailed sandaled *caligae* on the cement pavement, echoed across the parade field and bounced off the barracks walls. A brilliant sun glared off their burnished chain-mail armor and the wide, protective cheek guards of their red-plumed helmets.

"Appointing an outsider is an insult," a Watchman somewhere in the ranks grumbled.

"We ain't forgetting Drusus anytime soon," another said.

Although I couldn't see the malcontents, I stopped and glared in their direction. The eyes of the troops who stood at attention before me looked down at the pavement of the parade ground in apparent unease, instead of staring blankly ahead.

I stepped closer to the formation and halted, smelling sweaty bodies and garlic on their breaths. After turning to my entourage who stopped behind me, I faced the troops again and surveyed the ranks.

The morning grew warmer with each passing minute— Rome was in for another scorching day. Sweat poured down my chest from inside my uniform. The scarf I wore around my neck as a guard from the chafing heat of my medal cuirass offered little protection. It was as if I were a prisoner in heated bronze.

I addressed the men. "I will say this only once." I paused to let the words sink in. "From now on, I will hold every man of this cohort accountable for his acts. Under your old commander, you turned into fucking slackers. No more! Disobedience to orders or infractions of rules and regulations will be met with swift and severe punishment!"

A groan erupted from the ranks.

"Silence!" roared the chief centurion behind me.

"Know this," I continued, "my loyalty to the emperor and Prefect Sabinus is absolute. I demand no less from you." I paused again.

Silence.

I turned to the officers behind me. "Prepare the men for inspection."

The chief centurion barked the command.

Slowly, I paced along the lines, inspecting each man. The laborious process took most of the morning, with dismal results. I placed one hundred fifty-nine troopers on report for failing to pass inspection.

This was only the beginning. I surveyed the men as their centurions barked commands and snarled insults and led them in riot drills—a fiasco. They failed to maintain a solid shield line—any mob could have smashed their disorderly ranks.

Heat rushed to my face. Clinching the hilt of my sword and cursing, I turned to the chief centurion. "I've seen enough. Stand the men down—they're a disgrace. You and the rest of the centurions are to report to my office immediately." I turned and walked away, kicking pebbles down the street.

I sat behind my desk glowering at the reeking, perspiring officers who stood fidgeting at attention. "Never have I seen a sorrier group of troops in my life!" Briefly, I stopped to allow the words to sink in. "I realize these are Watchmen, and not legionaries. But they're dressed and armed like soldiers. Therefore, I expect them to look as sharp and perform in the same disciplined fashion. Do I make myself clear?"

"Yes, sir," the centurions answered glumly in unison.

I leaned slightly forward. "Your men—my men, will comply to all rules and regulations and follow standard training procedures. Discipline shall be enforced immediately." I jabbed a finger in their direction. "Any centurion who disobeys my orders will be broken to the ranks. By the gods, if you can't lead, then you will follow!" Lowering my hand, I studied the face of each of the ten centurions. Some remained passive; others stared in fear or hatred. Only one appeared to be pleased, Casperius Niger, who slowly nodded his approval. I remembered him as an Optio. He had been a member of the thirty Watchmen I had led on that infamous raid of the thieves' hideout beneath Rome a few years earlier. It was after we had killed or captured the bandits that we discovered the note leading to Gallus as the head of a conspiracy to kill Emperor Claudius.

"We have a lot of work ahead of us," I resumed. "Return to the parade field and begin at once. Dismissed!"

That afternoon the backs of many rankers incurred the stinging pain of a centurion's vine cane as I observed their drills on the parade field. They knew I was watching. No doubt the centurions, their commands laced with strings of profanities and threats, took out their dislike for me upon the backs of their men. This pampered lot deserved the boot and the rod if any discipline was to be instilled.

* * *

The first two weeks, Crispus and I traveled around the Trans-Tiberina District at all hours of the day and night, making dozens of surprise inspections of patrolling Watchmen. Upon discovering infractions or misconduct, I admonished or relieved the violators on the spot and reprimanded the centurion in charge.

One evening, Crispus and I, and an escort of picked troopers, stumbled upon a squad of bucketmen, extorting money from the proprietor of a wine shop along the *Via Portuensis* Road. I placed the entire detail of ten men under arrest and court-martialed them the following day.

Only in firefighting, the original function of the Watch, did the Seventh show competence. During the same period, under my close surveillance, the units quickly and efficiently used their tar-lined rope buckets and cart-wheeled water pumps to extinguish a dozen tenement fires.

Gradually, the Seventh began to improve. My inspections had the desired effect. After a long wait, I publicly praised appropriate conduct, which raised their pride and instilled confidence. The men grumbled, but soldiers always complained. So long as they obeyed orders, I didn't care. Due to the incompetence and poor leadership, I sacked centurions of the First and Third Centuries. The Seventh Cohort required further discipline and training before they gained my confidence in their abilities to be an effective police unit. There was progress, but the road to professionalism demanded by the emperor was still over the horizon.

One humid day, as I reviewed the daily reports in my spartan-like office, Casperius Niger, the tall and swarthy centurion from Tuscany, unexpectedly reported to me. Conducting the investigation into the death of Drusus, he had proved to be the best centurion under my command. Because his ideas on discipline were similar to mine, I promoted him to the command of the First Century, traditional assignment of a cohort's best centurion. Casperius snapped to attention, saluted, and gave a fitness report on his unit.

When he finished, I was about to dismiss him when he peeked over his shoulder to the office door and hallway. No one was about. His olive skin tightened over his lean face as if troubled by a problem. "Sir, may I say something personal?" he asked in a slow, Etruscan drawl.

"You may, providing it's honest and not disrespectful." Puzzled by his request, I nodded to a stool by the desk.

He sat and leaned slightly forward. "I've listened to the men comparing you with Drusus," he said in a lowered voice. "The younger ones are doing a lot of complaining, but the old veterans are praising your name. You're no friend like Drusus, but this cohort needed a commander like you."

"Thanks for your confidence."

"Well, I've known you about five years, sir, and I like how you handle the men. You're fair but keep a tough stick on them, if you know what I mean."

"It's my duty, Casperius."

His narrow lips curled in disgust. "Drusus did his, too."

"In a perverted manner of speaking, yes," I remarked dryly. "I know the ones he considered his pretty boys, whom, shall I say, 'loved him?'"

"Aye, he had his pets—not centurions, which made discipline impossible," he added. He rubbed the hilt of his short sword in a circle motion with his stubby fingers.

"I know."

He wrinkled his thick brows. "The centurions gave up, disgusted. Why crack the vine cane when Drusus kept interfering and playing favorites?"

"Didn't anyone report his activities to Prefect Sabinus?"

"No, sir, because the superiors weren't much better. The centurions had little doings on the side, too." Niger's jaw tightened.

"Go on."

"The men went unsupervised, and Lord Sabinus was too busy to inspect the Trans-Tiberina. With all these foreigners living there, it's like a different land. He depended on Drusus's lying progress reports instead of using spies, or better yet, his own eyes. And you saw how poor their discipline was on your first day in charge. They would have been chased by the first dung eater pelting them with a brick. But now, that's changed," he added with a satisfied grin, glancing to the vine cane lodged inside his sword belt next to the dagger. "My lads know what I'd do if they disobeyed orders. They fear me more than the dung eaters—just like it should be in a fighting force."

"That's comforting, but we still have lots of work ahead of us."

He grinned, revealing long, white teeth. "Aye, so we do, sir. They'll get a lot more of the stick on their miserable backsides and up their arses before I'm through."

* * *

The search for Drusus's assassin or assassins continued. Many suspects were arrested and questioned. All denied the murder, even under the questioning of Abroghast, the supreme rack master. At last, a pair of accused thieves named his killers. Sabinus's spies verified the information and was later confirmed by Scrofa's beggars, who had overheard three men bragging about Drusus's death in one of the local wine shops. Although offered twice the amount of gold, the mendicants, with their vast knowledge of Rome's caves, failed to pinpoint the hideout.

* * *

The Julian Festival was celebrated in recognition of Julius Caesar's victories over the Gauls more than one hundred years before and his enemy, Pompey, during the last ten days of July. Garlands in a rainbow of colors adorned the closed public buildings and temple. An army of state slaves scrubbed the streets unusually clean around the Forum, temples, and amphitheaters. Hundreds of bronze and gilded statues, gracing the Imperial Capital's squares and buildings, were polished to a blinding sparkle. Special events each day included theatrical performances, chariot races, and gladiator shows. The festival's celebration culminated with mock naval games given in the great basin, the *Augustan Naumachia*. Gladiators would reenact the Battle of Salamis, in which the Greeks defeated a huge Persian fleet off the coast of Athens over five hundred years before.

Rumors pervaded every dingy wine shop, sleazy back alley, and market place that three thousand trained gladiators would fight to the death. Although pecuniary in most financial matters, when it came to gladiatorial games, Emperor Claudius threw all costs to the Aeolian winds. His love for blood and gore in the arena knew no bounds. On dozens of occasions, he had violated the Augustan Law of using no more than one hundred pairs of gladiators fighting in one day. In superb physical condition, thousands of trained fighters, drawn from the Imperial and private training schools of the empire and skilled in the arts of slaying one another for entertainment, were about to add further color to the spectacle. Only Rome could feast upon such blood lust.

And Rome was hungry for the dawn.

* * *

In the darkness of early morning, hundreds of slaves scurried over the marble stands of the great basin, as task masters scolded and fretted over last-minute details. Everything seemed ready for the naval games and the final day of the festival.

Crispus, now a centurion and my aide-de-camp, gazed with me across the artificial lake that mirrored the stars above and the glimmering torchlights of workers below. The smell of pitch wafted through the stadium.

"What's on your mind, Marcellus?" Crispus asked. "You're unusually quiet."

"Thinking how peaceful this time of morning usually seems to be," I answered, bracing myself against the chill of a slight breeze swirling across the lake's surface.

"Aye, not for long."

"Soon, the sky will wax blue with the harsh light of the sun, and the murky waters and those scabby man-made islands in the basin's center will lay naked before the empire."

"You're sounding like a philosopher again," Crispus said.

I exhaled, disgusted with the whole matter. "I'm growing too cynical, I suppose, but what waste. We'll see slaughter, gore, and carnage on a scale so grand that surely this bizarre circus will be our terrible legacy to Rome's children—even if it never occurs again."

"Sometimes, there are events we can't control," Crispus reminded me, "and this is one of them."

"You're right of course," I said, "but there's something wrong with a civilization that slaughters men like cattle for amusement."

"But you're here, and nothing is going to change." Crispus turned away and spat at the shadowy outline of a spider scurrying along on the marble walkway.

I bit my lip. "Yes, and I'm part of it—no better than the rest. I was once told a thinking man shouldn't be a soldier—at least not of Rome."

"Don't tell that to anyone else—you'll lose your position—maybe your life."

We slipped away from the basin and hiked to the location of the Seventh Cohort.

I gave last-minute instructions to my centurions. Throughout the festival, the cohort had been held in ready reserve, providing squad-sized patrols in the neighborhoods surrounding the naval stadium and the public park known as the Grove of Caesar. The bulk remained on alert on a wharf by the banks of the Tiber, near the foul-smelling marketplace of the fishmongers. Placed in strategic positions around the area were other elements of the Watch and City Guard. Since the stadium was constructed in the Trans-Tiberina District, security surrounding the Augustan Naumachia was the responsibility of the Seventh.

Suspecting Tribune Drusus's murderers would be among the celebrants at the games, tension permeated the ranks of the Seventh. I overheard five or six bucketmen murmur they would find them. "May Jove have mercy on the bloody bastards," one said, "because we won't!"

After leaving Centurion Casperius Niger in charge, Crispus and I joined Sabinus in the Watch prefect's box at the arena. As part of a show of strength, he expected all his tribunes to attend him at the games. Scattering an army of cats, fighting over the remains of rotting fish by the entrance, we reached the secret passageway leading to Sabinus's booth.

Only upon entering the stadium could one truly appreciate its size and grandeur. During an earlier occasion when I stood at one end and viewed the far end— fifteen hundred feet away—the people appeared as ants. When I looked directly across, the distance was over eight hundred feet. It felt like a lake, not a manmade pond. Close to the center island, about four hundred feet away, two hippos created twin wakes as they paddled along. A water bird slapped footprints upon the calm water's surface as it raced to become airborne, then suddenly disappeared in a cauldron of white water without a hint of its fate. Nearby, an Egyptian crocodile slumbered against a guard's stand carved into the wall, as if staking out its territory, and waiting for him to take a careless step.

Divided into three terraces sloping towards the turgid basin, the Augustan Naumachia held over two hundred thousand souls. The *Alsietina* Aqueduct fed the huge oval-shaped basin, bringing water from the mountains northwest of Rome. Protected from beasts and gladiators by a bronze trellis, the lowest level sat nine feet above the water's edge. At fixed intervals along the wall, Praetorians stood guard duty in partial concave enclosures. This assured no gladiators or criminals would escape or hurl excrement into the crowd. After all, condemned men have little to fear and appreciate a dung-splattered senator as well as the next person.

The Great Imperial Box sat midway above the water's edge, about the center of the stadium. The enclosed seats of the city magistrates, including Sabinus's, and the Vestal Virgins sat adjacent to the emperor's section. Aurelia was attending the games as well, sitting alongside Sabinus. Eleyne would accompany Aurelia as her guest. Normally, my wife would not attend the games, but Aurelia had persuaded her to come to this event.

"It's almost time, Crispus," I said. "All eyes will be focused on the lake."

He snorted. "Aye, and it will turn into a sea of blood."

In the basin's center rose two large islands, shaped like hourglasses, and connected by a narrow bridge. Despite their size, ample room remained for maneuvering of two dozen half-sized war galleys and smaller boats in the surrounding waters.

The sun peeked over the distant hills, splashing the city in a brilliant morning light. A pale-blue haze settled over the western horizon, beyond the gray aqueducts snaking into Rome. The day's heat loomed almost as early as the dawn, followed by stifling humidity. Fountains surrounding the edge of the basin sprayed the heavy scent of saffron perfume as the noisy, jostling, and sweaty crowds entered the arena. My cuirass and bronze helmet became an oven. But the refreshing fountain mist cooled my face. How fortunate Sabinus's box rested beneath a shaded red and white striped canopy.

Ushers took numbered tickets made of flatbone from the festive crowd and escorted paying customers to reserved seats on the middle level. Retained for the nobility and wealthy, where the scent of blood was stronger, was the cushion-seated lower level.

White tunic vendors wandered through the aisles hawking cushions to soften the hard, wooden benches and marble seats of the mid and upper sections. Others peddled wine and Gallic beer, sweetmeats, and pastries. Free bread was distributed to all, and sales of programs were brisk. Bookmakers in portable booths near the passageways took last-minute bets. Although they bought hand fans and sun hats at robber prices, the rabble sitting in the harsh sunlight were in a festive mood.

The main event consisted of a naval battle fought by two fleets: the Blues, representing the Greeks, and the Greens, the Persians—the same colors used by the racing teams in the *Circus Maximus*.

Crispus and I reported to Sabinus, who greeted us with an air of gravity. Required to wear the clothing of a magistrate, even for the public games, he wore a white linen toga with a purple-trimmed *laticlavius*, drenched in perspiration.

Sabinus enjoyed the races and animal hunts but had little interest in gladiatorial matches. He appeared strictly for the sake of the emperor. Excusing himself from the consul and city prefect, he stood and motioned Crispus and I to follow him. We climbed the stairs to the secret subterranean passageway between the first and second levels. The smell of rodent droppings pierced my nostrils, and I noticed they were scattered along the tunnel floor. Dust motes drifted upwards in the sun rays that gleamed through the entry way.

"Good day for the games," Sabinus said in the dark coolness of the tunnel.

"Yes, sir, it is," I replied, puzzled by his attempt at small talk. What was his real motive?

He grinned half-heartedly. "I even placed a small bet on the Greens—Candra's team."

"Good chance his side will win," I answered, puzzled by his real intentions.

His lips curved into a frown. "For our sake, they better."

"Sir?"

Sabinus glanced to the opening and back to us. "I never wanted to send Candra to the arena, he was a loyal slave protecting Eleyne. But he gave no choice. By touching Gallus, a Roman citizen, I would have to summarily execute him or send him to the school for gladiators where he would have a chance to live. Now, I fear for his life—this isn't a typical gladiatorial match."

"You mean it won't be the usual man-to-man situation, Lord Sabinus?" Crispus asked.

"Indeed, Centurion Crispus, it's to be a full-fledged battle, as if it were Salamis, only on a smaller scale."

"But why this type of fight?" I asked, realizing the ramifications of Sabinus's statements.

"This is a preliminary bout," Sabinus answered. "The Emperor Claudius plans to conduct greater naval games after the canal from Fucine Lake to the River Latis is completed."

Fucine Lake huddled in the Marsian Hills sixty miles east of Rome. Every spring the huge lake flooded the surrounding countryside, destroying valuable farmland.

During the last ten years, thirty thousand slaves labored in building a canal between the lake and the River Latis, five miles away, to drain off the overflow. After tunneling through a solid mountain of rock, almost four miles long, the great ditch was nearly completed. Some considered the cost of three thousand slaves lost as cheap if it curtailed the flooding.

"Next year," Sabinus continued, "he'll sponsor a massive naval engagement on the lake involving nearly twenty thousand criminals."

"He'll have to clean out every prison in the empire to find enough," I said.

Sabinus nodded, and his lips tightened into a thin line. "True, and the lessons derived from today's events will be applied on a grander scale. He's expecting successful results."

"But Candra could be overwhelmed by sheer numbers," I said, knowing the mob would turn ugly if he were slain.

"Exactly," Sabinus answered. "The emperor won't have the time to grant him quarter—even if he's inclined to do so."

"By Melkart, if it happens," Crispus said, "the mob will go mad—you know how they worship Candra, sir."

"I do," Sabinus replied. "I've seen his name prominently displayed all over the city."

So had I. The posters claimed Candra was everything from the *darling of the maidens* to the *Lord of the Masses*.

"Are the troops in place?" Sabinus inquired.

"Yes, sir," I answered. "They have their orders."

Sabinus studied me intently. "Give me an honest opinion. Will the Seventh hold ranks if there is a riot?"

"They will, if we receive reinforcements in time," I answered without hesitation. "You've seen my reports."

He wrinkled his heavily lined forehead and exhaled. "I'm impressed, Marcellus. They've made significant progress since you've taken command. If there is trouble, I'll require every manjack trooper. The First and Fourth are only moments away, and so is the City Guard. If the mob moves your way, you need only give the signal."

"They'll contain the mob until reinforcements arrive," I answered, determined not to fail Sabinus.

"Good. If it comes to that, you shall hold at all costs."

"I will."

Below us two dozen galleys moored quietly at the north end of the basin next to the gray-stone jetty. By afternoon I pictured their holds swollen with gladiators. Stacked neatly at one corner of the dock laid dozens of flimsy flatboats. Approximately one hundred black Africans milled about the dock preparing canoes for one of the events—the hunt. To the rear a massive iron gate led to the chambers holding the condemned and the gladiators.

We returned to Sabinus's box, where he took his place next to Aurelia who wore a silk, white gown and matching stola. Eleyne, dressed in an emerald, ankle-length tunic, belted at the waist, sat to her left. Chulainn and a female mute slave, who attended to Eleyne, stood with the rest of the other guests, slaves at the far back next to the wall. Eleyne, whose pale neck was encircled by a slim, gold necklace, turned back to where Crispus and I were standing behind Sabinus. She motioned me to her side, and I bent down, my head level with hers.

"I know I told you this earlier," she whispered, "but I said another prayer to God asking that Candra's life be spared."

"I share your hope, darling," I whispered in reply. I didn't tell her I doubted Candra would survive the day.

"I had to come to the games, Aurelia didn't have to persuade me. I can't explain it, but my heart tells me this may be a critical day for all of us." She touched her fine nose with a long, delicate finger.

I was about to ask her to explain when Sabinus turned me and said, "Marcellus, the games are about to begin, you are on duty."

I snapped to attention. "Yes, sir!"

I took my place behind his chair next to Crispus. His eyes gave me a questioning look.

"Later," I said out of the corner of my mouth.

A brassy fanfare sounded, drawing all eyes to the Imperial Box. Emperor Claudius, who grew more emaciated and sickly with each passing day, appeared beneath the great, purple awning. Beside him stood his scheming wife, Agrippina, and her sunken-eyed, fourteen-year-old son, Nero. Missing from the Imperial Family was Britannicus, Claudius's son. The multitudes jumped to their feet and cheered the emperor with extended arms. *"Ave, Caesar! Ave, Imperator!"*

Dressed in a billowing gold and purple toga, the emperor slowly limped to the edge of his box. The people silenced as he raised his hand containing a purple, silk handkerchief. His entourage followed behind, including the president of the games, Gallus. By co-sponsoring the games, an expensive undertaking for even the wealthiest of men, he had ingratiated himself with the old man. If the games proved successful, he would obtain a higher position with the Imperial Government, such as governorship in the provinces. Then, he would recoup his expenses by collecting higher taxes. Gallus wasn't missing a Chaldean's trick.

After finishing a brief speech on the glories of Julius Caesar, the emperor nodded to Gallus.

The crowds hushed in expectation, and an eerie silence descended the Naval Arena. A gust billowed the emperor's silk canopy, and colorful streamers snapped above the top rows of the stadium. A hawker's cry drifted into the silence from a distant section, as Gallus stood majestically.

He stretched forth his hand displaying the blood-red handkerchief, apparently savoring the fact that all eyes of the world that mattered were upon him. Every ear strained to hear the ceremonial words.

"LET THE GAMES BEGIN," Gallus commanded in a loud voice heard across the basin. He dropped the weighted scarlet cloth into the lake. A cheering wave began on both sides of his stand and rippled to the far, distant side of the Augustan Naumachia.

Gallus nodded to the cornus players. A long blast swelled from the circular trumpets, joined by a deep-throated hydraulic water organ. The spectators cheered again and took their seats.

* * *

The morning passed quickly. A contingent of Praetorians herded hundreds of chained criminals onto the jetty five hundred feet away for the first event. Unshackled and armed with cheap swords, the prisoners were forced onto canoes stacked upon the dock. I realized why they hadn't been placed in the waters before the games. Within minutes after setting sail, the little vessels, constructed with a thin layer of whitewashed pulpwood, began dissolving and sank.

As murderers and thieves alike struggled to stay afloat, the crowd screamed for their deaths. As if on cue, submerged crocodiles, deliberately starved prior to the games, surfaced and attacked the condemned, savagely tearing them apart to the mob's cheers.

Standing behind Sabinus's chair, I glanced towards Eleyne's back. Her body stiffened, and she gasped. She shook her head, loosening strands from her simply coiffed jet hair.

Aurelia leaned toward and whispered something to Eleyne. She raised an arm, and her hand gently stroked Eleyne's shoulder.

For a few seconds, my wife relaxed, nodded to Aurelia, and mumbled, "Thank you."

Aurelia straightened and turned back to Sabinus. But thereafter Eleyne seemed to stare straight ahead, not moving a muscle in her body.

Torn limbs, entrails, and shredded clothing floated and mixed with the lake's bloodied waters. Those escaping rowed frantically for the islands, only to melt into the jaws of frenzied beasts—although one swimmer circled dazed, treading water for some time.

The surface churned with hungry animals. Victims screamed. The murky, brown waters between the dock and the islands became a sickening red slick, reeking of the smell of blood and bodily fluids, lazily drifted with the current to the south end of the basin, draining into an

111

underground cistern. Was this the ideal of Roman justice? I doubt if the writers of the constitution, the Laws of the Twelve Tables, had envisioned this kind of butchery five hundred years before. Like so many other things, the laws of Rome had been perverted.

After the premier slaughter ended, a wrestling event followed pitting gladiators against crocodiles. On the heels of this carnage came the hippopotamus and crocodile hunt by spear-wielding Ethiopians—a bloody spectacle lasting the rest of the morning. The losses on both sides were about even.

During the noon break, Crispus and I were invited by Sabinus to join Aurelia, Eleyne, and him for lunch. Upset by the bloodshed she had witnessed, Eleyne could not choke down her food. I did not blame her.

Meanwhile, Gallus's servants scattered lottery tickets through the crowd, redeemable for jars of wine, food, and money. A small villa on the seashore near Puteoli was the grand prize. A mad scramble for tickets broke out into fights between wealthy and poor alike. For a treasured ticket many a man emerged with a torn toga and bashed head. But Gallus triumphed as the rabble shouted his name in praise. Condescending, he took a half dozen sweeping bows, and the delighted crowds rained flowers upon his person.

But the morning's slaughter would pale beside the carnage to follow in the afternoon. Ironically, based on the success or failure of those coming events, Gallus's and my careers hung in the balance.

CHAPTER 13

When the noon meal ended, Crispus and I, who had
been invited to dine with Sabinus, Aurelia, and Eleyne,
resumed our positions behind Sabinus. I had received a
report from a courier that the Seventh Cohort was standing
by on alert, but so far, activity outside the arena had
been quiet. Trumpets sounded, and the iron grate raised
behind the dock, about five hundred feet away. An army
of gladiators emerged, their armor clanking and glistening
in the sunlight. In four long columns, two thousand of the
empire's best swaggered down the wharf to the awaiting
galleys.

Those wearing blue ribbons represented the Greeks,
and those wearing green were called the Persians. In
reality, they came from all over the world. Black Africans
from Nubia and Meriotic Sudan mixed with Thracians
from east of Greece. Scythians, who roamed the steppes
of Central Asia, stood alongside Celts from Britannia
and Gaul. Flaxen-haired Frisians, of Western Germania,
swapped tales with Scandians born to the far north.

Eleyne turned to Aurelia. "Look, it's Candra." She
pointed towards the gladiators.

Following the legion of fighters, well-known favorites
emerged singly. The crowds applauded, but only Candra,
the big Indian of the Persian Greens, received the wild
ovations of the multitude. A loud chant erupted as soon
as he appeared. "Candra! Candra! CAN-DRA! Spectators
streaming up the aisles back to their seats turned and
joined the chanting crowds in roaring welcome to him.

As if caught up in the moment, Eleyne stood and took
up the cry.

Stopping midway on the dock, he twisted his dark,
scarred face about, peering into the crowd. Spectacular
in a white loincloth and a leather covering that protected

his left shoulder, Candra's coppery skin glistened with oils accenting his every muscle. Dragging at his side, he pulled a large fishing net with one hand.

Candra responded to the still-cheering crowd, raising his long trident in salute. Escalated to a frenzied pitch, the shouts created a deafening roar. Spectators threw garland after garland of assorted flowers—some of which Candra speared and waved. When he placed one around his head, a thunderous applause added to the pandemonium.

Eleyne applauded as enthusiastically as the rest of the mob.

"I've never seen anyone," I shouted to Crispus, "including the emperor, receive such an outpouring of admiration."

"If the Emperor wore a loincloth as well as Candra," Crispus said in an equally loud voice, "he'd get a riotous ovation, too."

"You're probably right."

Only when Candra lowered his forked weapon and stepped aboard the ship did the audience settle down.

Eleyne sat and turned to Aurelia. "I don't know if I can watch. I'm so afraid Candra will die." She bit her lips to keep back the tears.

"I know," Aurelia said. "We can only pray that somehow he will find a way to survive."

When the remaining gladiators and slave oarsmen had embarked, the mooring lines were released, and the vessels set sail. In single file the galleys, three-banked oared triremes, glided silently towards the Imperial booth. Meanwhile, small boat skirmishers flying colorful streamers from top masts dashed to the islands from the boarding dock. Beneath the eyes of the old monarch, the triremes formed into four squadrons of six galleys each, one squadron behind the other. Quietly, the rowers paddled in position against the current that gently flowed from east to west, keeping the ships in place as the gladiators presented themselves to the emperor. Two squadrons flew blue pennants from their sterns and the other two, green.

As Claudius and Gallus sat in cushioned curule chairs, the combatants stood and pointed their weapons skyward in homage. "We who are about to die, salute you!" they proclaimed in ragged unison.

Claudius nodded to Gallus. He stood and raised a white, silk handkerchief. Scanning the basin, as if making certain all eyes were upon him, he opened his bejeweled fingers and watched the delicate napkin flutter slowly toward the sluggish waters. A large, silver, half-man, half-fish image of Triton, son of Poseidon, jutted through the surface and sent a ripple in front of the Imperial seats. Sounding from the silver conch held in its hand, a loud, mournful tone signaled the beginning of the fight. Instantly, the god submerged leaving a trail of bubbles and a foaming wake. Two Green flagmen and two Blue, standing on each side of the emperor's dais, raced along the lower walkway of the stadium to the far side, carrying oversized, silk banners streaming in the wind. A roaring cheer rippled in their wake as the squadrons slowly paddled to the opposite ends of the basin.

"At least the spectators on both sides of the stadium," I said, "get an equal chance of viewing the same amount of slaughter."

"Aye, pitting one Blue squadron against one Green on each side of the islands," Crispus agreed, "is the only fair way to go."

Gradually, the hot afternoon sun began its journey to the west. Climbing out along the wooden masts, overhanging the stadium's top rim, a detachment of sailors from the Misenum Fleet, installed blue and white canvas awnings. The protective coverings shielded the sun's glaring rays from reflecting upon the water and blinding the thousands of hatless spectators.

Crispus and I watched the vessels of the Greens and Blues nearest the emperor's box gliding towards one another. Mounting three banks of forty oars on each side, the galleys of both squadrons sailed in two staggered columns, three abreast, giving them more room for maneuvering. Men crowded the wooden decks wearing a variety of armor and carrying assorted weapons. As the ships approached one another, the gladiators went down on one knee bracing themselves for the oncoming shock when the vessels collided with one another.

Fitted into the bow, each ship mounted an iron ram shaped into a four-pronged beak. The sinister weapon barely cut the water's surface ahead of the prow.

To the crashing sounds of ramming ships and the cries of more than a thousand gladiators, the Blue and Green squadrons clashed in front of the Imperial section. Claudius clapped his hands enthusiastically and laughed like a gleeful child playing with a new toy. Spittle dripped from the side of his lips.

Locked together in a death grip, two galleys struggled to free themselves as gladiators from the Green ship stormed the vessels of the Blues. The battle turned into a scene of mass confusion—a spectacle of screaming, bloodied, hacking, sweating bodies in a sea of blue and green ribbons.

"Look, there's Candra." I gripped Crispus's arm.

"Where? It's hard to tell one gladiator from another."

I released his arm and pointed. "Over there, the big, tan one with the trident."

He nodded. "Aye, now I see him!"

Eleyne turned in my direction and back to the battle. She touched Aurelia's shoulder and pointed. "It's Candra."

Barely discerning his glistening hulk in the disarray of ships, I watched Candra, wading into the thick of the fight. His vessel was the second of the Green squadron to ram a Blue's ship. As he boarded, the mob's wild cheers swept across the waters. Deftly wielding his trident and net, he battled a group of long-haired British and Scandian savages. Flinging his net around the ankles of a bearded Briton, he yanked him off his feet, slamming the Celt onto the deck. Before the stunned warrior raised his weapon, Candra plunged the trident through his chest, to the cheers and jeers of the crowd.

Eleyne gasped and turned her head away.

Rolling over the dead man, Candra pulled his tangled net free. At that moment, a screaming, redheaded Teuton jumped into his path challenging him with a massive two-handed long sword. He lunged at Candra, who deftly stepped aside. The Indian threw his net but missed. The tall Scandian swung his blade, nicking Candra's shoulder. He reacted as if he had been stung by a bee—a nuisance.

My wife twisted her head about just as the hairy-faced barbarian circled around and raised his weapon about his head. Slashing downward, the sword blade caught the prongs of Candra's trident, bending the outer claw. Candra managed to veer it to the left, twisting his fanatical opponent to the side and knocking him off balance. He pulled the trident back, and with a lightning thrust drove it between his ribs. The barbarian crashed to the blood-smeared deck, on top of the slain Briton.

Eleyne's hand flew to her mouth, her body shaking. She pressed a fist into her stomach. Once again Aurelia reached over and rubbed a hand on my wife's shoulder. She faced Aurelia, her eyes closed and lowered her head. Despite the noise of the crowd, I heard her say, "I can't watch any longer—I won't!"

In spite of Aurelia's soothing words, Eleyne kept her eyes closed and slumped in her chair.

Sabinus seemed oblivious to the matter or refused to acknowledge Eleyne's plight.

The slaughter continued as Candra and his comrades slew one gladiator after another. Gradually the ships drifted away on the current from the Imperial section until I could no longer discern Greens and Blues.

As the afternoon waned, the battle took its toll. Three Green ships on our side of the basin sunk, many fighters drowned in their heavy armor. With the Blues in pursuit, the surviving Greens sailing from the opposite side of the stadium came to the aid of the remaining three ships. Outnumbered and surrounded, they totaled one-half their original strength.

One vessel closing upon another launched a catapult of fiery embers. The searing flames arced high, trailing wisps of smoke over the ship and towards the grandstands, provoking screams of terror from the lower spectator section. Instead, the enemy firebrand dropped and steamed into the water below them. Their horror turned to laughter and sighs of relief.

Once again, the crowd picked up the chant, "CAN-DRA! CAN-DRA!" His huge physique dominated all others. His ship rammed another Blue vessel marooned on a sandbar near one of the islands, and he and his comrades stormed aboard. Taking on all comers, every challenger met a sudden and vicious death by the two-handed sword he had taken earlier from the dead Scandian. It seemed impossible for an opponent to find his weak spot. In a matter of minutes, a pile of bodies surrounded Candra.

Being in the Magistrate's Box, close to the battle, I found myself caught up in the excitement. Although I tried to suppress the feeling, there surfaced from deep within a primitive corner of my soul the reality that I *enjoyed* the violence—the slaughter—as I yelled for Candra. I caught myself cheering over and over again for Candra and for the Greens to murder the Blues.

Eleyne straightened her slumping body. She must have heard me, because she turned, and although I couldn't hear her over the mob's roar, she mouthed the words, "How can you cheer for death?"

She was right. I kept reminding myself this was not a battle of armies, but of senseless slaughter for the sole purpose of pacifying the blood lust of the mob. Criminals, gladiators that they were, deserved a better fate than being needlessly killed for the amusement of the masses. Yet, I kept on shouting my encouragement.

Eleyne turned away, her lips puckered. She shut out the sight with the palms of her hands.

"Look," I said, pointing at a vessel listing to the port side, "Candra's ship is taking water."

"They better get out of there before it sinks," Crispus said.

My wife jumped to her feet and screamed. "Candra, get out!"

She turned to Aurelia. "Will this madness never end?" She slumped again in her seat.

Aurelia pulled her close. "Don't look, Eleyne, don't look."

Eleyne leaned her head on Aurelia's matronly shoulder.

The captain ordered the surviving gladiators to re-embark. The oarsmen backpaddled the mortally wounded galley, freeing themselves from the stranded sinking Blue vessel. A groan and squeal of sliding metal erupted from its wooden side. By his gestures I knew the ship's commander ordered the trireme to head for the island, in the center of the basin, and the galley limped away from near our box, struggling with one splintered bank of oars. The listing triremes managed to reach the big island and beach themselves. Only two other Green crafts managed to land.

"The Greens can't last much longer," I said to Crispus, concerned for Candra's survival. "They're fighting a delaying action. This could be their last chance to turn defeat into victory."

"Gods, it doesn't look good for Candra," Crispus grimly agreed.

The Blues pursued the Greens relentlessly ashore.

Skirting the waiting crocodiles and hippos, the remnants of the Greens slowly retreated up the island toward the bridge and the island fortifications, valiantly fighting every step of the way.

"The Greens still have a chance," I said, "if they destroy the bridge and block the Blues from crossing."

"Aye, but that'll take time," Crispus said. "Those wooden legs are pretty thick—they'll take a lot of hacking before they drop."

Up to now, quarter had not been given to any fighter. As the number of gladiators on both sides diminished, a murmur grew among the crowd to spare this or that gladiator. The emperor, who had the power to give or take life, ignored all appeals of clemency by the spectators.

The last to retreat, Candra covered the withdrawal of the few survivors to the smaller island. He fought like a madman as the remaining oarsmen chopped away at the bridge's foundation with axes and swords. When they had nearly hacked through the rope, the Greens reformed at the fort and urged the big Indian to cross. Quickly, he looked about and hurried to the other side.

Before the Greens could finish their work, Blues crossed the bridge, which stood precariously on its nearly severed wooden legs. Cornering most of the Greens by one of the small island's turrets, the Blues slew them one by one.

Trapped like a wild animal and surrounded on the barren island, Candra towered about his fallen comrades, blood streaked and alone.

"Gods, how much longer can Candra last?" I said, the muscles throughout my body tightened.

"Over there, Candra!" Crispus exclaimed, as if he could be heard.

Apparently, Eleyne did. She raised her head from Aurelia's shoulder, looked toward the battle, and gasped.

Crispus pointed to five or six gladiators, who managed to move close enough and inflict several small wounds, before being slain or disabled by Candra's huge sword.

Suddenly, the bridge collapsed with the weight of too many Blues. Groans of frustration rippled through the crowd downwind, as their view was fogged by heavy smoke from a nearby burning ship.

"Where is Candra?" Eleyne said. "I can't see him!"

Crowds emptied from the lower sections and charged through the aisle way towards a clear view, only to provoke the other sections, whose vantage points were blocked by their presence. The smoke shifted, and once again the spectators, including those in the Magistrate Box, could see the bloody battle.

"He can't go on forever," I said. "He must be exhausted."

"Aye, but he's not through, yet," Crispus said. "Look there!"

The spark of battle still lived within, prompting him to greater efforts. He turned from side to side, holding the weapon in front of him. But Candra's movements grew stiff and defensive against the sea of Blue armbands. Most of his opponents stayed just out of reach, taunting him with thrusts of iron. They seemed undecided as to who would next attempt to slay him. They kept probing for a weakness with feints to his right and left, but Candra, always there, blocked the fatal blows. He seemed oblivious to the perspiration mixed with blood pouring from his face.

I admired this valiant warrior, who had devotedly guarded my wife, and his incredible will to live.

"To your right, Candra! The Frisian!" I shouted, although he was too far away to hear me.

"Watch out, Candra!" Eleyne yelled.

The broken-nosed German edged around the towering Indian's right side. Covering his torso with a dark shield, the barbarian lunged at Candra thrusting his sword up towards the throat.

Eleyne screamed.

Before his blade touched, Candra swung around, and the edge of his sword caught the Frisian's. Forcing it to the left, Candra's sword sliced through the Frisian's neck, decapitating him. Spinning like a rolling ball onto the pavement, the head came to a halt at the turret's base. The rest of the body crumpled into a bloody, convulsing heap.

Then from behind, a British dagger slammed into Candra's side, deep between the ribs.

"No!" I yelled, in unison with two hundred thousand voices.

Eleyne screamed again.

"Oh no!" Aurelia shouted.

Candra dropped to his knees and writhed as he tried to extract the weapon from his body. Struggling, he managed to pull it out and drop it. He tossed back his head and glared at his assassin. The Briton hesitated, as if Candra challenged the barbarian to finish him off. The black-haired fighter kicked away Candra's sword. He pointed his own long sword towards the emperor.

Again, the crowd sprang to their feet, screamed for mercy, and stomped in unison. Everybody, including those who had wagered on the Blues, raised their thumbs and handkerchiefs. A sea of white cloth fluttered about the entire stadium. In unison the pulsating tidal wave of humanity stomped and demanded, "MER-CY! MER-CY!"

121

Eleyne and Aurelia shouted the same.

The demands, absolute in their pleas, surely would draw the greatest pleasure of the crowds if the emperor granted mercy.

"The mob will go mad if the emperor doesn't spare Candra's life," I barked to Crispus. "Be ready to return to the cohort at once if it happens!"

Claudius turned to Gallus, who must have been delighted in seeing Candra dying. He shouted something into the emperor's ear. Growing impatient, the crowd screamed for a decision. No doubt Gallus reminded Claudius how the giant had the audacity to shove him during Vespasian's victory feast and should have rightfully been crucified. The emperor hesitated, and Gallus leaned again, whispering in his ear. The aging monarch seemed to make up his mind. He stared at the Briton and turned— thumbs up. Then after a split-second pause—thumbs down.

Eleyne crumpled, head against her lap.

With a swift slice, the Briton beheaded Candra. Blood gushed from the stump of this twitching body. The bearded fighter let out a guttural cry. He grabbed the bloody head by its long, black hair and raised it for all to see. A sudden shocked silence, and then a loud groan and screams of rage erupted from the spectators. The Celt hurled Candra's head into the channel where an open-jawed crocodile lunged and snatched it in its jaws.

Eleyne continued screaming. "No! No!"

I wanted to weep but dared not.

Eleyne leapt from her seat. She fled from the Magistrate's Box followed by Aurelia and a number of servants through the emperor's private tunnel exit used by him and his guests. I wanted to follow and console her, but duty prohibited that luxury. Now, I had to brace myself for what I knew was about to follow.

I looked back at the carnage, not seeing it. Gods, how long could a nation tolerate this kind of barbarism? How could Rome consider itself a civilization and condone genocide in the name of justice and entertainment? An empire like that could not survive. How could I remain loyal to Rome? I couldn't answer. So ingrained in my soul, I was torn between my sense of justice and loyalty.

And disgust, because I, too, had cheered the butchery.

Gallus had his vengeance on Candra, but at what cost? I hated him all the more.

My attention snapped back to the present. Crispus and the other tribunes looked at me strangely. I nodded to them and they back to me.

The slaughter on the island continued between the Blues and the skirmishers from the small boats, even as the mood of the crowd turned ugly. Clinched fists shook at the emperor. Candra's bravery had been adored by them, and they would not forget his wasteful death. Nearby, the mob rained trash and cushions into the aisles and the basin and pulled down posters and decorations. Praetorians stationed about the arena were pelted. Pocked with filth, the nobles in the Imperial Box became alarmed by the screamed obscenities and curses at Claudius.

"All right, Crispus, let's get out of here. Time to test the mettle of the Seventh!"

As we headed for the secret tunnel, a squad of Praetorians charged into the lower rows of nearby hecklers and indiscriminately bashed their skulls with thick, wooden truncheons.

Instead of silencing the crowds, they incited them to bolder acts. Like drifting embers of fire, fights erupted throughout the stadium, no longer a mere isolated riot. Praetorians rushed to the main trouble spots, but the mob overwhelmed them.

The crowds headed for the exits and poured their rage into the streets. Crispus and I returned to the Seventh Cohort as rioting quickly spread.

Where was Eleyne? Had she stayed with Aurelia and the emperor's entourage, protected by the Praetorians? I prayed she had the sense to stay with them and not endanger herself by fleeing home through a rioting mob bent on revenging Candra's death.

Could we protect the emperor from this? The Praetorians would hold their ground, but would the Seventh Cohort?

CHAPTER 14

The surging mob tore up the park surrounding the stadium and smashed the hastily shuttered little businesses. Betting booths were ransacked and plundered, while shady Chaldean fortune tellers were reduced to poverty. Looters carried away armloads of sweet melons, fresh bread, and steaming sausages from cook shop stalls. Others hauled long-stemmed wine amphorae, thumping away on the rut-worn, stone streets. Dragged from their tiny cubicles beneath the stadium tiers, prostitutes were viciously raped and beaten on the street amidst the oblivious mob. Young toughs tore bricks and paving stones from adjacent buildings and streets, and then hurled the heavy objects at anything that moved.

I saw neither Eleyne nor Aurelia and their retinue. I had to give my full attention to the unfolding anarchy.

Although held in reserve, the chaos unfolding outside the arena required immediate action by the Seventh Cohort. I gave orders to disperse and scatter the rioters down side streets as quickly as possible, to summarily execute anyone caught looting.

Word arrived that the First and Fourth Cohorts waited in prearranged locations nearby, along with three more from the City Guard, ready to reinforce us upon our signal. By means of strategically placed flagmen, including one on top of the fish market building, we kept in touch with the other units. However, this was the jurisdiction of the Seventh. We were expected to handle the situation, requesting reinforcements only as a last resort. By rights, one well-trained and armed cohort should prove sufficient to deal with an unruly, undisciplined mob.

In less than two hours, Apollo's blazing chariot would sink behind the hills beyond the Tiber's west bank, and we would have more trouble after dark. At the far end of the plaza, opposite the stadium, the Seventh grimly waited. In the hazy late-afternoon sun, the cohort appeared as one dark-armed monster. Long shadows from the ranks crept across the dusty, gray tenement walls bordering the square.

The throng fanned out into the plaza. To the shouts of Bucketmen, they spotted the Seventh. I passed orders to the centurions to alert the men. Casperius Niger waved the flagman to signal the other cohorts the Seventh was preparing to engage the mob. Grouped one behind the other, tightly formed skirmish lines, one hundred men each, faced the oncoming rioters.

Earlier, I had placed Casperius Niger, my best centurion, in charge of the advance units. In the rear, Crispus commanded two centuries kept in reserve. To better direct the troops, I managed to commandeer horses for Niger, Crispus, and myself.

The screaming throng edged its way towards our chain-mailed troops. Mounting my gray dapple, I rode to the second rank from the front line. I took my place to the rear of its center for the best vantage point and gave the signal to advance. Circular cornus sounded a sharp note from the rear, and the cohort standard raised smartly. In one resounding thud, the Watchmen snapped their truncheons and protective oval shields to the front. On command, long-stemmed *tubicen* trumpets sounded the advance. A blast of three short notes followed. Long, wooden truncheons went parallel to the ground, thrusting from between painted scarlet shields crisscrossed with gold lightning bolts. Twenty drums boomed a slow death cadence.

For an instant, the mob halted, dead silent. A handful dropped their stones and knives and vanished back into the crowd. The centuries deliberately marched forward, across the plaza at a pulsating half step. The echo of clanking chain-mail armor and hobnailed sandals added to the ominous sound of the drums. The angry horde pressed forward again, to the cries of, *kill the Bucketmen*, disregarding the threat of bristling clubs and swords carried on each watchman's baldric.

The gap between mob and troops closed. A crash exploded as the masses slammed into the Seventh's shields. The line held while troopers clubbed and shoved back the swarm of people with truncheons. Crushed underfoot by the retreating mob, bloodied victims screamed as they tried to escape the head-bashing troops.

As the multitudes retreated, a watchman motioned to a group of ragged, young brawlers. "Over there—it's them!" he shouted. "They killed Tribune Drusus! Get them!"

"Shut your fucking mouth, Rufus Furius!" Casperius Niger ordered. "Hold your places men—tighten your ranks!"

For a moment, Furius hesitated, looking in Casperius's direction.

"You heard Centurion Niger," I barked. "Stand fast!"

Furius glared at me and glanced to the rioters. "Mars be damned!" he barked. He drew his short sword and slashed his way into the desperate mob.

"Return to the ranks!" Casperius commanded. But it was too late. One by one, men along the same skirmish line heeded his cry, drew weapons, and joined the attack. Soon, entire centuries charged the crowd in a hacking frenzy. Blood spurted everywhere as the fighters ignored all orders given by the commanding centurions and myself to cease and desist.

With the exception of the reserve centuries, led by Crispus, discipline collapsed. Individual actions resulted in troopers being cut off from help. I watched helplessly as a woman leapt upon an isolated soldier's back, but when he desperately whirled to dislodge her, she slit his throat.

The rest of the Seventh plunged into the frantic crowds, slashing and chopping at will. Casperius bolted his mount into the midst of his men, slaying one in an attempt to restore discipline. Too late. Caught up in the carnage and slaughter, countless innocents sprawled, blood spattered, headless, limbs missing on the plaza's worn stones.

I shouted above the noise to restore order to the ranks. But my offers of rewards and threats of certain punishment were ignored as the lines continued to disintegrate. When the formations crumbled, the mob encircled pockets of

Watchmen. Although surrounded by a group of thugs, my horse's sharp hooves kept them from yanking me off. After cutting down a couple who had slipped around Casperius's blind side, I spurred my mount in the direction of the reserves, praying Crispus's troops would hold.

I motioned for Crispus and his men to join me, then called the flagman to signal the other Watch cohorts and the City Guard for reinforcements. Bruised and cut, I led Crispus and his troops forward. The outnumbered reserves valiantly held together, but eventually were overwhelmed, engulfed by civilians rushing between their ranks.

In the space of a heartbeat, I saw Crispus, attempting to rescue a young woman and her baby. He reached down to his right side, grabbed the child from its mother, and placed it in front of him. He then reached down for the mother and pulled her up behind him. Suddenly, the surging mob broadsided his horse. Crispus lost control of his chestnut mare. Like an overturned wagon, the horse lost its balance and fell on its side, throwing Crispus, the woman, and child to the pavement. The mindless mob trampled their bodies like pieces of rags. I hurried to Crispus's rescue, followed by a squad of slashing Watchmen. As I approached Crispus, the troops cleared the area of stragglers and ringed us. Dismounting, I kneeled over his crumpled body.

His bloodied face quivered, and his breathing grew shallower. He choked on the blood pouring from his mouth and nose, and his eyelids rapidly swelled. I held him in my blood-stained arms. Somehow, his body didn't seem as heavy as I expected. He groaned in an attempt to speak.

"Don't say anything, we'll get a *medicus* here. You'll be all right." We both knew it was a lie. In the distance an overpowering drum beat signaled the arrival of the First and Fourth Cohorts and the City Guard in force. Their disciplined ranks wheeled into action.

"The woman and boy . . . ?" Crispus struggled to ask in a choking voice.

I quickly scanned the area. Two limp, blood-stained bodies swirling with flies lay behind him. The horse, recovering from its fall, stood nearby munching on a discarded loaf of bread. "They're safe," I lied.

"L . . . looks like the . . . joke's on me," he rasped, coughing blood.

"Don't say any more—you'll be all right."

"Horseshit . . . to the end . . . I have to . . . keep you honest."

"That's enough, friend." My eyes clouded with tears, and I turned away.

"B . . . best friend . . . you've got."

"The very best," I said.

"W . . . what are you . . . going to do . . . without me?" Crispus tried to grin, his voice fading rapidly.

"I'll manage. You're going to survive," I insisted, refusing to believe he was dying.

"You'll be alone . . . Marcellus. One . . . grave robber to . . . another, p . . . promise me . . . something."

"Anything," I answered, puzzled by his request.

"T . . . trust no one—including . . . Sabinus—he's still a Roman."

I looked about before answering. The troops had pushed the crowd far back, allowing them to escape down several side streets. "I promise, I won't." Crispus was wiser than I in many ways. Until now, I still retained too much of my idealism about the goodness of people and the world.

"O . . . otherwise," he gasped, "Rome will destroy you. Don't let it . . ." He coughed more blood. A sickening gurgle echoed in his throat. His eyes stared vacantly at me, the spark of life fading into dullness. He went limp. Gone.

I would have wept if I hadn't been approached by about ten Watchmen.

"Sir, we need your help," one of them said.

I glared up at their haggard faces and recognized Rufus Furius, the first to break ranks. A sense of rage and revulsion shot through every pore in my body. I peered deep into his pathetic eyes—right to his miserable soul and reviled by what I saw.

"Not now!" I barked. "I will deal with *you* later, Furius!" I waved the group away. I wanted to scream: *He died*

because you refused to hold ranks! Your heads will roll!
Instead, I turned my back to them.

No longer could I control my emotions. In a burst of tears, I broke down and wept, not caring who watched. Pure, unadulterated rage for the world swelled my insides. I wanted to destroy Rome with my bare hands. Soldier or not, I had lost my dearest and closest friend. I had persuaded Crispus to transfer to Rome, and now pangs of regret wreaked havoc with my conscience. Had he stayed in Britannia, he would still be alive. Never would I have another friend like Crispus. May the gods watch over him wherever he might be.

I recovered my wits a moment later, once again the soldier within took command and carried me to the troops. The First and Fourth Cohorts and the City Guard restored order, but too late to save the countless innocent lives lost and the enormous property damage.

* * *

By early evening, a detail of state slaves had been dispatched to the riot area to remove unclaimed bodies and wash away blood from the streets. Carted to the river's edge outside the city gates, corpses were cremated on mass funeral pyres. Cautiously, shopkeepers surfaced to clean and salvage what remained of their destroyed businesses.

During this time, my duties had kept me so busy, I had little time to think about Eleyne's safety. I prayed she was with the emperor's party and that she had stayed with them until the worst of the rioting had passed before returning home. I was certain Aurelia would make her see the wisdom in such a decision.

Exhausted, and still reeling from Crispus's death, I rounded up the remnants of the Seventh Cohort. After receiving the centurions' casualty reports at my office, I ordered the cohort confined to barracks pending full investigation of their conduct. About the same time, I received a message from Sabinus to report to him at once.

Ignoring the wreckage scattered about the streets, I trudged to the Office of the Watch Prefect on the *Via Lata*

Road. As Commander of the Seventh, I was accountable
for the actions of the men, and no excuse would suffice.
Despite my weariness and the searing pain of headache,
which I felt not only inside my skull but in my eyes,
ears, and teeth, I attempted in vain to contain my anger.
I failed. Heat rushed to my face, and my lips curled
into a murderous frown as I glared at the approaching
Watchmen. The ten men took one glance and shunned me.
Never had I made a lonelier trek in my life.

Claudius cared little for the rabble as he called them,
but I knew the afternoon slaughter railed his sense of
justice. His demand for what the Jews called a scapegoat
was inevitable. Political reality dictated that Sabinus give
him one. The emperor could not afford rebellion. Sabinus
had to take steps to stabilize his own position, placed in
jeopardy by the riot. I knew his decision the moment we
came face to face.

Except for the flickering glow of a single oil lamp, his
office remained dark. For some reason I thought of Eleyne
and the nights we spent together by candlelight. Young
love was as fragile and fleeting as the ebb and flow of the
candle flame before me.

"You won't find an answer in the flame," Sabinus said,
bringing me back to reality. "At least, I didn't."

I jolted. *Did he read my mind?*

Sitting at his hardwood desk, Sabinus momentarily
studied the scowling, black marble bust of Cicero, nearly
invisible in the room's obscured light. I stood before the
prefect, examining his haggard face. The night had taken
its toll, his shadowed eyes full of anger and sorrow, and his
hair grayer and thinner than I remembered.

A sense of shame enveloped me. I had failed when
he had depended on me the most. A sickening sensation
settled in my stomach as I waited for Sabinus to speak.

"What happened?" he inquired simply.

"They broke," I offered in a woodened voice. "I failed
to maintain discipline, and they got out of control." I
explained the circumstances leading to the carnage.

Sabinus clasped his hands together on the desk and leaned forward. "I'm not an unreasonable man, and I know the problems you've encountered with the Seventh. If any man could have restored their discipline, it was you."

"Had I the time," I said, knowing my answer was a poor excuse.

"Unfortunately, no explanation is acceptable to the emperor."

I nodded. "I accept full responsibility for their actions."

"Do you have the names of the men who instigated this disaster?" Sabinus asked.

"Yes, sir."

"They will be severely punished, but . . ." He took a deep breath. "You know in the end you'll be held responsible for their conduct."

"I know. I've given orders for their court martials. Executions are a foregone conclusion, and only await the signatures of you and the emperor."

"And so it must be done," he said. "I have received reports that an estimated five hundred or more were needlessly killed—Watchmen and civilians alike."

My eyes drifted back to the candle's flame. "Roman . . ."

Sabinus seemed puzzled by my look. "Go on—no one can hear but me."

"Roman justice," I said as our eyes locked, "Roman sense of right and wrong. How can we agree on the disaster of five hundred innocent lives outside the Naval Arena, and not care a god's curse for the thousands of bodies still stinking less than a half mile from here?"

Sabinus stood quietly, stepped to the window, and looked out beyond *Campus Martius*, the great parade Field of Mars, and across the river. "Why must so many die every time?" he whispered as if thinking aloud. "True, there *must* be a better way. Even as I speak, hundreds of funeral pyres line the banks of the Tiber."

I sensed his resolve to support Rome, and yet the language of his eyes and hands supported my observation of true Roman justice.

For the first time, I became aware of the odor of pine-scented wood and burning flesh. The acrid stink of burnt hair drifted on the night air—a unique stench I will remember for a lifetime.

"It'll go on the rest of the night," he said. "A cryptic reminder." He returned and slumped at the desk and stared into space.

"Aye, the Watch will never live it down," I added bitterly.

"The people fear us, and well they should," Sabinus said. He glanced up to me. "We shall be known as butchers—no better than the Praetorians," he whispered. "You know well their record. It's possible the emperor will disband the Seventh and discharge the lot, although I think not."

A moment of silence passed between us. My eyes fell to the dark blood upon my uniform. "Crispus is dead."

Sabinus closed his eyes and lowered his head.

"You have been my retainer for many years, Marcellus. And what I do now saddens me. But if I'm to discipline the Watch, then I must start at the top." His eyes opened and twisting in my direction, locked with mine. "You know what that means?"

"Yes, sir," I answered as the taste of bile rose in my throat.

"An example must be made," he added, "much to my regret. If I am to maintain credibility with the Senate and the emperor."

My face grew hot and knuckles turned white when I clenched the hilt of my sword. Although I had expected it, I did not deserve this fate. Would I be executed? Crispus was right, Sabinus was still a Roman. I wanted to lash out at anybody and anything—including him.

Why was I being punished? It *was* the logical—political—thing to do, and were I in his place, I would have ordered the same. But it was no consolation.

At that moment, I hated Sabinus with my entire being. Fortunately, I managed to suppress my heated passions, and eventually steadied myself. To lose self-control again, so soon after grieving for Crispus, was stupid and, perhaps, fatal.

"However," Sabinus said, drawing me out of my thoughts, "I shall see that you are not executed."

I exhaled a breath I didn't know I was holding. At least Eleyne would not be left a widow in a hostile city. "I'm grateful for your sense of justice, sir."

"Unfortunately, you have one remaining choice—exile."

"Lord," I said slowly, "unlike others, who would consider the penalty a disgrace worse than death, I accept the punishment as honey from the gods."

At long last, I could return to Hispania—home. After witnessing Candra's death, Eleyne would have no qualms on fleeing the city's cruel boundaries.

"Before I leave your office, may I ask if you had any word from Lady Aurelia as to her and Eleyne's safety?"

Sabinus said he had dispatched a messenger to the emperor's palace home. The courier returned and informed him that his wife and Eleyne stayed with the Imperial entourage until the worst of the rioting was over before returning to Sabinus's home, under Praetorian escort.

I was relieved to hear that and prayed that Eleyne, who was probably still grief stricken over Candra's death, would have sense enough to stay with Aurelia. She needed someone who she could trust and who would console her.

"Thank you for the information, Lord, it places my mind at ease."

"Then perhaps your leaving Rome is for the best, my friend." Sabinus shook his head and exhaled. "I'm sorry. There is no other way."

"Aye," I answered, biting my lower lip.

"Will you be returning to Hispania?"

"Yes, and it's just as well. My mother's health is failing—she needs me," I said. "The latifundia is an excellent place for Eleyne and me to raise our sons." No truer words were spoken.

"Indeed, I envy you. No longer must you concern yourself with the city's turmoil." Sabinus gestured to the office window. "Forget Rome. There is nothing more soothing to one's soul than the peaceful countryside."

Placing a parchment roll upon his desk, I offered a list of those men in the Seventh whose bravery during the riot merited they be spared.

He nodded. A long pause followed, and I sensed, too, he was uneasy with a task that had drawn out too long.

I had lost everything my father struggled for. I had failed Rome and my family.

Sabinus extended his hand and forearm. "Will you not clasp my hand and arm?"

A silence passed between us.

"Are you, Sabinus, the man, my friend?" I asked. "Or are you, Sabinus, the emperor's man?"

His hand wavered slightly. "There is but one Sabinus—the Roman—there shall never be another."

I did not reach out to him, although my heart cried out to do so. I watched as he lowered his hand to his side.

"It is finished between us," I heard a distant voice say; the words were mine.

I turned to leave and paused as the senator called, "Farewell, my friend."

I stepped into the night.

CHAPTER 15

After leaving Sabinus's quarters, I returned to the
Augustan Naumachia. Painful though it was, before I
could pick up Eleyne and take her home, I needed to
sort out the day's events and better understand why
the calamity occurred. I trudged past damaged booths
and shops littering the adjacent park and climbed to the
empty stadium's top row of cement benches. A bright, full
moon in a cloudless sky filled with a barrage of winking
stars lighted the city in a false dawn. A soft breeze teased
the limp-wavering purple streamers above the emperor's
podium. In one grand view, I surveyed the surrounding
silver hills of the city, and the murky waters of the basin
below. Carefully, slaves stepped between the aisles,
cleaning up the rubbish left by the spectators. More
glided in canoes on the glassy water, fishing out debris.
Crocodiles lined the two islands' artificial beaches in
peaceful repose. Nocturnal hippos fed upon the vegetation
lining the shore.

Standing in quiet solitude, I tightly wrapped the sagum
about my shoulders, bracing against the night chill. I
leaned over the top guard rail and studied the devastated
shops, overturned statues, and shattered monuments
in the plaza beyond. In the distance, columns of smoke
drifted above the funeral pyres along the Tiber, blotting
out the lustrous moonlight. Sounds of wailing mourners
floated on a mild breeze. A child's cry stabbed my being
as sharply as if a Cretan arrow had pierced my heart. I,
too, experienced the pain of losing someone close to me.
Fearing he would think me strange, I'd never told Crispus I
had loved him like a brother.

In less than twelve hours my world had fallen apart.
Until the first light of day I stood motionless, deep in
thought. The sun glared over the red horizon, and then

slipped behind the lid of smoke hanging above Rome. The old days and life had vanished forever. Would the new day bring a new beginning?

As I was about to leave for Sabinus's house to see Eleyne, a runner dispatched by Sabinus found me and said that my wife had returned home, despite Aurelia's protests to stay. Even though the worst of the uprising had passed and she had Chulainn to protect her, the streets of Rome were still dangerous. I prayed they arrived safely at our residence.

* * *

Tired and full of despair, I went home. However, any further personal agony and bitterness had to wait. Certain that Candra's death had devastated Eleyne, I had to put on a strong front to console her.

A worried Porus greeted me at the door. "Master! I'm so pleased you're not injured. After last night, I—"

"Never mind me, where is the mistress?" I stepped into the small vestibule.

"Lady Eleyne is gone."

"*Gone?* Where?" Gods, I needed a bath. Porus's words about Eleyne and the accompanying dangers had not registered in my mind. I removed my helmet from sticky hair, caked with dust and perspiration.

"The cemetery of the aliens, the catacombs, to be with her Christian friends." He took my cloak.

My head snapped in Porus's direction as I awoke from my daze. I fully comprehended the ramifications of Eleyne's acts. "But why? That's nearly five miles from here. Didn't she realize the streets are still dangerous?"

"I don't know, sir," Porus answered, shaking his head. "She was very upset after returning from the games. The Lady Aurelia pleaded for the mistress to stay with her, but she refused. Is it true Candra was killed?"

"Yes," I answered controlling my emotions. "How long has she been gone?"

"She left early this morning when you did not return."

"Gods, what is wrong with her—the streets are still full of looters and bandits." Why would Eleyne leave the safety of our home to be with a religious cult of questionable and suspicious origins? Something was painfully awry.

"Chulainn is with her," Porus said. "I'm certain she's safe."

"Where are my sons?" I glanced to the atrium where they usually played. "Don't tell me they're with her, too?"

Porus motioned over his shoulder. "They're in the nursery, sir. Imogen is taking good care of them."

Relieved, I pulled off my cuirass and sent it crashing to the tiled floor, no longer caring if the breast plate was damaged. There were no inspections in exile.

"Porus, I'm going to Eleyne." I glared at him menacingly, suspecting his sympathies were with those people. "You will take me to their meeting place."

He grimaced and looked away. "Yes, sir, of course."

"Good. Bring me a shrouded cloak. I won't waste any more time changing clothes."

"At least it will hide your uniform," Porus said. "Soldiers terrify Christians, especially after last night."

"They have nothing to fear from me—I've been relieved of my command."

"Thundering, Zeus, no!" He paused for a moment. "I'm sorry, sir."

I'm not.

* * *

Outside the city wall, near the Appian Way, we entered the subterranean burial chambers. Guided only by our small lanterns, Porus and I passed entombed bodies marked by simple slab wall markers and through the shadowy maze of cold and dank narrow passageways. A large vault loomed ahead, lighted by a dozen acrid pitch torches. A cloud of wispy smoke drifted up to the smudge-covered ceiling. Two hooded sentries dressed in simple robes blocked our entry. Challenging us, they asked for a *sign.* I glanced to Porus, not understanding their request.

He hesitated as the suspicious guards visually inspected me. Their eyes settled on my soldier's boots.

"He is one of us," Porus said.

With the edge of his leather sandal, Porus made the simple outline of the top part of a fish in the dirt.

The bottom was completed by one of the guards. "Pass in peace, my brothers," he said solemnly.

Several primitive drawings decorated the walls of the stifling, smoke-blackened chamber. A silent crowd congregated in the center stood listening to a man speaking about their God.

"It's Marcus from Judea, the one they call John-Mark," Porus whispered. "He's writing about the life of our Lord Christus."

John-Mark was dressed in a simple, homespun, woolen robe. His brown beard speckled with gray concealed a youthful face, but not the gleam in his copper eyes.

As he spoke, I searched the room for Eleyne. Adorned in a dark-blue stola, and shrouded in a lighter-blue, woolen mantle, she stood a few feet from John-Mark. Next to her hovered Chulainn, strong and wiry, wearing a cloak with a cowl. Her eyes, full of hatred, fixed on mine. It was if they warned: *Stay away from me, Roman! You are one of them.* The crowd appeared to be protecting Eleyne, drawing closer to her and John-Mark.

I gazed about, studying the worshipers. Only two or three couples wore rich clothing. The majority were slaves, ex-slaves, and poor plebeians dressed in simple garb. Despite leading miserable lives and experiencing the horrors of the riots, their faces radiated with hope. Did their religion promise something better in the future? Perhaps in another life? Certainly not in this one.

Etched in charcoal, crude pictures depicting stories of Christus and other prophets, which Eleyne had told me about, peered down upon the group from the domed ceiling and high masonry walls. Two images stood out in my mind. One portrayed a naked, young man, Christus, wearing a long, soft beard, hanging from a tree on top of a mound. Below him, a gathering of people knelt in prayer, and a short distance away a detail of Roman auxiliaries kept guard. Christus's pain-ridden face searched the dark heavens for something or someone. Crucified, he hung alone on the hill—a feeling I knew all too well.

In another picture, draped in white robes, he appeared ghost-like, hovering above an empty tomb or cave in a grotto. This was the resurrection scene described to me by Eleyne. A raising from the dead—unbelievable. How can people believe such drivel? Yet, the gullible do. Beneath the pictures, inscribed in Greek and Latin were the words, "This is life!" Whose? The smoky pulsating torchlight gave the simple etchings a warm supernatural countenance, which perhaps inspired these plain people.

John-Mark's strong voice echoed throughout the maze, and my mind turned to his words.

"I have come out of Ephesus to Rome," he preached, "so that you might know what our Lord has done. He is risen these many years past, of that I am certain." He turned in my direction as if reading my thoughts. "For I have seen the empty tomb and heard His words. The Anointed One was not in the tomb. His linen clothes, before you now, laid draped within the sepulcher. The napkin shaped upon His face laid folded neatly nearby—and he was gone. He *is* risen." John-Mark nodded to me. For a moment the hair on the back of my shoulders and arms stood on end, and a chill flashed through my body.

"Come this morning," he resumed, "and see the blood-stained cloth, and know the truth, so that you might bear witness for those who will not see it. Then return to your homes, your families, and tell them—He lives."

The group stepped closer, whispering excitedly as they viewed and touched reverently the simple piece of white, homespun cloth. I jostled my way through to Eleyne as John-Mark continued to speak.

Hostility flamed in her sea-blue eyes. She raised a hand and jabbed a finger towards me. "Why did you come here? Go away!"

"Eleyne, I'm sorry about Candra," I blurted, "but your place is with me—I need you." I reached for her hand, but she shoved mine away. A few worshipers cast side glances at us.

"No!" She glared defiantly, narrowed her eyes, and pinched her black tapered brows together. "These are my people. Here, I'm safe from Roman butchers."

Stunned, for a moment I said nothing, attempting to understand why she had turned her anger against me. I, too, was an alien to Rome. "Do you know what you are saying? Would you leave our sons?"

"Why shouldn't I?" she answered in a calmer voice. "You would be free to raise them as little Romans to grow up and slaughter innocent people." She gestured toward the entryway.

"That's not true—where did you get such a mad idea?" Our voices were easily overheard by all. Many exchanged whispered comments or admonished us with their glares.

"From the horrible games—isn't that proof enough?" She turned to John-Mark and then the worshipers gathered around the shroud. "Why don't you leave now, without me! I'm sure you'll find a Roman woman who'll be delighted to become their mother."

My breath caught in my throat. The muscles tightened in my shoulders and arms. "I don't want any woman except you—my wife! You're the only mother I want for our sons. Don't you understand?"

Eleyne violently shook her head. "No, I don't!"

By now, the gathering openly stared at us. John-Mark seemed to falter, no doubt puzzled by our harsh whispers. Then he, too, fell silent as all present turned towards the family drama before them.

"Eleyne," I said in a softer tone, "I love you very much. You're the only woman I want at my side."

John-Mark approached and touched Eleyne's arm and looked into her eyes. "Your husband is right, Eleyne. You cannot stay here and hide from life. Our Master did not mean for us to bury ourselves within His teachings to escape from the world or our responsibilities to our families."

"But the Romans are so cruel," she rasped. "Look what they did to our Lord, and to Candra!"

John-Mark nodded and sighed. "The Lord knew He would die."

He turned to the people who were watching us intently. "It's to His death we owe our salvation. He allowed it to save humanity, and in so doing brought light into a world of darkness."

The Christian leader turned back to my wife and touched her arm again. "No, Eleyne, the Lord does not want His people to run away from life."

He pulled his hand from Eleyne's arm and gestured to the worshipers. "On the contrary, He wants His people to go forth and spread His word—to spread the Good News, each in his own way."

He motioned to Eleyne. "You are to convey it to your husband, your children, your household. You cannot teach them his peaceful ways if you hide." He made a wide gesture with his hand toward the gathering. "For all those here know and believe, they need no one to tell them the Word."

John-Mark paused. "No, Eleyne, you must return to the outside world."

Eleyne shook her head and gesticulated with her hands. "But I hate Rome! Dear God, I know it's wrong to hate, but I do."

"Come now, did not our Lord say that we must forgive and love our enemies?"

"I know, but how can I? After what they did to Candra . . . and . . . what they did to my people in Britannia." She began to weep and slumped in my arms.

"Marcellus, please for the love of God, take me out of Rome," she sobbed. "I can't stand this horrid place any longer."

"That's what I plan to do, beloved," I answered in a soothing voice. "We are leaving. Sabinus has relieved me of my command."

"Oh, Marcellus," she said as if the words snapped her out of self-pity. She straightened and pushed my hands from her shoulders. She arched back her head until her tear-streaked eyes met mine. "How could he?"

"It's a long story, which I'll explain later. I promise we'll leave Rome within the week."

"Where will we go?"

"Hispania—home. You'll find happiness there."

"Hispania?" muttered someone in the gathering. A low murmur arose from the congregation.

"Yes," Eleyne said. "Anyplace, so long as we're out of Rome!"

"I am sorry you lost your command," John-Mark said as he stepped closer. He paused as his bronze-like eyes pierced mine as if seeing straight into my soul. "I have heard many good things about you from Eleyne and others." He looked toward Chulainn and Porus.

I snorted. For the span of a heartbeat, I clinched my hand into a balled fist. "I doubt if you'll retain the same opinion when you hear the details of the slaughter."

Eleyne frowned and nodded.

"We have received tragic news, and the perpetrators will answer before God."

"Yes, they will," Eleyne said, her voice crisp with anger.

"They already have," I said. "I doubt if anyone else will be as forgiving as you—especially, the people."

John-Mark looked about and pursed his lips together before he answered. "Whether they do or not, there is One who will know and forgive you."

I slapped a hand against my thigh, loud enough to startle the people around us. "*Your* God—you mean? Your promises are as hollow as the echo of your voice."

Eleyne gasped. "Marcellus, how can you say that?"

"He is the God of us all," John-Mark said in a calm manner.

"If he has the power, why didn't he stop the massacre?" I asked. It was all I could do to keep my voice under control. "I can't believe in a God who willingly allows so many deaths."

A murmur rippled through the gathering as if in disbelief of my accusations.

"I do not pretend to have all the answers," John-Mark said patiently, "but we know from His teachings there is a definite reason for everything He allows, and no doubt it is the same in your situation. In time you will see."

People nodded in agreement.

"I regret I'm not so optimistic," I said, the muscles growing tighter throughout my body.

"Marcellus, please try to understand John-Mark," Eleyne pleaded.

"How can I?" I replied.

"You must have faith in yourself, and place your trust in the Lord," John said. "You will see."

"But I don't believe in your God—any god."

John-Mark smiled. "Yes, I hear, but do not believe you. If not, you would not be so adamant in your denial, with bitterness in your voice. Just as Peter denied knowing our Master on the night He was betrayed. You believe, Tribune, but are afraid to bare your soul before the world. That is understandable, especially for a soldier. You are a good man, and one day you will be welcomed into His kingdom. For the Lord has a place in Heaven for all soldiers who repent."

He turned to Eleyne, gently took her hands, and locked her fingers into mine. "Go now—your place is with your husband. Go in peace and love."

John-Mark gave us a blessing—a fish-like sign with his outstretched hand, and we departed.

* * *

Within a week, Eleyne, the children, and I, along with the household slaves, boarded a ship in Ostia for Hispania. The crew had cast off the last lines when Gallus arrived with his entourage on the dock. Gloating in the early morning sunlight, he approached the quay's edge as the ship eased away from its mooring. He had escaped all blame for the game's failure. Motioning to one of his freedmen to come forward, the servant handed Gallus a small, leather pouch. Removing a handful of sesterces, a smirk came to Gallus's powdered face. Suddenly, he hurled the coins onto the ship's deck, scattering them at our feet. He glared at Eleyne, who stood a few steps away from the wooden railing. "Enjoy your new reign on the farm, Princess!"

PART II

58-69 AD

CHAPTER 16

JUNE, 58 AD

After leaving the Imperial Capitol in disgrace, my first impression upon returning to Hispania was how much our family's great estate had changed since my boyhood. Soon, I understood it was I who was different. We can never return to the memories of youth. By custom and law I was head of the household, and responsible for running the latifundia. But I had not been home since joining the army. I admired Mother for the efficient way she had managed the lands since father's death many years before.

While posted on the frontier and later, in Rome, I had neither the time for nor interest in the burdens of managing a big cattle farm. I lived on a tribune's substantial salary and money sent by mother from the ranch earnings. Thank the gods for her business sense—she had amassed a fortune. She became my tutor and was thorough. The latifundia prospers to this day because of what I learned.

Mother died about a year after Eleyne, my sons, and my abrupt homecoming. She had lived far longer than I had expected. Her appearance alarmed me when I introduced her to Eleyne before our wedding. I was certain she was wasting away and would be dead within the year. Obviously, the gods thought otherwise.

Despite her lingering illness, Mother continued supervision of our properties until about a week before her death. I wore the black band of mourning on my arm for one year.

Over the next six years I watched my sons grow, and the cattle farm prosper. Yet, I missed the capitol, the only city—Rome. Despite its decadence and corruption, I could not purge its grip from my soul.

As promised, Sabinus corresponded with me and kept me briefed on the events in Rome. He never mentioned the slaughter of the Julian Games or my exile. He left unspoken the fortune in gifts he bestowed on numerous senators demanding my head, who generously condescended to my resignation and the decimation of the Seventh Cohort as adequate punishment. I learned about this from a spy whom I had paid a substantial sum of gold.

Shortly after my departure, Claudius appointed Sabinus Procurator, Governor of Moesia, a province north of Greece bordering the River Danubus. The emperor probably held him responsible for the riots as much as me. Sending him to a place as remote as Moesia, on the far reaches of the River Danubus, was the same as being exiled.

Two years later the old monarch died. Rumors abounded that his fourth wife, Agrippina, fed him poisoned mushrooms. She didn't waste a moment in placing her son, Nero, on the throne. Manipulating old Claudius, Agrippina had controlled the government for years. Did the empress believe she would continue to rule when the seventeen-year-old youth became emperor? If so, she was badly mistaken.

A year after Claudius's death, I received a letter from Sabinus saying Claudius's son, Britannicus, had suddenly died, one day shy of his fourteenth birthday. He had lost favor when his father married Agrippina—a tragedy. I had known him to be a decent young man who would have made a good emperor.

Based on the rumors I had heard, I wasn't surprised when Nero degenerated into a tyrant. Thank the god, Melkart, I was in Hispania.

For the first five years, Nero's reign was fairly peaceful. Together his advisors, the Stoic philosopher Seneca, Burrus Afranius, commander of the Praetorian Guard, and his mother kept him under control.

The murder of Nero's mother ended any further notion of a tranquil rule. When he failed to drown Agrippina on a collapsible bottom-boat, she swam ashore in the Bay of Neapolis. Nero and his Praetorian Guards searched the surrounding resorts and villages for her. Early the next morning, they found her shivering in a fisherman's hut and put her to the sword. Later, Burrus died of a throat abscess, and Seneca retired because he refused to work with Burrus's replacement, the conniving Sofonius Tigellinus.

* * *

One hot June afternoon, Chulainn and I rode back to the house, a half mile from the cattle pens. I was happy to be through another year with the *Herradero*. Like all branding days, seemingly mass confusion reigned. After herding the young calves into hot, dusty corrals, each young steer was chased, roped, and restrained by four or five struggling slaves. Another group of workers seared their flanks with hot irons, then clipped and tagged their ears. When cut loose, the animals blatted as they scattered other calves and slaves alike before scampering out the open gate onto the narrow plain and tree-dotted foothills.

As we cantered along the dusty road, a hot sirocco wind blowing across the Mediterranean from Africa swirled around our stubbled faces, churning up the iron-red earth. Although my tunic and wide-brimmed straw hat were drenched in perspiration, I relished the summer heat. But Eleyne, pregnant again, suffered miserably. The nights did not bring respite, sometimes hotter than the day—a contrast to the cooler climate of her native Britannia.

I approached the house, a sprawling, whitewashed adobe villa, built on a grassless plateau overlooking the gray, rocky coastline. As far as the eye could see, stretches of white-pebbled beaches intermittently dotted the shore below. I left my mount with a stable slave and dismissed Chulainn. After rinsing the dust from my face and limbs at the trough, I strolled along the seaward side of the house overlooking the cobalt sea. Passing the manicured bushes and evergreen trees bordering the mosaic stone sidewalk,

I paused at the bed of red Persian and white Alba roses, Eleyne's favorite flowers. They were irrigated from one of the ranch's many underground springs. I plucked a just-blooming bud of a Persian Rose and entered through the portico.

Fanned by her mute slave, Imogen, Eleyne sewed on a tapestry where she sat in the shaded garden near the bubbling fountain. The slave's effort to cool her proved ineffective. Eleyne's face was flushed, and she perspired. Leisurely, I stepped along the short, tiled walkway, canopied by a vine-covered trellis, until I reached her cushioned, marble bench. Eleyne turned and gave me a halfhearted smile as I laid a flower next to her side. She glanced at the bud but remained expressionless. I bent down and kissed her.

"How are you feeling?" I asked.

"Sweltering," she answered.

For a few seconds, I softly stroked her abdomen, protruding through the light-green tunic, and sat next to her.

"Don't get so close!" she snapped. "I'm too hot." She picked up the bud and carefully inhaled its fragrance. I moved to the wooden bench across from her.

"I almost wished we were back in Rome." Eleyne picked up a white, cloth napkin from the small, three-legged, wooden table between us and wiped the moisture from her face and hands. She examined the soiled cloth, cricked her mouth in disgust, and threw it against one of the sea horses carved into the table's legs.

"I know," I said. "The sirocco's arrived early this year. Our June rains never came."

"Well, I hope we have an early fall—I'll die if this weather continues. Our Lord said we must endure all this for His sake, but He was never with child. And I feel like I've been with child all my life instead of five months." She glared at me as if her situation was entirely my doing. Wisely, I said nothing.

"Maybe you should spend a few days by the beach where it's cooler," I said.

"That would be nice," she answered with a grimace. "But riding a donkey down the cliff side is too bumpy."

"That's easy to remedy. I'll have a cushioned litter built and use our strongest slaves to carry you down the trail."

A smile brushed her pale lips. "Will you? Oh, you're a darling."

Although a necessity in Rome, there had been no need for a litter here. It was eighty miles to Malaca, the closest major city. For goods not manufactured or raised on the latifundia, we rode by horse and wagon to the nearby fishing town, Abdera, to pick them up.

"And Chulainn will oversee your transport," I added. "If they value their lives, they'll use the utmost care."

Apparently, Imogen was excited about the prospect of accompanying Eleyne. She fanned hard enough to breeze me.

I ordered wine, and when it arrived, I eagerly drank the tart Baetican vintage. Eleyne sipped only water from a blue-enameled earthen cup.

"By the way, where are the boys?"

Eleyne glanced in the direction of the sea. "Marcellus and Sabinus rode their ponies down to the beach."

Inwardly, I shuddered, muscles tightened about my shoulders. "They're too young to be going down the steep path from the cliff by themselves."

"They're not alone, silly." She smiled. "Avalos and Hamilcar are with them."

Relieved, I felt the tightness leaving my body and slumped a little in my seat. "Then they're in good hands." Avalos was our horse trainer, a retired Spanish cavalryman from the Roman army. Hamilcar, a local young man, was his assistant. His people had worked for our family for many years.

"How long have they been gone?"

"About an hour. Avalos wanted to drill them in riding on the beach's soft sand."

I grinned. "He has done a good job in training them these last several years."

"Considering Marcellus is only nine and Sabinus eight, he has turned them into excellent riders."

"When they are a little older and bigger, I will see they get full-size horses."

"Just be sure the animals are well broken, we don't need any unruly mounts to start with." I reached over and touched her hand. "Not to worry, I'll see to it. But right now, I have no doubt they've stopped somewhere on the beach to do a little fishing."

She glanced again seaward. "I noticed they carried sling lines and hooks around their saddles."

"Maybe we'll have fish for dinner."

Eleyne sighed. "Probably caught by Avalos and Hamilcar."

I chuckled. "Of course."

As I relaxed, hoof beats from a galloping horse reined in front of the villa. Porus scooted to the door in response to the hard knock. He returned and announced the army courier as the rider entered the garden. The soldier bowed to Eleyne and saluted, handing me a rolled parchment bearing an Imperial Governmental seal—imprinted with Sabinus's signet ring.

"I come from Malaca, sir," the dusty messenger said, "and have instructions to wait your reply."

"Very well," I said. "In the meantime, we'll see you're properly fed and share one of our good Baetican wines. You've ridden a long way."

Porus motioned the grinning soldier to follow as he shook the rust-colored dirt from his scarlet tunic and mailed armor.

When they left the garden, I turned to Eleyne, the muscles in her face appeared tight and set. "Please Marcellus, don't open it!"

"Why?"

"I'm afraid what's in the dispatch—it looks too official. Leave it alone!"

"You must be joking—you've seen Sabinus's seal before." I pulled out my dagger and sliced opened the letter. Slowly, I read the message. I paused and locked my eyes with my wife's. "You're right—Sabinus wants me to return to Rome."

"I *knew* it. What does he say?"

"He's been recalled to Rome."

"You mean Nero is relieving him as Governor of Moesia?" she asked. "What has he done—embezzled the taxes?" Theft of taxes by provincial governors was an all too common occurrence.

"He hasn't been accused of anything. At long last, he's been appointed to the position of city prefect."

"What happened to that old drunk, Publius Secundus, who cheated him out of the office?"

"Murdered by one of his slaves."

"Oh, dear." Eleyne made a sign in the shape of a fish in front of her chest. "May God have mercy on his soul."

Imogen momentarily stopped fanning.

"He probably deserved his fate," Eleyne said as an afterthought. "He was cruel to his slaves—even when we were in Rome. Still, I will pray for him and the poor slave that, no doubt, Nero executed."

I hesitated for a moment. A chill ran through my body. "Then you better add prayers for the souls of another four hundred."

"Four hundred! No, Marcellus, no!" For an instant she cupped her hand over her mouth. Alarm registered in the slave's expression. She stopped fanning.

"The entire household," I said.

"But why?"

"To assert his powers as emperor. Nero had revived the old law under which all slaves of a slain master are executed as punishment." I exhaled. My hands stiffened, and I barely held onto the parchment. "It's just the beginning."

"God save us and the Roman people from such a horrible creature."

"Sabinus says since Tigellinus became Nero's chief advisor, the emperor has grown worse. He thinks the ex-fishmonger is playing on his fears of the Senate. At the same time, Nero is relinquishing more of his responsibilities to Tigellinus so he can spend time racing chariots and take singing lessons."

"I don't like it, Marcellus. Everything has been so quiet—so peaceful. It seemed Nero might have been a just ruler, but this massacre—"

"There's more," I said, scanning the rest of the letter. "Gallus is an intimate friend of Tigellinus."

"That's not so remarkable," Eleyne said in a barely audible voice as she eyed her tapestry. "Any place there's corruption, you'll find Gallus." After thinking a moment, she looked up. "Why was Sabinus appointed city prefect?"

"He doesn't say."

She fixed her sea-blue eyes on mine. "He wants you to return, doesn't he?"

I nodded.

"Why?"

"He wants me to take charge of the entire City Guard." I dropped the message on the bench beside me.

Eleyne gasped, snapping both hands to the side of her face. "I still don't understand. Why you?"

"He doesn't trust anyone else. He has supreme authority, but the force has been under supervision of a field commander since the days of Augustus."

Eleyne glared long and hard. "Isn't once enough? Look what Sabinus did to you last time."

I raised my hand and gestured toward her. "He allowed me to live—he could have ordered my execution."

"If you return this time, he may not have a choice."

I lowered my hand and focused on her angry face, the tight muscles around the jaw line, the defiant jutting chin. For several minutes, I remained silent, thinking. I came to a decision, one she wouldn't like. "I've decided to return to Rome, and you're going with me."

Startled, Eleyne's eyes narrowed, and a sneer came to her lips. She shot a forefinger in my direction. "Let me remind you, if you've forgotten, not only am I your wife, but a *princess* and true Queen of the Regni. You are *my* man, *my* consort. I don't take orders. I give them."

Imogen, who stood behind flagging her fan, insolently nodded in support of her mistress. I shook my head thinking how Eleyne was like all women—wife, princess, lover. She wore the helmet of one or all three when it suited her purposes.

"Nevertheless, this is a summons, and Sabinus needs me," I said a few seconds later.

"*Needs you?* What about our sons and me?" She touched her abdomen. "And the baby? Do you think we need you any less?"

"A few minutes ago, you said you wouldn't have complained if we'd stayed in Rome."

She ignored my reminder of her earlier comment. "Doesn't your family come first? Don't we matter at all?"

I took a deep breath, stood, and walked a few steps away. I halted, turned, and faced Eleyne. "You matter— gods, how much you and the boys mean to me. I regret receiving this letter, but it's something I can't explain. It's some inner feeling pulling me back."

"You're moonstruck, like a mad Druid, that's what you're feeling."

I gestured to the parchment lying on the bench. "Perhaps, but I'm going. I know the risks. Sabinus wouldn't have written me if he didn't believe my presence wasn't important. Don't you see? With Aurelia dead, there isn't anyone he trusts except me. He knows my loyalty, and honest advice on all matters."

"Didn't you learn anything from your last experience?"

I returned to my seat and sat down. I smacked a closed right fist into my open left palm. "I detest Rome and its rulers and corruption as much as you do—my loyalty isn't to them. But I am loyal to my friends, family, and myself. I know why Sabinus did what he did."

"As Commander of the City Guard, you'll be in greater danger than before."

After unclenching my fist, I rested both hands on my thighs. "If that's the situation, I'll resign immediately and leave Rome."

Eleyne shook her head. "I don't believe it. You'll stay until they carry you out. You can't be so naive to think you'll get away so easily? This time they'll kill you!"

Heat rushed to my face, the muscles tightened in my jaw. "I'll watch my back like a wolf. I'll recruit my own spies and won't be surprised by anybody or anything."

Eleyne folded her arms across her chest. "Well, I'm not going and neither are the boys. We are staying here!"

I narrowed my eyes and stared into hers. "You will go—your place is at my side."

"And see you killed? Never!"

I stood again and walked the length of the garden path and back toward Eleyne, struggling to keep my annoyance under control. I returned to my chair, and we argued for the rest of the afternoon. Dusk fell before Eleyne spoke in a voice of resignation, "So I can't stop you? You've made up your mind?"

"Yes, the moment I read his letter—I'm sorry." My insides churned, knowing her concerns. I prayed she would still change her mind. But if she didn't, I would go without her. The thought of leaving her behind tore at my spirit. After eleven years of marriage our love had grown and matured. Not only was she my wife and lover, but a dear friend and companion.

Our lives had settled into a domestic routine like many other marriages, but I didn't mind. Had I wanted to, as master of the household, I had the right to take my pleasures with any slave woman. Because I was content with Eleyne, I did not. Only once did Eleyne complain, unjustly. She accused me of showing too much attention to a house girl. I had complimented the young woman on an occasion for her efficiency and beauty. Furious, Eleyne took my remarks as a proposition. After I convinced her that she was mistaken, Eleyne's anger quickly subsided. However, the temptation to take the wench had crossed my mind.

Nonetheless, Eleyne's Christian charity did not lend itself to taking chances, and she sold the poor girl. I had no say in the matter, because Eleyne originally purchased the walnut-eyed girl with money from the dowry given her by Sabinus and Aurelia. By Mars, sometimes I thought Roman law gave women too many rights.

"Where will you stay?" Eleyne asked, pulling me from my thoughts.

"Probably at Uncle Budar's home on Vatican Hill."

"Of course. It's a very pleasant place, isn't it?"

"Aye, better than living within the city. He said if I returned to Rome, I could live there. I'm going to take him at his word."

"Well, if you must go," she said in a calmer voice, "then I guess I'll follow—I won't stay here without you. I know I've been acting like a shrew, darling. Can you forgive me?"

"Yes, dear lady, always," I answered, relieved that she had changed her mind.

She smiled. "I'm glad. Besides, I don't want any hussy house slaves tempting you—you're still mine."

Her servant nodded and smirked in agreement. If Imogen had not been Eleyne's favorite slave, and such a good nurse to the boys, I would have sold the wench in a moment. I kept a sober face, delighted Eleyne had changed her mind—gods love her.

"Besides," she continued, "I've heard rumors that Paul, the apostle of Christ, was brought to Rome under house arrest. If we must return to that wicked city, then I want to meet him," Eleyne added in a resolute tone. "He's a great teacher and healer—I can learn from him." She studied my face as if looking for a sign of disapproval and smiled when she saw none.

"We'll tell the boys about the move when they return from the beach," I said.

She sighed. "Yes, so we will. I hope they will understand. I'm afraid they won't like it."

"I know," I said quietly, "but they will have to adjust to it."

She nodded.

I stood and moved to Eleyne's cushioned bench and sat beside her. She sighed and rested her head on my shoulder. "The flower is lovely," she whispered.

CHAPTER 17

At dawn, our ship, *Orion's Sword*, quietly approached the harbor of Ostia two miles north of the Tiber's mouth. The only ripple striking the passing ship's hull was the mirrored surface of the Tyrrhenian Sea. Brooding on the horizon, Ficana Hill sat cloaked in a sullen grayness of overhanging clouds, overlooking the river like a Greek acropolis. In the depressing light, the distant Alban Hills vaulted black and purple.

The ship arrived none too soon for Eleyne. We had encountered two raging storms crossing the normally tranquil summer waters of the Mediterranean. Because she was less than six months pregnant, I had feared she would give birth prematurely—fatal for the child and possibly, Gods forbid, herself. Eleyne was dressing in the cabin below.

On deck, the household slaves struck their small goatskin tents, which provided temporary shelters during the ten-day voyage, and repacked the last of our baggage. Chulainn stood on the stern near the tiller with my noisy sons, Marcellus and Sabinus. Teasing him, they kept Chulainn's hands full, jumping on his shoulders and attempting to wrestle him to the splintery deck.

"That's enough, you little monkeys," Chulainn said in mock anger.

He sat on the two and rasped their short hair with his knuckles. Surrender quickly followed, and the three laughed together.

They waved to me where I stood amidships by the railing, dressed in my ceremonial officer's uniform. I grinned and waved back, regretting I had not joined their fun. Sometimes, I make the mistake of acting too dignified. I chided myself for not being more uninhibited like the children. It would have been a soothing balm for the soul.

The squatting merchantman glided past the massive stone, three-story lighthouse guarding the harbor's entrance. Nesting in the building's minute cracks and crevices were gulls who had splattered its walls with droppings. They seemed oblivious to the blazing light from the tower's beacon. Built on an island of concrete, only the great lighthouse of Alexandria, Egypt, surpassed the structure in size and grandeur. The small island acted as a breakwater to the entrance of the encircling mole. We slid between the protective arms of the harbor and entered the busy anchorage.

Over one hundred ships of various sizes lined the stone quay. Most were coated with protective black pitch. The surrounding waters reeked of filth and garbage dumped from countless vessels. Squawking seabirds circled, dived, and fought over prized tidbits before a victor emerged and flew away. Wide-beamed merchantmen, hoisting one square center sail and a smaller sprit raking sharply over the bow, ruled the harbor. Nearby bulging two-storied warehouses stood framed by red brick porticoes. Sweaty dock workers, freedmen, and slaves alike busily unloaded cargo, hurrying up and down gangways from vessel prows. Ship masters shouted orders to crews. Cursing foremen drove stevedores and dock workers. Money changers, sea-captains, and merchants haggled over the price of goods. The deafening noise, carried on the sea breeze like invisible fingers, reached into every dock, slip, and quay of Ostia's turbulent harbor.

At one end of the dock, troops from the City Guard's Ostian garrison marched into view—dressed in chain-mail armor and red-plumed, old-style republican helmets. The entire contingent of four hundred mustered for the occasion, officially welcoming my return to Rome. Displayed prominently in front were the cohort standards, gilded dolphins, and the emperor's image, dressed with laurel garlands.

At the head of the formation, Casperius Niger, my centurion from the Seventh Cohort of the Watch, sat astride on a well-groomed black gelding. Promoted to the rank of tribune, he wore a silver cuirass as part of his uniform. Transferred to the City Guard, he was assigned commander of the Ostian Cohort.

Then I spied an unwelcome menace among the crowded dock—Gallus. He sat in a plush, silk-lined litter, surrounded by an entourage of retainers, freedmen, and slaves. Shoving aside the hatless workers, his people threatened bodily harm to anyone who failed to show respect as the senator passed by. What had brought Gallus to Ostia? Surely, he had not journeyed here to greet us. After all these years, his hatred still lingered, as did mine.

Affectionately, he stroked the belly of a furry, white cat sprawled in his lap. As the litter moved along, a slave handed him a highly polished, silver mirror. Gallus snatched the mirror and handed the slave his pampered cat, which immediately clawed his face. He admired himself in the mirror, touched his hair foppishly, and pushed an invisible strand back into place.

As I leaned on the railing, the soft touch of Eleyne's hand rubbed against my left arm. "Is that who I think it is?" she asked.

"Yes, it's him," I said, glancing to her pale face, meeting her eyes. Eleyne wore a bright-green and orange, full-length tunic. A gold torc encircled her white neck, and two silver bracelets dangled from each wrist.

She glared at Gallus. "Has he come to throw more coins?"

"Perhaps he's part of the welcoming party."

"That's not funny."

"It's not meant to be. I'm as puzzled as you."

"Where is Lord Sabinus?"

"I didn't expect him. The Guard was sent to welcome us."

She sniffed. "If he wanted you to return so much, he should be here. If not for you, then for my sake. He once considered me part of his family. After all, you had to get his permission to marry me."

"A city prefect doesn't publicly welcome a military tribune," I said, "especially one he forced to resign. Not even for the sake of one he considered a daughter." I took both Eleyne's hands and looked into her eyes. "He'll welcome me and you, too, in his own way."

For the length of a few heart beats Eleyne smiled, but then pulled her hands away. "How silly."

Before I could answer, the harbor breeze picked up. I caught a whiff of fetid dead fish and coughed. In the distance, I spotted a group of fishermen gutting a new catch of tuna on the dock. They threw the entrails into the putrid water quietly lapping against the pilings. Screeching seagulls instantly appeared and dived upon this newly discovered feast.

"On the contrary," I finally answered, "it would be considered a sign of his weakness and my strength. He must stay in Rome where he can keep an eye on the main bulk of the City Guard. If he came to Ostia, they might swear their allegiance to someone else instead of him— that's seven thousand men. Remember what happened when the Legions of Dalmatia along the Danubus pledged allegiance to Scribonianus during Claudius's reign?"

"But he was forced to commit suicide," she said. "Honestly, do you believe the Guard would pledge you their fealty? They don't know you."

"Apparently, my reputation with the Watch, tarnished though it might be, has preceded me to the City Guard, something I never envisioned. I know from reports I received from Sabinus, they had heard of the terrible reputation of the Seventh Cohort before I had taken command. They also were informed of my efforts to retrain and ultimately hold them together on the day of the riot and massacre during the naval games. And the Guard certainly knew about the punishment the Watchmen received for disobeying orders. As their new commander, I'll have the power—if I want it."

"And be crushed by Nero?" she said. "You're not on the frontier."

"Very observant, my dear." I gave her a catty grin. "It's not worth losing my head for something I never wanted."

"Good, I love your head too much."

I gave her full cheek a gentle kiss. "So do I."

Stevedores snagged lines tossed by the crew from *Orion's Sword* and secured them to iron rings set in concrete at the wharf's edge. Scampering over the sides and down the gangway, they began unloading a consignment of a hundred jars of garum, a foul-smelling Spanish fish sauce.

"In any event," I continued, "I'm not so ambitious— probably one reason for my recall. As city prefect, Sabinus is the lawful supreme commander of the Guard. I'm only an extension of his authority."

"A powerful one."

"Aye, but I'll use my office for the good of the people. And, unless he's changed, Casperius Niger can help."

"Why him?"

"He was the only reliable centurion in the Seventh Cohort, and trustworthy—like Crispus."

"Don't you remember Crispus's words about never trusting a Roman?"

The sounds of breaking jars, spilling vinegary Gallic wines and olive oil, and the grinding roll of marble blocks over wooden rollers to waiting river barges echoed along the quay. For the length of a few heartbeats, the noise interrupted my thoughts as to how I should answer Eleyne's question.

"I haven't forgotten," I finally said. The memories of that terrible day of slaughter, and of holding my dying friend in my arms, flooded my memory. The sight of his broken body was as vivid as if it had occurred yesterday. I turned from Eleyne and blinked the tears away. Facing her again, she placed a delicate hand on my shoulder.

"I'm sorry," I said.

"Darling you don't have to apologize for anything. He was your best friend. Only despicable Rome should be sorry." Her hiss showed her contempt.

"No matter, Casperius is considered as much a foreigner as we are, even though he is Italian born."

"Why?"

I glanced in Casperius's direction and back to my wife. "He's Etruscan—Rome's ancient enemy. They were defeated hundreds of years ago and became Roman citizens, but old fears about them still exist." I shrugged. "Sheer madness."

"Can you be certain of his loyalty?"

"Unless I'm mistaken, he'll place his allegiance in Sabinus and me."

Eleyne studied the cohort as it stood on the dock. "You once said officers considered malcontents were sent to Ostia." She fixed her cobalt eyes on me. "Is that why Casperius is here?"

"More than likely. He must have done something to displease Prefect Secundus before his death. Now that I'm the Guard commander, I'll transfer Casperius to Rome."

I took Eleyne's hands and steadied her on the still rocking ship. Then I released one hand and led her down the gangway.

When we disembarked, Casperius Niger dismounted. Accompanied by an escort of guardsmen, he greeted Eleyne and me after we stepped off the gangway. Darker and harder than I remembered, his olive face had the affable grin of a lynx. "Welcome back, sir," he said heartily while saluting. "And you, too, Princess," he added in deference to Eleyne, who smiled.

"Thank you, *Tribune* Casperius Niger," I replied, noting his rank as I tried to adjust my shaky sea legs. "It's indeed a pleasure. I hadn't expected to see you again."

"They can't hide a good man forever, can they?" he answered in a slow, Etruscan drawl.

"Aye, you were the only decent centurion under my last command."

A smirk came to his face. "They were a bad lot. But despite them and the politicians, I worked my way up the ranks. Lord Sabinus sent the garrison to welcome you, and I've turned out every manjack of them."

"I'll take a closer look."

Eleyne stayed behind with the family and slaves as Casperius and I stepped over to the formation.

The troops formed four squares, ten men deep and ten wide. Upon our approach, the senior centurion called the garrison to attention, and junior centurions echoed the command down the formation. Clanking shields and the slamming of hob-nailed sandaled shoes to the pavement rumbled the entire length of the jetty. After a brief inspection, we returned to the front ranks.

"The men are in good spirits today, Casperius," I said.

"They got paid, just before you arrived."

"That explains it."

Casperius frowned. "Not exactly. They think you had something to do with it."

"Why?"

"Usually, the Ostian Garrison is seldom paid on time. Today they were."

"I don't see why they believe I had any part in their being paid. Sabinus probably put a flea in someone's ear at the treasury so they would be in a good mood when I arrived."

"No matter, the troops think it's an omen from the gods that you'll be a good commander. You know how superstitious soldiers are."

I loudly complimented Casperius on the strength and fitness of the men as I turned and faced them.

"Soldiers," I barked, "I will now administer the oath of allegiance."

In a voice only I could hear, Casperius leaned over and said, "Sir, they're willing to swear their allegiance to you, and no one else. They know about your bravery."

"That's suicide," I answered sharply, "especially here where there are so many witnesses. Let there be no mistake, my fealty is to Sabinus and the emperor."

He shrugged. "As you say, sir. But if you change your mind," he added, "say the word, and they'll swear to a man."

I administered the oath.

When I finished they gave a rousing cheer, "*Ave, Reburrus! Hail, Reburrus!*" Drawing their legionary swords, they banged their weapons against rectangular shields in a show of loyalty—to me. As the din of the noise grew deafening, the activity on the docks paused, and all workers, sailors, wharf officials, and others looked our way. Becoming alarmed, I immediately silenced the troops. News of the ovation would race to the emperor's ears, not to mention Sabinus's, and be misconstrued as a sign of treason. Everyone hearing the oath knew it had not been sworn to me but to the emperor and Sabinus. Nevertheless, my position had been jeopardized. I would need a convincing explanation for Nero and Sabinus.

No sooner had the noise subsided than Gallus and his haughty retinue approached. As a senator, his rights of protocol could not be ignored. He barely acknowledged Casperius. And what did he think of the Guard's acclamation? It was in his power to report the truth or distortion to Nero.

Both of us were forty and had managed to keep our weight trim. But Gallus's blond hair had lost its luster, replaced by a sickly yellow shade. Receding gray strands sprouted at the temples. Deep lines crept across his narrow forehead, and wrinkles surrounding the edge of his eyes, fanned like the web of a spider. His pursed mouth was set permanently in a razor-thin frown. A light film of white powder masked his face, with a touch of kohl applied to the narrow eyelids. Light-pink rouge accented his cheeks. A fine, linen toga, trimmed in purple and lined with gold thread, draped his slight build—each fold meticulously in place.

"May I offer my congratulations to the new commander of the City Guards?" he said in a voice dripping with honey. "The Guard's newfound loyalty to you is most impressive and shall be duly noted in the right places."

"Then you know from your own military experience how troops react when they've been paid on time. We both know the credit goes to Nero and not me. You heard me administering the oath to the emperor."

"I shall inform the emperor of the facts as I see them," Gallus snapped.

"Naturally, you'll report the truth. I hear Nero doesn't appreciate lying—not even from his friends."

"Are you saying that I would lie to his Divinity?"

"Of course not." I grinned. "You know when the truth is in your best interest."

For a moment he glared, and then a smile, as affable as a snake, rippled along his lips. He snorted. "One should always be honest with the emperor in affairs of state, but that is not why I am here."

"To what do I owe this visit?" I asked.

He cleared his throat. "I realized we have had our differences in the past, but I pray they can be forgotten."

"Can they?" I said. I thought it possible when the sun shines in Hades.

"Really, my dear Marcellus. What is past cannot be changed, and I regret the animosity, which developed between us."

"Both of us know the reasons."

He shrugged. "We were caught up in the hatreds of our fathers—they had nothing to do with us. Now, I ask for a new beginning, this time to culminate in a lasting friendship."

I didn't believe Gallus any further than I could toss a horse. Something ominous lay behind his newly found benevolence. He never did anything without expecting to benefit tenfold. I kept my suspicions under my tunic.

"Perhaps," I said after a brief pause, "it's possible."

"Of course, it is," he said. "I have many friends at court. Tigellinus is my dearest friend, and the emperor takes note of my opinions, too."

"Oh?" He would attempt to use me to get what he wanted. "I'm only a soldier—I stay out of Imperial intrigues."

"Oh, come now, my dear man, of course you are joking? Prefect Sabinus may be your patron, but he is at Nero's bidding, and one word from me—"

I raised my hand. "What do you want, Gallus?"

He stiffened and studied me for an instant. Apparently, judging the time right, he looked about, and his eyes narrowed slightly. "I have a proposition, but this is not the place for discussion. Perhaps tonight at the palace." He continued in a louder voice. "The emperor is having a feast. Come as my guest, and I shall personally introduce you to Nero—an opportunity you must not ignore. Otherwise, you will have to wait months—if ever."

"You're most generous," I answered in an equally civil manner, "but I must decline. I'm due to meet Prefect Sabinus upon arriving in Rome. He may have other plans."

A sneer rippled over Gallus's mouth. "Surely you know the emperor has requested the prefect's presence?"

A request from Nero was a command. "Then I shall be his guest, if he invites me—I'm duty bound to Sabinus. Besides . . . ," I grinned, "I'm no politician. Why would his Divinity bother with a poor soldier like me?"

"Naturally, you are right," Gallus said. "You are just a soldier. However, we can still be friends."

"Of course," I lied.

"We must speak about the proposal soon. I assure you it is an opportunity only a fool would ignore."

Gallus turned away and strolled back to his litter. Halting in mid-stride, he faced me again. "The emperor shall hear about the Guard's devotion to its new commander. You *are* a politician, or you would not have obtained your rank, but a diplomat, you are not!"

"Beware of him, sir," Casperius said, as Gallus's entourage disappeared among the sea of dock workers. "He's no fool."

"And neither am I."

* * *

Casperius Niger led the century of honor guard of one hundred men, escorting my family and me the twenty-two miles to Rome. Eleyne and my sons rode in a canopied wagon drawn by four horses while I rode next to Casperius. The rest of our household rode behind us in baggage carts pulled by mules.

Considered a hardship post, Ostia would not be a long-term assignment for Casperius. He was scheduled to rotate from Ostia to Rome during the Ides of August. Neither officers nor troops at the seaport were posted there for more than four months. Primarily trained to arrest felons and quell riots, duties of firefighting were considered hazardous and unpopular among the ranks of the City Guard—fit for only the Watch.

"Of course," Casperius explained, "at the Calends of December, they'll rotate me back. Then I can't complain I was kept in Ostia permanently, which is what the Imperial bureaucrats want!"

I facetiously reassured Casperius I wouldn't put a stop to the routine by the bureaucrats. He didn't laugh.

Enroute, Casperius briefed me on events in Rome and the deteriorating situation under Nero. Although I had learned much about Nero through my correspondence with Sabinus, I had underestimated the emperor's tyrannical lust for power.

"Has Lord Sabinus written to you about Nero's murdering ways?" Casperius asked.

My chest tightened, and for the length of a heartbeat, I pulled back on the reins of my horse, jolting him to a halt. I kicked his sides, and he moved forward. "You mean the thirty senators who were falsely accused of treason?" I asked returning to Casperius's side.

"The same. They were executed or forced to commit suicide."

I still hadn't forgotten how much this bothered me when I'd received Sabinus's report. Most of the senators were honorable men. "Gods only know how many more will be slaughtered before he's finished."

Casperius exhaled. "Lord Sabinus has to watch his back."

"All of us have to watch our backs."

So far, Nero had confined his terrorism to the Senate, tragic enough because its ranks contained many noble men, excluding Gallus.

During the journey an oppressive humidity lingered in the air, and the sun never cracked the rust-iron clouds. The worst of seasons, only critical business kept Sabinus in Rome during the summer. Usually, he resided at his rambling villa along the foot of the cool Apennines. Because Nero was giving a feast tonight, the nobility had remained in the city, or they all would have escaped to the milder temperatures of the country or the seashore. Only the poor were trapped in Rome during the summer. I planned to send Eleyne to Budar's coastal villa near Antium, south of Ostia. The tasks ahead would prevent my joining her.

It was late afternoon when we reached Uncle Budar's estate, across the Tiber from Rome, before I reported to Sabinus. I turned and moved back to the wagon where Eleyne and the boys rode behind Casperius and me. The dust from the long trip failed to hide her drawn face and drooping eyes.

The boys, nine-year-old Marcellus and Sabinus, age eight, their faces and tunics streaked with dust, looked about their new surroundings. The oldest had been three and the latter two when I was exiled to Hispania. I doubted they had any memory of living in Rome.

Marcellus squinted his dark eyes and stared at the palatial mansion. He turned to Eleyne. "Is this where Uncle Budar lives?"

"Yes, it is, Son. It is our new home," she answered in a tired voice, her shoulders sagging.

He glanced toward the Tiber and to Rome in the hazy distance. He scratched his straight nose and sniffed. "Rome's ugly."

"I know," Eleyne said. She motioned to Budar's villa and to the lush greenery of the adjacent park on Vatican Hill. "But it is nicer here and cooler."

"Hispania's better," Marcellus said. He shrugged and turned to his younger brother.

Sabinus vigorously nodded his long, narrow face. "It is."

"I know you don't like it," I said approaching the wagon, "but for now, we will be staying here."

The boys frowned. I reached over and touched young Marcellus's shoulder and then Sabinus's. "Don't you fret, we will return to Hispania next year for the summer, I promise."

Sabinus smiled. "Really?"

"You mean it, Da?" Marcellus asked.

I grinned and nodded. "Yes, really, I mean it." I prayed I would keep my promise.

Marcellus and Sabinus turned and slapped each other on the shoulder, something they did when happy.

Eleyne gave me a half-hearted smile. "Thanks for promising the boys." She pulled a silk cloth, tucked in her girdled waistline, and wiped her face. Tucking it back under her belt, she shook her head and sighed. "I'm so tired. The baby has been kicking me—I need to rest. Please convey my apologies for not coming with you to see Lord Sabinus."

"He'll understand," I said. I bent over and kissed her cheek.

Dusk fell before Casperius and I arrived at Sabinus's home at the end of Pomegranate Street on Quirinal Hill. We were led to his study, a room that opened onto the garden. The place, illuminated by several olive oil lamps, was lined with wooden cupboards filled with hundreds of scrolls from floor to ceiling. In one corner sitting on a pedestal was the bust of Cicero, and in the recess of another stood the bust of a brooding Nero. We stood before an aging, heavily wrinkled man, dressed in a white, linen toga, sitting behind an ornately carved sandarac wooden desk. Nearing sixty, Sabinus was almost bald, a white crown of hair surrounding his ears and scalp. Casting his deep, brown eyes upon me, I felt the command of his personality. We saluted, and he gave Casperius and me a spirited greeting. After pleasantries, he asked Casperius to wait in the atrium and close the door behind him.

Sabinus and I studied one another for a long moment without saying a word. He stood, stepped around his desk, and shook my hand firmly with both of his. "Welcome back my friend, I have missed you."

"Likewise, sir."

"I know you were wronged six years ago," he said gravely, "but what I did was a reaction to the events of the moment."

"Events neither of us controlled."

Sabinus shook his head. "That's no consolation for the damage wreaked upon you and your family. Unfortunately, time can't be altered, but I will do what I can to alleviate past wrongs."

Strange, even though I left Rome in disgrace, I looked forward to returning to my home in Hispania. And no doubt it also saved my marriage. Nevertheless, my failure to control the destructive actions of the Seventh Cohort, which led to the riot outside the naval arena, was still a painful memory. For a second my muscles tightened. Yet the healing process of time had turned what anguish remained into a fading memory.

"There's no point of dwelling on the bitter fruits of the past," I said, "I want to continue with my life, serving you as before."

Sabinus nodded and motioned for me to be seated across the desk from him. "And you shall. You are a general in everything but name, with all the privileges and benefits going with the position. I did not recall you only because you are the best man for the job—I need someone whom I can trust."

"I'm grateful, sir. Your faith in me won't prove unfounded."

He patted my arm. "You have already shown your loyalty and trust."

"There's another matter that needs clearing up immediately," I said.

Sabinus eyed me quizzically. "What is that?"

"Gallus met me at Ostia."

"So I heard, and the troops hailed you."

"Weren't you told I simply reaffirmed their allegiance to the emperor and you?"

"Gallus reported the actions of the Ostian troops, and explained you administered the proper oath. Tigellinus's henchmen, who Gallus did not know were there, confirmed your actions—Nero was pleased."

I hadn't realized I was so tense. The muscles throughout my body relaxed so quickly I caught myself slumping in my chair.

"What's wrong?" Sabinus asked.

I shook my head. "It's nothing. I'm just relieved to hear this piece of good news."

"But we must remain alert," Sabinus said. "Depending on who is most influential on a given day, Nero has a reputation for abruptly changing his mind. He could get it into his head at a later time that you and the troops were disloyal."

"I'm aware of that." I prayed to the gods, including Eleyne's Christian God, Nero would not.

I changed the subject. "Gallus was very friendly today. He said he wanted to resolve old differences."

"And I gather you are wary as to his reasons."

"Wouldn't you be?"

Sabinus placed his thumb and forefinger to his chin, pulling the skin almost to a point. He nodded before lowering his hand. "I am. Since my return from Moesia, young Senator Gallus has been amiable to me, too. His motives are always suspicious, and my spies are seeking his reasons."

"Does he have as much influence as he claims?"

"He and Tigellinus are considered to be *intimate* friends—a dangerous alliance, because Tigellinus's powers go beyond his authority as Praetorian prefect. Nero depends heavily upon his advice."

"Why did Nero recall you to Rome?"

"To do his bidding, I suspect," Sabinus answered.

I winced. "Surely you're not?" Then I realized had he refused, it probably would have meant his execution.

Sabinus exhaled and momentarily looked around his office. "I have had to learn old Claudius's tricks. He was a survivor, and so am I. Of what value would I be as a dead martyr? By living, I help the vast majority. I am still influential, and so long as I take precautions for my own safety, I am determined to minimize the tyranny at court."

"Doesn't that mean sacrificing your beliefs?"

He slammed a hand on the table, the sound echoing through the room and outside in the garden. "My beliefs, my values are nothing compared to the thousands of lives at stake."

Sabinus stood and paced about the room as if attempting to calm himself. He took a deep breath and stared at the tiled floor. "I have compromised where necessary."

"I'm disgusted to have to say this, but you were wise to do so."

He returned to his chair, sat, and studied my face. "Not only wise, but necessary. There are too many lives at stake. Had I declined, I would have signed my death warrant. I cannot stop the murders of senators, some of whom are my oldest and dearest friends." He paused, and his face tightened. It seemed as if Sabinus would be overwhelmed with grief, but he quickly recovered. "At least I can help their families in retaining properties and prevent their disgrace. It is a terrible burden to bear, and sometimes I am ashamed because I do not speak against him. At once I am afraid, but at the same time it is better I am chief magistrate, rather than one of Tigellinus's cronies."

I understood why he requested my return. He had spoken to no one but me about his true thoughts. I sensed that inner turmoil wracked his soul, and he was paying a terrible price.

"By the way, my friend," Sabinus continued, "when you return to your uncle's home, take a look in the stables. A present and a token of my friendship awaits you. It will be obvious to all when you speak it is with the authority of the chief magistrate of Rome, and more importantly . . . you are my friend."

Sabinus smiled. "Right now, join me as my guest at Nero's feast."

CHAPTER 18

The guests admitted to the Palace of Tiberius, residence of the Emperor Nero, had changed in composition since I had left Rome. A motley assortment of characters, which Claudius would have barred, mixed with the nobility, wealthy freedmen, and foreign emissaries—all of whom flattered him unashamedly. Nero was known to enjoy the company of charlatan high priests, effeminate mimes, scarred gladiators, wiry charioteers of his favorite racing faction, the Leek Greens, and blonde-wigged, divorced women from great families.

I commented on my observations to Sabinus as we strolled through the cavernous palace halls.

"They appeal to Nero's deviant nature and his quest for excitement," Sabinus answered.

I snorted. "Being the butt of his jokes is very profitable these days."

Sabinus crinkled his nose. "If necessary, they would wallow in his shit to obtain his favors."

Scattered in the great dining hall, guests chatted in small groups, as they waited for the emperor's arrival. The sweet scent of verbena wafted in the air. Clustered in the huge triclinium, in dozens of delicate long-necked vases, fresh roses and irises neutralized the odor of hundreds of bodies, sweltering in the evening's humidity.

After being congratulated by numerous dignitaries on my new command, Sabinus and I were led by a slave to a set of dining couches near the emperor's dais. As we reclined next to one another, an army of slaves began serving the guests smooth-tasting Sentenian wine, cooled by mountain snow.

Lights from a thousand candles illuminated the dining room. Gallus, dressed in a scarlet dining toga and wearing a crown of sulfur roses, lurked amidst the shadows dancing on marble and alabaster walls and ceilings. His cold face watched the diners as if studying and remembering, misplacing nothing in his mental archive for future reference.

As he stood between the naked statues of the helmeted Diomedes and bearded Hercules, his lusty gaze fixed upon an infamous, scantily clad beauty, attended by her nearly naked, young male slave. Beads of sweat formed upon Gallus's brow and upper lip. I was about to credit him for his exquisite taste in women, but when she fluttered away in a wake of colored silks, Gallus's eyes remained upon the tanned boy. I should have known better—his preferences for young men had not changed.

Gallus approached Sabinus and me—his eyes meeting mine. A tall, thick-jawed, swarthy man dressed in the scarlet, white, and gold trimmed uniform of a Praetorian officer followed. His yellow, hawk-like eyes, set beneath shaggy eyebrows joined at the base of a thin, straight nose, told me unmistakably he was Tigellinus.

All eyes settled on the two when they stopped before our black-lacquered table.

"Ah, Marcellus," Gallus said in a sugary voice. "What a pleasant surprise. How fortunate you came after all. Greetings, Lord Sabinus," he said as an afterthought with a nod of the head.

Gallus turned to the dark stranger and gestured. "I want you to meet my friend, the noble Sofonius Tigellinus, Praetorian Prefect and Friend of Caesar."

I stood and shook his hand. Tigellinus's clammy grip was as limp as the dead fish he once hawked. The cold eyes of the former fishmonger from Greece sliced through mine as if lopping off the head of a codfish.

"Greetings, Tribune," the Praetorian prefect said coldly. "I've heard much about you."

No doubt from Gallus, his vast network of secret police, and my service records. "And I of you," I answered. "Your fame grows with each passing day." I yearned to wipe the grease off my palm from his hand shake, but feared he would notice, and refrained.

"You know I live only to serve Caesar," Tigellinus said.

I looked about and noticed several guests murmuring in agreement.

Provided Nero allowed him to control Rome.

"Your service to the emperor is well known," I said.

Tigellinus glared as if reading my tone of voice. "Since we are *only* soldiers," he glanced to Gallus, "you and I know it's essential to guard against the enemies of the state."

I nodded. "Your diligence is legendary. I hear the Senate gives public thanks every time you expose a traitor. I didn't realize Rome had so many."

"It's only proper," Tigellinus said. "The emperor has numerous enemies. I won't hesitate to exterminate their filthy carcasses even when they appear in the most extraordinary places." He glanced to a sober-faced Gallus.

"Yes, don't they?" I said, immediately regretting my reply. Sabinus scowled, but as he averted his glance I detected a subdued smile.

The edge of Gallus's thin lips curled into a frown.

The Praetorian prefect studied me for the span of a few heartbeats. "I'm not like these perfumed clowns," he answered loudly, gesturing towards a couple of senators at the next couch, "who snivel at the voice of Caesar. I cater to his wants, yes, but those who dare to oppose him or me—I crush like beetles under my boots."

Gallus nodded, as did Sabinus, but I suspect not as eagerly.

"Under the circumstances, only a fool would oppose the emperor," I said.

A wry smile appeared on Tigellinus's weak mouth. "You learn quickly, Tribune. You have no ambitions like these buffoons, do you?"

"Contrary to what you may have heard." I glanced to Gallus, "As a soldier, I have no interest in politics or Imperial intrigue."

"Wise indeed," Tigellinus said in a jovial voice. "I like you, Tribune. I shouldn't because you mocked me, but I do. You, I don't fear."

"I'm not mad. What is the City Guard to the power of the emperor and the Praetorians?"

"See that you keep your oath to Caesar," Tigellinus warned. "It would be a shame if you disappeared. There are few honest men left in Rome." He abruptly turned away. Gallus trailed him like a puppy. He shot a smug look over his narrow shoulders.

"Marcellus," Sabinus said, "do not play the fool's game with Tigellinus—you will lose."

"I hate groveling."

"No one says you have to. He knew by the tone in your voice you attempted to play him for a simpleton. He holds the Cast of Venus and the powers of Jupiter."

A haughty court chamberlain entered at the end of the triclinium. Scanning the room, he pounded his black, wooden staff on the mosaic floor, signaling the arrival of Nero. The guests sprang to their feet in a flurry of clattering sandals.

Six tall Praetorian guardsmen puffed on brass, circular cornus. The metallic sounds echoed through the Great Hall. Twenty more guardsmen, wearing white ceremonial garb trimmed in silver, swaggered ahead of Nero's entourage of slaves, freedmen, and the bejeweled Petronius—philosopher and advisor to the emperor. Next followed a dozen prancing young girls and handsome boys dressed in diaphanous, white tunics. Guests lecherously eyed male and female alike. The milky-white youths daintily tossed red and white rose petals in the pathway of Rome's First Citizen and the Empress Poppaea. The Imperial couple strolled in to boisterous cries of, "*Ave*, Caesar! Hail, Caesar!"

Nero wrinkled his nose and shrugged. Dressed in the Greek manner, he wore a flowing tunic adorned in a flower pattern of blue and purple iris. A brilliant-purple, ankle-length garment girdled around the waist. A garish, silk scarf covered with spiral designs, dyed a blue woad, draped his neck.

As she walked next to her husband, Poppaea's sky-blue eyes searched the room rapidly, perhaps for a new lover.

She had left her first husband, Otho, for Nero. Sprinkled with gold dust and glistening in the candle light, Poppaea wore her hair in platinum rows piled atop her head. Devoid of the cruelty for which she was known, her smooth, ivory face bore the image of an innocent nymph.

"See that woman?" Sabinus whispered, motioning to a female in her mid-twenties, standing with Poppaea's ladies-in-waiting behind the Imperial couple.

"The one wearing the yellow chiton and dusky, brown hair?" I said.

"That is Acte, the freedwoman."

"Isn't that Nero's mistress?"

"The same. At one time he wanted to marry her."

"What stopped him?"

"Petronius advised against it. She would be bad for his image, and beneath his station."

"Why hasn't Poppaea gotten rid of her?"

"She doesn't perceive her as a threat. Acte knows her place—thank the gods. It is rumored she is a Christian."

Nero and his wife reclined on a purple, silken couch on the dais at the head of the hall. Just below them was three couches filled by a group of dwarves dressed in outlandish costumes as effeminate actors, brutish gladiators, and heavily mascaraed young men. They were all smiles and clapped enthusiastically as they gazed upon the Imperial couple.

As the applauding guests resumed their places, Nero clapped his hands. "Wine!" he bellowed in a crisp, deep voice. The chief steward nodded, and a slave rushed to the monarch's side with a gem-encased, long-stemmed amphora. Carefully, he poured the dark-red nectar into the emperor's jewel-encrusted, golden cup. Another slave approached and tasted the vintage to ensure it wasn't poisoned.

Nero took the goblet in his fleshy hand and raised it to his mouth. "Drink and enjoy!" he proclaimed. "Let the feasting begin!" He consumed the wine in one gluttonous gulp, sloshing wine down the sides of his lips and onto his thin, bronze beard.

Servants appeared with huge platters of food, including everything from roasted flamingos to sides of steaming goat meat. Huge, colorfully decorated dishes trimmed with plumes of feathers contained delicacies pleasing to the palate. Slaves flooded us with rivers of wine, and dancers streamed onto the floor. They gracefully wandered about the cavernous marble room, causing candle lights, as they passed each table, to wink like expanding ripples from a rock tossed into a glassy pond. The tables before the emperor's guests groaned with the weight of a fifty-seven-course dinner.

"Nero feasts like this every night," Sabinus said.

"Then this is just another boring banquet for him," I answered.

"It is."

Scanning the dining hall, an expression of pleasure came to Nero's round face as he held out his cup for another refill. At twenty-four, his appearance was not conducive to being worshipped like the gods on mighty Olympus, as he wished. Dominated by a strong forehead and overhanging eyebrows, his dead-blue eyes gave the illusion of a perpetual scowl. Layered in four rows, one behind the other, his frizzled, dark hair copied the same style worn by charioteers in the Great Circus. His neck and jowls were thick and ugly. Fortunately, Nero had not commanded the people to venerate him as a god, but his sniveling lackeys acted as if he had, making flattering comparisons with Jupiter and Mars.

Yawning and shoving away an offered dish by a slave, the emperor slowly scanned the diners with a polished emerald mounted on a delicate, ivory handle. Having peered through similar stones on occasion, I knew one side made fat people appear thin, and the opposite side the reverse. The glass was cut so thin that one could see through it. Nero toyed with the jewel, turning the clear stone this way and that, playing with the height of his guests by slowly rolling the ivory stem. His scowling eyes gazed through the green stone upon our table. He turned and said something to Tigellinus. A sadistic grin rippled across the Praetorian prefect's mouth as he nodded. He sent a slave to our table.

"The Divine Caesar," the slave announced, "commands your presence, Commander Reburrus."

I glanced to Sabinus.

"Guard your words carefully," he said.

I had been in the Emperor Claudius's presence on many occasions and usually felt at ease, but I had no idea what to expect from Nero. A wrong phrase would jeopardize my life. If not by Nero, certainly, by Tigellinus. Determined to suppress my fears, I confidently strode towards the emperor. Halting at an appropriate distance before his solid gold table, I gave a sharp salute and looked him in the eye.

"Welcome to our court, Commander," Nero said in a formal voice. "Our reports indicate you have served Rome with bravery and honor. That . . . ," he popped a small honeycake in his mouth, "pleases us."

Smacking noisily, he gaped through the emerald jewel and rolled its stem repeatedly with forefinger and thumb.

"I'm honored, Caesar," I answered in an even voice. "As my family has in the past, my sole ambition is to serve Rome and my emperor."

"Is that so?" A menacing look flashed through Nero's eyes. "Why did you invoke the name of Prefect Sabinus after mine in the oath at Ostia?"

Alarmed by his question, my face grew hot. I attempted to relax my tensing body. Every word had to be carefully chosen. "As is obvious to everyone, Caesar is very busy with the affairs of state." For a moment, I hesitated. My heart pounded so loud I could have sworn everyone about me heard it.

"Go on," he commanded, "we are listening." His eyes locked with mine as his little fingernail dug loose something stuck between his teeth. Those within earshot quieted to hear if another head might roll.

"However," I continued, "such mundane affairs as policing the city have been traditionally the responsibility of the city prefect. What I emphasized first and foremost is that the troops must be loyal to your Divinity—at all times. However, in normal duties, such as policing the city, their orders come directly from Prefect Sabinus, through me, and given in Caesar's name. In carrying out their daily assignments, not only must they obey Caesar, but remain obedient to Prefect Sabinus and me, their immediate commanders."

Nero sat silently for a moment studying my face, as he scratched an armpit and digested my words. I prayed my expression did not betray my thoughts. He looked about slowly. The room remained quiet as the dead as he eyed Sabinus, and again, me. My explanation had been awkward and unconvincing.

Nero nodded. "You appeal to us."

I caught Tigellinus's wrinkled look of disapproval out of the corner of my eye. As evinced by his smirk, Gallus, too, did not share the emperor's enthusiasm.

"Tribune," the emperor continued, "you are a man of unusual integrity."

The crowd breathed heavily, disappointed, I sensed. Nero picked up a large-boned chunk of beef, toying with it, as he had with me. He took a large bite. "We rarely see your kind in Rome," he said through bulging cheeks. The emperor flicked a piece of torn meat with a finger. He glared at a few chosen senators and back to me. "Rome needs more men like you."

The emperor seemed to tire of gnawing on the shank and flung it to the pack of dwarves gathered for his amusement. A minor skirmish ensued for the prize morsel. He waved me away with a greasy hand, and I withdrew, relieved the audience was over. Soaked in sweat, I took my place next to Sabinus.

"Your answers to Nero were very good," Sabinus said, "but from time to time you seemed to lose your path of thought. What was going through your mind?"

"It isn't every day," I answered, "when I stand before an emperor whose emerald-glazed eye flickers from pea-size to egg-size in rapid succession. I didn't know what to expect."

"Fortunately, you caught him in a good mood."

After dining on a course of roast peacock and drinking several cups of wine, I went to the lavatory and relieved myself.

Returning from the latrine, I spotted Gallus loitering in the shadows of a marbled column. Nonchalantly, he stepped in front of me.

"What do you want?" I demanded.

"Remember the proposition I mentioned this morning in Ostia?"

"Senator," I said impatiently, "any proposal by you has the smell of rotten eel."

"That depends on one's senses," he said. "After all, I'm about to offer you an opportunity even Jove himself would relish."

Although I expected the scheme to be corrupt, he piqued my interest. "I'm listening."

Gallus placed a hand conspiratorially on my forearm. I shrugged it away. "Your new position gives you power few men possess. It is you who decides whether the City Guard scrupulously enforces all laws of Caesar, or . . . shall we say, *selectively* implements certain edicts, if you understand my meaning."

"Are you expecting me to condone criminal activity?"

"Oh no, nothing so plebeian," Gallus answered quickly. "The thought never crossed my mind. However, if the Guard provides greater protection in specific sectors of the city on certain days, particular parties could arrange rewards for the protectors."

My breast filled with anger as the wine loosened my inhibitions. Withdrawing the Guard from one part of Rome to reinforce another section would leave the exposed district wide open to Gallus's bandits, who had been in his pay since his father's death. I glanced around and saw Tigellinus quietly approaching us. At this point I didn't care if he heard what I was about to say to Gallus.

"Obviously, you forgot that Prefect Tigellinus said I was an honest man, and he is right."

Gallus sniffed. "Empty words on his part."

I clenched my fists and then relaxed them. "Perhaps they are but know this. I don't care what your scheme involves, I will have no part in it; not now, not ever!"

The senator's face grew scarlet, something that his makeup couldn't hide. Apparently, he was about to answer me when he saw Tigellinus. He froze.

Tigellinus brought his full attention upon us. "What is this all about?"

Ignoring the prefect, Gallus turned to me. "I'm not one to be trifled with. You will regret this, Marcellus Reburrus."

I grabbed for a sword at my waist that was not there, but Gallus seemed to get the idea. "I am not easily intimidated."

"I didn't hear everything, Senator Gallus," Tigellinus said, "but I heard enough."

"He's mistaken, I swear," Gallus replied, giving me a black look.

The Praetorian prefect viewed Gallus with contempt. "It's not Tribune Marcellus Reburrus who has made the mistake. If anyone regrets this day, it will be you, Anicius Gallus, for trying to bribe this one."

"I made no such offer. Besides, he is nothing." Gallus gestured with a hand in Tigellinus's direction.

I stepped back a few paces, as Tigellinus admonished Gallus. "It was obvious to me. This man has the backing of Sabinus's money and power and the emperor's approval. More importantly, he has principles, something you lack. He can't be bought. I suggest if you can't buy him, you should discreetly kill him."

"Don't tempt me," Gallus said. A sneer crossed his mouth.

"Then I suspect you shall suffer the worst end of it." Across the room, Nero laughed heartily at some unrelated amusement. The conversation stopped as Gallus glanced at the emperor and then Tigellinus.

"You're not the source of Nero's diversions," Tigellinus said. "Another poor soul has the privilege."

Gallus crinkled his mascaraed eyelashes. He raised his wrinkled hands to the candlelight above, spreading his fingers. He tilted his head back and examined his smooth, polished fingernails. "Why, my dear friend, I don't have the slightest idea what you are talking about."

He and Tigellinus walked away, and a small knot of people gathered to ask me what had happened. I shrugged it off as a misunderstanding and returned to my couch.

Unfortunately, Gallus found another more insidious way to take his revenge.

CHAPTER 19

We lost our baby three weeks after returning to Rome. The daughter we both wanted was lost forever. It happened on a muggy morning, the first week in August. The baby was not due for another two months, and Eleyne hated being confined to the house as custom dictated. Four days following our arrival in the city she went to the home of a Christian elder and offered to visit the homes of the sick and dying. "I know little about the healing arts," she told me after she had returned from the call on the leader, "but I can pray for them. That seems to help, even if only a little bit."

During the years we had lived in Hispania, Eleyne went among our household slaves and local villagers near the latifundia to nurse and pray for them. She told the people about her Christian God and Christus. Whether she converted any of them to her faith, I couldn't say. But I know they appreciated her good work. As I traveled about our lands, people inquired about her, and asked me to convey their regards.

That fateful morning before I left for my office at the Praetorian Barracks, Eleyne received an urgent message concerning one of her friends in the Subura. Agnes, the fuller's wife, had gone into labor, and her life was in danger. The baby was breeched, and if the midwife could not turn its head towards the birth canal, both mother and child would die.

"She needs me," Eleyne said. "I'm more valuable there than I am with boring household routines."

"But what about your condition?" I protested. "Every time you go out, I'm concerned that something will happen to you."

She crinkled her black eyebrows together. "I'm perfectly capable of taking care of myself. This isn't my first child."

"How could I forget?" I said, grinning. "You didn't get pregnant by yourself."

She playfully slapped my face. "Then you know I must go to Agnes. It's strange, but when I help others, I feel better, too. At least I can be near and pray for her."

As household patriarch, I could have commanded her to stay home, but Eleyne was headstrong enough to disobey me. Despite the trappings of Roman clothing, jewelry, and education, she was a Celt at heart. Like other Celtic women, no man ruled her unless she gave consent, and the situation was to her advantage. An intelligent and sensible woman, Eleyne would not be refused, and the household would be happier if I gave permission.

"All right," I said, "maybe the midwife will have turned the baby by the time you arrive."

"I hope so."

"Be careful," I added.

"You needn't worry," she answered. Smiling, she touched my forearm. "I'm taking along my own midwife just in case, and Chulainn, with an escort of slaves. After all, I have our baby to consider."

"Why is the woman necessary?"

"It's just a precaution. I don't know anything about Agnes's midwife, but some of them are so inept they couldn't deliver a litter of kittens. If she's knowledgeable, they can exchange secrets."

"Is that the only reason?"

Eleyne sighed. "I want her with me in case I get sick, she'll know what to do. But nothing will happen, I'm riding in the sedan. The sun's too bright, and the streets are too crowded and dirty to walk."

I wished her well and good health and luck to her friend, Agnes, and left for the Praetorian Camp.

Later that morning I traveled to the barracks of my old unit, the Seventh Cohort, in the Trans-Tiberina section. Unfortunately, I was all too familiar with this section of Rome.

Crowded with dilapidated, wooden tenements, a week rarely passed without a couple of apartments in the area burning to the ground. Only the gods knew why a major fire hadn't destroyed the district and other parts of the city. During the day, heavy foot traffic congested the area as the people shopped and conducted business in the hundreds of tiny shops and open stalls lining the narrow, twisting lanes. Ideally suited for criminal activities, the crowded conditions allowed robbers and thieves to strike and flee with near impunity.

Representing Flavius Sabinus, I met with Annaeus Serenus, the Prefect of the Watch. We reached an agreement where the City Guard cohort would use the Seventh's station dungeon instead of transporting prisoners through the teeming streets and across the river to Latumiae Prison. Although little more than a mile and half away, transport of prisoners by arresting guards required more than two hours. As a result, too many guardsmen were removed from patrol for an extended period of time. Rather than waste two hours on minor arrests, the guards tended to administer gutter-side justice—a throttling and a form of *escape.*

Detaining felons at the local *stationes* holding area increased in importance. Recently, Nero gave Sabinus jurisdiction over all criminal cases within a one-hundred-mile perimeter of Rome. Overwhelmed by the increased volume in minor cases, he delegated the responsibility for their trials to district junior magistrates where the offenses occurred. A *Trestiviri Capitales* was assigned to each Watch station where minor offenders were prosecuted. Sabinus presided over the court proceedings of only major offenses.

Five years earlier, Scrofa the beggar king, had died, and the current leader refused to cooperate with the Guard or the Watch. I missed old Scrofa's help; he cared for his people, while this slime bag did not. I had to develop my own network of informants and spies. A scummy lot by nature, they had their own foul reasons for helping the Guard. At best their information was questionable.

I left the precinct office and entered the courtyard. As a groom handed me the reins to my horse, a commotion echoed in the courtyard entrance. Under the gray stone arch, gesticulating excitedly with his hands, Chulainn argued with two sentries blocking his path with crossed javelins.

What's he doing here? Something's wrong.

"Let him pass!" I barked. "He's my slave!"

Chulainn raced down the brick-lined passage, darted between the horses of my escort. He tripped a few steps away in front of my path. Panting, he leapt to his feet. "Sir!" he exclaimed, "Lady Eleyne has been hurt in an accident!"

My first impulse was to vault my horse and rush to her aid. Somehow, I kept myself under control.

"Calm down, man," I said in an even voice, "what happened?"

"She fell from her litter," he gasped. "She screamed she was losing her baby."

For a split second I was stunned. "Did she lose it?"

He shrugged and rasped, "I don't know. We placed her back into the litter and took her home right away. I told Porus to fetch the family physician, and then I ran here to tell you about it. I'm sorry I couldn't get here sooner."

"Considering how far you had to run, it's a miracle you made it here in less than an hour." I realized he must have literally ran from the west side of the Tiber to reach the Praetorian Barracks here at the east end of the city.

There was no time to waste. "Let's go!" I grabbed the saddle pommels and flung myself onto the gray gelding's back, feet straddling the side of its girth. I gave Chulainn a hand up behind me. Wheeling the mount around, I jabbed my spurs into his sides. Bolting past the sentries, I plunged into the crowded lane, scattering pedestrians, leaving my escort far behind.

As we darted down the way, I turned and shouted at Chulainn, who was holding his arms about my waist. "Briefly, tell me when and where my wife fell—the rest of the details can wait."

"The accident happened as we walked up Vatican Hill about ten blocks from the house," he shouted back. "She was knocked off the litter by a gang of thugs fleeing from the City Guard. She fell onto her face and stomach right over a big stepping stone."

"Stepping stone?"

"Aye, the ones that cross Mercury Street just past where we turned off from the Triumphant Way. Her stomach slammed right onto the center stone of the three in the crossing."

"Good gods, if those are the ones I think they are, they're like jagged teeth! She could die!" My voice started to choke at about the same time. I veered my mount around a cluster of people by a cook shop who shouted obscenities at us. I had to find the bastards who did this to Eleyne, but my duties could wait—I had to get home. I feared she and our child might be gone before I arrived.

*　*　*

Porus's glum face, as he stood by the front door, wringing his hands, said it all. "The baby is dead, sir. I am sorry."

Much as I prayed against it, his dismal words were not surprising. "What about my wife?"

"She has lost a lot of blood."

I charged into the house, forgetting to dismiss my arriving escort. My hobnailed boots echoed down the hall as I rushed to our bedroom cubicle and barged into the dark, oppressively hot room. The only light, a bronze, three-headed horse lamp rested on a small table by Eleyne's bedside. As Eleyne slept on the goose-feather mattress, the sputtering, yellow light illuminated her gray, perspiring face, one side covered by abrasions. Miraculously, her delicate nose appeared untouched. A bloodstained linen blanket covered her from hips down. The midwife slowly messaged her abdomen below the gown, which was pulled above the waist. She and Imogen, who was assisting her, wiped Eleyne's face with a wet sponge. The women looked in my direction and wearily bowed.

The family physician, Soranus, a short Alexandrian Greek dressed in a bright-green, silk mantle, left her side and blocked me.

"I want to see my wife," I demanded. "Get out of my way!"

"Commander Reburrus," he said, "she is barely alive . . . you mustn't disturb her."

"Get out my way!"

Unflinching, he stood his ground. "With all due respect, my Lord, do you want her to die?"

I could have swatted his needle-thin body away like a fly, but his last question stopped me like a fortress wall. I refused to endanger Eleyne's life. "But I must see my wife," I pleaded weakly.

"In due time," he offered in a friendlier voice. "She is very weak and requires complete rest. You must wait until she awakes."

"But she may never awaken," I said, afraid and shaken.

"That is possible, I regret to say," he answered. "However, we must not take any chances—the fall greatly injured her."

I told the physician that Chulainn had described the fall including Eleyne's fear of losing the baby. "Did she lose the child because of the fall?"

Soranus pursed his thin lips and nodded. "Yes, Commander, she fell face first. Her abdomen smashed onto a large stepping stone." He gestured toward Eleyne's slumbering form. "The fall's impact induced birth, and the baby was too small and badly injured to survive. Its skull was fractured. Also, your wife's right arm was broken above the elbow." Tightly wrapped with a dressing, Eleyne's arm was splinted to long boards from elbow to wrist. "If there is any consolation," Soranus added, "the break was clean and should heal nicely—with rest."

I clinched my sweaty fists and shook my head. "Will she recover?"

"I don't know—it's too soon." He glanced from me to Eleyne. "Her uterus was injured, and she lost much blood. Fortunately, the hemorrhaging stopped before you

190

arrived—thank the gods. However, she must be confined to bed for many weeks if it is to heal."

"I pray to the gods that she will recover."

He placed his thumb and forefinger to his receding chin for a moment, silently pondering his reply. "If she stays free from infection and further bleeding, she has a good chance. My greatest concern is her rising fever."

"Fever?" A thousand questions and worries raced through my mind.

The little physician crinkled his nose. "Had one of your Roman quacks attended, your wife's chances for recovery would be slight, but with me the odds are far greater. Maybe one in three."

I despised his smugness and wanted to strike him. "Why are her chances better with you?"

"It is something as a soldier you can appreciate—cleanliness."

"Army hospitals are clean," I said, puzzled.

"If you have noticed," Soranus answered slowly, "my hair is short, and I do not wear a beard." He pointed to his pale face. "I keep my fingernails short and clean, and I wash my hands with soap—something you Romans should copy from the Celts." He made a gesture rubbing his hands together. "When I wash my hands in hot water and boil my instruments, infection seems reduced. Boiling water seems to purify whatever evil spirits inhabit the hands and tools."

"Unusual methods. Is that what they teach now in Egypt?"

"I was not taught hygiene in Alexandria," he answered in a voice dripping with contempt. "I learned from an Indian physician, whom I encountered when I was surgeon to a wealthy merchant in Parthia. They have practiced the technique for generations, as taught by their master, Susrata. It works."

I poked his scrawny chest none too gently. "Then pray you succeed with my wife, because you'll be substantially rewarded."

Startled and wide-eyed, Soranus quickly regained his composure and stepped back. "Thank you, my Lord," he replied with a bow, showing a true interest for the first time.

"If you fail . . . ," I gave him an evil look, "the reward won't be in gold."

"I shall do everything in my power to ensure your wife's recovery—reward or not. I am at your beck and call."

"Of course, you will stay until she awakens?" I glared.

He met my eyes, seemed to measure me, and, perhaps pondering his fee, nodded. "Naturally, I am as concerned about her as you, Lord Reburrus."

I glanced to Eleyne's bloodstained sheets and back to the physician. "Didn't you say you could reduce infection?"

"Of course."

"In the army, soldiers aren't kept in bloody blankets. Remove these at once." Soranus nodded to the silent Imogen.

After the bed linen had been changed, Soranus stepped aside with a slight bow and motioned the women away. I moved to her bedside. Kneeling, I took her hand and studied her ashen face, viewing the abrasions on her face and hands. I touched her forehead, which burned with fever, and listened to her shallow but steady breathing. She moaned at my touch but did not open her eyes. Feeling helpless to do little more than watch, I prayed to all the gods, including her Christian God, that she would live. It was ironic that Eleyne had gone to pray for the safe delivery of another woman's child, but could not prevent the death of her own. Now she was fighting for her life.

As I got to my feet, I thought of something and turned to Soranus. "Couldn't my wife's fever be reduced by packing her in snow? I've heard stories that it can."

He cocked his head to one side as if pondering the question and nodded. "Yes, Lord, combined with sponging, it does lower in some instances. However, the expense and distance to the mountains—"

"Damn the expense! If there's a chance it'll break her fever, then I'll get it!"

Soranus gestured in the direction of the room's entrance and back. "The Apennines are far away. The nearest snow is at least eighty miles, if it hasn't melted. And the heat—"

"I can get there and back in one day, Commander."

Startled, I turned and discovered a perspiring Casperius Niger standing in the doorway. "What are you doing here, Casperius?"

"I heard about your wife, sir. Came to see if there were any duties I could assume while you stayed with her."

"You already have, Casperius," I said. "Take my horses and chariot and ride to Mount Corno. Use army courier post horses as relief. Chulainn will follow in a wagon."

"Tell your slave to meet me outside of Amiternum, on the Caelian Road," Casperius said. "By then I'll have the first sacks of snow." He saluted and left for the stables without further comment.

Casperius would use the teakwood chariot, a gift from Sabinus presented to me upon returning to Rome. Paintings, depicting the army battling devil-like Germans, embossed the car's body. The oakwood axle and wheel spokes sparkled with shining, silver plate. Bronze and gold-trimmed dolphins with twinkling amethyst eyes, decorated the yoke and pole. A gift worthy of a general returning in triumph. I now dispatched it on a journey far more important than any fleeting victory.

Both of us were aware of the conditions entailing this long and hazardous journey. After traveling part way on paved roads, the remaining trip consisted of a jolting kidney-breaking ride over a haphazard series of narrow, rutted wagon paths and goat trails.

After Casperius Niger departed, I turned about and spotted the crumpled blanket that contained the tiny, blood-encrusted corpse of our baby.

"I'll get rid of it," the physician said, noting my glance.

"No!" I picked up and handed the small bundle to Imogen, who returned from disposing the sheets. "See that she is cremated at once."

She nodded and took the child.

"Imogen!" I called. She paused. "Have her ashes returned to me." My voice choked off further words. Again, she nodded and carried our daughter away.

I sent for Porus and gave orders for a servant to stay with Eleyne day and night. "If there is the slightest change in her condition," I said, "summon me and Soranus at once."

A few minutes later, I dispatched a messenger to Sabinus, informing him of Eleyne's accident. Since arriving at Budar's home, I had placed my servants into positions of authority. As he had been in my previous homes in Rome and Hispania, Porus became chief steward, to the consternation of Budar's staff. But my uncle had allowed it. Now, at a time when I knew he would have wanted to be here, he was on business, in the city of Mediolanum Northern Italia.

Leaving the physician with Eleyne, I trudged into the triclinium and called for wine and two cups. Dutifully, Chulainn, who had waited outside the cubilicum, followed. Porus removed my hot armor before I took a seat. I found his devotion to our family . . . touching. Shoulders slumping, as if distraught by the loss of Eleyne's child, my loyal servant, now in his early fifties, shuffled from the room. Wearily, I dropped onto the cushioned couch.

"Sit down," I told Chulainn, who stood silently by with his hands clasped behind his back.

We sat in silence. Chulainn appeared uncomfortable sitting in the presence of his master. I was too consumed with my thoughts to worry about Chulainn's feelings. In concern for Eleyne, I had not fully obtained all the details surrounding her accident.

When the slave brought a vintage Tusculum, I took a long drought, letting the white liquid burn its way down my throat.

"Give Chulainn the second cup," I ordered.

Both he and Chulainn raised eyebrows and exchanged glances. Customarily, slaves didn't drink or eat with their masters. After hesitating the span of a couple heartbeats, the servant gave Chulainn the cup and departed.

"It's all right, Chulainn," I said. "Pour yourself a cup—you deserve it as much as I."

"That's kind of you, sir." He took the pitcher and poured the wine into the silver cup, diluting it with a small amount of water. Sipping at first, he then tossed his head back and drained the vessel.

"Chulainn, tell me again what happened this morning. Hold nothing back." I gestured for him to refill his cup.

He did, and gripping it between his hands, leaned forward. "As I said before, it was an accident."

Returning from the Subura, Eleyne and her entourage of slaves and German litter bearers had left the city beneath the Arcadian Arch. They crossed the River Tiber over the Neronian Bridge, traveled a short distance along the Triumphant Way, and turned onto Mercury Street, which trailed up Vatican Hill to our home, adjacent to the public Gardens of Nero.

"The street was crowded as usual," Chulainn said. "The other slaves and I kept forcing a passageway through the mob. I heard a cry from somewhere behind us shouting, 'Assassins! Stop them!'

"I turned and spotted four men running. Their faces were partially covered by mantles and hoods and were shoving everyone out of their way. They knocked down an old woman hobbling on a crutch and a boy carrying live chickens by the legs, scattering them. Close behind a squad of ten guardsmen chased them, but the stinking crowd hampered their way."

Chulainn hesitated, his hands started to shake.

"Easy man, go on," I said softly.

He nodded, wrapped one hand around the other, and held it firmly in his lap.

"I knew I had to get our people out of the bandit's path—they were heading our way. I ordered the litter bearers, carrying the mistress, to head for an open space next to a tenement wall. It was across from an alley way."

"Is that where the jagged stepping stones cross the street?"

"Yes, sir, the same."

Heat rushed to my face, shoulder and arm muscles tightened, knowing what came next. I had to keep myself under control. I could not show my true feelings in front of a slave. "Go on."

"We passed the mouth of the alley, but the assassins saw the entry about the same time. They headed in our direction." He huffed. "They didn't give a damn that we were in the way. The bastards bounded right into the litter carriers."

Chulainn unclenched his hands and slapped them on his thighs.

"Big as they were, the litter bearers were spun off balance by the impact. They stumbled and lost control. Mistress Eleyne screamed and was thrown from the cushions onto the filthy rocks."

Chulainn paused, his hands shaking as he attempted to hold them together again.

Even though I felt my heart pounding like a hammer, I managed to keep myself under control—it was important for Chulainn to finish his story. "It's all right, what happened wasn't your fault."

Another minute passed before Chulainn brought his hands under control. "The mistress used her right arm to break the fall, but she slammed onto the high stones, her stomach took the full force." He paused and exhaled. "Her face struck the edge of the rock ahead of her and legs grazed the rear one. The dirty bastards stumbled over her body and disappeared down the alley. No one recognized the mistress as your wife, sir. Except for the people of our retinue, there was no attempt to aid her."

"Typical of the damned mob! Go on."

He swallowed and nodded. "At first the mistress didn't say a word—I thought she was dead. Then, thank the gods, she groaned, and I ordered her placed in the litter and rushed home. As the bearers lifted her into the litter, she screamed her water had broken, and soon she would give birth. That was later confirmed by the midwife who was with us."

"I remember Eleyne telling me she would be with her. Go on."

"As I ran with the litter bearers carrying the mistress, she complained of bleeding. I had to get her home right away and tell Porus to send for Soranus." He shrugged. "You know the rest, sir."

I curled my toes attempting to remain calm, which grew more difficult with each passing minute. Incensed by the bearers' clumsiness, I wanted to execute all of them. But realized the absurdity of my thoughts. The collision with the fleeing assassins had been enough to strike down even the strongest slaves.

Chulainn's face tightened. "Sir, the litter bearers are terrified."

"Why?"

He gulped. "They fear you'll blame them for the mistress's injuries, and they'll be punished."

"Tell them not to worry—they're faithful slaves." I knew I was wrong, but in my anger, I found their clumsiness unforgivable. Although I gave no order, Porus, sensing my displeasure, sold the Germans the next day to a slave buyer from the marble quarry at Carrara.

"What about the woman, Agnes?" I asked as an afterthought. "Did she lose her baby?"

"No, sir, the girl was safely delivered."

I flinched.

When Chulainn finished his story, I got up and went to the library. I returned minutes later and gave him a pass permitting him to travel outside of Rome and a pouch filled with enough gold for a dozen wagons of snow. I dispatched Chulainn with instructions for the snow merchant to send a wagon load every day until notified to stop shipping.

At this point I stood. I wanted to scream, but I wasn't about to let the slaves hear me. Instead, I threw my cup against the wall, splattering the leavings of wine. Its metallic sound echoed as it bounced and rolled back to me across the mosaic floor. I kicked, and it spun off toward the entrance to the dining area. I picked up Chulainn's from the table and hurled it to the wall with the same effect.

A slave rushed in, halted, stood wide-eyed, before bowing his head and silently waiting for instructions.

"Clean up the mess, and then tell Porus to come here," I said.

Porus arrived, and I ordered him to send a messenger to the Praetorian Barracks, billet of the City Guard, to fetch the cohort commander of the troops involved in the chase.

Once the messenger had departed, I asked Porus where my sons were.

"They are with Diogenes in the Gardens of Nero."

"At least they weren't here when Eleyne was brought home."

"Actually, they were here," Porus answered.

"Where?"

"In the usual place, the household gardens where Diogenes was teaching them their lessons," Porus said. "But as soon as the mistress was brought home and I saw her condition, I sent for the physician. Then I went out and told Diogenes to take your sons to the park."

There was a door in the back part of the wall that surrounded our house and private garden, adjacent to the public park. "A wise move, I don't want young Marcellus and Sabinus to see their mother until after I have explained to them how she was injured."

Porus nodded. "That was my guess. I believe young Marcellus and Sabinus did not have time to notice anything before Diogenes took them away. I told their tutor they were not to return until you sent someone for them."

"Do you know where they might be? That's a big park."

"Most likely by the pond. I suggested to Diogenes to continue their lessons there."

"Send someone now to bring them back," I said.

"I will personally see to it."

* * *

The boys returned and found me near the opened roof area by the shallow pool that caught rain water, the impluvium. The tutor, Diogenes, stood at the entrance, and I waved him away. Marcellus, the eldest, and Sabinus, wearing dusty tunics, ran over to where I sat on a cushioned bench. "Da!" they cried.

I raised my arms wide. "Here, give me a hug." They bent over and wrapped their arms and hands around my legs. I motioned to them to sit beside me, Marcellus to the right, Sabinus to the left.

Sabinus's pale, long face, smudged with dirt, leaned back, his dark-brown eyes looking into mine. He smiled.

"Diogenes took us to the park, Da, we had fun. He said we could play after we finished our lessons. We did."

I grinned. "I can see that. Good for you."

Marcellus shook his short, black, curly hair. "Why did he take us to the park, Da?"

"Didn't you like it?" I asked.

He looked about and seemed to hesitate, his piercing-blue eyes studying mine. "I did, but most of the time we don't go to the park until later. I heard a noise from the house. Then Porus came out to us."

"Is that so unusual?" I said.

"He whispered to Diogenes and then told us to go to there. Is something wrong?"

I glanced to Sabinus then Marcellus. "You are very smart for your age, Son. Yes, Mum is very sick."

Marcellus shook his head. "Mum sick? No!"

Sabinus's eyes widened. "What kind of sick?"

I took a couple of deep breaths. How do you explain this to a couple of young boys? "Remember I told you she was going to have baby?"

"Yes," they said in unison.

"She's been badly hurt in an accident. The baby was born too soon—it died." I didn't believe it necessary to tell them bandits had been involved. Their mother was injured and that's all they needed to know.

The boys released their hands from my legs. They stood back, mouths opened.

"Will Mum live?" Marcellus asked.

Sabinus grabbed my leg again, holding tight with his little hands. "Will she get better?"

"Soranus is doing his best to keep Mum alive," I said. "But it will be awhile before she is well."

Although the boys were familiar with death, witnessing the passing of three slaves at the latifundia to accidents and disease, this was personal. They had lost a sister and could still lose their mother.

Sabinus sniffled. "I don't want Mum to die." I rustled my hand through his straight, auburn hair again.

"Me neither," Marcellus said. He, too, snuggled against me. "Can we see her?"

"Not now. She's asleep."

"When can we see her?" Marcellus asked.

"Later, when she's better." I smiled. "Enough of this for now. It's time for you to have your baths. We can talk about this at dinner. Perhaps we will have some good news about Mum then. In the meantime, I have business to take care of." I called for Porus, and he escorted the boys to our private bath.

* * *

Cornelius Martialis, Commander of the Twelfth, offered his condolences on his arrival at my house. I motioned to a wooden couch, cushioned with a leather backing of zebra hides. Young for a junior commander, Cornelius was bright, promising, and, above all, a trustworthy officer, according to Casperius Niger.

"It's about the assassins, isn't it, sir?" He rested a shiny, brass helmet on his right thigh and leaned forward.

"Aye. Did an assassination actually occur?"

"No, sir, the would-be assassins failed. But I'm certain they're the same ones who injured your wife." He hesitated. "And killed your unborn child—their descriptions fit in both incidences.

My muscles tightened. "Who are they? Who was their intended victim?"

Martialis squinted his pale-brown eyes. "We're not sure who the suspects are, but they appeared to be Roman citizens, probably from the mob."

"Describe them."

He shrugged, glanced away, and thought while stroking his broad, clean-shaven face with long, thick fingers. "They had short hair and wore no beards. So they probably aren't foreigners."

"Are you sure? Weren't they wearing hoods?"

"The hoods slipped back from the heads of a couple of them as they ran from my men."

"Any additional description?"

"One was a three-letter man."

"A convicted thief turned assassin."

"Yes, sir, the branding scars on his forehead were fresh. The letters FVR for being habitual thieves were still pink and barely healed."

"I'll ask Lord Sabinus to have his court clerks check the records during the last four months for all criminals branded as thieves. Any further information, Cornelius Martialis?"

"Two wore white, ragged tunics, maybe Italians— Samnites from the south like me," he answered. "Unfortunately, they all got away." Cornelius rubbed a big hand over his olive face, and squared jaw.

"As to the intended victim," the tribune continued, slowly turning his helmet on his thigh, "he's Apollonius the cement merchant, from Neopolis."

This sounded like Gallus's work. He had many building interests. I knew he was deeply involved in the Imperial intrigue that raged within the palace and city. Apollonius may have been the target of one of many political factions. If Gallus had any part in this, it was doubtful he would have employed such incompetent assassins. However, he couldn't be ruled out. "Apollonius holds the government cement monopoly," I said.

"Excuse me, sir," Cornelius said, "I don't understand."

"Like most Neapolitans, Apollonius is Greek. He's hated by the local merchants because he is not Roman and has the nerve to hold a government franchise."

"Makes sense. Imperial contracts are worth a fortune."

"Indeed. He bribed enough government officials for the privilege. In the process, my wife was nearly killed and our daughter born dead."

My mind turned to another matter of importance. "I'm sending a dispatch with you to the commander of the Ninth Cohort. Effective immediately, the first two centuries of his cohort are reassigned to patrolling the Trans-Tiberina under your command."

"Yes, sir."

"My reports indicate even the poorest shop owners are being extorted in that district. If nothing else, perhaps our increased presence will prompt people to step forward and give information leading to arrests."

"Don't bet any sesterces on it, sir. They don't tell us anything. They fear and hate the Guard more than the parasites and thieves that suck their blood."

"Perhaps we can at least create an illusion that the streets are safer."

"If they see enough of our men patrolling, it might work, during daylight. But forget the nights—they'll never be safe, even if we could double the Guard and the Watch."

I dismissed Cornelius and returned to Eleyne's room. I stood silently and prayed to the Horse Goddess, Epona, to ride swiftly with Casperius Niger on his journey to the Apennines for the precious snow for her recovery.

Nothing else mattered.

CHAPTER 20

Eleyne's fever raged as day drifted into night. No longer perspiring, her skin burned to the touch. Imogen and the midwife attempted to cool her body with wet sponges and compresses to little success.

Soranus, the physician, stayed with her throughout the day and night. Despite his ministrations, Eleyne became delirious.

"I don't know how much longer she can last," Soranus said. "Even if she survives, the prolonged fever may damage her brain."

That possibility tore at my soul. *She could revert to child-like behavior or worse.* I stayed at home while Eleyne hovered near death and prayed to the gods for a recovery free of madness. Sabinus sent a message of encouragement and hope.

Periodically, I checked with Soranus. Each time I entered Eleyne's room, the sight of her emaciated face made my heart pound so loud I thought those around me could hear it. Pitifully, Imogen glanced at me through her dark-ringed eyes as she dabbed Eleyne's cracking lips with a wet sponge.

Knowing I was in the way, I left feeling helpless—lost.

More than twenty-four hours had elapsed since Casperius Niger and Chulainn had left Rome. *Were they encountering unforeseen problems? Had all the snow melted?*

The Italian peninsula was experiencing an unusually hot summer, and there had been heavy flooding from melting mountain snow packs. If snow on Mount Corno, one of the highest peaks in the Apennines, was exhausted, Casperius would head to the Julian Alps in Northern Italy. The trip required at least five days—without rest—too long for Eleyne's survival and would probably be melted.

I had to remain optimistic he would arrive in time, and ordered the portable bathtub, stored in a closet next to the slaves' quarters, for packing Eleyne with snow when it arrived.

* * *

Late in the afternoon of the second day, clattering hooves and rumbling wheels halted in front of the house. Seconds later the doors burst open and Casperius Niger, haggard and sweating, dragged in to the atrium a big, leaking goatskin sack.

"I've got it, sir!" he puffed, "I made the best time I could, but the detours slowed me down." He dropped the bag. The protective hay and slushy ice spilled from the sack on to the mosaic-tiled floor.

"Don't worry, my friend," I answered. "I'm grateful you returned so quickly." *Thank the gods!* A sense of relief ran through my body. I didn't realize how tense I had been.

I motioned two slaves to take the heavy bag from Casperius. "Carry it to the mistress's room at once. Then get the portable bathtub. Imogen and the midwife will know what to do."

"There's more in the chariot," Casperius said, "but it's mostly slush."

"No matter. It's a start, and it's cold. Porus!" I shouted.

He scurried in from an adjoining room. "Yes, sir?" He saw Casperius handing the bag to the slaves. "You brought the snow, sir! Thank God!"

"Save your praises for later, Porus," I said. "Send a slave for Soranus. Have a couple others retrieve the rest of the bags from Tribune Niger's chariot. Her women will place her in ice." I prayed that the relief hadn't arrived too late.

"Right away, sir." Porus hurried from the atrium shouting orders to passing slaves.

Casperius shook the gray-red dust from his tunic and cuirass as he and I hiked to the atrium. Motioning for him to take a seat on the couch, I called a slave to bring wine and food.

"You don't realize how much this means to me," I said. "I'm in your debt."

Casperius wiped sweat from his face onto his sleeve. He reeked as if he had ridden through every sewer and mud-hole on his journey. "My privilege, sir. You owe me nothing. I would've returned sooner if it weren't for the quarantine."

"What quarantine?"

"The pox. So far, it's confined to one town, a village outside Reate on the Salarian Road. Must be sixty miles northeast of here."

"You think it will spread?"

He snorted. "I doubt it. They're not letting anyone in or out, and I gave the pesthole a wide detour. Crossed two swollen rivers and a swamp to get around."

I said a silent prayer in thanks and asked him if Chulainn had gotten through. Niger said my slave had arrived a couple hours later after driving like the furies. They found snow from Mount Corno had been kept in a storage cave, near the mountain's foot where it was cooler and lasted longer. Casperius had to deal with a fat merchant who held the Imperial monopoly on all snow from the mountain.

A slave arrived with a glass pitcher of wine and two silver goblets and placed them on the small table between Casperius and me. We remained silent until the servant poured our drinks and departed. We raised and tapped each other's cups and took deep swallows.

Casperius exhaled, looked at his drink, and nodded, appearing to be at ease, the muscles in his face relaxed.

I held my cup on my thigh and asked, "Any problems getting the amount we needed?"

He took another gulp and answered with a telling grin. "There would have been, but I convinced him to see things my way."

"What happened?"

"I didn't have any money, so I told the nose-picking bugger that your slave was en route with the cash. He wouldn't believe me—figured I was playing the Greek. I told him I'm not a thief."

"What changed his mind?" As if I didn't know.

Casperius placed his right hand on the hilt of his short sword. "I pulled out old Scorpio and pointed to the crest of eagles on my helmet and said, 'In the name of Rome.' When he wouldn't budge, I threatened to cut out his fat, stinking heart. Somehow, that carried more weight than the eagles," he said, grinning. "Then I repeated Chulainn would be along anytime. He *believed* me that time.

"But then he demanded a stamped receipt with the eagles," Casperius continued. "The hilt knob of my sword has an eagle on it. So I slammed it into his forehead and held up a brass mirror for him to see the imprint. I got the snow."

I raised my cup in salute. "It served the fat bastard right." I looked past Casperius toward the front of the house. "How far behind is Chulainn?"

"I'd say about an hour. I whipped those nags ahead until they almost flew like Pegasus."

"I appreciate your efforts, Casperius." I leaned over and clasped his shoulders.

Minutes later, Soranus arrived. Casperius stayed behind, as I stood and followed the physician to Eleyne's room. By the time we entered, Imogen, the midwife, and female slaves had already placed my wife in the round, flat-bottomed vessel. Still delirious, Eleyne was packed by the women in the melting, straw-riddled, gray-white snow and slush, matching the ashen color of her naked body. Pleased by the servant's work, Soranus made a few minor adjustments.

"I hope the snow hasn't arrived too late," the physician said. "She is still burning with fever. All we can do is wait and hope the snow will bring it down."

Although grateful for Casperius's efforts, I was not good company as we dined together that evening. My thoughts continued to return to Eleyne's condition—I could not keep her out of my mind. Her fever had dropped within an hour of being placed in the ice, but she remained in a state of delirium. Eleyne once said her God aids the faithful in times of crisis. For the first time, I prayed He would help her now.

I could not sleep and stuck my head into Eleyne's bedchamber five or six times during the first night after the snow's arrival.

Gaunt-faced Soranus, who had stayed by her side since her removal from the tub, silently shook his balding head. "She's still delirious. Fortunately, the fever is beginning to subside. If it continues at this rate, it should be gone by morning."

As dawn drove away the night's shadows, fatigue caught me like a deer in a snare. Still wearing a dinner tunic, I passed out on my bed.

My eyes snapped open to a gentle tug on my shoulder. "Sir," Porus said, "the mistress is awake."

I bolted upright and set my leaden feet on the tile floor, still doubting my ears. "Are you positive?"

"Oh yes, approximately an hour ago. Soranus wanted to be certain she was out of danger before waking you."

I glanced to the sun-lit doorway. "What time is it?"

"About noon."

"Good gods, so late!"

I rushed from my room and an instant later entered Eleyne's dimly lighted cubicle.

Eleyne's unbraided hair hung to one side of her exhausted face. Clothed in a pale, yellow gown, she rested on clean, linen blankets. Half open, her eyes stared blankly into the darkness of the invisible ceiling. The smell of vinegar used in cleaning up after the sick and wounded lingered in the room.

Soranus approached. "Lord, I have good news. The worst is past, though she will need a lot of rest."

"Can I be with her?"

"Of course, but she is very weak." He glanced to Eleyne and lowered his voice. "There is something you should know."

His last remark sounded ominous. "What's wrong?"

After peering over his shoulder, he lowered his voice. "I do not know how much the fever has affected her mind. When I attempt to question her, she turns away from me. I know your wife hears but she is ignoring me. I fear she suffers from melancholia."

"So? She was gloomy after giving birth to our sons. I expected some grief now after losing our first daughter."

"No, it is worse than the usual bereavement and after-birth melancholy. She will recover physically, but her mind is another matter."

I poked his bony chest shoving him away from me. "You better be wrong, physician, very wrong."

Quietly, I approached Eleyne, and she turned her head. She blinked her eyes five or six times. A quivering smile crept across her small mouth. "Marcellus, darling?" Slowly, she extended a hand. I grasped it. The cool warmth of life swelled in the little palm and fingers.

"I'm here," I answered. Bending down, I gently kissed her chapped lips. Eleyne, her body shaking, tried wrapping an arm around my neck, but groaned and limply dropped it to her side.

"Don't exert yourself," I gently admonished. Grabbing a stool, I sat next to the bed. "You've been very ill." Nearby hovered the hefty, middle-aged midwife, apparently ready to drive me away at the first sign of distress.

"Is it true?" Eleyne asked. "The baby is dead?"

I exhaled. "I'm afraid so."

Her eyes clouded. "I know I should thank God for saving my life, but . . ." Tears streamed down her cheeks. Trembling, she turned her head away. "I wish He had taken my life instead." She wept.

Reaching over, I stroked her long hair, attempting to comfort her.

"I wanted her so much," Eleyne sobbed. "Now, I just want to die—I have failed you."

"You haven't," I said softly. Her melancholia had never been this severe. "Your God wouldn't want you to think such things, would He?"

"I don't care what He thinks!" she rasped. "I want to die."

My chest tightened—I couldn't believe my ears. I took Eleyne into my arms and gently rocked her. She turned her head, and I looked into her tear-reddened eyes. "Darling, no one wants you to die. Neither I, nor our sons, or the household. Everyone loves and needs you."

"I don't care." She sniffled and pulled away from me. The midwife approached and handed Eleyne a linen cloth to wipe her tear-stained face and blow her nose.

This was not the Eleyne I knew—resourceful and self-reliant. I did not understand. *Why does she want to die? The baby's death is not her fault.* In her state of mind, I doubted if she would listen to reason, but I had to try snapping her out of her spell.

"That's enough," I said in a firm but soft voice. "I love you and so do our sons. This wasn't your doing, it was an accident, caused by fleeing criminals."

She threw the cloth, barely missing me. A fierce animal look flamed in her dark-blue eyes. "Go away! Leave me alone!"

I stared in disbelief.

"Will you leave me alone?" Eleyne rasped.

The midwife wrung her beefy hands, and then said as *politely* as a drill-centurion, to get out.

Given Eleyne's state of mind and condition, I agreed. "All right, maybe you'll feel better, later." I got up and headed for the door.

"No, I won't! I hate you. I hate . . ." She trailed off into a pillow of muffled sobs.

Struggling in an attempt to conceal my alarm and frustration, I glanced her way once again and left the room. Later, not knowing what else to do, I drank myself into a stupor.

* * *

The following week, as I hopelessly waited for Eleyne to recover from her depression, the family was struck with another tragedy. A messenger came to the house with news that Uncle Budar had died of a stroke. He was returning to Rome, from his business trip, and spending the night in the town of Arretium at a friend's home when he was found dead the next morning.

My heart had leaped into my throat upon learning the news, and I wanted to weep, but could not. There was too much to be done. Immediately, I sent Porus with a detail of slaves to fetch the body. Arretium was more than one hundred miles to the north. It would take them two to three days to reach the town and another to return with the body. In the meantime, I arranged for one of Rome's more reputable undertakers to take care of Uncle Budar's remains. In an earlier conversation, Uncle Budar told me he did not want a formal funeral, he had little use for the gods. He wanted to be cremated, and his ashes sent to Hispania to be buried alongside my mother and father.

Only when the urn containing his ashes was placed aboard a ship with a captain I trusted, and upon returning home, did I lock myself away and weep. The old man had been in his seventies when he crossed the River Styx. He always said, I was the son he never had. Although he left his house and other properties to me, I always considered the home on Vatican Hill to be his, and that his shade still roamed the place.

* * *

Three months later, on a cool November afternoon, my duties finished for the day, I returned home from the Praetorian Barracks. As always, I planned to look in on Eleyne. Although I had nearly given up all hope that her condition would improve, I still wanted to see her. During the last few months, Eleyne had barely asserted her will to live. Bedridden because of injuries suffered during the accident and birth, she had lost weight. However, Soranus's main concern was the recovery of her sanity. He said the legendary Hippocrates, whom the Greeks call the Father of Medicine, believed one's mental state greatly affected the body. After witnessing Eleyne's deteriorating condition, I agreed. Wasting away, she seldom ate, caring little about her appearance. She refused to take a bath or allow the maids to sponge her. When the smell became too foul, I ordered the servants to bathe her—by force.

Not only had the baby's loss affected her mind, but she had never forgiven me for returning to Rome. The loss of the child aggravated her festering hatred for the city.

Soranus attempted everything in the art of medicine to heal Eleyne. Keeping my wife alive was in itself a miracle. But he did not possess the skills to overcome her low spirits. I spent a greater part of my evenings with our sons in her room. In their childlike ways, they attempted to cheer their mother—to no avail. She seldom said anything to them.

Nothing to me.

"Master!" Porus exclaimed, upon greeting me at the door, "The mistress is well! A miracle."

"Impossible," I answered. "She was so sullen this morning."

I hurried to her room. She sat in bed, propped by a number of pillows. Imogen and another maid brushed her hair and adjusted her bedclothes. Although pale and visibly tired, a certain glow radiated from around her face. A smile formed at the edges of her full lips. I ordered the women to leave. Sitting down beside Eleyne, I reached over and took her into my arms. She felt as light as goose feathers. Careful not to squeeze too hard, I gave her a tender hug.

"I've seen him, darling," she said, drawing her head back. "He's in Rome."

CHAPTER 21

"Who?" I asked, puzzled by her seemingly inappropriate remarks. "Does it involve your recovery?"

"*Everything*," she answered. "I've seen Paul, the chief apostle of my faith."

I knew about the Jew from the city of Tarsus, in the eastern province of Cilicia. The first time he came to Rome, he was tried before Caesar on a vague charge brought against him by Jewish leaders in Judea. He had outraged them by claiming his right as a Roman citizen to be heard in Rome instead of their gods forsaken land. Subsequently, the complaint had been dismissed by the emperor as groundless. He had returned to Rome about a week ago for his own reasons. Paul's appearance had been expected months earlier, but a dispute among the Christians, which required his advice, delayed his arrival.

"Who told Paul you were ill?" I asked.

"Imogen brought him. She went to one of the elders, who told Paul about me. Poor girl, she was so worried."

"I appreciate her concern," I said a little annoyed, "but as a slave, she presumed too much by asking him. After all, we have Soranus."

Eleyne touched my shoulder. "Don't be silly, Marcellus. Imogen is a Christian, too. She heard Paul had healing powers like the Master."

"And he cured you?"

She nodded with a smile.

"What kind of trickery did he employ? I won't have you under any spell."

"He didn't use any tricks." She beamed and patted my hand. "He simply looked at me, with his soft, brown eyes and asked if I believed in God. Of course, I said I did with all my heart."

"Is that all? Nothing else?"

"He placed his hand on my forehead."

I snorted. "Then he did cast a spell."

"Marcellus, look at me," she said patiently. "It's me, Eleyne. Do I sound like I'm under a spell? Can't you see I'm well?"

"Yes, I know you are. It's so sudden—so unbelievable." I shuddered not knowing what to think.

"Does it really matter how I was cured?"

I hugged her again. "No, not at all. I'm just overjoyed you are." I could not help thinking some witchcraft was behind her recovery, but I didn't care.

Eleyne pushed me slightly away and stroked my stubbled chin. "I know my faith in God cured me. I'm sorry I said those awful things about not caring for Him or for you or the boys."

I took her hand in mine, so light and fragile, I was afraid I would crush it. "You don't have to apologize, it was the fever."

"At least He knew I didn't mean it, and whatever you think of God, I'm well."

She was right. I didn't care who cured Eleyne—her God, or the God of Mount Corno. I had sent the ashes of our daughter to the Sacred Mountain to be scattered as an offering for the snow, which had spared Eleyne's life. Silently, I thanked her god, too. Together, we sat for a long time holding one another, lost in thought.

* * *

Eleyne's recovery brought about a gradual but significant change in her life. Although she had prayed and administered to sick Christians and non-Christians alike before the accident, I had sensed a little disdain for those who had not yet converted to what she called, *The Way*. That attitude vanished overnight. If someone was ill or in need of food, clothing, or shelter, Eleyne was there to help. It did not matter whether they lived in the slums of the Subura or the Trans-Tiberina or in the shadow of the wealthy mansions of the Esquiline, Eleyne would find a way to aid them.

Because Paul had cured her, Eleyne began spreading the word about his life, deeds, and conversion to Christianity. Whenever possible, she visited him at the home of one of the sect's elders, where he was staying, and returned to our house inspired by his words.

She would have passed Rome's pestilent summers among the city's disease-infested tenements had I not insisted on her spending that season with me and our sons in Hispania. I had to remind her the Christian sect taught the importance of family devotion. Reluctantly, she conceded.

After previously living six years in exile on the latifundia, Eleyne admitted that she regarded the great cattle farm as her home. She could never return to her native Britannia again. Because she was the rightful heir to the Regni throne, Eleyne was still considered a political threat to the appointed ruler, a Roman lackey. She no longer had an interest in becoming a tribal monarch. Although I feared she might someday desire to return to Britannia as a queen and spread the message of Paul.

* * *

JULY, 64 AD

We had spent the last six summers in Hispania since my recall to Rome. Late one July morning, Eleyne and I journeyed back to the ranch from the fishing village, Abdera, where she had picked out the tunny we would eat for dinner. Ignoring the raised eyebrows and frowns of the local population, she often rode to town on her little dapple mare. Having been raised on the nearby latifundia, I knew the villagers considered it unladylike for the mistress of a great estate to ride a horse like a man, especially when she dressed in a Celtic tartan tunic and breeches. Eleyne had never forgotten her riding skills as a Briton. She freely rode her mount about the surrounding countryside, telling the people about Christus and Paul.

When we arrived home, Porus greeted us as usual at the door. "There is a courier here waiting to see you, sir. He has a message from Rome."

As the three of us entered the atrium, I said, "Why didn't he leave it like the rest?"

"He wouldn't say, Lord," Porus said, "except that he would wait for your return."

Daily, I received documents from Sabinus and Casperius Niger, whom I had promoted to my second-in-command, keeping me abreast of the City Guard's activities. Sometimes they asked for my opinion or clarification on one policy or another. In any event, Sabinus made the final decision. Despite the messages and the heat, Hispania had been an ideal escape from the city's hectic pace.

The messenger, a soldier smelling of horse sweat wearing a dusty tunic, breeches, and carrying a long sword at his side, stood by the edge of the impluvium in the center of the room. He snapped to attention and saluted. "Urgent message from Prefect Sabinus, sir. I have been ordered to wait for your answer." He held out a parchment scroll, bearing Sabinus's seal.

For a split second I froze, before I took the document from his hand. It had to be a serious matter to require an immediate response. I would need time to study the message before giving a reply.

"Very well," I said. "By your appearance, you have ridden long and hard from Malaca and need something to eat and drink. I will give you my answer once I have read the prefect's message." I turned to Porus. "Take him to the kitchen, he could use a good meal."

Porus nodded to the courier to follow him.

Eleyne and I took seats in the wicker chairs next to one another near the water catch basin in the center of the room.

"What do you think is in the message, Marcellus?" Eleyne asked. "I didn't like the sound of that soldier's words."

"Only one way to find out. It certainly won't be the usual answers to my request for more manure rakes for cleaning out the horses' stalls or wax tablets and scribe quills." Although Sabinus approved the annual budget for the City Guard, I was responsible for approving operational expenditures. And the messengers never left until I signed the appropriate spending authorization.

Opening the parchment, I scrutinized the letter and shuddered. I choked out the words, "By all the gods!"

Eleyne leaned toward me and said, "What's wrong, Marcellus? Your face is white."

"It's Rome," I stammered. "A fire has destroyed nearly the entire city."

Eleyne shot both hands to the sides of her face and gasped. "Merciful God, are you sure?"

I took a couple of deep breaths. "It's all here in Sabinus's handwriting. He says the city suffered the worst fire in all its eight hundred years. The fire burned for nine days. Gutted the Capitol."

"The reports *must* be exaggerated." Eleyne lowered her hands to her lap.

I shook my head. "No, they're not. He says thousands died and as many are homeless. The City Guard, the Watch, and the Praetorians combined their efforts, but couldn't halt its spread. Raging firestorms made that impossible."

Eleyne raised a hand to her mouth. "Oh, Marcellus, all those poor people. The children—hundreds—maybe thousands must have died." She fell silent and regarded me. "When did this happen?"

"The fire started a little more than two weeks ago. He wrote this about four days later, after the worst of the fires were extinguished and sent it on the next ship leaving for Hispania from Ostia."

"And it takes about eight to ten days for the message to reach us."

"Depending on weather and currents, yes."

"Does this mean you're returning to Rome?"

I placed the scroll on the small table in front of my chair, reached over, touched her hand, and nodded. "At once. Sabinus orders my return. I would leave in any event—my place is with the men. Don't worry." I pulled

216

away, but she grabbed my wrist. "I'm not expecting you to follow—at least not for the time being."

She sniffed. "You're not leaving me behind, Marcellus. I'm going with you."

Eleyne's answer did not surprise me. "Why should you? For all we know, the fire destroyed our home, and the city is still in chaos. There may be food riots and worse."

"I'm not going to idly stand by while you're in Rome. The people, especially the poor, need any help we can give. They've lost what little they had."

"What can you do?"

Her eyes focused squarely on mine. "The same as before. I'll nurse the sick and injured and find food and shelter for the homeless—I'll do whatever I can." She released her grip. "It's the Christian way."

I raised my arm and jabbed a couple of fingers in her direction. "You're taking a lot upon yourself."

"Don't stop me from doing my part, Marcellus." Eleyne stood, walked to the edge of the impluvium. She seemed to study the moated sunrays that streamed down from the opening in the center of the roof onto the placid pool of shallow water. She turned back to me.

I closed my eyes and pondered her words. As head of the household, I could have forbidden Eleyne from returning to Rome. But she was a strong woman and had survived her share of the painful blows of life and could stand the shock of seeing a gutted city.

I opened my eyes and studied her for the space of a few more heartbeats. "All right," I said, "you can come, but I promise it won't be a pretty sight."

She raised her head and turned to me. "Can it be worse than Briton villages sacked and burnt? More hideous than seeing everyone put to the sword by Roman soldiers? Or men slaughtered in the arena to satisfy a blood-thirsty crowd?"

"Yes."

She stepped back to her chair and sat. Leaning over, she placed a hand back on my forearm. "When do we leave?"

"Tomorrow. We'll ride to Malaca, and sail on the next ship to Ostia. The boys are coming with us."

"But Marcellus is only fifteen and Sabinus fourteen. Do you think they're mature enough to see such terrible destruction?"

"Under Roman law, they became grown men and citizens at fourteen. They'll have to learn to deal with it, especially if they are to one day serve in the army. Believe me, thousands of children in Rome are already having to adjust to the horror of a destroyed city, our boys can do no less."

"Yes, but I still don't like it."

"We can't leave them behind. Regardless of what Roman law says, they are still too young and immature to stay by themselves with only the slaves and Arajo. He's a good steward, but his place is to run the latifundia in our absence, not to supervise our sons."

She sighed. "Very well, I hope you're right about this."

A sick feeling lay in the pit of my stomach. Regardless of the stink, congestion, and recalcitrant population, I realized how much I cared for the city. Rome did not deserve this horrible fate. At the same time, I was concerned for the men of the City Guard and their well-being. How did Casperius Niger, my second-in-command, deploy the troops? What were our losses? Did my home on Vatican Hill survive? Those and many other questions raced through my mind.

* * *

Early one August morning, the merchant galley fetching my household from Hispania wove its way up the barge-choked Tiber River to Rome. Eleyne and I stood amidships at the wooden rail along with other passengers. In the distance, we saw the city's blackened skeleton emerged through a gray, dusty haze. Mixed with smoke and soot, the smells reeked of human filth and the sickening, rancid odor of rotting corpses.

Eleyne's light-blue, long tunic draped with a stola and yellow mantle, fluttered in the noisome breeze as did the scarlet army cloak hooked to the shoulders of my uniform. She squeezed my arm tightly. "Oh, Marcellus, this is worse than anything I could have ever imagined. Could our house have survived?"

I heard nearby passengers murmuring similar questions. A couple of sailors, including the tiller, cursed openly, more in shock than anger.

"I don't know," I answered, shaking my head. "We'll learn soon enough. From what I was told by the garrison commander when we docked in Ostia, most of the destruction was inside the city walls."

"I pray to God you're right."

I turned toward the ship's bow where our boys stood with Chulainn and saw them whispering to one another. Hovering a few steps away were the rest of our household servants, who appeared stunned by the city's destruction. Porus shook his head.

Eleyne and I leaned against the ship's rail in shocked silence.

My sons left Chulainn's side and came over to us. Young Sabinus, taller than me and Marcellus, looked at his mother, then me. He shook his head, strands of auburn hair falling over his pale forehead. "I don't believe this," he said in a voice little more than a whisper.

The dark eyes in young Marcellus's olive face seemed to focus on the destruction. "I never liked Rome, but no city deserves this." He ran long, narrow fingers through his black hair and shook his head. He had my coloring but his mother's slighter features.

Eleyne and I glanced at one another and nodded.

Suddenly a woman wailed and pointed in the direction of the blackened Aventine Hill, standing in forlorn desolation beyond the wharves. "My home! My beautiful house is gone! Great Goddess Minerva, why didn't you call on Mother Juno to stop the burning?"

"Oh, the poor woman," Eleyne whispered, on the verge of tears.

Merchants groaned at the loss of their businesses. "I'm ruined!" one exclaimed. "There's nothing left of the Emporium! Years of work—a heap of ashes!"

"The whole city is destroyed," another said, "at least the parts that count."

I turned my head away. My throat tightened. I could not speak. Fury and sadness swelled inside me. There was only one Rome. More than mortar and brick, it possessed a soul of its own. Now, lying close to death, could the grand old lady survive and rebuild? Sabinus was right: like a beautiful but moody woman, you may love or hate her, but you'll never get her out of your blood.

Sensing my sorrow, Eleyne held back her own tears and touched my face. "You love Rome, don't you?"

"I guess I do—more than I realized," I answered in a voice little more than a whisper.

"I saw it in your face," she said softly. "You've never hidden your emotions very well."

"I know."

The boys nodded.

"The city will rise again," she said, "you'll see. Much as I doubt it, I pray to God that Rome will be a better place to live."

I hugged Eleyne. "Gods, I'm glad you're my wife." I pulled away from her, turned, and clasped the shoulders of Marcellus and Sabinus. "I'm proud to have both of you for my sons."

The boys grinned and in unison said, "Thanks, Da."

Eleyne smiled, and together we turned, hand-in-hand, to scan the Tiber's bank, determined to survive whatever fate brought our way.

* * *

Outside the city walls, thousands of homeless people clustered along the shore of the Tiber and the Appian Way, living in goatskin army tents and spindly, thrown-together shacks. Acrid smoke from hundreds of campfires drifted over the river stinging our eyes and causing breathing difficulties. Strangely enough, the children laughed, shrieked, played games, and chased about as if it was an ordinary day.

"Look at the youngsters amusing themselves," I said to Eleyne. "They don't seem to see the city's devastation."

She placed a scented cloth to her nose and coughed. "That shows how much you know about little ones."

"What's wrong with them?" young Sabinus asked. "It doesn't seem natural."

"They're scared to death," Eleyne said. "Play is how they hide their fears. But they can't escape from their dreams, and they wake up screaming. No, Son, they're aware."

"I'd wake up screaming, too, if I was them," young Marcellus added. "Not afraid to admit it."

I touched his shoulder. "You're wiser than you know."

The long process of recovery and rebuilding had begun the day following the extinguishing of the last fire. Yet a calm prevailed among the refugees. Near the Ostian Gate, thousands waited in long lines for bread distributed from wagons under the watchful eye of armed Praetorian Guardsmen. News had reached our ship in Ostia that Nero had opened the city granaries to feed the survivors. He had ordered the Praetorian Guard to distribute thousands of tents from the arsenal at their camp.

As the ship glided towards the soot-encrusted stone dock, I counted at least a hundred barges moored along the river. An army of slaves shoveled loads of ashes and rubble onto barges, from an endless stream of wagons and carts lining the jetty and backing into the city. In turn, the black, wooden vessels hauled the debris downriver to the south and dumped it at sea. On the wharf where we were about to debark, more slaves combed the charred rubble of a burnt warehouse like maggots on a dead carcass.

"Look, Marcellus," Eleyne said, "there's Casperius Niger."

"Just as I expected." When we arrived at Ostia, I had the commander of the Ostian Garrison send a courier to Rome to notify Niger of our pending arrival.

The boys grinned and waved in his direction. They had always regarded Casperius Niger with affection. He had shown a liking for them ever since we first returned to Rome after my exile.

"Look, he's got a broken arm," young Marcellus said.

Tribune Casperius Niger stood squarely on the pier before a ceremonial century of the City Guard. A series of wooden splints encircled his left arm, tightly wrapped in a linen cloth. Scabs dotted his face. I waved to him as he called the detail to attention. The crisp appearance of their red tunics and shiny chain mail and armor notwithstanding, the men appeared haggard and drawn. Dark rings circled eyes sunken from long, sleepless hours of duty.

"I'll ask him how he broke it, and let you boys know later," I said. "In the meantime, when I go ashore to meet Tribune Niger, you will stay with your mother. I'm now on duty."

After the ship moored, I left Eleyne to attend to our sons, servants, and baggage while I debarked and received the troops. Standing on the pier, my legs nearly gave out. After being at sea for ten days, it took a few moments to adjust to being on land again. Even as I approached the men, I staggered a few yards before I could walk in a straight line. With a loud stomp of hob-nailed sandals, they snapped to attention.

"Welcome back, Commander," Casperius said after I had stepped onto the dock and exchanged the usual formalities. "You missed one hell of a fire."

"So I heard. What about you and the men? What's your condition?"

Casperius frowned. "The men are exhausted. They've been on almost steady duty since the fire erupted, but things are settling down."

I motioned towards the troops and back to Casperius. "Place them at ease."

Casperius passed the order to the centurion in charge who barked at the men to stand down.

"Once I receive a full report," I said to Casperius, "we can begin relieving the men on a rotating basis—they need rest—lots of it. And that goes for you, too, my friend."

Casperius winced as he attempted to raise his splinted arm in salute. "Damn, I keep forgetting I'm not supposed to move this arm—it's near mashed."

"I noticed."

"Pretty sight, eh?" Casperius grunted. "Don't know if I'll get full use again, but it's not as serious as it could've been."

"Let's do a quick inspection of the troops, and you can tell me how and where you injured your arm."

As we stepped along the front of the formation, giving the men cursory looks at their uniforms and weapons, Casperius filled me in on the details. "It happened at the foot of the Esquiline—nearly got caught by a falling building—escaped just in time."

"You're lucky to be alive."

He snorted and grimaced. "Takes more than a few flying timbers to keep me from duty."

"Good man."

When I finished the inspection, I saw Eleyne, our sons, and the rest of my entourage off to Vatican Hill with an escort of twenty guardsmen. I motioned to the groom who held the spare mount Casperius had brought along for my use. He led the dark bay gelding toward me as it snorted and its buttocks drifted from side to side, the pendants on the bridle jangling in the breeze. The groom soothed him with some quiet words. Taking the reins, I said to Casperius, "We'll head for Lord Sabinus's headquarters, but first I want to see what's left of the city."

We mounted our horses and left the river front with the troops following behind. Casperius and I zigzagged down the rubble-strewn avenue, passing the shattered remains of a temple. Workers and slaves shoveled mountains of ash and cinders and threw burnt timbers into the cluster of parked carts and wagons. These, too, would be driven to the docks and loaded aboard barges. I turned about and ordered the centurion to send a squad of ten troops ahead of us to clear a passageway. The people scattered at our approach. I looked about and saw among the ruins hundreds of refugees picking through the rubble, attempting to recover belongings or bodies of loved ones.

"I read Lord Sabinus's report," I said, "but I want to hear it from you. How did the fire start?"

"Commander, we know it first started somewhere near the Circus Maximus," Casperius said, "but it took off like Jupiter's thunderbolts, spreading through the whole city. We couldn't control all the fires—there weren't enough of us. Most of our men were needed just to keep order among the panicking mob and control the looting. Had to leave most of fires to the Watch, and later the Praetorians, when Nero ordered them to give a hand."

He continued his grim narration about the storm of flames raging through Rome for three days. "With a life of its own, it blew winds fed by timbers and wares, roaring and feasting at its whim. The heat was so intense we couldn't get near without burning ourselves. You could smell scorched flesh everywhere. A few of the men got too close and were trapped by falling timbers. They died horrible deaths—still haven't got their screams out of my mind. We had to demolish a ribbon of houses for a firebreak before the blaze was finally stamped out at the foot of the Esquiline and the Quirinal. Sabinus's house was scorched and blackened but remained standing with little internal damage.

"Altogether," Casperius said, "the fire leveled three districts and reduced seven to blackened ruins. Thousands of shops, mansions, tenements, public buildings, and temples have been razed."

I cursed to myself and wondered if this was some sort of punishment by the gods, and if so, why? "What about the barracks?"

Casperius looked about and spat. "The fires completely bypassed Castra Praetoria, so the Guard and the Praetorians had a place to return. Of course, we've seldom seen the camp during the past weeks."

"Altogether how much remains of the city?" I waved towards the charred ruins.

"Only four of Rome's fourteen districts survive intact."

"Which ones?" I looked back towards the Tiber.

"The Trans-Tiberina across the river, most of Quirinal Hill, the Janiculem, and the Capitoline."

Upon hearing the report, I held my reins tighter than usual. My horse came to a sudden halt, jolting me backwards. I loosened my reins and kicked him in the sides. We rode forward. "Anything else saved?"

"The Forum and parts of the Esquiline survived, too, and areas south of the Circus Maximus and Caelian Hills between the Appian and Ardeatian Ways."

"How did Vatican Hill fare?"

Casperius glanced at me as if knowing why I asked. He grinned. "You're in luck, Commander. Like most of the areas outside Rome, your home wasn't torched."

I nodded, quietly breathed a sigh of relief, and said a silent prayer in thanks.

"Did the Palatine escape the blaze?" I inquired as we approached the hill. A haze of dust and smoke, churned by the activities of the workers at its foot, partially obscured the emperor's residence.

"Yes, sir." Casperius related that due to a concerted effort between the City Guard, the Watch, and the Praetorians, much of the palace was saved, including the House of Livia and Tiberius and part of the venerable quarters of Augustus. Unfortunately, fire gutted the adjacent Temple of Apollo.

Riding along, I studied Rome's devastation—the shattered remains of a great city. Lost forever were many of Rome's splendid historical monuments. No longer would citizens sacrifice at legendary King Servius Tullius's Temple of the Moon or the Altar of Holy Peace dedicated by Evander to Hercules. They would never again pray in the temple at the foot of the Palatine, which legend said, was consecrated by Romulus, the city's founder, to Jupiter the Stayer. Nothing remained but ashes of Numa's sacred residence and Vesta's shrine containing Rome's household gods across from the Temple of Saturn.

As I looked around, I said to Casperius, "It's amazing the Guard and the Watch saved as much as they did."

Casperius winced and grabbed the hilt of his sword, then released it. He spat. "Our efforts were nothing compared with the loss of people. Thousands died, mostly from fallen buildings or while trying to escape. Countless numbers were trampled to death or trapped beneath the rubble of burning buildings. Thousands more suffocated from smoke inhalation."

Casperius told me his men had supervised the disposal of the dead to prevent the spread of disease. State slaves dug giant pits for mass burials and cremations outside the city, leaving no time for relatives wishing to conduct private rites or to search for loved ones.

As we approached the Palatine and Sabinus's headquarters, I noticed its scorched but standing walls and pillars. But the once extensive garden at its foot was a clump of ashes being cleared away by a small army of slaves and shoveled into nearby carts.

Casperius continued his story. "Nero has contracted two architects, Severus and Celer, to supervise the rebuilding."

"He chose wisely," I said. "They're Rome's greatest designers."

"They must be," Casperius said, "because the work has started. The emperor gave orders to *clean up and embellish the city.* Of course," he said with a snort, "he confiscated the choicest land east of the Forum for his newest home. They're going to build what's called the *Palace of Gold.*"

Army tents still sheltered the homeless who remained at the mercy of nature's fickle elements.

Casperius pointed to an area covered with cinders beyond the Circus Maximus and growled, "As if that weren't enough, the emperor's planning to erect a pompous golden statue to himself, nearly one hundred feet tall, I'm told. He'll call it the *Colossus of Nero,* but the people already have other names for it—none of them complimentary." He grinned. "Already heard about one clod who wants to trim its golden toenails."

Exhausted, the men of the City Guard suffered from injuries and fatigue. Given little time for food and sleep, they had exceeded the limit of human endurance. But they had obeyed.

After hearing the report from Casperius, I was proud of them. No! I was honored to serve with such men. From the first day their numbers diminished from injuries, illness, heat exhaustion, and death. Now they could be relieved, properly fed, and rested.

Unfortunately, the end of Rome's greatest fire was the beginning of a greater tragedy.

CHAPTER 22

Upon completing a survey of Rome's destruction, Casperius and I reported to Sabinus's office on the Palatine. We entered the well-lighted room that contained a large window overlooking the Circus Maximus. The heat of the city and smell of charred ruins drifted on a faint breeze. We saluted the prefect, sitting behind his desk. A half dozen scrolls were stacked to one side. Deep lines creased his forehead and black, heavy bags underscored his sunken eyes. A two- or three-day stubbled growth of a gray beard covered his face. He wore a dyed-white, leather corselet, bordered with gold fringe over a scarlet tunic. A gold, muscled cuirass protected his chest. Sabinus skipped the usual greetings.

"Welcome home, Commander Marcellus Reburrus, if one can call it that." Sabinus motioned to a couple of stools, and we sat across from him.

"I regret I didn't arrive sooner," I answered while wiping the sweat from my hands along the side of my breeches.

"It would not have made any difference, but your troops performed in an exemplary manner." He nodded to Casperius. "Tribune Niger is a good man."

Casperius sat straighter. "I'm honored, sir."

"Did the emperor comment on their performance?" I asked.

Sabinus grinned. "He was impressed by Centurion Cornelius Martialis's status report, which was far superior to one filed by the Praetorians."

"Another good man," I said. "That must have infuriated Tigellinus."

The prefect scratched his nose. "If so, he kept it to himself, but you are probably right."

"Is there anything to the rumors I've heard?" I asked.

Sabinus narrowed his eyes. "Which rumors?"

I looked toward the door that opened out upon a wide corridor. Footfalls clattered on the mosaic floor, and a slave walked by. Soon his steps faded away. I waited for the space of a few more heartbeats before answering, "Nero played his lyre from a tower in the Garden of Maecenas while Rome burned. The story is sweeping through the streets and refugee camps."

Sabinus shook his head. "Utter nonsense. He returned to Rome immediately upon receiving news of the fire. He ordered the Praetorians at once to combat the flames."

"We would have lost more of Rome if he hadn't," Casperius said.

"Indeed, Tribune Niger," Sabinus continued. "Nero did not go near the gardens. I reported to him at Esquiline Field east of the city when he arrived from the coast. I'm not surprised his enemies spread that piece of trash. Nero heard the same gossip and turned his dogs loose to find the source—for once I hope they are successful."

Again, I glanced to the door and back to Sabinus. I leaned forward and whispered, "Unfortunately, his reputation for depravity gave the rumor mongers the excuse they needed."

Sabinus seemed alarmed by my open remark. He glanced at Casperius Niger and wiped the perspiration from his balding head. He motioned me closer and placed a hand on my forearm. "Marcellus, I know the destruction of the city must be a shock, but these are dangerous times— made more so by this calamity. It is not safe to think such thoughts, let alone give them voice."

I nodded, and Casperius agreed.

The senator related how Nero asked Tigellinus, his secretaries, and Sabinus himself their advice on feeding and sheltering the thousands of homeless people. Over the objections of Tigellinus, the emperor concurred with Sabinus's suggestion that the city's wheat supplies, which had survived the inferno, be opened to the state bakeries and bread distributed to the hungry.

"I informed the emperor, if he did not, food riots were a certainty," Sabinus added. "Nero was visibly shaken. He needs the mob's support."

I wiped the sweat rolling down the side of my face with the back of my hand. "I can imagine the look on Tigellinus's face."

"There is more," Sabinus said. "I suggested sheltering the homeless in the Field of Mars, using surplus tents and blankets from the Praetorian camp. Tigellinus protested, but was overridden by Nero, who stood very firm. By the gods, I was proud of him."

"Did Tigellinus object to using the Praetorians in fighting the fires?" I asked.

"No, he realized the city must survive, especially since our guards fought alongside his Praetorians in saving the Palatine. Faenus Rufus persuaded Tigellinus it made good sense."

Since my return from exile, I had seldom encountered Faenus Rufus. It was he who had warned me of Drusus, the corrupt Watch tribune, when I first arrived in Rome with Sabinus years before. Faenus transferred to the Praetorian Guard during my exile, and eventually was appointed to the position of co-Praetorian prefect.

"Thank the gods," I said, "for having an ex-Watch officer as an ally."

"Exactly. Tigellinus knew the Praetorians had to participate in fighting the fire if he was to remain in Nero's favor. After all, someone must be left to pay taxes."

"At least he's making the effort, sir," Casperius said.

"That's true, Tribune Niger, but the rumor about the lyre playing is so bizarre," Sabinus said in a voice that trailed away. He shook his head and looked out the window. He sighed. "I fear one day his enemies and historians alike may record such tripe as fact." He paused, and then continued in a lower voice. "Despite the terrible crimes Nero has committed, the burning of Rome is not one of them. Although, he loves to sing and play the lyre, he put his instrument away to deal with the blaze. I know because I was there. Nero sent commands to outlying towns to provide aid for Rome in the way of men, additional food, and provisions."

Sabinus looked at Casperius and then focused his eyes on me. "We have work ahead of us. The investigation into the fire's cause has begun. Tigellinus and the Watch prefect are conducting their own. I assigned Casperius Niger to head our own inquiry until you returned. He can fill you in on the details."

Casperius nodded. "I already have, sir."

"Very good," Sabinus said. "Now, I must leave. The emperor expects me and the rest of the court present . . . ," he lowered his voice, "for one of his abominable recitals."

* * *

Although the investigation of incendiarism was within the jurisdiction of the Watch, I knew the prefects of the Praetorian Guard, the City Guard, and the Watch distrusted one another. It didn't surprise me to learn they would conduct independent probes. Sabinus wanted me to see what mine would reveal. He told me the prefects, including himself, feared the repercussions resulting from such devastation. During the following three days, on more than one occasion, Annaeus Serenus, the Watch prefect, approached me ostensibly to clarify questionable details noted in my preliminary report. I included his statements, along with my observations, for Sabinus's judgment. Serenus assured me, his report likewise noted overpowering winds were to blame for the lack of containment within my areas. Politicians—what an abomination.

On the fourth day, Tigellinus delegated Faenus Rufus to continue the inquiries for the Praetorian Guard. The emperor required the Praetorian prefect to be at his beck and call, leaving little time for the investigation. Fortunately, Rufus was an honorable man, not cut from Tigellinus's dirty cloth.

Three mornings later, Rufus and I conferred in his spacious office at the Praetorian Barracks, which looked out onto the camp's huge parade field. Through the open door and window came shouts from snarling centurions putting troops through their drills. Moated columns of dust roiled on the sunbeams coming through the window. A half dozen cabinets, filled with canisters containing scrolled records, lined the office's brick walls.

"Did you know," Rufus said to me across the desk from where I sat, "Tigellinus removed your men from their posts along the Caelian when he attempted to save Gallus's lost estate on the Viminal?"

My chest tightened as a frown crossed my lips. "Yes, I did. And because my men were pulled from their posts, the Caelian's contained fire rekindled and raced into new areas. I'm naming Tigellinus in my report as the party responsible for the fire reaching Nero's estate."

Rufus's face, which reminded me of a bear, flushed as he quickly grasped the document's consequences. For a moment he eyed me. "Perhaps we can work something out—I'm not ready to fall on my sword for Tigellinus."

I gestured with a hand. "You're not to blame for his actions."

"No, but I'm second-in-command." He looked in the direction of the door and back to me. "Tigellinus will denounce me for failing to carry out his orders. He'll use me as his sacrificial goat." He shook his head. "What's worse, Nero will believe his every word."

"What do you have in mind?"

"I'll file a neutral report," he said in a low voice, "and I ask that neither of our reports indict or criticize the other's forces."

I understood his meaning and nodded. "Agreed."

Later, I reported to Sabinus and informed him of what Rufus had proposed.

Fearing many innocents might be injured by the political sword, Sabinus suggested I *temper* my formal report even more than Faenus Rufus had proposed, but also file a separate unofficial one to him containing all details and names.

Arsonists started the fires, rumors said. But reports confirmed the conflagration began in a shop near the Great Arena, the Circus Maximus. My investigation could not substantiate arson as the cause. No survivors lived to point an accusing finger. The proprietor of the silk shop

where the blaze ignited died in the flames. Like most fires
in Rome, it probably started from a spark flying out of
a cooking brazier and landing in a corner of the shop's
tinder-dry room. But gossip continued to persist that the
fire was deliberately ignited.

* * *

Ten days had passed, after I assumed the investigation
from Casperius Niger, when Sabinus presented my
amended report to Nero. Later, in the afternoon, I arrived
at Sabinus's court office, eager to learn of Nero's reaction
to the document.

I waited only a few minutes before Sabinus arrived
clothed in a white and purple magisterial toga. After the
usual salutations, he dropped wearily to the leather,
cushioned chair. An expression of disgust crossed his
aging face. "The emperor is a fool."

Quickly, I turned to the open door listening for footfalls
or other noise from the hallway. None. "Sir, do you know
what you're saying? Isn't that treason?"

Sabinus glared at me, his face tight, lips pressed
together in a thin line. He exhaled. "You are right, I must
choose my words carefully. But you will understand why
when I tell you what Nero did with the report."

"What about it?"

"Naturally, I handed him the narrative." Sabinus
paused to pour a cup of diluted wine from a small amphora
on the desk. He leaned back and took a long drink—
something he rarely did. He exhaled and resumed after
a short pause. "Nero flipped it to Tigellinus without the
decency of a glance." Now his pallored face changed into a
field of deep furrows. "You know what that means?"

I nodded. "Tigellinus tells Nero what he wants him to
hear."

"Of course," he answered waving a wrinkled hand.
"When I tried to explain the findings, Nero shoved my
attempts aside. All he spoke about were the rumors
accusing him of burning Rome." Sabinus refilled his

cup and rapidly tossed it down his throat. "Then he became downright nauseating, ranting about the pain he experienced upon learning about the destruction of his beloved gardens." Sabinus took another long drink.

I tightly grasped the hilt of my sword. "We should have known better than to believe he cared about learning the truth. I suspect finding a scapegoat, as the Jews call it, is more to his interest."

"Exactly. My spies say that at the instigation of Gallus, Tigellinus planted the idea into Nero's mind."

"Any victim in particular?"

"I'm just speculating, but most likely he'll target foreigners or sects unpopular with the mob."

I snorted. "Anyone who doesn't have the power to fight back." *Such as the Christians.*

"In any event . . . ," he sighed. "There is little I can do outwardly without losing my own head. I will have to employ subterfuge. I do not wield the influence I once did."

His remarks startled me. This was unlike the Sabinus I once knew. He was never one to give in so easily. But shrewd politician that he was, he valued his life more than his pride. Sabinus had said before, he could do more good alive than dead.

"Through no fault of your own," I said. "But whose troops will undertake the arrests once he decides on his prey? I don't like using mine to arrest innocent people."

"This is Tigellinus's scheme, and he will take credit for the success. He will use the Praetorians for his dirty work."

Relieved to a degree, I was concerned about his intended victims.

"If my spies discover whom he plans to arrest," Sabinus went on, "then I will quietly warn them to flee Rome."

"Since Senator Gallus is Tigellinus's friend," I said, "you know he'll stick his hand in this somewhere—especially if he smells a profit."

"I daresay he will. Gallus lost millions in the fire and has to recoup his losses."

"I heard that the only properties he saved were his pet cat, a ledger containing the accounts of his debtors, and his prized collection of campaign trophies."

"The only possessions that he holds dear in his life," Sabinus said. He grew silent, and his eyes seemed to glaze over. "The real questions at hand," he resumed in a distant voice, "is what will Nero do, and when?"

CHAPTER 23

Rumors spread that Christians had fired the city.

Through bribery and special sacrifices to the emperor's glory, influential sects like the Cult of Isis guided the accusing finger away from themselves and towards the group least likely to defend itself—the Christians. They were attacked and beaten on the streets, and an avalanche of public outcries demanded that the arsonists be punished.

Because they quietly worshipped in secluded grottos and caves beneath the city, the Christians had become objects of fear and suspicion. Many Romans believed the sect had a morose contempt for all mankind. Rumors persisted they performed blood sacrifices and ate human flesh, especially their own infants. Among Rome's poorest people, they lived mostly in the unaffected Trans-Tiberina District, and the Christians had lost little in the conflagration. Sabinus sent a secret messenger to the Christian community warning their members and leaders to flee. They ignored his advice.

Although not Christians, the boys and I more than once accompanied Eleyne to their services in a huge burial vault beneath city streets. Disguised in shabby clothes, with a hood obscuring my face, I witnessed the rites, and found no truth in the malicious tales. A loaf of bread, symbolizing the body of their Messiah, emerged as the so-called flesh they ate. Instead of blood, the Christians drank wine donated and blessed for the meeting.

Except when Paul or any other prominent members preached, the worship consisted of stories and singing praises about their Christ and God. Tales glorified and enhanced Jesus's so-called miracles. I didn't believe the accounts of His raising from the dead. But since Paul had cured Eleyne of her deep despair, I found the Christians more perplexing than ever. Their meetings closed with admonitions against committing acts of murder, thievery, and adultery—the same laws Rome expected her subjects to obey. Afterwards, the faithful gathered for a meal called the *love-feast*. Every member contributed something—even if all they could afford was a jug of water.

Eleyne had not converted young Marcellus and Sabinus to Christianity. By Roman law, as head of the household and therefore chief priest, it was I who decided which gods the family would worship. I had tolerated Eleyne's god, but I told her in no uncertain terms that our sons were to respect all gods. They were old enough to decide which ones to believe, if any.

She didn't like that but acceded to my wishes. I did allow her to teach the boys the Christians' beliefs. However, I had their tutor, Diogenes, discuss the traditional Greek and Roman gods and those of my family, including prayers to my ancestors. Eleyne seldom spoke of the gods of Britannia, revered by her people. And every morning, I required the boys to make offerings to the household gods at the little shrine near the front door, a function Eleyne no longer performed.

My wife kept herself occupied nursing the sick and injured, the homeless, Christian and non-Christian alike. Without hesitation, she withdrew money from her private funds, part of the dowry Sabinus and Aurelia had given her at our wedding, to buy medical supplies and clothing for the needy. Although drawn and tired from long hours spent in service, Eleyne's enthusiasm never waned.

"Do you realize attending the Christian worship is becoming dangerous?" I said as we reclined in the triclinium during a late dinner.

"It's no different than before," she answered, nibbling on a green olive.

"On the contrary. Tigellinus's spies are attempting to find evidence linking your sect to the fires."

Eleyne dropped the olive pit into the iron-red earthen platter from Samos and wiped her hands on a linen cloth. "We have nothing to hide. He will find no such evidence."

"That isn't the point." I tore off the small leg from a roasted quail smothered in spices and asparagus sauce. "If they find none, it'll be fabricated. Nero has to blame someone for Rome's destruction."

"And so it's us?"

"Most likely. The accusing rumors gain strength daily." I couldn't keep the worry from my voice. "But that's not all, Eleyne. If his spies have attended the services, they'll report your presence and that of the boys."

Eleyne shook her head. "What's the difference? The boys no longer worship with me. Diogenes has seen to that. They prefer Rome's cruel gods and those of your ancestors." Eleyne slapped a thin layer of honey on a piece of flat bread.

My face grew warm. "That was their choice. They are legally men. In the meantime, the Praetorian prefect may use you to compromise me," I said, though it was the least of my fears.

She dropped the bread onto the platter. "That's ridiculous. I'm no threat to Rome. Does being married to a Christian jeopardize your position as commander of the City Guard?"

"It well might, but I'm more concerned for your life. Like other Christians, you haven't sacrificed to the genius of the emperor—that's a treasonable offense."

The effort entailed no more than pouring a little grain and wine in a brazier at the base of his statue, but the Christians spurned all idolatrous images, especially Nero's.

"You mustn't worry for me," Eleyne said. "Up to now, no one has bothered us."

True, the Imperial government hadn't until now actively sought the all-but-penniless Christians. Only when arrested in conjunction with some other offense were they forced to sacrifice. Those who refused were executed as traitors.

"That's about to change," I said quietly.

Eleyne slammed her cup on the small table of striated blue marble, the golden liquid splashed onto the mosaic floor. "Those unspeakable pigs! How can they do that to innocent people?"

"Easily." I looked into her sea-blue eyes, appealing to her common sense, to her long experience of life in Rome.

Eleyne gazed back, still for a moment. "When will they start?"

"No official word has come to my attention yet. But I may not hear in enough time to warn your friends."

* * *

A week later, I received ugly reports from my informers. Gallus had compiled a list of enemies, business competitors, and foreign merchants he planned to eliminate.

Gallus did not wait long to make his move. By late September, the persistent rumors of Christians torching the city inflamed the population.

My spies warned of impending trouble, but they could not pinpoint the specific date and time. An attack in the Trans-Tiberina District was a certainty, but by whom? Would we be dealing with a mob incited to riot and led by a group of organized criminals? Or a scattering of disgruntled people banding together on the spur of the moment and disbursing once they had vented their anger and looted every shop in sight.

I placed all cohorts on alert, and ordered Octavius Quartio, the lumpy-faced commanding tribune of the Thirteenth Cohort, to double his patrols in the Trans-Tiberina, the unit's regularly assigned area. Based at the Praetorian Barracks on the northeast side of Rome, the City Guard's responsibility included policing the city by day and quelling riots. Their jurisdiction partially overlapped the duties of the Watch, who fought fires and policed the city, day and night. Unfortunately, the City Guard and the Praetorians were billeted in the same camp, and their spies had infiltrated our ranks. They wasted their time if they expected to uncover any treason among my men.

I reported to Sabinus's office upon learning of Gallus's latest scheme. "Do you realize," I said, "Gallus has devised a plan to destroy his competitor, the foreign merchants, by linking them to the Christians?"

"I have received the same reports," he answered, sitting at his desk. He waved me to a chair across from him.

"You know he's greedy for their franchises." His enemies held state monopolies in lumber, cement, marble, and lead—the commodities needed for rebuilding Rome.

"Absolutely, and I immediately requested an audience with Nero to make him aware of the plot."

"What was his reaction?"

Sabinus clasped his fingers together and exhaled. "By the gods, Tigellinus refused my admission. As city prefect, I have the right to see the emperor at any time. But surrounded by his bullying guards, the Praetorian prefect said he decides who sees Nero and who doesn't—and I'm not included."

I took a deep breath and refrained from pounding the table with a clenched fist. "He knew why you were there."

"No doubt. You know what plan Gallus has devised?"

My lips tightened. I studied his lined face and the dark circles around his eyes and nodded. "Aye, far worse than the usual methods of assassination, unforeseen accidents, or treasonous accusations."

"Unlike most of the nobility, the merchants and contractors aren't afraid of working for a living."

Both of us knew Roman aristocracy held the alien merchants in disdain. "Unfortunately," I said, "their demise will receive little sympathy from the Roman people."

"Precisely. Gallus and Tigellinus are depending on it."

"I can figure the rest," I said. Once his enemies were executed, Gallus would buy their great estates cheaply at state auction and recoup his losses. Through Tigellinus, he had gained preference in obtaining future state monopolies previously held by his prospective victims.

* * *

One hot evening during the first week of October, carrying torches and wielding clubs, thousands from the tent camp crossed the Sublician Bridge to the west side of the Tiber. Heading south on the Campanian Way, the noisy mob converged on the Christian quarters in the Trans-Tiberina District. Then, as if rising from the ashes, armed bandits appeared with clubs, swords, and knives. Inciting the crowds to kill the Christians, they scattered through the narrow streets, a mixture of tenements and river warehouses, beating, maiming, and killing any suspected Christian or foreigner. Their bloodlust only whetted, the mobs broke into closed businesses, Christian or otherwise, looting and butchering the proprietors and families living in rooms above and behind the shops.

More than an hour passed before the Thirteenth Cohort arrived, and with the assistance of the Watch, brutally restored order. But they reached the area too late. Nearly one hundred innocent people died in the rampage before the rioters dispersed, and the perpetrators were killed or arrested.

I hurried to the area, leading a detachment of troops from the Twelfth Cohort. By the time I arrived, caged wagons rolled past my contingent in the opposite direction carrying the surviving prisoners to Latumiae Prison. In the fluttering light of crackling torches, I began the nasty job of surveying the Trans-Tiberina's damage.

Casperius Niger rode with me. "Not a pretty sight, is it, Commander?"

I spat. "Not at all."

Ruined goods and garbage littered the narrow streets and alleys in front of smashed shops and shuttered stalls. Isolated fires, brought under control by bucket brigades of the Watch, dotted the area. Pools and splotches of blood clotted the gutters and walls. State slaves hurried about, gathering and hoisting bodies into oxcarts, for burial in the lime pits outside the city. A few of the area's braver souls warily darted about the street searching for injured loved ones or neighbors. Others hastily ascertained the damage and boarded up their businesses.

I discovered the Thirteen Cohort Tribune, Octavius Quartio, sitting at a splintery table surrounded by a small group of centurions and clerks, at his makeshift command post, a dingy tavern called the Galley and Lighter.

Squeezed between two warehouses on Neptune Lane near the Tiber, the pest hole was a known hangout for sailors, longshoremen, and thieves. Asellina, a middle-aged widow, owned the bar. Besides wine, her three serving wenches, Aegle, Maria, and Zymrina sold their favors to customers in the tiny rooms above the wine shop. Outside, painted in red letters on the whitewash walls, they advertised their names and prices.

Quartio staggered to his feet when I entered the place and approached him. His breath reeked with wine as he gave a preliminary report of the incident.

"Why did the cohort wait so long before restoring order, Tribune Octavius Quartio?" I inquired, with a thin hold on my temper.

"My men were scattered through the district on patrol," he slurred. Quartio wiped the sweat from the jagged eyebrows sinking above his deep-set, piggish eyes and belched. He swayed on his feet. "It took . . . took time to send runners and . . . and gather them for redeployment."

"Did you not keep at least a century on standby at all times?"

"Of course, sir."

"The Trans-Tiberina isn't that big," I reminded him acidly. "If you had properly deployed them, it would have taken no time at all to muster five hundred troops." During the alert, I assigned five hundred guardsmen from the Thirteenth on duty at all times to the Trans-Tiberina.

"Due to the . . ." Quartio hiccupped. "The . . . enormity of the . . . situation . . ." He belched. "I fi . . . figured I ought to wa . . . wait till all men reported . . ." He sucked in his breath. "In from their patrols."

"Why didn't you send the standby century to the Sublician Bridge? They would have easily blocked and held the crossing until reinforcements arrived. That was part of the riot plan."

Quartio winced. "But I—"

"I expect a detailed report on my desk first thing tomorrow morning. The entire fiasco—and your failure to follow standing orders. In the meantime, I hereby relieve you of your command."

The tribune stiffened "But s . . . sir—"

"Shut up!" I growled, grabbing the hilt of my sword.

I turned to Casperius. "Tribune Niger, you shall head a full inquiry into this matter, starting now."

"Yes, Commander," he answered. He grinned like a cat who had just caught a mouse.

Facing Quartio, I said, "Tribune Quartio, you will give Tribune Casperius Niger your full cooperation. There is no excuse for what happened tonight."

I feared the situation in the days to follow would only grow worse.

CHAPTER 24

Though it was nearly midnight, Eleyne was waiting for me at the front door when I returned home. I handed my helmet and cloak to one slave and my cuirass to another.

"Is it true? Was there a riot in the Christian quarters tonight?" she asked.

I snapped my head in her direction. "How did you find out?"

"One of the elders rushed to the house almost three hours ago with the news. Your message this afternoon only said you would return late."

Eleyne and I walked through the dimly lit atrium and down the hallway. Except for our footfalls and sputter of olive oil lamps illuminating the way, the household remained silent.

"I was told about the riot just as I was about to leave for home," I finally said. "There wasn't time to send you word."

I related news of the disaster.

"Did you know friends of mine were murdered by those horrible people?" Eleyne paused at the entrance to the cubiculum. Her face tightened, and for a moment I thought she would weep, but she choked back the tears.

For a long minute I drew Eleyne close and held her. "I'm sorry."

"I know," she answered softly.

In the bedroom, I dropped to a stool by the bed and pulled off my boots.

"What are you going to do about stopping all this?" Eleyne asked in bitter voice. She removed the white palla covering her green night shift and sat on the goose-down bed.

"I'm taking every step necessary to ensure it doesn't happen again," I answered, barely able to keep my eyes open.

"Is that all?"

"I've started an investigation."

Eleyne jabbed a finger at my chest. "Can't you do more?"

"What happened to the Christians tonight was unconscionable. I hate it, but it's not just your damn Christians that died. Good men—my men—were also lost. But you don't mention them at all." I threw my boot across the room. "I've done enough for one night—my mind has turned to mud, and I can't think."

Eleyne sat, her face sullen as if hurt by my rebuke.

I leaned over and placed a hand on hers. "Look, I didn't mean to snap at you. It's just that things are set into motion no one wanted. They're taking on a direction and life of their own and will have to play out to the end. We'll talk about it in the morning, when we're both in a better mood."

Eleyne nodded, but turned her back to me, slid under the blankets, and fell asleep.

* * *

About a week later I told Eleyne about what my investigation revealed.

Evening drew an ash-gray curtain across the sky, and rolling thunderheads snuffed out the dim afterglow of sunset. Heavy darkness draped Rome as lightning flashed silently in the distance.

I stood watching from the balcony of our house as thunderbolts rocked the earth. The first rains of October were approaching the city. Nearly a week had passed since the riots, and Eleyne wanted to talk once again about the attacks on the Christians. But I used the approaching storm as a moment's distraction to collect my thoughts.

Strolling outside, Eleyne placed an arm about my waist and leaned her head on my shoulder. A sudden crackle and a brilliant flash of lightning illuminated everything. She tightened reflexively. In that instant, the hills of Rome were silhouetted against the horizon, and beyond black-purple clouds dragged in a slanted, gray curtain of rain.

A fresh, cool windswept before the storm, carrying the scent of rain. Angry clouds churned, and thunder rumbled, as if Jupiter and the gods raged upon Mount Olympus. Pelts of rain fell as we retreated into the bedroom just off the balcony to continue watching nature's display.

"Marcellus," Eleyne said, "I didn't know about your men being killed. Their poor families . . . my heart goes out to them. But my friends are Christians, and I need to talk about them, too. I know you're not telling me everything."

"All right," I said, "I'll tell you what I can." I sighed. No longer could I delay her questions.

Jagged bolts of lightning slashed to the earth, and rain plummeted from the sky, dancing upon the black striated marble of the balcony.

"Gallus is behind this," I said.

She gasped and pulled away from me. "I might have guessed."

"He instigated the whole tumult in collusion with Nero and Tigellinus. This is only a strong suspicion, but I'm positive it happened."

Her shoulders slumped. "What lead you to believe this?"

"I was investigating why the Thirteenth Cohort was so slow in responding to the riot."

"And were they?"

My chest tightened. "Unfortunately, they were. I found substantial evidence to prove their commander, Octavius Cuartio and ten of the mob's leaders were on Tigellinus's payroll. He ordered Quartio, who was a habitual drunk, to ignore the carnage until the last moment. Tigellinus despises the Christians and used the mob to rid the city of them."

"Tigellinus is a monster!"

I nodded.

Eleyne stepped closer and touched my shoulder. "What else did you do?"

I grabbed her delicate hand and placed it to my lips for an instant before releasing her fingers. "I confronted Quartio with the evidence. In spite of his denials, I sacked him."

"Why didn't Tigellinus stop you?"

"He dared not interfere lest he give credibility to the charge implicating him in the carnage."

"What about the mob leaders, were they arrested?"

"The ones that weren't killed were either arrested or fled the city. Those captured were tortured and confessed that nameless intermediaries paid them to incite the populace. There is no doubt in my mind that Gallus played a major part in this catastrophe."

Silence filled the room after I finished.

Soon, sheets of chilled rain lashed desperately, driving us to the warmth of our bed. We snuggled beneath the heavy quilts. Eleyne wore a woolen nightshift, while I was clad in a long tunic. She laid her head against my chest as I placed my arm around the back of her head. Despite heat from two braziers placed on iron tripods near the bed, the room remained chilly.

"Why can't you protect the Christians?" Eleyne asked. The red glow of the brazier reflected in her ivory face.

I focused my eyes on hers, which I barely saw in the dim light. "Sabinus's spies warned your friends before the rampage, but they refused to listen."

"They're too poor to flee." Her lips tightened. "They don't have anything, and there isn't any place to go."

"They can hide in the catacombs."

"To be hunted like criminals?"

"It's a matter of survival."

Eleyne raised her head and shook it before lowering it back on my chest. "Our Lord taught us we can't run away from our problems."

How ironic. She repeated the same words John-Mark chided her with twelve long years ago, when I found her hiding in the catacombs after the riots in the naval arena. I stroked Eleyne's freshly washed, jet hair. It was scented with rosemary. A few thin gray strands appeared at the temples. But at thirty-five, she was still a stunning woman.

"If they stay, their murders won't solve anything," I said.

Eleyne sighed. "Are you sure the information is true? Your spies have been wrong before."

"Positive. I confirmed their sources."

"What about our sons? What about you?"

My shoulders stiffened. So far, my sons hadn't been endangered by the growing mob violence, but how much longer? I had seriously given thought to sending them to Hispania where they would come to no harm. "I am thinking about them, but don't forget yourself."

"Never mind me, I can take care of myself."

I pulled my arm from underneath her head, raised up on my elbow, and stared at the outline of her pale face and jet hair in the flickering light of the smoky brazier. "Can you? Can you stand up to Tigellinus?"

"He wouldn't dare arrest me." She sniffed. "After all, I'm your wife. And Lord Sabinus wouldn't tolerate it."

"Oh? Wouldn't he?"

"Of course not."

I cupped my chin with a palmed hand on a raised elbow. "My dear, if Tigellinus can condemn to death senators at the raising of an eyebrow, he can have your pretty head as well. Neither Sabinus nor I could stop him. That's how much influence he has with Nero."

Although I could not see her eyes, I felt them glaring at me. "Why would Tigellinus arrest me?"

"Because as I explained before, you're my wife and a Christian. And now, Gallus is involved."

Eleyne shook her head. "That doesn't answer my question."

"What better way at holding me accountable than by your imprisonment and perhaps the boys?"

"He wouldn't—not our sons!" she said in a rush, then paused. "Do you really think he would?"

"He's capable of doing anything, especially when there's a fortune involved."

"Gallus," she exclaimed, bolting upright in the goose-feather bed. "It's always Gallus. Can't you do anything to stop him?"

"Short of murder, no." A low rumbling thunder rolled overhead.

"I don't expect you to kill him. But there must be something!"

"So long as he is under Tigellinus's protection, there is little I can do, except keep him under close surveillance." I came to a decision. "That's why I'm sending you and our sons back to Hispania."

A whistle escaped through Eleyne's nostrils. "Oh? When was that decided?"

"The moment I received news Gallus's scheme had Nero's blessing."

"And if I refuse?"

I feared losing my patience. "You may not care about your life, but our sons are in danger, too."

She reached over and laid her small alabaster hand on my arm, her fingers warm to the touch. "There are others in danger," she said, "people that I have aided—what about them?"

"My concern is for you and the boys."

"You should be as concerned for our slaves. What of Chulainn, Imogen, and their little daughter?"

"As much as I care for Chulainn and his family, they're still slaves."

"They're equals in the eyes of God," Eleyne retorted. "Regan is barely two, she has as much right to live as anyone else."

"What does Chulainn's daughter have to do with this?" I asked.

"You mean you haven't heard?"

I shook my head.

"Regan is dying."

I studied her in silence. "Chulainn mentioned last week that Regan was sick but didn't seem too concerned."

"It wasn't serious then, now it is. She's wasting away. She can't keep any food down, and she burns with fever."

"Has Soranus seen her?"

"Yes, and there is nothing he can do," Eleyne replied. She turned away. "And neither can I—my prayers have been futile."

I pulled Eleyne close to me. "I'm sorry." I had thought Regan was suffering from just another childhood illness. Children always seem to be coming down with something.

Unfortunately, any fever could be fatal. It was common knowledge that only half of all children survived to age five. My duties, especially the investigation of the fire, had consumed all my thoughts and energy. Household affairs I left to Eleyne, the customary role of a Roman matron.

"Then you've done all you can do and must leave," I said. "As much as I value Chulainn and his family, your life is far more valuable to me."

She pulled away from me. "No child, especially Imogen's, should die," Eleyne said in an angry voice. "To me, Regan is like the daughter I lost."

"What else can you do for her?"

There was a long pause only interrupted by the muffled sound of distant thunder. "We have one last hope," she answered. "And I promise no matter whether she's cured or dies, I will leave Rome when it's finished."

"What does it involve?" I asked, already knowing the answer.

"I must take Regan to see Paul. He's back in Rome and speaks tomorrow night at our services."

I sat up in bed. "Is he mad? He couldn't have returned from Greece at a worse time."

"What difference does it make? He's Regan's last hope."

"Tigellinus's spies are everywhere—they won't let Paul out of their sight."

My thoughts turned to the Christian leader. He had gathered a sizable following for the dead Jew during his previous stay in Rome. When he left the city, he reportedly journeyed to Greece or Asia Minor. I feared his return at this perilous time would once more put his life and those of the Christian community in jeopardy.

"If he attends the meeting," I continued, snapping out of my thoughts, "your chances of being arrested are multiplied tenfold! Stay home!"

"No, Marcellus," Eleyne answered firmly. "I'll return to Hispania, but you won't deny me this chance to save little Regan. After all, Paul cured me, and he may be able to do the same for her. I must take that chance."

I could forcibly lock Eleyne in her room, but if the child died she would never forgive me. I was stymied by her determination.

"All right," I said. "Needless to say, Chulainn goes along for protection. The streets aren't safe after the sun sets."

Despite the risks to Eleyne, I was gambling that my concerns for her safety were an overreaction on my part.

* * *

The storm ended the following evening. I would arrange for passage on the next ship to Malaca out of Ostia the following day. Eleyne and the boys would be packed and ready to go at a moment's notice. Chulainn and Imogen's daughter had reached a crisis. She would either be healed or dead. Departure could come none too soon. With each passing day the seas grew worse. Soon the sailing season would end until the following spring.

Eleyne had left earlier for the meeting carrying a bundled up Regan and escorted by an anxious Chulainn. The boys, who had always liked and respected Chulainn, had been concerned about his daughter, and had initially waited up with me. Soon they grew bored and sleepy and went to bed.

When the hour grew late, and Eleyne failed to return with the child and Chulainn, I sent Porus to fetch them.

He didn't return until three hours later, well past midnight, fresh scratches on his wrinkled face and patches of mud streaking his newly made woolen cloak.

"Master," Porus gasped. "Terrible news. The mistress and Chulainn and his daughter were arrested."

My heart shot up into my throat. I barely breathed and took several deep breaths before asking, "Where?"

"In the catacombs, by the Praetorians."

"How long ago?" I asked, trying to keep my wits about me.

"Nearly two hours, sir," Porus's voice waivered. He seemed on the verge of collapse.

"Where did they take them?"

"Latumiae Prison."

"Get my horse and your mule and send a slave to Prefect Sabinus with the news. You can fill in the details on the way."

"But sir, I saw . . . ," he mumbled a reply as he hurried away.

As we traveled to the prison, Porus rode beside me and related the story. "I used the cover of a moonless night to sneak out of the city. I hiked along the Appian Way and kept to the shadows that surrounded the tombs lining the road. Three times I avoided patrols of the Watch, ducking behind those pretentious monuments." He paused and sighed. The hooves of our mounts, striking the tufa stone pavement, echoed off the walls of the surrounding buildings.

"Go on," I said.

He swallowed and cleared his throat. "I left the highway and moved toward a grove of poplars. You know the place, sir, the hidden entry leading to the underground gallery where we worship."

I nodded.

A couple of shadowy figures stepped out of a dark alley into our path, startling the animals to a halt. Both pulled knives from their tunics and waved them in front of us.

Robbers!

I pulled out my sword. "Don't stop," I said. "Trample them!"

Porus and I kicked our mounts forward. I swung my weapon down toward one bandit, but he and his partner jumped to one side before I could strike him. The two fled down the alley on the opposite side of the street.

I looked back to make certain they didn't have second thoughts, sheathed my weapon, and then asked Porus to continue with his tale.

He nodded. "I looked about before I approached and stopped about two hundred feet from the brush-covered entrance. My eyes strained to pierce the darkness. It was like ink, but was impossible to see more than a few feet. Then I heard metal clanking on metal—sounds of armor and dived into a nearby thicket. I was afraid I'd made too much noise and wanted to flee. Somehow, I managed to remain silent." He licked his lips and glanced toward me.

"Don't stop now, continue."

"I saw no sign of movement. After a few minutes, I recognized the silhouettes of two Praetorians patrolling near the entrance carrying javelins. I concluded the other guards had fanned out and surrounded the cave. I was too late to help mistress Eleyne and Chulainn. It was impossible to flee, I had no choice except to stay hidden."

My stomach churned, knowing what fate must have befallen on Eleyne and the rest.

"It seemed like hours," Porus continued, "but I'm certain no more than a few minutes passed, when I heard women screaming, followed by curses from the Praetorians. At least a hundred troops herded the Christians out of the cave with clubs and javelins.

"In the light from the soldiers' torches, I caught a glimpse of the mistress's face—she was terrified. The guards shoved her and the other Christians past the bushes where I hid. Chulainn seemed very shaken, walked by her side. Still he attempted to soothe her fears as she held Regan in her arms."

Shit! I wanted to shout and many other profanities but kept my anger under control. Why did I let her go there?

"I kept to the shadows at a safe distance," Porus continued, "and followed the Praetorians. They drove between two and three hundred Christians to prison."

When Porus and I arrived at Latumiae, I headed for the office of the tribune in charge of the prison and demanded the release of my wife and servant.

"My orders are to release no one, including your wife," the haughty tribune said.

At one time, Latumiae had been under the jurisdiction of the city prefect, but the Emperor Claudius transferred the prison to the jurisdiction of the Praetorian prefect. No longer did Sabinus or I have authority within its confines.

I attempted to force my way past the tribune's office, but two burly Praetorian guardsmen blocked my way with crossed lances. I stormed out of the lockup.

Outraged and frustrated, I rode to Sabinus's home. It was now more than an hour after midnight, and his chief steward turned me away at the door. "Lord Sabinus is not here, sir, and I don't know when he will return."

"Didn't my slave relay the message about my wife and the child?"

"Yes, sir, and I shall see that Lord Sabinus gets it as soon as he returns."

"Where did he go?"

"He didn't say."

I found the steward's conduct puzzling. Even in Sabinus's absence, I was welcomed at his home—day or night. Something sinister had occurred. Sabinus seldom stayed out this late. Had Tigellinus arrested him on a trumped-up charge—the same fate of other senators?

I proceeded straight for the palace to see Praetorian Prefect Tigellinus. While his mansion was being rebuilt, he had commandeered the living quarters used by the Praetorian tribune on duty with the palace detachment.

Dressed in a white, silken night tunic stitched with gold thread, the Praetorian prefect stood by the open mahogany door to his apartment. The shadowy light of a couple of oil lamps lit the entryway. "What do you want, Commander Reburrus?" Tigellinus asked. A wry grin crossed his weathered face. He knew well enough why I awoke him in the middle of the night.

"Your troops have arrested my wife and servant and his dying daughter."

He raised his eyebrows. "Did they? The charges?"

"For incendiarism and being Christian."

His face muscles tightened. A frown crossed his thin lips. "Those are serious allegations."

"Sir, you know perfectly well she's innocent of arson, and since when is it illegal to be a Christian?"

"I grant you, my troops *may* have acted over-zealously in charging her with arson, but . . . " He paused and scowled. "For too long, the plotting Christians have committed seditious acts against Rome and the emperor. Especially, refusing to sacrifice to the genius of our beloved emperor. I will no longer tolerate their crimes. And lately they have appeared in the strangest places. Imagine even the wife of a trusted commander and personal friend of Lord Sabinus, belonging to that abominable sect. Incredible!"

"Prefect Tigellinus, my wife has always been loyal to Rome—even when taken as Imperial hostage years ago."

"If true," he answered evenly, "she will have no qualms sacrificing to the Emperor's genius—before loyal witnesses."

"Her religion prohibits her from making votive offerings to anyone but her God. She can't do otherwise."

Tigellinus cupped his hand over his mouth as he yawned. Then he shook his head. "Pity. Her Christian friends had no qualms about sacrificing Rome to please the same God."

"We both know the rumors implicating her and the Christians are lies."

He twisted his mouth into a sneer. "Are they? My sources say otherwise. Remember, the emperor in his infinite wisdom divines what is truth and what is false—who am I to question him?"

"Since I'm her husband, why haven't you arrested me?"

"Because your loyalty is unquestioned, and we know you have no use for her God." He seemed bored with my questions, and his eyes flicked impatiently toward the bedchamber.

"If I guarantee she won't leave the house or attend further meetings, couldn't you release her?" I asked. "It's in your power."

"Tribune Marcellus Reburrus, Rome's enemies are everywhere," he intoned with a wave of the hand, "especially among this seditious sect who pray to the dead Jew. I won't risk the chance of releasing even one, unless . . . unless she sacrifices to the emperor."

A girl of about ten peeked playfully through the chamber drapes behind his back as I asked, "If she doesn't?"

"For her sake, pray to the gods she does. She holds herself prisoner, Commander, not I." He turned on his heels and slammed the door behind him.

Fuming and full of despair, I left Tigellinus, knowing his parting words rang true.

CHAPTER 25

During the next three days, rumors abounded about the fate of the Christians snared in the mass arrest. My spies failed to learn how long they would be imprisoned before the persecutions began. However, one brought me word that Eleyne had received the clothing I had sent her, including a gold stola, a gift from Sabinus, befitting her station.

Despite protests and threats, the authorities at Latumiae Prison spurned my requests to see Eleyne. I encountered the same resistance at Sabinus's residence. The steward insisted his master was not home, and he refused to see me at his office. Tigellinus ordered his Praetorians to arrest me if I came near his quarters.

Late afternoon of the third day, I received a confidential message by courier from Faenus Rufus. He said he would attempt everything in his power to secure Eleyne's release. Grateful for his concern, I recognized his efforts to remain secret. He loathed Tigellinus and the tyranny he subjected to all in Rome. Under the Praetorian prefect's leadership, the Praetorian Guard had changed from protector of the emperor to an instrument of terror feared by the people.

Although Sabinus had refused to see me, he remained my commander-in-chief, from whom I received orders. He sent word that Nero had invited him to a party in the rebuilt gardens at the Palace of Augustus. I arranged for my daily inspection patrol of the City Guard to cross his path on the way to the palace.

At dusk Sabinus's entourage left his home on Quirinal Hill. Scouts forewarned my escort of thirty mounted guardsmen as he approached the noisy, crowded Forum. Darkness crept over the city, and people jostled one another as they fled homeward before Rome's criminal elements claimed the streets.

Riding in an open litter, Sabinus entered the Forum from the slum-infested Subura. His slaves and servants shouted at passersby to make way for the City Prefect, but the indifferent mob ignored their admonitions. Nonchalantly, we rode in his direction as if on routine patrol. Unlike Sabinus, my contingent had no problem plowing through the vast ocean of people. No one likes being trampled by horses with iron-shod hooves.

I halted before Sabinus, and for a knowing instant, our eyes locked. From his litter his glazed eyes stared through me without acknowledgment, like a stranger. I was seized by loathing and despair.

"Lord Sabinus," I said, "what has happened to my wife?"

"This is not the time or place to discuss her situation," he answered sharply. "You are blocking the way."

Heat rushed to my face, acid filled my stomach. "I'll move once you name where and when we can talk about Eleyne."

Sabinus's face darkened, the edge of his lips curling downward. "I give the orders, not you."

I motioned my troopers to surround his litter. His followers moved out of the way, intimidated by the horses.

The prefect's hawk eyes stared into mine. "You know I can arrest you for mutiny."

"I'm aware of your power, Prefect Sabinus," I said as I motioned to my guard, "but these men are loyal to me. All I want is to speak of my wife, Eleyne, the woman who you once treated as a daughter."

Sabinus looked about as my horsemen turned their mounts outward and shoved back his people. He seldom used an escort of troops—an error on his part.

Displaying no emotion, Sabinus nodded. "Very well, you deserve at least that courtesy. I will send a messenger when I return home."

"Thank you, sir."

Before I departed, the troops cleared a pathway through the crowds to the Sacred Way and palace for Sabinus.

* * *

257

That evening, after Sabinus had attended the feast at Nero's and returned home, I reported to him. His steward hustled me into his study where a lone, flickering lamp illuminated the tablinum. For a moment an air of treachery filled the room. He could still arrest me, but he was too honorable to set a trap in his own home.

"Marcellus," a tense voice called out in the darkness. Sabinus stepped forward but did not offer a handshake or an embrace. A coldness enshrouded the library as he moved to his ancient writing desk. A slave lit the small, gold-plated olive-oil lamps sitting in bronze tripods at each end of the desk. Sabinus dismissed him with the arching of an eyebrow, and I took a chair in front of his desk.

The dim, blue-white flame cast a ghostly pall on his face. Visibly shaken, Sabinus's bloodshot eyes contained a look of despair.

"Tonight I have witnessed," he said, "one of the most horrifying spectacles in my life. I have attended countless games, and seen men slaughtered in many ways. Some deserved their fate and others not, but never have I seen a more repugnant, degrading scene than tonight. And in this case the victims were truly innocent."

"Eleyne?" I asked instantly. "Were she and Chulainn among—"

He raised his hand to silence me.

Sabinus placed both hands to his face and rested his elbows on the table. A hush engulfed the room. Although eager to ask more about Eleyne, I sensed something ominous and waited for him to finish. Sabinus raised his head, and his dull eyes met mine.

He related his story without interruption. After the usual banquet, and a ghastly serenade by Nero, the emperor invited his guests to the new gardens for a special treat, as he called it. Illuminated by hundreds of torches, exotic flowers dazzled the imagination in a rainbow of colors. Manicured shrubbery and statues imported from all over the empire, bordered pathways and sculptured fountains. The warm night seemed made to order by Nero. A cheerful flute teased strolling lovers, and the fragrance of a thousand flowers scented the air, somehow making the stars above seem close enough to touch.

"Pathways scattered throughout," Sabinus said, "were blocked by strings of colorful ribbons, to guide the guests to a central point."

Sabinus hesitated. "But upon arrival, I felt uneasy. I heard a muffled scream."

Ushers, dressed as laughing clowns, followed by all-too-serious Praetorian guards, had prodded the stragglers forward.

Then in the dancing illumination of orange and amber lights, startled guests saw the victims. On an open stretch, along a straight, mosaic-inlaid path disappearing into the tall, distant cypresses, stood sixty newly made crosses cut from pitch-bleeding pine. Men and women alike, stripped of their clothing and dignity, hung like sausages in a butcher shop, groaning in pain and gasping for air. Blood trickled from spike wounds in their hemp-tied wrists, down the sides of their emaciated bodies, and along dangling legs and feet.

"Amongst all the beauty of the world," Sabinus whispered, "such a sight will forever pervert my memory of the night."

He related how the stench of sweat and excrement, of stale blood and sweet roses wafted through the crowd of guests.

"Large bundles of dried faggots had been piled high for kindling," he continued, "these surrounded the base of each cross. The captive guests realized what was about to occur. Some attempted laughter, pretending to enjoy the spectacle, but the groaning and agonized faces of the victims dampened the festive occasion."

The dancing flute now shrilled a bizarre note of the macabre. Some guests could not mask their horror—a fatal mistake. Others radiated pleasure bordering on ecstasy. Nero's spies scattered among the crowd to report any undesirable reactions—to the emperor's displeasure.

With the greatest of difficulty, Sabinus maintained his composure. I continued to listen in dread, forcing myself not to interrupt.

"But it was only the beginning," Sabinus continued. "No one noticed Nero had disappeared. A short time later he thundered into the gardens driving a gilded chariot, pulled by four snorting, white horses."

Dressed in flowing lion skins, Nero reined up at the center of the ghastly line of crucifixes—thirty posted on each side of the path. He leapt from his chariot and motioned impatiently towards a bush. Six hidden slaves emerged carrying a ladder and hurried to the cross where a slender female was nailed. She wore a mask depicting Diana, the huntress. Deftly, they slipped the ladder behind her buttocks, resting it against the wooden beam.

Eagerly, the boisterous Nero, who snorted more like a pig than roared like a lion, climbed the ladder. He paused only when he had slid between her blood-smeared legs.

Slaves struggled to maintain the ladder's balance and prevent him from falling. Two other slaves jumped upon the kindling and held the cross, beginning to lean slightly to one side. Nero fondled the young woman's breasts and body as she struggled to breathe. Hiking up his lion skin, and covering them both, he coupled with her.

"Silently, she endured his animal lust," Sabinus related. "I glanced to the other guests and surmised revulsion and horror from their eyes. Yet, none were as horrified as I. I was certain I recognized the golden stola I had given Eleyne," Sabinus said.

I sat dazed, not realizing that I clutched a drawn sword. Had anyone but Sabinus told me this disgusting tale, I would have killed him.

"When the woman refused to return his groans of pleasure," Sabinus said, "Nero ripped off her mask and slapped her. Then his eyes searched the crowd and locked on mine. Seeing me swaying in shock, he roared in laughter."

"Was it—"

"It was not Eleyne."

I breathed in relief, and suddenly, the heavy exhaustion from the days of strain dropped upon me like a blacksmith's anvil.

"Then he moved on to other crucifixes and committed more revolting acts," Sabinus said nearly choking on his words. "None were spared. When Nero finished," Sabinus continued, "he rode to the standing guests, halted, and announced the criminals being crucified in his beloved gardens were the perpetrators who burned Rome. For the guests' pleasure and amusement, they had the honor of witnessing their executions. Nero received a rousing ovation."

Sabinus recognized eight of the victims as prominent merchants, all whom were branded Christians. Nero gave credit for the arrests to *the diligent investigations of our Praetorian Prefect, Sofonius Tigellinus.*

Tigellinus stood on the edge of the crowd feigning a bow of humility. Nearby, Gallus beamed his pleasure.

"At a nod from the emperor," Sabinus added, "a century of Praetorians emerged from the shadows and heaved flaming torches onto the bundles at the base of each cross. The dried packets exploded, and in minutes flames towered to the top of the crosses. The heat was so tremendous it forced the guests back. We heard the poor souls' screams above the fiery, howling roar—and then, silence.

"Nero laughed, and the horrified, terror-stricken guests followed suit. As the flames billowed higher, one by one the flimsy crosses burned through, and their victims toppled into the burning heap, creating one long, narrow funeral pyre.

"Afterwards, Nero returned to the palace, followed by his guests. I excused myself as soon as I dared.

"I discarded my clothes and bathed immediately to rid myself of the stench of burnt flesh, but I . . . " His eyes clouded, and he seemed near tears. "I'm a weak man, Marcellus. I haven't the courage to stand up to Nero."

"And what if you had?" I said. I echoed his own words of long ago. "You're no good to Rome dead." Right now, Eleyne was more important to me than Rome would ever be.

"Rome wouldn't be any worse than it is now. I had influence until Nero began attacking the people— Christians, merchants, even petty thieves. Now—"

"In the name of Jove, can't you at least obtain Eleyne's release?"

"No," he said, exhausted.

"Surely," I said, "you have some influence left. Can't you appeal directly to the emperor?"

"No, Marcellus, it's no use."

"Then why did you summon me?" My stomach churned, quill bumps raised upon my arms and back. Rage grew within my being.

"To reassure you for the present, Eleyne, has remained unharmed. Forgive me for the tale I just told, but you have a right to know about Nero's crimes."

"I must see her."

"You will make no more attempts." His voice was flat, a command.

"Why?"

"I can't say. My warning is enough."

Heat rushed to my face. My ears filled with noise like roaring tidal waves crashing against a rocky shoreline. "And if I disobey your order?"

"Don't be foolish," he answered harshly. "I would place you under arrest, and this time I won't back down."

His candor shocked me. He saw the anger and pain in my face.

"You know I don't condone this monstrous persecution, but I'm in no position to stop Nero and Tigellinus."

"What about Eleyne—my wife? Is she to die like the others—crucified?"

Sabinus reached over and placed his still-powerful hand on my elbow. "Nothing will happen to Eleyne, I promise. You know she means the world to me. But Nero's message was clear—Eleyne's life is in jeopardy and depends solely upon our behavior—yours and mine."

"Your promise?" I roared. "Nero's message is a damn lie!" I shoved his hand away and leapt to my feet. "By the gods, you ignored me, refused to see me, treated me like . . . like . . . and now, you *promise* me? You bastard, I could—"

For the space of a dozen heartbeats he bowed his head and turned away. "I told you I am weak. It wasn't Eleyne

on the cross—but I believed it was her and watched her
being raped. And I did nothing. Eleyne has done so much
good for others as a caring and courageous woman. I was
sickened, but I acted the coward. I was afraid to speak
out."

Sabinus paused and lifted his head, fixing his gaze
upon me. "I will live with my cowardice and shame until
I die. But neither you nor the cursed gods will by foolish
actions bring harm to Eleyne, my *daughter*, Eleyne." He
still cared, and that alone tempered my rage.

I left Sabinus's home angrier and more frustrated than
before. Where else could I turn for help?

* * *

I nearly discarded the message from Gallus waiting on
my return home after midnight. I was grateful I changed
my mind. For the first time in days a glimmer of hope
returned. Gallus said he could obtain Eleyne's release.
What irony. Whereas my patron failed, my adversary
offered hope. What was his price in return? I hated him
still, but for Eleyne's freedom, I would try anything, pay
any price.

I headed for Gallus's new home east of the walls on
Pincian Hill. Untouched by the fire, the palatial mansion
once belonged to one of Gallus's victims, a prominent
merchant holding the state's lead monopoly.

I stood across from Gallus as he sat at a desk in his
new trophy room. Ignoring me, he gazed at a parchment
laying on the flat surface, filled with obscene drawings.
Assorted weapons, taken from Rome's conquered enemies,
hung on the wall, including a plain, black hardwood club.
Wearing no makeup, Gallus's once youthful face revealed
the ravages of time and debauchery. Drab and limp, yellow
hair, receding at the temples, replaced his once-blond
locks. Cavernous furrows crossed his forehead, and thin
lines tracked from the corners of his washed-out, blue
eyes. The deep-set battle scar on his cheek coupled with
his natural smirk, stamped his malice plainly on his face.

Finally, bored with his little game, Gallus peered up from the scroll. "Greetings, Marcellus, I have been expecting you."

"I'm curious to hear more about your proposal," I said.

He grinned. "Since your wife is involved, I assume you're more than just curious."

"Come to the point!" I snapped. Then I forced myself to grovel. "Go on, please."

"My dear Marcellus, you were never one for wasting words." His voice grew stern. "It is within my power to obtain the release of Lady Eleyne. Once I give the word, she will be discharged in a matter of hours."

A surge of relief and excitement welled within me. I called on all my strength to maintain my self-control. "What is the price for her freedom?"

"Nothing."

I studied Gallus in stunned silence. He lied. By freeing Eleyne, I would again be under an unknown obligation. One I would be compelled to honor. We both knew it.

"You never grant favors," I said, "without expecting something in return. I haven't forgotten my repayment of your loan at one hundred percent interest in Britannia."

Gallus brushed off the remark with a wave of the hand. "That was long ago. I assure you I want nothing that is yours."

In other words, don't interfere with his schemes. I had no doubt he would extract a heavy price at a future time, and I would pay it. "By what means," I asked, "do you intend to free her?"

He glanced toward the entrance before he turned back to me. "For a fee, there is a magistrate who will sign the appropriate documents."

"Of course, what other way is there?" I shook my head. "But she'll never sacrifice to the emperor."

He raised his thin eyebrows as in mock surprise. "No one is asking her to do any such thing. The judge and two hand-picked witnesses will testify she did."

"You must have reached far inside your toga for him."

"Far enough."

"But why?"

"Never mind," he growled, "I have my reasons. Be grateful I did."

"I am." I exhaled, hating myself.

"It so happens she is here—not free, mind you—but here." He motioned for me to follow and stepped into an adjoining room with a stone wall. He swept aside a velvet curtain and gestured to me to look through the peephole. My heart pounded when I saw her. Eleyne sat amongst the flowers between pink Numidian columns of a *peristilium*. I was too far away to call her, but close enough to see she was unharmed. Chulainn stood near the peristyle, leaning against a pillar, hanging his head. In my concern for Eleyne, I had forgotten Chulainn, and his wife's desperate plea for help.

Then I saw little Regan peeking from behind the bench where Eleyne sat. She scooted out and nearly tripped on her long homespun tunic. She squealed and crawled onto Eleyne's lap and giggled. She was no longer ill. Was this the work of Paul?

"Her release," I said turning to Gallus, "includes her servant, Chulainn, and his daughter."

Gallus moved to the peephole without answering. A few seconds passed. "It goes without saying the child is to be freed. She is innocent, and I hate to see children suffer. As for your man servant, I am impressed by his loyalty to your wife. He was willing to do anything to see her free." Gallus lingered, staring blankly at them. "Loyalty, and a willingness to do anything, are virtues I greatly admire."

His voice dropped and spoke softly, as if thinking aloud. "His skin was . . . so . . . soft, and . . . " He caught himself. "Of course, he is to be freed, too. But should you ever decide to sell him, send for my slave buyer, immediately."

Gallus escorted me to the entrance of his house and paused briefly. A dark expression crossed his face. "I have arranged this favor for you. In turn, the time will come when I shall ask you the same. When that hour arrives, remember this day." He grinned and gave a slight mocking bow of the head.

* * *

Gallus kept his promise. An hour before dawn, I waited outside Latumiae Prison, enduring the jail's overwhelming stench. When the iron door swung open, I caught Eleyne's small, cloak-draped figure and Chulainn's wiry frame. He carried his daughter asleep in his arms. Stiffly, they trudged to the lane where I waited with a litter and an extra horse.

Although I had observed them wearing clean clothing at Gallus's home the night before, their garments now reeked of prison filth. It did not prevent me from giving Eleyne a quick embrace and a pat on Chulainn's back. Despite foul-smelling clothing, his face was scrubbed and clean shaven.

Regan's face was a healthy pink. Chulainn smiled.

"Thank God you came," Eleyne whispered, her gaunt face riddled with pain. "I don't know much longer I could have endured that foul place. We found Paul—Regan is healed."

"I'm glad for all of you, darling," I said. "But let's get quickly away from here. This place sickens me."

I whisked them home. Chulainn said nothing during the trip and avoided my eyes. I knew the unspoken wound he had suffered to protect his mistress.

The entire household, including young Marcellus and Sabinus, awoke early to welcome us. Chulainn's mute wife, Imogen, pregnant with their third child, gave him an awkward hug. For a moment, Chulainn stood near tears, then met her embrace with equal tenderness.

Before discussing her terrible ordeal, Eleyne quietly ordered a bath.

When Eleyne departed in Imogen's company, Chulainn and I went to the library. I motioned for him to take a seat in front of the desk from where I sat. As the pulsating light from two lamps sitting on tripods lit his haggard face, he licked his chapped lips, swallowed, and reluctantly spoke.

"The mistress and I," Chulainn said, his eyes avoiding contact with mine, "traveled to the catacombs. The place was lighted by the lanterns of hundreds of worshipers."

Paul, who had been expected to address the gathering, never arrived. By the time the services concluded, rumors circulated that Tigellinus had placed the apostle under arrest.

"We were disappointed," Chulainn said, "and the faithful began to leave. Within a few minutes one of the members returned shouting, 'Guards! Run for your lives.'

"There were three entrances to the great vault. People crowded and clogged the passageways trying to escape. But it was impossible. The Praetorians blocked all exits. Few worshippers resisted, which saved our lives."

Chulainn swallowed. "The troops were eager for slaughter."

My heart leaped into my throat, and I took several deep breaths. I wasn't surprised by the Praetorians' action. "Go on."

"I would've fought them if the mistress hadn't ordered me to stop. Seven guards surrounded me sticking their javelins in my face."

"You were wise to refrain, I know those butchers. Continue."

He nodded. "After we were herded through streets to the prison, they stuffed us like cabbages into stinking dungeon holds. We took turns sitting and standing in the dark and filthy cell. It was so stifling we could hardly breathe. Except where you sat or stood, there was no place to relieve yourself.

"We received one meal of maggot-infested food in three days," Chulainn said bitterly, "and little water. There wasn't enough for all. Little Regan suffered badly. Her breathing grew shallower, and her face turned gray. I thought she would die at any time."

I balled my fists and shook my head. "How did the Lady Eleyne withstand the conditions?"

Chulainn nodded. "The mistress endured everything without complaint. She was more concerned about Regan and constantly comforted her. She attempted to help others who didn't fare so well, especially the children. Like my daughter, they suffered the most."

On the night before Eleyne and Chulainn's release, Paul was shoved into the cell by two burly guards. Despite the cell's cramped conditions, everyone crowded around the Christian leader, asking questions about his arrest and for his blessing.

Eleyne managed to push her way to Paul's side. "He recognized the mistress at once," Chulainn said. "'The baby,' is all she said. Then Paul nodded and laid his hands on Regan's cheeks and his lips moved in silent prayer. He removed his hands and whispered something to the mistress who thanked him. At first, I didn't see any change. Then the color returned to Regan's face, and her breathing grew stronger.

"When she awakened and started crying from hunger, I knew she would live."

"I'm thankful for the both of you," I said.

Chulainn swallowed. "It wasn't over yet. The night was on us when guards carrying torches arrived and yanked nearly sixty men and women from prison, including us."

I shuddered, and chills ran through my body.

"As the Praetorians escorted us and the other Christians through a tunnel and out into the Forum, a soldier suddenly pulled the mistress and Regan out of the line. My daughter broke free from his grasp and ran to my side, screaming. She would not leave me. The soldier seemed confused and looked about. I followed his gaze to a commander on horseback. Even in the torchlight, I recognized Tribune Faenus Rufus. He nodded his approval and spared the three of us."

"Thank the gods, he did," I said. "I plan to see him later. Go on, Chulainn."

He nodded. "Tribune Rufus ordered the mistress to remove her golden stola and give it to him. She refused, but he warned her that if she did not obey, she would be crucified."

I jolted. "What happened?"

"She complied and was left wearing only a white, woolen undershift. A guard grabbed the mistress and dragged her into the dim light of the hallway. I feared the worst."

He exhaled. "Thank God, the centurion in charge of the escort ordered the guard to stop and return the mistress, my daughter, and me to a cell.

"A few hours later, the door opened, and the guard ordered the three of us out. I was afraid the centurion had changed his mind. They placed the mistress and Regan in a private cell, and other guards escorted me to Senator Gallus's house for questioning." Chulainn paused. He swallowed hard and licked his dry lips.

"You don't have to speak if you don't want."

"Gallus then said that before the mistress was crucified he would have her."

My face grew hot. *That filthy bastard! He deserves death!*

"He threatened crucifixion again," Chulainn continued, "and I begged him to spare my daughter and Lady Eleyne. I said I would do anything to save their lives."

'Anything?' Gallus had asked. I could only nod. He said, 'Your mistress by force, or you willingly—either would be amusing.' He parted the robe from his otherwise nude body and stepped closer to me and forced me to kneel. He ran his fingers through my hair," Chulainn struggled to go on, "and made me . . ."

"Say no more," I said, sensing the outrage he endured. I tried comforting him, grateful for his loyalty, but when I reached across the desk and touched his shoulder, he pulled away.

"I'm sorry, sir," he said an instant later.

"Someday, Gallus will pay for your humiliation, I promise."

After a minute of silence, Chulainn resumed his story. Later, Eleyne joined him in Gallus's peristyle, and afterward both returned to prison. The turnkey said Eleyne's detention had been a mistake, and she and her slave and the child would be released. When the door to freedom sprang open, Eleyne whispered, *Thank you, Lord, for our deliverance.*

When Chulainn finished his story, I told him of the prisoners' fates. He smashed a fist into his other palm. He fled to his room.

* * *

Later, after Eleyne had bathed and dressed, I went to the bedroom. Imogen had finished combing her hair, and Eleyne motioned for the mute servant to leave. Eleyne's impassiveness gave way to sobs. I took her into my arms.

"Marcellus!" She softly wept and later fell asleep.

I held her the rest of the morning. I swore my revenge to the gods, cursing her dead Jew who allowed this man named Gallus to live.

CHAPTER 26

64-69 AD

During the next five turbulent years, my fortunes and
that of Sabinus fluctuated like the ocean tides.

Within days after Eleyne's release from prison, I sent
her and our sons, along with Chulainn and his family, to
Hispania. As their ship moved away from Ostia's dock and
headed for the open sea, I turned away to hide the tears
sliding down my cheeks. Although I had made the right
decision, it had been gut wrenching. I missed my family
already, not knowing when I would see them again. My
only consolation was the remoteness of the latifundia, sixty
miles from the nearest seaport, which would keep them out
of sight and harm's way.

The situation in Rome grew worse. Nero's neglect
and greed inspired a series of conspiracies against his
life. Some, patently fabricated by Tigellinus, allowed the
emperor to seize the estates of prominent and blameless
noblemen. The Stoic philosopher, Lucius Seneca,
was forced to commit suicide while many others were
executed. Sabinus and I stayed quietly in the background,
performing the mundane duties of city administration and
law enforcement.

Because the emperor had neglected to visit legion
garrisons strung along the empire's frontier, he failed
to hold the loyalty of the army. Then he made the fatal
mistake of allowing their pay to fall into arrears. Only the
Praetorians, commanded by Tigellinus, and City Guard,
which I led, were paid on a regular basis.

During this time, a period of approximately four years,
I had corresponded with Eleyne and our sons, young
Marcellus and Sabinus, and managed to spend three

summers with them. But before each time I left for Rome, the farewell to my family became a prolonged, heart-breaking experience full of long hugs and tears. Still, I refused to allow them to return to the city, and I'm glad I did.

* * *

68 AD

After I returned from my last leave, events in Rome reached a critical stage. After two unsuccessful revolts in Gaul and Germania, the commander of Hispania's only legion, General Galba, then past seventy, declared himself emperor and marched on Rome. The rumors I had heard when in Hispania were true when I returned to Rome just ahead of Galba. I served under the old man as a young cavalry sergeant in Germania. The Senate sentenced Nero, who earlier went into hiding, to death in absentia branding him an enemy of the state. Galba's agents promised a substantial bonus to the Praetorian Guard if they pledged their allegiance to the still vigorous Legate. They did, and the army followed suit. Not wanting to be executed as a traitor, I had little choice but to include my troops.

Nero fled to a freedman's house in Rome's suburbs. Because Tigellinus was dying from cancer, there was no one to protect the emperor from the wrath of the Senate. Too cowardly to open his own veins or take poison, Nero whined and begged his mistress, the freedwoman, Acte, to cut his throat with a dagger. Groveling to the end, he died at barely thirty-two.

When Galba arrived in Rome, he immediately dismissed Sabinus as city prefect and chief magistrate, replacing him with one of his own men. I was transferred to the fleet at Ravenna on the northeastern coast of Italy. My orders stated the purpose was to broaden my experience and value as a commanding officer. I had been field commander of the City Guard too long. In reality, Galba feared the loyalty of the city troops, which I still retained. The emperor demanded this for himself. Although I had a reputation for unquestioned loyalty to the throne, the emperor was not impressed, and decided such fealty was better suited for an officer in the navy. He kept me far enough away to have little political influence in Rome, but close enough to be well within his reach.

Instead of being angry and resentful, my whole body sagged in relief. I was grateful for the opportunity to leave Rome and thanked the gods. I had spent too many years in a high-profile position, subject to the scrutiny and political foibles of madmen and murderers.

However, to further ensure my loyalty I was ordered to return Eleyne from Hispania to Rome. Although angry, she knew neither of us had a choice. Fortunately, three months earlier young Marcellus, now twenty, and young Sabinus, nineteen, had been appointed as tribunes in the army and assigned to the Twentieth Legion based safely in Britannia.

When Eleyne returned to Rome, I worried that her life could be in jeopardy once again. Would Galba continue the persecution of Christians?

* * *

69 AD

One rainy January morning during the seventh month of Galba's reign, the Praetorians murdered the emperor in the Forum, after he refused to pay the bonus he had promised them. Marcus Otho, a foppish nobleman, pledged the troops the same bribe if they acclaimed him emperor. He decided to move against the old man when he discovered Galba had not kept his promise to adopt and make him heir to the throne.

After Galba's death, Emperor Otho recalled Sabinus and reinstated him as city prefect, but I was left to languish with the fleet in Ravenna. I was second-in-command in name only. The real authority remained with its commander, Admiral Lucilius Bassus.

No sooner had Otho claimed the Imperial purple than the bejowled commander of the Upper Germania Legions,

Aulus Vitellius, declared himself emperor. His father, Lucius Vitellius the Elder, had been one of Sabinus's closest friends during the reign of Claudius. He marched south in early spring to Northern Italy and defeated Otho in a bloody battle on the plains north of the River Pedus, near the village of Bedriacum. Otho committed suicide, and Vitellius announced a general amnesty.

Although relieved that Vitellius was not taking any reprisals, I wondered how long the peace would last. Too many rumors floated about. I suspected more conspiracies loomed on the horizon. I prayed I was wrong.

Emperor Vitellius replaced men of the Praetorian and City Guard, loyal to Otho, with his own troops. Sabinus as city prefect, found himself in command of frontier troops, alien to city life and of dubious loyalty.

At least Eleyne, who was still in Rome, came under Sabinus's protection. She stayed in seclusion at our home on Vatican Hill.

Within three months after Vitellius took the throne, Sabinus's younger brother, Vespasian, commanding the legions fighting Jewish rebels in Judea, proclaimed himself emperor. Three years before, when the Jews revolted and nearly destroyed three legions, Nero had recalled Vespasian after he had earlier forced him into retirement. A soldier's soldier, Vespasian was the only general the mad Emperor Nero had trusted to crush the rebellion. Now, leaving four legions under his son, Titus, who commanded the siege of Jerusalem, Vespasian commandeered the legions of Syria, Egypt, and the Danube garrisons, and marched to the west.

I had known Vespasian for many years as a no-nonsense man and leader. If anyone could restore order to the empire, it was him.

* * *

69 AD

On the first of December, Admiral Bassus, commander of the Ravenna Fleet, relinquished control of his ships to the forces of the self-proclaimed Emperor Vespasian. The fleet of Misenum, based at the northern end of the Bay of Neapolis, quickly followed in swearing its fealty.

The admiral sent me to southern Italy as inspector general on tour of Misenum, to affirm the loyalty of the fleet for Vespasian. In reality, Bassus wanted me out of the way. Because Sabinus was Vespasian's brother and my patron, Bassus feared I would ingratiate myself and replace him as commander of the Ravenna Fleet—an absurdity. Sea duties reaffirmed my preference for the cavalry and infantry. I love the ocean but only when gazing upon it from a beach.

I had sent a message to Eleyne that I would be coming to Misenum but told her to stay in Rome. Even though I missed her, the times and roads were too dangerous to make the long journey down the Italian coast.

My inspection of the Misenum Fleet ratified their loyalty to Vespasian. But on the fifth day, as I completed the final review of the fleet's condition and the fitness of their command officers, I received a secret dispatch from Sabinus. Breaking the seal, I read the message. Sabinus wrote of intrigue, executions, assassinations, and political power plays threatening the safety of Vitellius. Finally, he had induced the obese ruler to abdicate after the defeat of his forces outside of Narnia, forty miles north of Rome by advance units of Vespasian's army. But the troops marched no further, and Sabinus didn't understand why. He was still in grave danger.

Puzzled, I wondered why he hadn't summoned me to Rome.

I reflected on why I was still loyal to Sabinus even though he had not always reciprocated that trust. Our friendship went back to when, as a newly promoted centurion, I became his retainer many years before when he brought me to Rome from Britannia. I appreciated the trust he placed in me and the leeway he allowed through the years. When others doubted my loyalty, Sabinus backed me when I had proved the elder Gallus conspired against the Emperor Claudius. Sabinus sponsored my admission to the Equestrian Order.

I would be forever grateful to him for clearing the way for my marriage to Eleyne after he thwarted Vitellius the

Elder's attempt to take her for his mistress. Sabinus's
influence allowed me to be promoted to the rank of military
tribune. And later, when I failed to control the Seventh
Cohort during the Augustan Naval Arena riots and was
exiled, he saved me from taking my life.

He had ignored my pleas when Eleyne was imprisoned
during the persecution of the Christians under Nero—
unforgivable. But I knew something beyond his control
halted him from coming to my aid, which forced me to
seek Gallus's assistance. I swore one day I would learn the
reason why Sabinus failed to get Eleyne released. But right
now was not the time to turn my back on him.

I burnt the letter. Knowing that any reply to his
message could be intercepted by Sabinus's enemies,
I didn't send a response. Instead, not waiting to learn
why Sabinus failed to recall me, I decided to cut short
the inspection tour. His letter convinced me he was in
grave danger. I bullied and persuaded Admiral Claudius
Apollinaris, the Misenum Fleet commander, of the political
necessity for me to sail his thirty ships and six hundred
marines to Ostia. A detachment of City Guardsmen was
still posted at the bustling seaport, and again, Casperius
Niger was in command. But I had no idea to whom he had
pledged his allegiance. If he remained loyal to Sabinus, I
would land unopposed. If not, I was prepared to fight. I had
not informed the admiral, but if need be, I would take his
marines with me to Rome and protect Sabinus.

More than a tempest brewed on the dark sea horizon
on that bleak December day. Risking the chance of
encountering a winter storm, I sailed the fleet north to
Ostia. A northwesterly wind bloated the sails of my ship
and carried us directly to meet the fate of Rome.

* * *

The following morning at high tide, the fleet entered the
harbor of Ostia, passing between the arms of its circular
mole.

As I leaned against the ship's railing, I said to Admiral
Apollinaris, "Looks like a reception's waiting for us."

"Aye, the question remains," the grizzled-faced admiral said, "are they still Vitellius's men, or did they swear to Sabinus and Vespasian?"

In the distance, the Ostian Cohort of the City Guard stood upon the curving stone quay. Assembled in full battle dress, the iron-plumed helmets and javelins of the port's detachment of four hundred men glistened in the noonday sun.

Despite the cold and my heavy armor, I perspired freely. "No matter," I said, "we're prepared for battle, but let's pray they'll stand down."

"If there's opposition, we can maneuver well enough to safely land the troops." The admiral paused, rubbed his hawk nose, and snorted. "And when they do, my marines will punch right through their ranks like a dagger through shit."

Well within the glassy water of the harbor, beyond the curly haired Colossus of Neptune, scows, barges, and grimy merchant vessels hugged the face of the dock like barnacles to a ship's hull. On the cool afternoon breeze, a mixture of sweet and sour spices and reeking sewage wafted towards us. Its source floating aimlessly in the turgid waters. Seagulls swarmed, dived, and fought over scraps of garbage dumped by smaller boats. The last hundred yards of dockside was cleared. Tiny boats, called lighters, were swatted away by scouting craft of the fleet to make room for our landing. With no intention of being caught between opposing forces, merchant crews of larger ships re-boarded and prepared to sail out of harm's way.

I dreaded the sentence fate dealt me. To order the ship's captain to sail away was within my powers, but clearly impossible. I considered the idea but discarded it.

"Signal the ships to prepare for battle," I said to the admiral.

"Hoist the battle flags!" Apollinaris ordered. On his signal, the main fleet within the harbor and the few remaining ships on the outside suddenly broke from a trailing formation and sailed into a flanking maneuver on both sides of the pier. A squadron of ten triremes, armed with *balistas*, stood ready to clear the pier of troops. Capable of firing spear-length shafts bearing two-foot-wide razor heads, the giant crossbows could slice through ten men at a time. For a moment the pier bustled with activity as soldiers formed into lines of interlocking shields bristling with javelins and swords.

As the ship's crew raised oars and the vessel drifted towards the pier, I grabbed the hilt of my sword. Suddenly, I recognized the powerful stance and erect shoulders of Casperius Niger. Would I be his commander once again or an enemy? The next few minutes would tell.

Dressed in chain-mail-covered blue tunics and breeches and wielding swords, shield-bearing marines crowded the triremes' decks. At a signal from our flagship, the galleys would dock in four lines, five deep. Four gangways placed between the decks of each ship would turn them into one big pontoon bridge allowing marines to charge across each gangway to the wharf. Relying on my past friendship with Casperius, and his strong loyalty to Sabinus, I hoped to avoid bloody confrontation. Everything weighed now upon our mutual faith and trust in one another.

Casperius barked a command, and dock workers hastily moved forward to the wharf's edge and hailed the ship's crews to toss mooring lines. I looked about the vessel's deck and saw the narrowed eyes and scowling faces of suspicious sailors and marines. Was this part of a welcome or a trick? Yet, if he intended to fight, would Casperius have called for the ship's lines? I stepped up to the admiral, who stood amidships. After a brief discussion, I turned in Casperius's direction and leaned over the oak railing. Cupping my hands to my mouth, I shouted to him on the dock. "Tribune Casperius Niger, this is Commander Marcellus Tiberius Reburrus! What are your intentions! Do you come in peace or to fight?"

"We *are* the peacekeepers!" Casperius shouted. "We're here to welcome you. Jupiter's balls, Commander, don't you know me by now?"

I grinned and whispered a sigh of relief. This sounded like the Casperius I knew. "Stand your men at ease, and I'll do the same."

Casperius signaled, and with a clang of shields his troops snapped to parade rest. I commanded the marines to do the same.

"I'll go one better, Commander," Casperius said, "I'm coming forward alone."

Casperius marched crisply to the gangway. He clutched his right fist to his chest. "Greetings Commander Marcellus Tiberius Reburrus," he bellowed. Without waiting for me to return his salute, he nodded to a flagman who thrust the cohort's red and gold streamers smartly into the crisp air.

The roar of the four hundred men deafened all with their cries. "VESPASIAN!! SABINUS! REBURRUS! VESPASIAN! SABINUS! REBURRUS!"

A chill ran down my back. The men had pledged their loyalty to the new emperor, Sabinus, and me. There was no turning back.

The marines followed suit. Between the two fighting forces, the banging of swords and shields rocked the ships and shook and threatened the very pier upon which the guard stood.

When the cheering and clattering subsided, I stepped from the gangplank onto the dock, relieved that we had avoided needless butchery.

Casperius Niger, squinting his dark eyes against the glaring sun, spoke in a voice that only I could hear. "You won't find this bunch to your liking, Commander."

"What's wrong with the lot?"

"Used to be Vitellius's men—dung eaters, every last one of them."

"How did you persuade them to Vespasian's cause?"

"When I received news Vitellius abdicated and Sabinus administered the oath of allegiance to Vespasian, I promised them they'd receive a bonus for their new *loyalty*."

I took a deep breath, glanced to the men, and then Niger. "Then it's official?"

"Aye, but there's more. You arrived too late."

"For what?"

His leathery face darkened. "Haven't you heard? Sabinus is trapped on the Capitoline."

My heart caught in my throat. "How could I have heard? I've been at sea. When did that happen?"

"This morning—four or five hours ago."

"Do you know the circumstances?"

He frowned, glanced to the men, and back to me. "I don't know all the details, but the Praetorians wouldn't let Vitellius abdicate. Sabinus went to the Forum to persuade them to change their minds, but he and his men were chased to the hill and encircled by the mob and the Palace Guard."

My chest tightened. *Good gods, are we too late?*

I would not stand idly by and leave Sabinus to his fate. The odds were against us, and even though the cohort had shouted their allegiance as our ship docked, I needed to make sure they would still follow me to Rome. We stood a chance of saving Sabinus's life if they did.

"There aren't enough of us," Casperius grumbled. He paused. "And I don't trust the men. Then again, if things boiled down to a fight, my men are as good as any. Even if they'd sell their own mothers for a few pieces of gold."

"We'll have to chance it. I'll promise them a bonus of five hundred gold pieces—one I'll pay myself. I've received word Vespasian's advance units, under General Antonius, are not more than two or three days away. Our best bet is to enter Rome after nightfall. All reports I've received indicate Vitellius's personal troops are a slovenly, undisciplined lot."

"At least mine are better," Casperius said. "I've flogged them into shape. When I received word the fleet was flying your pennant, I assembled the troops because I figured you had a plan for using them somewhere."

"That's right, but for a moment I thought you intended to fight me."

"After all these years? Are you mad?"

"Maybe, but politics and civil war make strange bed fellows. Now, it's time to address the troops."

I surveyed the men behind Niger. Although still at parade rest, they appeared more casual than I would have liked. Several gawked about instead of looking straight ahead. They needed a flogging, but there wasn't time. I had to work with these troops.

The rescue of Sabinus would require the support of the Ostian Cohort. Whether they fought for gold or Caesar, the only crucial point was that they fight—to the death, if necessary. Keeping their dubious loyalty in mind, I returned to the ship's forecastle, where I could be better seen, and addressed the men.

Silently, I scanned the men on the dock below. The ship gently rocked back and forth at its mooring. Quickly, I surmised what most likely would appeal to their vanity.

"When I last landed in Ostia," I began, "Rome was strong, and I had the power to command your allegiance. Now, Rome is in peril, and I'm asking you as patriots to follow me. We win or lose with Sabinus. Whether we stand here or go to his rescue, our fate is his fate.

"Years ago, city troops like you wanted to swear allegiance to me, alone. I ordered them first to swear to Sabinus. I'm asking you take the same oath, not only to me and Sabinus, but one to our new emperor, Titus Flavius Vespasian, who now rules Rome—your Rome. Break the link in that line, and you are nothing but outcasts and traitors."

I pointed to the northeast and shouted, "At this moment our commander, Sabinus, is besieged on the Capitoline. Without your help, he will be slaughtered by Vitellius's Praetorians. Are we going to allow the Praetorians to murder our commander—the brother of the new emperor?"

A loud murmur rumbled from the men.

"For sure that's what they'll do," I continued. "No, we shall not let that happen!" I waved a clenched fist. "We will march to Sabinus's rescue and hold the city until the emperor arrives. The risks are great, but rewards are greater. Outcasts and traitors? Or duty, honor, and glory?

"One is rewarded by flogging and death, the other is crowned with gratitude of our new emperor. Not only does a large reward in gold await each of you—five hundred gold *aureii*—but one greater than any treasure. The glory of

Rome, the glory of the emperor, and the undying gratitude of the people."

There was an overwhelming quietness, except for the lap of waves and seagulls cawing. I gestured for the cohort's standard bearer to come forward. He hiked up the gangplank, crossed the ship's deck, and halted before me. I took the standard from his grip and thrust it high above me, its battle streamers snapping. Knotting my other hand into a fist, I commanded, "For the glory of Vespasian!"

Then Casperius struck out a cheer. "VESPASIAN! SABINUS! REBURRUS!"

"VESPASIAN! SABINUS! REBURRUS!" the troops resounded. Like a tidal wave, their clamoring grew louder and louder until they roared to the rhythmic beat of swords striking shields.

When the troops quieted, I debarked from the ship and issued orders for the march.

Admiral Apollinaris, caught up in the spirit of the war cry, stepped forward from behind me. He said he would sail his marines north and attempt to link up with Vespasian's march and join it.

We began the journey to Rome on the Ostian Road.

As we entered the Ostian Way, Casperius and I advanced to the head of the troops. The first mile was lined with mausoleums and poplar trees. Four hundred men, wearing chain-mail armor, carrying short swords and javelins, marched at a route step in columns of three, stretched down the lane behind us. The loud clatter of armor and hob-nailed sandals echoed through the countryside.

Casperius looked about and moved his head closer to mine. "Do you really believe all that shit you spouted?"

I grinned, glancing toward the brooding peak of Ficana Hill and again to Casperius. "They're marching aren't they?"

"For a minute you had me worried. And by the way, thanks for scaring the piss out of me with your dramatic port entry!"

* * *

Late in the afternoon as the cohort passed the fallow truck gardens lining the highway, the temperature dropped rapidly. Thunder from the north erupted through black clouds, followed by heavy rain.

A half hour later we received a dispatch from one of Casperius Niger's couriers. The rain-drenched messenger had managed to escape Rome through a hail of javelins. The thick jaw messenger spouted, "Three Praetorian cohorts repelled the advance units of Vespasian's cavalry, north of the city."

"What about General Vespasian's army?" I asked.

"His main force is about a three-day march to Rome. When the Praetorians learned Sabinus had fled to the Capitoline . . . ," the messenger said. He turned his head in the direction of the city and back to me. "They returned to Rome and surrounded the hill and ordered a dawn-to-dusk curfew, upon pain of death."

"Now, we must to rescue Sabinus," I said. "It's more important than ever."

CHAPTER 27

Early in the evening, after force-marching a hard twenty-two miles in the drenching torrent, we reached the outskirts of Rome. Expecting to be challenged at the Ostian Gate, I signaled the cohort to prepare to fight, but there were no guards. We entered the desolate city. Slogging our way through the flooding streets and past boarded-up shops, we did not encounter the usual lamp-carrying pedestrians or noblemen returning home from dinner parties, accompanied by armies of retainers. The death-enforced curfew was confirmed by the occasional sight of bodies sprawled in the overflowing gutters. Even criminals sought sanctuary from swords of marauding troops.

The Watch, still charged with night peacekeeping duties and fire prevention, patrolled uneasily, and stood aside as the cohort passed through the winding, narrow streets. We hadn't spotted one Praetorian detail. Near the entry to the Forum, the main approach to the Capitoline, the cohort encountered a squad of Watchmen barricading the Sacred Way.

By the fluttering light of smoky torches, a haggard, rain-drenched optio raised his sword in challenge. "Halt!" he ordered. "Stand where you are!"

Heading a detachment of only ten men, strung out between the imposing Basilica of Julia and the Basin of Curtius, the squad leader remained undaunted by the size of our force. "I command you—go no further!"

Tension mounted. "We could easily wipe them out," I said to Casperius. "But let's try to avoid bloodshed."

"Aye, Commander," Casperius said, "I'll see if I can put some sense into his thick head."

Casperius approached the bearded optio and received his salute. "Optio, the Watch is under the jurisdiction of Prefect Sabinus and the City Guard. As tribune of the

City Guard, and your superior officer, I order you to stand aside."

"I'm sorry, sir," he declared, "but I have orders to let no one through." He stood firmly as rain rolled off the cloak snugly wrapped about his large shoulders.

The cohort's senior centurion barked orders for his men to prepare to throw javelins and clear the way.

"Don't you recognize who this is?" Casperius said, gesturing in my direction.

The optio squinted in the hissing light of a torch moved near my face. "Commander Reburrus, sir, but he's navy," he answered uneasily.

I stepped forward next to Casperius. "I *was* navy, but I am again *your* supreme commander, and hold authority over the Watch."

Casperius nodded.

"But sir—"

I cut off the optio. "And as such I can relieve you as I choose. Use common sense, man. You'll accomplish nothing by getting yourselves slaughtered."

The optio's scarred eyebrows puckered, and his round face contorted. He looked to his men and then ours—four hundred raised javelins. He hesitated for the space of five or six heartbeats, no doubt realizing his refusal would change nothing, and pinched his lips together. He saluted. Exhaling heavily, he stood aside and returned to the barricade as ordered.

The cohort marched forward as the rain gradually receded to little more than a crisp, gray mist.

Rounding the west end of the Basilica of Julia, we saw the Capitoline tower into view, crowned by the Temple of Jupiter Greatest and Best and the Temple of Juno. The cohort trekked passed the basilica to the Temple of Saturn where I ordered a halt. In the rain, the Capitoline appeared nearly unguarded. Only a thin picket of scarlet cloaked Praetorians, hunching against the cold and dampness, patrolled at the foot of the south end of the hill. Despite our size and noise, the Praetorians seemed oblivious to our appearance. I gave the order to move at a dead run. The men slammed through their midst, like a sword through a melon, racing up the fabled steps of *Clivus Capitolinus* to the Citadel.

Sabinus's defenders lining the wall of the rocky Capitoline covered our charge, hurling bricks and tiles on the Praetorians below as we surged up the narrow steps. Not until the cohort was safely inside the main gate, and all men accounted for, did we relax.

Greeted by a cheering crowd of soldiers and civilians, handshaking and backslapping occurred all around. In the billowing torchlight, I recognized Cornelius Martialis and received a crisp salute and hearty welcome. Now senior centurion of the City Guard, his once-youthful features had hardened into a grizzled face. But the glitter in his eyes still remained.

Cornelius grinned broadly. "Commander Marcellus Reburrus, I didn't think I'd see you again. Figured you were too smart to join us."

"Where is Prefect Sabinus?" I inquired.

"In the temple, sir. You're the last person he expects to see."

"No doubt, but I'm not going to allow him to stay trapped like a wild animal—that goes for the rest of you. Why is he still here?"

"He won't leave. We had the chance earlier, when the rain was heavier, but he refused—he even sent for his son, the young Sabinus!"

"That's madness."

"Aye, and a number of men have deserted. More would've if you hadn't arrived."

I nodded. "I'll find Sabinus. In the meantime, I need a place for my men to dry off and get a few hours rest—and food if there's any."

"Yes, sir. They can use the chapel of Minerva. We've stripped it of some of its old timbers for firewood."

I encountered Sabinus in his magistrate's toga as he slowly walked out of the torch-lit temple. Completely bald at seventy, bearing a face crisscrossed with lines and wrinkles, he had become an old man.

"Marcellus," he said in a surprised tone, as we shook hands, "this indeed is a pleasant surprise." Weakly, he clasped my shoulders. "I am pleased to see the troops, but why didn't you stay away?"

"And leave you at the mercy of the Vitellians? I could no more do that than cut off my right arm."

"I did not send for you because my brother betrayed me."

"Vespasian betrayed you? Why?"

"He has never forgiven me for holding the mortgages to his lands. I loaned him the money many years ago."

"Why is he holding it against you now?"

"He has planted rumors that I want the Imperial purple."

"You? I don't believe it."

"Pure nonsense. The purple is his for the taking. What few of my comrades left with influence will scurry to the mantle threads of my brother's emerging powers. I didn't ask for your aid because Vespasian may use your presence to validate the rumors. I don't want you suffering my fate."

"It's too late for that, now that I'm here. You don't have to die—why not leave? With our forces together, we can hack through the Praetorians and escape. Now! Tonight!"

"And abandon Rome? Never!" He paused for a moment, lowering his eyes and studying the temple steps. He seemed lost in thought, perhaps in conflict with his conscience.

He looked up at me again. "I am as much a prisoner as Vitellius. That is what the Praetorians have made of him. The power has passed to my hands. Until Vespasian arrives, I must remain as a symbol of his authority, no matter how dangerous the threat may be."

I wanted to grab him by the shoulders and shake some sense into him, but didn't. "You realize it could mean your death."

He shrugged. "Regardless of my fate, my brother is the best man to become emperor. If anyone can restore order to the empire, it's him. This may sound trite, but I am the bridge between the old regime and the new. No matter how precariously it may hang between the two sides of a bottomless pit, it must not fall."

"For once you must think of yourself," I insisted. "Rome will survive, whether you preserve the power or not. Don't be a martyr for a city and an empire that doesn't give a damn whether you live or die."

Sabinus placed a hand on my shoulder and looked me straight in the eye. "Marcellus, I am very old and have seen many things in my time. I know what Rome has done for me and to me and what she thinks of me. But there are many faithful servants within the government. Why do you think the empire continues to flourish despite the likes of Nero and how it stood in this last year of turmoil?"

"Only the gods know, it's a miracle the bureaucracy still works."

"It survives because loyal civil servants, freedman, and slaves keep the government functioning."

"All the more reason to leave, Lord Sabinus—the empire can get along without you."

"No, Marcellus, I won't," he said quietly. "What I have done is not because of the emperor, but for the majority of good citizens and free people throughout the empire—they are the ones who matter. It is they I serve. Would you want me to be any different? Would you rather see Gallus the Younger or his kind in my position?"

"Of course not."

"I am too old to change the habits of a lifetime, foolish as it may be. No, I will stay and die if necessary. My beloved wife died five years ago. Perhaps, it is time I join her."

Sabinus had sent me a letter in which he said Aurelia had suffered severe headaches, ultimately leading to her death. Her physician suspected she died from a brain tumor.

Slowly a broad grin crossed his somber face and seemed to transform Sabinus into a lighter mood. "Who is to say I won't survive? After all, the Capitoline represents Rome's strength in times of crisis. It has endured far greater calamities than this. Don't despair, Marcellus, there is still hope."

288

Arguing with Sabinus was pointless. In an earlier period, the Capitoline had held out against attack, but the construction of new tenements on one side of the towering hill since the Great Fire five years before placed the citadel in danger. Literally, the hill could be bridged from apartment roofs.

A short time later, Praetorian reinforcements arrived, blocking any further escape. But like the earlier sentinels, soon they, too, became lax. The resuming downpour and an icy, sharp wind sucked away their vigilance.

Certain there was no present danger from attack, Sabinus and I entered the Temple of Jupiter to dry off. As we stood around the smoky brazier beneath the marble pedestal that held the bronze giant of Rome's supreme god, he related how the present situation evolved.

"Since the first of December," Sabinus recounted, "Vitellius knew his cause was lost. He came and asked that I intercede of his behalf with General Vespasian, hoping my brother would spare the lives of him and his family. He appealed to the memory of my close friendship with his late father, Lucius the Elder."

Sabinus agreed to help, believing enough blood had been shed, and negotiated an agreement with Vitellius. He would abdicate, and in return his life would be spared. The former ruler would receive a payment of one million pieces of gold and be allowed to retire at his retreat on the coast of Campania. Witnessed by members of the nobility, the treaty was concluded in the Temple of Apollo, as Vitellius requested. It was a sad day for both Sabinus and Vitellius. The former emperor, because he was humiliated, and Sabinus, because he pitied the son of his old friend.

"Early this morning," Sabinus said, "I called together at my home delegates from the Senate, senior civil servants, and men from the City Guard and Watch and administered the oath of allegiance to Vespasian and myself. No sooner had I finished when a messenger arrived with astounding news—the Praetorians and mob refused to let Vitellius abdicate! The Praetorians feared losing their paymaster and being replaced by Vespasian's troops."

Dressed in gray mourning clothes, Vitellius appeared in the Forum with his family, and made a short speech from the Rostra announcing his resignation. The former emperor proclaimed he was depositing all aspects of Imperial Insignia at the Temple of Concord and then retiring as a private citizen to the house of his brother, Lucius the Younger.

Except for the Sacred Way, both troops and populace blocked all avenues of departure. Fearing the mob and troops more than abdication, Vitellius reluctantly accepted the fact that he could not leave and returned to the palace.

The news turned the gathering at Sabinus's home into chaos. "I found it embarrassing," Sabinus said as he continued his narrative. "Half the Senate and part of the City Guard were present. Now, in effect, we were opposing the will of the Praetorian Guard and the people of Rome. But I could not turn back."

The assembled nobility and tribunes from the City Guard urged Sabinus to action. He had been reluctant to take up arms and cause another bloodbath, but ironically, he did so to prevent one.

"I concluded," he went on, "it was too dangerous to disperse and go our separate ways. As individuals, we would be at the mercy of the Praetorians and the mob. Worse yet, there was no guarantee Vespasian's troops would arrive in time for our rescue."

Sabinus assembled a force of less than three hundred troops, noblemen, and retainers, and boldly marched to the Forum. They never reached the plaza. At first, jovial mobs were happy to let them pass. But at the small Fundane Lake reservoir on the Quirinal, they encountered a desperate band of Vitellian troops. In a brief but violent skirmish, the Vitellians got the upper hand.

Alarmed by the clash, Sabinus's party turned westward to the Capitoline, with a raging pack of swordsmen nipping at their heels. "We retreated up the Gemonian Steps," Sabinus continued, "through the Grove of Refuge to the Citadel, on the southern height of the twin-peaked hill. I managed to form the senators, knights, and guardsmen still with me into a defensive perimeter around the crest of the hill."

Many so-called Flavians, sympathizers with Vespasian's cause, melted into side streets and alleys on the way. While a handful of women with children stayed near their husbands, cowardly men fled. Even camp followers remained, including the buxom Verulana Gratilla, who was attracted by the excitement. A prostitute, well known to the troops for years, she nonetheless proved to be a good fighter and an extremely brave woman.

"The Capitoline was quickly besieged," Sabinus related, "but not before I smuggled a message to Vespasian's advanced forces. General Antonius is at their head, thirty-five miles to the north." He grimaced with macabre humor. "I resorted to secreting the letter in the coffin of a dead man ready to be carried out of the city for burial."

By that evening, a stinging rain sapped the will of the Praetorians to maintain a close vigilance on the Capitoline. Without leadership, they soon grew careless. In his dispatch, Sabinus summed up the perilous situation at hand—they were without food and other provisions. There was no hope for victory unless relieved by Vespasian's troops. His message implored General Antonius to march on Rome as quickly as possible.

* * *

The torrential rains had not relented since the arrival of the Ostian Cohort, and the number of Vitellians reinforcing the original pickets melted away. But we numbered too few to defeat them, and our only hope was delay until Antonius's troops arrived. At best, his legions were not expected for another two days. At worst, they would never arrive.

I used this time to send a message to Eleyne by a man chosen by Casperius.

"I don't trust any of them," Casperius said, "but if any man can get through, he will. Just don't expect him to return to this trap."

"I don't care if he doesn't, so long as he tells Eleyne that I'm here in Rome."

We waited for the dawn to tell our fate.

CHAPTER 28

Exhaustion seeped through every pore of my body, but I couldn't sleep. As the rains waxed, I huddled at the brazier attempting to dry my uniform. About midnight, a slave delivered a message from Gallus, asking to see me at his home without delay. How did he know that I was with Sabinus? He must have received word from spies or his Vitellian cronies that I was with the force that smashed through the Praetorian blockade. And why did he want to see me? Had he decided to call in my debt to him? I couldn't forget he had obtained Eleyne's freedom from prison nearly five years earlier.

I handed the wax table encased in citrus wood to Sabinus. Carefully, he examined the letter.

"What do you think Gallus is scheming, Lord?" I asked. "Personally, I smell treachery."

He squinted his eyes and nodded. "No doubt he is planning something putrid. However, it might be worth learning what is on his mind. You could use the information against him later."

"A pleasure I'd relish."

"If you decide to see him, we will create a diversion. The women and children can escape with you. Thank Jove, most of the husbands persuaded them to leave."

"It's worth seeing Gallus if we smuggle out the families. I never understood why they joined their husbands and fathers in the first place."

In recent months, I had learned from my spies that Gallus's world was falling apart. Three times during the last year, he had backed the wrong men for Imperial leadership. Certain that Nero's days were numbered after the failure of the Pisonian Conspiracy, Gallus quietly loosened his ties with Tigellinus and his emperor. Gallus clearly feared their close association would jeopardize his life when the next emperor assumed power.

It was common knowledge that upon Nero's death, Gallus pledged his allegiance to the aged legionary commander and new emperor, Galba. But Galba's impecunious nature thwarted Gallus's attempt to gain influence with the old man.

Otho was another matter. The foppish, young aristocrat borrowed heavily from Gallus and anyone else foolish enough to loan him money. When Otho became emperor, a delighted Gallus believed not only would he be repaid but would regain his influence at court. His disassociation from Prefect Tigellinus had been a wise move. Otho executed the dying, cancer-ridden ex-Praetorian prefect upon taking the Imperial Office.

But within days of assuming the Imperial purple, the Army of Upper Rhenus declared Vitellius emperor. Discreetly, Gallus distanced himself from Otho until a victor emerged from the latest power struggle.

When Vitellius arrived in Rome, Gallus again pledged his allegiance. But Gallus had lost millions of sesterces in his loan to the ill-fated Otho. Because three emperors had been elevated in less than one year, he cautiously decided to wait and see what befell the empire before further investing in its future.

In the meantime, Vitellius proceeded to bankrupt the treasury, and a grateful Gallus offered sacrifices to the gods for not having offered his services and loans.

Rumors said that Gallus had little time to savor his wise move. News of Vespasian's declaration for the Imperial purple alarmed him. Should Sabinus's brother emerge victorious, he would lose his head in the Proscriptions. Gallus had to act quickly if he were to survive.

* * *

Leading women and children through the misting rain, we escaped by the unguarded north end of Capitoline Hill. Again, the Praetorian security had been lax. Deftly, the group snaked its way down the rocky slope to the home of one of Sabinus's loyal clients, where I left them in safety. Had I more time, I would have gone to see Eleyne at our home on Vatican Hill, which so far, had been free of the turmoil found in the center of the city. I crept along Rome's back streets, avoiding Praetorian patrols, until I reached Gallus's home on Pincian Hill.

In his trophy room, Gallus sat among unusual weapons displayed on eagle-clawed tables in bronze tripods and lining frescoed walls. Inserted among the Dacian battle axes and British Celtic and German long swords, rested a common, wooden club. Black and heavy, long and thick, it was the same I'd noticed years before when I pleaded for Eleyne's freedom. Although studying the assorted weapons, my eyes kept returning to the blunt stave.

Gallus no longer applied makeup to his face. Like a living death mask, a dark, gray pallor covered his drawn features. His breath reeked of strong wine. A jewel-encrusted, gold wine cup and a small amphora jug rested on the desk in front of him. Dressed in a yellow and purple, fringed tunic of silk, Gallus leaned back in a velvet-lined mahogany chair. He rested his leathery, wrinkled hands on the cushioned, wooden arms. We were the same age. But at forty-nine, I was still firm-muscled and vigorous, if a bit lined and graying around my ears.

"I see you're still interested in the club," Gallus said as a grin cracked his dried face like a raisin.

"It doesn't fit with the rest of your weapons."

"You think not? It has special meaning for me, and . . . for you."

"Why?"

"Obviously, you don't remember."

Puzzled, I frowned.

"Maybe you wouldn't. You used it years ago."

A small shudder rippled through my body as the painful memory, blunted by many passing years, returned. "Aye, now I remember."

"You should. You used it to bash to death a poor, unfortunate soldier in the *Fustuariam*," he said.

Stunned by the visible reminder of the execution gauntlet and Avaro's death, I didn't ask the obvious question as to why he had kept the cudgel.

"Did you know," Gallus said, interrupting my thoughts, "one of the city cohorts was annihilated in Terracina?"

"Yes, I heard," I answered. I forced my mind to the present matter, realizing Gallus probably had revealed the weapon's past to unnerve me. Did he think I was that vulnerable?

"They disobeyed Sabinus's orders," I said.

Reports said the butchered cohort fled Rome only to be slaughtered by the Praetorians commanded by Lucius the Younger, brother of Vitellius. Incredibly, they failed to post a guard after joining the populace in celebration of the winter solstice, Saturnalia. The Praetorians penetrated the coastal city south of Antium, during the early hours of morning, murdering troops still in their drunken slumber.

"Were they not attempting to join Vespasian's forces?" Gallus inquired. He grabbed a filled cup and gulped down its contents.

"His forces were nowhere in the vicinity," I replied. "There had to be another reason."

Gallus grinned, revealing his brown, wine-stained teeth. "How perceptive you are, Commander. Of course, you're right."

"You mean, they were—"

"Since the fools are all dead, there isn't any reason I shouldn't tell you. I solicited their tribune to look after my interests in Terracina where my holdings are vast. I needed his cohort for protection, but after their destruction, I thought of you. I heard you were marching to Rome."

"Go on," I said, suspecting what would follow.

Gallus refilled his cup and noisily gulped the dark-red wine. Finishing, he wiped his mouth with a hand and belched. "I'm well aware of the situation on the Capitoline and know you're trapped. Trapped because the soon-to-be emperor's brother is a proud but stubborn old man."

"It's true, what am I doing here, when I could have escaped?"

His bloodshot eyes narrowed into lizard-shaped slits as he jabbed a finger in my direction. "I know you. You'll return to your men, because you won't abandon them to their fate and allow them to die needlessly."

"What do you want from me?" I demanded, tiring of his game.

"I have a plan to save your life and Sabinus's."

"What about the rest?"

He met my eyes and glanced away. "A few—perhaps even most, at least everyone of importance."

"What is your price?"

Gallus nodded. "I knew you would see things my way. You'll succeed where the other cohort commander failed. Protect my lands and interests until peace is restored."

"And in return, you'll arrange an escape?"

"And a generous reward for your services."

"How much?"

"One thousand pieces of gold a month for life, and my best properties in Hispania will be transferred to your name."

It was all I could do to refrain from laughing in his rotting face. Once he had coveted my family's estates. Now he proposed a different bargain. Greed. It was only his total motivation. Even when losing, his goal was to cling to whatever remnants of power he still possessed.

"You've backed the wrong men," I said, "and they've fallen. Do you honestly expect me to do your bidding now?"

"I want you to save my fortune—what's left of my estate," Gallus answered in a desperate voice. "When Vespasian reestablishes stability, I'll prosper again."

I leaned over his desk, enduring his overpowering alcoholic breath, and glared into his yellowing, bloodshot eyes. "Help *you* prosper? You, a bloodsucker and parasite on Rome for over twenty years? Do you take me for a fool? Once he's in Rome, you'll be at the head of Vespasian's death list."

"Don't you realize it is within my power to save Sabinus's life?" Gallus said. "If I do, he'll be forever in my debt. Vespasian won't proscribe me. I admit Sabinus eluded me once before, but now I'm willing to save him if you'll agree to my proposition."

His remark about Sabinus piqued my curiosity. "When did he *elude* you?"

"At this point, it doesn't matter."

When I started to leave, he sputtered, "Very well, there's no sense fencing the details. The persecutions have passed. The night your wife was arrested, I was after bigger fish. She was caught in a net thrown for the senator."

I re-approached the desk as he poured another cup of wine. "Then my suspicions were right. The raid was your idea."

"Quite right, and only by accident did she fall prey. I was after Sabinus."

"Sabinus, a Christian?" I voiced, incredulous.

"Didn't you know?" Gallus seemed genuinely surprised. Then he grinned and erupted into laughter. "My good man, you are indeed naive. How could you fail to see all these years?"

My gaze broke from his. Now I understood why Sabinus had been reluctant to offer help in obtaining Eleyne's release. Because Nero would have arrested him as a sympathizer, he dared not reveal his concern for the Christians. It explained his horror at the appalling deaths suffered by the Christians at Nero's gruesome garden party. Had he explained his predicament to me, I would have understood. But the longer I thought about his dilemma, the more I realized he had made the right decision. I might have attempted something irrational to free Eleyne and jeopardized all of us.

I forced my attention back to Gallus. "That still doesn't change things."

"Let's not be stubborn about this, Commander," Gallus snapped. "I considered arranging an accident for you, but deep down I believed you a reasonable man."

"Assassinations were always your favorite game," I answered with a sneer.

"Sometimes they don't succeed," he answered flatly. "For instance, take the Neapolitan cement-merchant,

Apollonius, a few years ago. The assassins slit his throat, but he didn't have the decency to die." He shook his head. "The Greek screamed so loud that your inept guards arrived in short order, and they had to flee."

"So it was your men who attempted to murder the cement merchant?"

"You'll never prove it, of course. Your incompetent guards couldn't catch my men even in a crowded market place."

Gallus's revelation meant his murderous plotting had indirectly led to Eleyne's injuries and the death of our baby. My long-suppressed hatred boiled to the surface. Acid poured into my stomach, and bile rose into my throat. A roar-like surf pounding the shoreline filled my ears. He confirmed every dark suspicion I had ever entertained about him. He had been the source of the misery Eleyne needlessly suffered. He had caused the loss of our unborn daughter. Eleyne still pined for her. Here sat the man responsible for more grief than I could endure.

"Now, if you insist on being obstinate," he threatened, "I can still arrange an accident to include Sabinus and your barbarian wife."

I said nothing, struggling to contain my growing rage, suppressing the shaking of my body.

"What's it going to be?" Gallus demanded. "Speak up." Silence.

"Can it be you're not in agreement? Do you misunderstand the gravity of such a decision?" He smiled and took another drink of wine. "I assure you not all accidents dispose of their victims neatly or with anything resembling dispatch."

Blind rage boiled upon me. No longer would I allow this incredible monster to exist.

Gallus stood and started toward the door to summon his guards. I grabbed for the nearest weapon, scarcely aware which, and lunged at Gallus.

Too startled to scream, he reached for the dagger inside his tunic, raising his arms and weapon to ward me off.

The force of my blow brushed them aside and smashed into his face. Stunned, he hurtled into the frescoed wall, bouncing off with a crumpling thud. Bejeweled swords fell and clattered around him on the tiled floor.

Maddened, I struck him again and again. Blood spattered his silk evening tunic, my hands, and face. Still he lived. He began crawling, trying to dodge my blows. Beyond mercy or reason, I dragged him by the folds of his tunic to the nearby atrium's fountain. I pushed him backwards over the edge of the marble fountain, into its foaming waters. Eels slithered away in fright as I grabbed him by the neck. Squeezing my hands tighter and tighter around his throat, I forced his head beneath the water. Sharp fingernails dug into my wrists in desperation. Bubbles flowed from his mouth, his bulging eyes glared at me. In a sudden burst of strength, he convulsed and nearly overpowered me. But no power on Earth or the Heavens could dislodge me.

At last I dropped his limp form into the blood-stained water. He was dead. I slumped to the edge of the fountain, done. I felt strangely hollow, drained of all my rage. It was murder. Not in the heat of battle, but in one unendurable insane moment. Then my glance fell on the weapon I had grasped even as I dragged Gallus from the fountain. The black club. The instrument Gallus had forced me to use so long ago on a fellow soldier.

Why had I used it instead of my sword? Somehow in some part of my mind, had instinct dictated Gallus was not worthy of dying by an honorable weapon? I had dealt him the death of a common criminal. Doubling on the curved edge of the found, I placed my face in my hands and wept.

CHAPTER 29

In spite of all the noise and scuffling, Gallus's dour guards never entered the room. This puzzled me, but only for a moment. No doubt they knew that Gallus would be on Vespasian's proscription list, and their fates were tied to his. They must have heard the commotion, but discreetly ignored it in hopes I would kill Gallus. Once I left, they would sack his home and flee.

Quietly, I slipped over Gallus's balcony unseen and disappeared into the cold, early morning mist. Encountering few pickets along the way, I safely returned to the Temple of Jupiter.

As dawn approached, Sabinus dispatched Cornelius Martialis with a message to Vitellius, demanding he order the Praetorians to withdraw immediately. A couple of hours later, Cornelius returned with Vitellius's reply. He no longer possessed the power to order their recall.

"They went on a rampage and destroyed the northern end of the Forum earlier today," Sabinus said.

By midmorning, three Praetorian cohorts had reinforced those surrounding the Capitoline.

"Look," Casperius Niger said, pointing in the direction between the Temple of Concord and Temple of Saturn.

"They're heading straight for the outer gateway," I said. The opening led to the sacred enclosure by the east side of the hill. Instead of keeping the tight formation normally expected of Roman troops, the Praetorians noisily ran in a spread-out, jumbled formation. Years of discipline kept them banded together, but without direction, their headless main body meandered around the contours of streets and terrain towards us.

"Casperius, post the troops on the roof above the portico and along the Temple of Jupiter's front," I ordered.

The area paralleled the ascending steps near the main gateway.

The enemy charged up the steps in a ragged, undisciplined manner. We easily repelled the Praetorians with a hail of stones and tiles hastily pulled from the temple floor. Fleeing before the deluge, they left behind a trail of bloodied and broken bodies.

"Good work, men," I said, walking among the regrouping defenders afterward. "I'm proud of you."

But this reality of fighting and killing fellow Romans disgusted me, especially when I heard the agonizing cries of the wounded and dying.

"They're coming again," a dusty and blood-spattered Casperius Niger shouted a few minutes later. "Man your posts."

The palace troops returned in a tighter formation, shields raised overhead.

"They've set fire to the portico," a centurion reported. The portico was supported by wooden timbers below and could not stand if the timbers began to buckle.

A cursing optio led the mob of Praetorians, bullying them into a loose-order charge with tribunes and centurions mixed with the soldiers.

"Our men are retreating." Casperius motioned with his head.

Flames roared up the dry, old timbers, protected earlier from the rain by a sturdy, tiled roof. Driven from the roof, the Praetorians pursued our troops uphill. Smashing down the charred gates, the palace troops would have succeeded in entering, had it not been for Sabinus's foresight. Earlier he had ordered the uprooting of hundreds of statues adorning the temple grounds, to be used by the troops as improvised barricades.

But the Praetorians persisted. "They're attacking us from three directions, sir," Casperius Niger reported. "One group is climbing the Gemonian Steps between the Records House and the prison to the east." Another detail approached from the southern side by way of the *Clivus*

Capitolinus. But the most critical assault came from the tenements on the north side near the Grove of Refuge.

The dry, wooden buildings had sprung up after the Great Fire five years earlier. Climbing story after story, enemy emerged at the tops of the buildings overlooking the temple grounds and its surrounding portico.

At that moment, Sabinus returned from surveying the battle. "The situation is very grave," he said. "I have ordered Quintus Atticus to set the apartments on fire."

"That's madness," I said. "The winds are continually changing direction. They could shift without warning and bring the flames back towards us and the temple." The rear of the Great Temple was adjacent to the area.

"No, we must burn the buildings now," he urged, "or we will be overwhelmed."

As he spoke, I saw his friend, Quintus Atticus, Consul of Rome, hurl five or six torches from the temple portico to the roofs of the apartments.

"You've made a grave mistake," I said.

Within minutes the winds veered towards us again, and the fire quickly leapt up the portico fringing the northern section of the Temple of Jupiter. Beneath the bleak cover of low, dark clouds, and despite a sprinkling of light rain on the city, the Great Temple caught fire. Patches of red and orange flames licked at ever-larger parts of the dried, wooden roof and gorged on its supporting rafters, like a beast devouring freshly killed prey.

I glared at Sabinus and shook my head before I shouted, "The fire will drive us right into the arms of the enemy!"

The command staff and guards fled the temple. The only escape route left open to us forced us into the midst of the attacking Praetorians. But our counterattack was so furious, they withdrew like a disorderly mob after losing so many men.

Steaming in the rain, fire engulfing the Great Temple grew until patches broke into a raging wall of flames enveloping the entire temple. In the intense heat, marble pillars supporting the roof and building disintegrated. Rain added its hissing voice to the carnage. Like a disgorging volcano, the great edifice collapsed in an explosion of billowing flames and smoke. An irreplaceable loss. Three thousand bronze tablets, texts of senatorial decrees and laws dating back to the early days of the Republic, stored in the temple for hundreds of years, gone. Rome's history wantonly destroyed.

The destruction of the Great Temple shattered Sabinus's will to resist. After our retreat to the Grove of Refuge and its smaller Temple of Juno on the second peak, he stood dazed and glassy-eyed. "All the sacred documents are lost," he said slowly.

The temple had represented Rome's strength and power in the world.

"Prefect Sabinus," I said, "we've got to get you away from here."

"No, we must carry on the fight." Sabinus gave a series of commands and counter-commands, jeopardizing our remaining defenses.

Disregarding his disjointed orders, I quickly established a perimeter defense around the smaller temple. To buy time as we strengthened our position, I left behind the remnants of a century of troops in the Grove of Refuge. I ordered troops, along with civilians, who had been Sabinus's supporters and refused to leave, to barricade from more fallen statues, iron tripods, old war trophies, and broken bricks.

Casperius and I went among the men and women manning the defenses of jumbled, broken artifacts armed with swords, spears, and broken pieces of tile and brick.

"We can't hold out much longer," Casperius said.

"I agree, but we've got to keep trying. Surrender is out of the question. If only Antonius's troops would arrive."

"I doubt if they will. If what Lord Sabinus says is true about his brother, Vespasian, than we are trapped and cut off from rescue."

I nodded, knowing Casperius was right. I looked toward the Grove of Refuge and pulled my sword from its scabbard. "Here comes the enemy."

The Praetorians chased remnants of the rear guard from the Grove of Refuge back to our defenses. We defended our position savagely as the Praetorians hurled themselves over the makeshift embankments. We slaughtered many in a bloodbath of carnage. The clashing of swords echoing metal upon metal, the screams of the wounded and dying exploded into an echoing roar heard throughout the city. The stench of coppery blood, emptying of bowels and bladders engulfed the battle scene like a sickening, invisible fog. But the enemy continued the assault. My face, sword, and uniform were covered in blood. I lost track of the number I hacked and sliced my way through as I ran from position to position, encouraging our people to hold tight. Hot, thirsty, and sweating, my hands sticky with blood, I don't know what kept me going except the fury of battle.

The Praetorians smashed through our perimeter. We had no reserves to hurl them back. Our defender's resolve began to flag, and in minutes they would overrun us. The woman, Verulana Gratilla, tore a javelin from a stunned soldier's grasp and charged, screaming and cursing. Her insane rage inspired a vicious counterthrust, quickly plugging the breach and stemmed the danger. For a moment, the Vitellian Praetorians retreated.

All of us suffered from the wet and cold, from hunger, fatigue, and wounds.

After quickly checking with Casperius, Cornelius Martialis, and other officers overseeing the defenses, I searched for Sabinus. He had disappeared during the last engagement. To my dismay, I found the once-brave soldier squatting and cringing, wild-eyed and in shock, in a small, dark corner of the chapel.

"Lord Sabinus," I said. He didn't reply. "Lord Sabinus, answer me—what's wrong?"

I glanced through the pillars of the temple entrance. The enemy attacked again using a barrage of fire arrows. Falling into our midst like shooting stars, they harassed our vague attempts at defense.

I knelt and shook Sabinus by the shoulders. "Hear me, Lord Sabinus. It's Marcellus. You've got to recover yourself—you must leave, now!"

He didn't recognize me. Then I heard a great noise outside—the war cries of attacking troops. With a promise to return, I had to race back to the life of defense.

I barely reached the top steps in front of the sanctuary when a fire arrow struck deeply into my left thigh. Blistering pain shot up and down my leg. I fell backwards onto the brick steps. I felt as if I had been smashed with a hammer. My screams stopped a wounded, running man in his tracks. But he only glanced dully at me, dumbly curious at such animal sounds roaring from the throat of a man. He ran on, probably lost in his own anguish.

Suddenly, Sabinus appeared and calmly smothered the fire beginning to engulf my breeches with his cloak. He laid me on the ground. Nausea overcame me, and the sounds of battle grew muffled and distant. Weakly, I raised my head and stared numbly at the smoldering thing in my leg—or someone's leg. Someone ripped my clenched hand from its shaft while scolding me like a child.

I managed to turn my head and watched as Sabinus quickly scanned the devastation. "Trumpeters, sound the order for assembly, including the civilians," he commanded. "I want a defensive perimeter thrown around this position."

Sabinus broke the feathered, wooden shaft from the embedded arrow, leaving the barbed iron head and smoldering, embered cloth in place. I tried to stand but passed out.

When I regained consciousness, both trumpeters lay dead, their bodies riddled with arrows. I had a second wound in my leg. The simple arrow wound was worse than the one lodged above—its V-head passed through my calf muscle completely. My vision blurred, but I clearly remembered Sabinus and Casperius Niger ordering a litter and men to carry me to a makeshift dressing area for the wounded.

Then as my thoughts blackened into nothingness, someone spoke next to me, "His leg must come off."

* * *

I awoke. After groggily searching about, I realized I was home on Vatican Hill. I looked about. Where was Eleyne? I had no idea how many hours had passed since being carried from the battle—or how many of us had managed to escape. A searing pain throbbed through my leg, and I viewed the bloody linen wrapped around my thigh and calf. I looked about and saw a soldier standing nearby. Obviously, he had been ordered to stay with me.

"Where is my wife?" I asked.

"I don't know, sir, haven't seen her."

"Find her," I ordered.

He turned to leave when a slave entered the room. He passed the command on to him.

Against the wishes of a soldier, I tried walking to the balcony window. Excruciating pain shot through my body as I stood. I fell to the floor but waved away the soldier rushing to my side. Despite the agony, I crawled until I reached the marble bench by the opening. Nearly losing my grip, I grabbed the seat's slippery edge with blood-smeared hands. Exhausted, dripping with sweat and gasping for air, I made another attempt. I pushed myself up on my good right leg and managed to straddle the bench. Again, pain lanced my thigh. Hanging over the other side, I lay there a moment to take several deep breaths. Using my arms, I pushed myself up and rolled over onto my back, exhausted.

A few minutes later, I managed to sit up and peer over the balcony railing to search for the scene of battle. As dark clouds crossed the afternoon skies in the distance, dots of flames licked at the tenements on the steep Capitoline. Below the hill a brighter glow flared now and then, like a dying campfire fanned by a sudden breeze. The glowing debris of the skeletal colonnades of the great temple, jumbled with broken men and women, fueled a pyre that only the Great Fire of Rome could rival.

Watching helplessly, I sensed—feared—the end was near. Hell itself seemed to conspire in the carnage splitting the earth asunder and gorging upon the ashes, bones, and the souls of hundreds, perhaps thousands. My eyes clouded, blurring all details into a distant, yellow fireball.

Holding the sides of the bench for support, I tightly closed my eyes. Being home and not at Sabinus's side to the end spawned a sense of grief and betrayal within me. Blackness again claimed me.

* * *

The dream. Gods, I pray it was a dream. I remember looking down at the slaughter from my villa. Too far to hear the screams and curses, or smell the stench of battle, but clearly seeing flaming arrows streaking down in golden arches from the surrounding tenements, onto the defenders at the Temple of Juno. Like colliding meteor showers, the arrows danced through the dark afternoon. I grabbed the marble bench for support, but it started toppling—or was it me? Lying on the cold, tile floor, I stared at the spinning wooden ceiling as hands moved my body to a softer place. Darkness.

Cool hands encompassed my forehead, or was it moist cloth? Cold and wet, like the murky waters of a flowing river. Then I saw *it* floating with the current towards me. A body, whose face I could not see, rolled over and over, until it bumped against me. KYAR. She sank into a void. Voices. Distant voices—laughing . . . crying . . . screaming. A fire burned my body, and I begged for water, but the voices only laughed—louder and louder. Death—the city laid to waste in ruins.

Then faces from the past drifted before me, fading in and out. Faces floated by on a sea of fire and wind . . . taunting . . . calling . . . summoning me to their world—old Gallus, snarling, his hair swept by the wind. Rix the Gaul, wearing a mountain cat broach, glaring at me with his one good eye and speaking wordlessly. The little beggar girl in the cave—piercing eyes terrified, screamed a shrill sound that merged with the cries of the tortured Druid priest, as Scrofa the beggar king and Obulco the torturer laughed on.

Marcellus, a wavering voice hissed.

I answered, but the voice merely whispered again, *MAR-CELL-USSS*. With each repetition of my name a new

louder voice, and floating face, joined in unison, *Marcellus!*
The Druid witch, Mugain, cackled, wagging a gnarled and
pointing finger. *Marcellus,* accused Avaro, the soldier I
had executed. Abroghast, the Tullianum Prison torturer,
appeared shoving slithering little monsters in my face. I
turned away and saw Candra fading in. He swung his long
sword cutting away a gladiator's hand and launched my
head through the air until it struck Crispus and knocked
him off his horse, as he joined the chorus, *MAR-CELL-USS!*

A soldier knelt in a shaft of purple light, and a fleeting
woman danced in and about the now motionless figments
of my dream. *MAR-CELL-USSS,* she hissed. *MARCELLUS,*
echoed the shadowed faces. A man floated toward the
soldier, and I saw a dagger sticking out of his chest.
An ashen-faced young Gallus raised a club, and all
the monsters raised theirs, and together they beat and
clubbed the kneeling man, chanting, *Marcellus! Marcellus!
Marcellus!*

And when they stepped back into the blackness, a long
figure, dressed in the uniform of my old decurion, Rufius,
beckoned me. He pointed to the sprawling dead thing, its
headless body bruised beneath a blood-spattered white
toga with purple trim. I moved closer against my will as
the intense shaft of purple light narrowed, away from the
corpse. All was in darkness except for the beam cast on
the severed, pale-white, bloodless face before me. Sabinus.
His eyes and mouth snapped open, and all the voices
screamed, *Marcellus!*

And then I fell, riding a wooden bucket down a black
well, racing past blurred faces and skulls embedded in the
walls. Down I dropped into a bottomless pit, swirling and
spinning, carrying with me the demons I had seen. Down
into the whirlpool we sank. Slow motion at first, past the
Poseidon's Eye, going faster and deeper and farther, until
torchlights and faces and bodies and boar's head rings and
the world of Druid darkness blurred into oblivion.

CHAPTER 30

When I awakened, an unusual silence pervaded the house. A searing pain shot through my head as I turned and spied Eleyne in a dark-blue, woolen stola and mantle, sitting by the balcony in the cold morning sunlight. Our eyes met. Making no sound she rose, and the tension drained from her pinched face. Padding across the room in woolen slippers, she came to my side.

I tried raising myself from the pillow.

"It's all right, Marcellus." She sat on a stool next to the bed. "Lie down, my love, you're still too weak."

Despite her reassurance, I feared the dream would return. But when she held my hand to her warm cheek, I knew this much was real.

"How long have I been here?" I asked in a scratchy voice.

"Nine days, and delirious the whole time," she answered. "I returned as soon as I received news that you had escaped from the Capitoline. I went into hiding with the other Christians when the mob rampaged through the city, but Vatican Hill was spared."

"Thank the gods you're unharmed." As I attempted to move myself, a dull ache shot up my leg along the left side of my body. Breathing heavily, I dropped my head back to the pillow, exhausted by the feeble exertion. "By all the gods," I rasped, "it's . . . it's a miracle I survived."

"Yes, darling," she said, stroking my hand. "You had me, and the entire household, very worried. They've remained silent as mice, making sacrifices for your recovery. For days you burned with fever and lingered near death. The physicians bled you repeatedly until I sent them away. All I could do is sit and wait . . . and pray."

"It seems your prayers and offerings were heard," I said. For the space of a heartbeat, I gripped her hand. "Thank you, dear, and thank our people, too."

"I will, darling. The worst is past, and you're going to live. Thank God, your leg wasn't infected with gangrene."

"Will I walk again?"

Eleyne hesitated and pinched her lips together for the length of a couple heartbeats. "Yes, eventually," she answered as if measuring her words, "with crutches. Your muscles were so badly damaged they'll never heal properly. It may be months before you can stand and walk on your own."

"That's better than losing the leg altogether." Inside, I wanted to weep, but I was too numb and weary to exert any outward emotion.

"How did I get home?" I asked, changing the subject.

"Sabinus's men sneaked you out through a hidden crypt in the Temple of Juno. Did you know the passage existed?"

"Yes, I vaguely recall its location. It leads to a cistern emptying into the Tiber—a very clever way of escaping indeed. But what happened to the others?"

"I don't think you're strong enough to hear the story."

The tone in her voice struck an ominous chord. A sense of urgency ran through me. "Please, Eleyne, it's important I hear it all. I won't rest until I know the whole truth."

She sighed, and with a firm grasp, held my hands in hers. "Very well, but it's an ugly tale. I had sent a couple of slaves to the Forum to learn what they could, and this is what they heard. After Sabinus's son and Vespasian's son, Domitian, escaped, the Praetorians overran your remaining forces. It was hideous." Eleyne's voice broke. "They hacked Casperius Niger and Cornelius Martialis to pieces and many others, too." Her puffy, bloodshot eyes clouded. She turned and pulled her hands away.

"There were few survivors," she continued a few minutes later, drying the tears shed with a cloth of Egyptian cotton.

"They disguised themselves as Praetorian soldiers. During the confusion of the battle, they overheard the password and used it to escape." She paused. "But Lord Sabinus and Quintus Atticus were captured unarmed."

310

The Praetorians manacled Sabinus and Atticus and marched them through the rain to the palace. Vitellius received the two in the forecourt at the head of the staircase. In spite of foul weather, the all-too-fickle mob gathered by the thousands and screamed for the deaths. As Vitellius spoke kindly to the old prefect and consul, the mob bolted through the loose guard around the prisoners. Before the Praetorians closed their protective shield around the two prisoners, the rabble grabbed Sabinus. The guard managed to save Atticus from the throng's wrath, but the crowd stabbed and hacked Sabinus to death. Decapitating him, they dragged his body to a spot on the Gemonian steps used for exposing a felon's carcass, where the mob further ridiculed and befouled Sabinus's battered remains.

"Enough!" I cried, "I can't stand to hear anymore." I turned, and thrusting my face into a pillow, wept. "What a senseless waste. The murdering bastards were never worthy of his justice and humanity. They don't deserve to survive—and neither does Rome!"

* * *

Five months later, in late May, Emperor Vespasian arrived in Rome after crushing the last Vitellian forces.

Within a week, I received a summons from the emperor to appear in the Senate for a reading of Sabinus's will. Only three days before, despite the long rehabilitation of my damaged limb, I took my first steps since collapsing and falling into a coma. Although my personal physician, the old Greek, Soranus, attempted to retie the torn muscles, the arrows had inflicted too much damage. He was fortunate to save the limb from amputation, and cursed the quack doctors who had bled me. Never again would I have full use of my left leg.

That morning, a litter carried me and Eleyne to the *Curia* as a cool, light rain swirled around us. "Stop right here," I ordered, and the sedan halted in front of the Senate building. "I won't be carried into the emperor's presence like an invalid."

"But you can hardly walk," Eleyne protested.

"Rubbish, I'm well enough."

After tightly wrapping a wool mantle around my white toga, two big German slaves lifted me from the seat. Chulainn handed me the crutches, and with his and the help of a strong, young Briton slave, I slowly and painfully hobbled into the hallowed chambers. Eleyne, the mute Imogen, Porus, and twenty other attendants followed.

Vespasian sat on a low dais, his body rigid, in a cushioned curule chair, as a group of advisors and freedmen hovered nearby. Five hundred members of the Senate reposed in a large semicircle before the ruler on ornate tiered benches. To ward off the cold winter wind outside, all doors were shut tight. Eye-stinging smoke from a dozen braziers wafted through the dimly lit chamber.

As I struggled to approach the dais, the emperor motioned with a flick of an eyebrow, and four slaves rushed to my aid. Four more scurried to fetch a bench. Moments later they returned with a horse-legged, wooden chair.

The emperor acknowledged my salute. "Please take your seat, Commander Reburrus," he commanded in a kindly tone.

"Yes, Caesar," I answered in gratitude. I had suffered enough pain and no longer cared about my undignified ride before him.

Vespasian ordered the proceedings to begin. Prior to reading Sabinus's will, the Senate approved a proposal by Domitian to vote that a medallion portrait of Sabinus's image be displayed in a prominent position in the Senate House, and his statue placed in the Forum of Augustus and honored with Rome's past heroes. An empty gesture for a man who dedicated his life to peace, and yet it would have pleased him.

The emperor nodded to Sabinus's lawyer, who came forward to the dais and bowed. "You may read the will of my brother, Titus Flavius, Sabinus," Vespasian ordered.

The advocate read that Sabinus had bequeathed all his property in Hispania to me.

I gasped, not believing my ears. I never expected to be included in his will but was gratified he thought so highly of me.

The emperor stiffened, but then nodded his head as if in approval.

After finishing the reading of the will, Vespasian addressed the Senate. "This costly and tragic war has decimated the ranks of the army, Praetorian and City Guards alike, and much of Italy, including Rome. Many months, perhaps years, lay ahead in the recovery and rebuilding of our forces and our cities if the empire is to survive. We need good men at all levels." He paused and fixed his eyes on mine.

"Marcellus Tiberius Reburrus, we bestow upon you our gratitude for your devotion to Rome, and our brother, the late Titus Flavius Sabinus. We have further need of your services and talents as chief peacekeeper of the city. No one qualifies better than you, Commander, for the post of city prefect and chief magistrate of Rome."

A murmur of approval swept the Curia. The emperor nodded to the Senate, and silence descended upon the hall.

"One must hold the rank of Senator in order to take command as city prefect," he continued. "Therefore, after long debate, the noble fathers of this august body, with our approval, unanimously voted you to the exalted position of senator. In addition, they have bestowed upon you the title, *Clarissimus*, Most Illustrious Citizen."

I couldn't believe my ears. Usually, the title was reserved for the most distinguished senators and the emperor. As one body, the Senate stood applauding. At that key moment, I didn't think of glory, power, riches, and honor—but of my sons. I recalled the humble origins and royal blood flowing in their veins from our Spanish ancestors from the Turdetanian Tribe, who centuries ago fought, but were never conquered by the Romans. We became allies and now filled the ranks of her legions. I recalled my father, the first to earn Roman citizenship in our family. And Eleyne, my beloved wife, mother of our sons, still a princess, and true Queen of the Regni. And a Roman—although she'd never admit it.

All my warrior ancestors played their parts in guiding my destiny to this offer. But unlike those before me, I could guide my sons away or towards Rome—forever.

I thought about the pain and needless death suffered at Rome's hands. Yet if only the right man could rise to power, he could make a better world. No Spaniard had risen so high, but a simple *yes*, and the path for my sons to inherit their seat in the world's most powerful forum would be assured and in such a place where anything was possible.

"Your offer is most generous, Caesar," I answered, "And I'm honored you place such confidence in me."

"Then it's settled," Vespasian said, again leading the Senate in boisterous applause.

I swallowed hard, took a deep breath, and carefully chose my words when the applause died down. "Great Caesar, I'm honored and deeply grateful that you have chosen me for the position of city prefect, and for admission to the Senate. They are offices to which I have never aspired. But please forgive me, Lord, I must respectfully decline the position of city prefect. As Caesar can see, I'm a virtual cripple and cannot adequately perform the duties required of such a high office. Therefore, with Caesar's permission, I'm retiring from Imperial service."

Vespasian studied me. His weathered, round peasant face of sixty years gave no indication of what lay behind those calculating eyes. A smirk gradually creased his face. "Naturally, you have our permission. Of course, we understand and are disappointed, but your health comes first. We are sorry because your services will be missed. Nevertheless, you shall be elevated to the rank of Senator, whether you stay in Rome or go elsewhere."

"I'm deeply honored, Caesar," I answered, bowing my head.

"What are your plans for the future?" the emperor inquired in a less-formal manner.

"I'm returning to Hispania, Lord Caesar."

"Of course, we should have guessed," he answered with a wry smile and a sigh of relief.

I wasn't surprised by Vespasian's reaction. I was sure he was happy that I would return to my homeland. He had offered the position of city prefect knowing I was too crippled to accept.

"Before I'm dismissed, may I ask a favor?" I said.

"If it's within my powers, I shall grant it."

"I request the surviving guardsmen who fought to defend Caesar's brother, Prefect Sabinus, be rewarded. And I ask that the remaining families of those fallen receive a pension. I need not remind the emperor many loyal men fought to save your brother, and your son, Domitian."

"They have earned the state's gratitude," Vespasian answered tersely, "and a benevolent compensation is forthcoming."

After Sabinus had warned me of Vespasian's avariciousness, I feared the pensions would be a long time in arriving—and paltry at best. Sabinus was right, Vespasian had betrayed him. His troops could have marched into Rome in time to save Sabinus. I received word General Antonius deliberately held back his final assault until he received confirmation of Sabinus's death. Although Sabinus had a son, Vespasian would be one of his brother's beneficiaries receiving a substantial amount of gold and land. Only after Antonius was informed of Sabinus's murder did he enter the city and defeat the Praetorians in a pitched battle costing thousands of lives.

Above all, Rome's mob had earned my disgust. Their murder of Sabinus I could never forgive, and their fickleness appalled me. When the advance units of Vespasian's army entered the city and captured Vitellius, the city hordes meted out to him the same fate suffered by Sabinus, ripping his body apart. So long as they gorged themselves on free bread and amused themselves with the bloodthirsty games, it mattered little to them who was emperor. I attempted in my own way, as a peacekeeper, to bring law and order to the city and protect the people. But

315

were the mindless hordes worthy of protection? My years
of service and struggles to protect them had been wasted. I
had nothing for them now except contempt and disgust.

"Are there any other favors we can grant you, Senator
Reburrus?" Vespasian inquired.

"No, Caesar, you have been most generous," I lied.

"Then good luck, and may Fortuna and the rest of the
gods smile upon you."

* * *

It was almost noon when we left the curia and headed
for home. The rain had stopped, but a chilly wind whisked
down through the streets and alleys, between the buildings
perched on the surrounding hills, as we crossed the near-
empty Forum in our litters. Although I was bundled in
woolen blankets, the chilly air crawled around my body like
a series of icy fingers, sending quill bumps up my back and
down my arms. I tightened the covers.

We crossed the white-capped Tiber, and about half-way
up Vatican Hill, I ordered the litter bearers to halt. The
wind whistled through the bending poplar trees lining the
avenue. The cold was so intense my face and ears felt as if
being attacked by dozens of needles.

Eleyne was in the litter behind me. Wearing a heavy
stola and mantle, she got out and ran to my side. "What is
it? Is there something wrong?"

"No," I said. Although I was sitting upright, I attempted
to turn my body, barely moving my legs. "Turn me toward
the city."

"But you're freezing, your face is red."

"I don't care, do as I ask."

"All right, I'll help you." Eleyne motioned to one of the
big litter bearers and then reached inside. With his help,
Eleyne pulled me about, and I faced in the direction of
Rome.

Shivering, I looked across the river, but for no more
than the length of a couple heartbeats. I turned away.

"Let's go," I said.

"That was quick. What were you looking at, Marcellus?" Eleyne asked.

"A city now dead to me. I will never cross the Tiber again. Once the weather improves we will return to Hispania."

Eleyne took my hand. "Rome has never deserved your loyalty let alone your love. You cared for her, but she was an ingrate, undeserving. Now you are in my care, the only true care you have ever had, forever."

I glanced beyond Eleyne in the direction of Hispania, seeing the broad latifundia in my mind's eye. I watched cattle peacefully grazing on the open range. Behind me, beyond the villa, steep cliffs overlooked the deep-blue Mediterranean, the surf pounding the pebbled beach at its base. Taking a deep breath, I knew this was where I belonged. My father had always wanted me to supervise our lands, and I will do so living in quiet retirement. I leave Rome to my sons, Young Marcellus and Sabinus, officers in the army. Perhaps, she will be kinder to them.

EPILOGUE

79 AD

My husband, Marcellus, is dead of heart failure. In the ten years following his retirement, his bitterness mellowed. But he regretted being so naive about how poorly the state treated loyal servants like Flavius Sabinus. Yet, when speaking of Rome, he spoke with affection.

He found it a puzzling irony that a Roman arrow, rather than a barbarian's, ended his career. Marcellus believed he had accomplished many things but regretted he had not done more for the people of Rome. Perhaps our sons' accomplishments will be greater than his. They are cohort commanders in the army he so loved and senatorial candidates. Neither the people nor the army deserved his love or care.

In his last hours, he was in little pain and at peace with himself. During the last year, his health deteriorated at an alarming pace, and he desperately wanted to finish his memoirs. I don't know if they are of any value, except in confirming the truth he witnessed in Rome.

Marcellus said he received word that Emperor Titus's court historians were *revising* the history of Rome, especially, the year of the four emperors. They placed the father of Emperor Titus, the late Emperor Vespasian, who died three months ago, in a light far more favorable than he truly deserved. They even erased all records of the attempted rescue by Marcellus and his cohort, who had attempted to rescue Sabinus from the Temple of Jupiter on Capitoline Hill. Why, my husband could not understand. I believe this particular piece of news was the final blow to his health.

Marcellus knew his time was short. He never came to terms with himself for killing Senator Gallus. Although Gallus was on Vespasian's proscription list, meaning anyone could kill him, my husband had an uneasy feeling that must have ached within his soul. I'm certain he believed God would forgive him. But he never expressed those thoughts to me.

Now he is at rest, buried on a hill overlooking the Mediterranean he so loved to admire from his study. At this moment, he would be pleased to know the seasonal rains are mild, the seas are calm, and Rome . . . his beloved Rome . . . is at peace.

AUTHOR NOTES

Keep in mind this is a work of fiction, not history.

We don't know a lot about Titus Flavius Sabinus, older brother of Emperor Vespasian. We know he was city prefect of Rome and the historian, Tacitus, says he was, "quite windy." He did die at the hands of the mob after being captured by the Praetorian guard.

However, there was no rescue attempt by elements of the City Guard, assigned to Ostia, or any other military unit. Only Sabinus and a few followers put up a futile attempt on Capitoline Hill, which failed. I took historical license by having Marcellus leading a rescue attempt. You could say that if history did not play out this way, it should have.

The temple of Jupiter Greatest and Best on the Capitoline actually burned as described in the novel. Most other events surrounding the battle for Rome are true. Vitellius was also murdered by the mob.

Vespasian did not arrive in Rome until September or October, 70 AD. For the purpose of the story, I moved this to May.

Marcellus Reburrus is a fictitious character. I wanted to use a Roman citizen for my narrator, but one who was an outsider with a different perspective. I settled on a Spaniard from the southern province of Baetica, one of the most Romanized provinces in the empire. Interestingly enough, by late first century AD and early second century, two of Rome's greatest emperors, Trajan (98 - 117 AD) and Hadrian (117 - 137 AD), both Spaniards, would rule the Roman Empire.

ABOUT THE AUTHOR

JESS STEVEN HUGHES is a retired police detective sergeant with twenty-five years experience in criminal investigation and a former US Marine. He holds a master's degree in public administration and a minor in ancient Mediterranean civilizations from the University of Southern California. He has traveled and studied extensively in the areas forming the background of this novel, which brings vivid authenticity to the unique settings for his historical novels, *The Sign of the Eagle*, *The Wolf of Britannia, Part I*, *The Wolf of Britannia, Part II*, *The Broken Lance*, and *The Peacekeeper*. He currently lives with his wife, Liz, and their three horses in Eastern Washington. He is currently working on another historical novel from the first century AD, *The Emperor's Hand*.

CPSIA information can be obtained
at www.ICGtesting.com
Printed in the USA
FSHW010453030519
57808FS